Christina Suss
2013

Sweetwater

Sweetwater

A NOVEL

Roxana Robinson

RANDOM HOUSE / NEW YORK

All rights reserved under International and Pan-American Copyright Conventions.
Published in the United States by Random House, Inc., New York, and simultaneously
in Canada by Random House of Canada Limited, Toronto.

RANDOM HOUSE and colophon are registered trademarks of Random House, Inc.

ISBN 0-375-50916-X

Printed in the United States of America

Book design by J. K. Lambert

This book is for my sisters

KATHY AND BETHANY

with love

ACKNOWLEDGMENTS

I would like to thank the following people for their patience in response to my inquiries: Sarah Chasis, Hal Crowther, Joan Jakobson, Steve Katona, Donald Kimelman, Robert Liberman and Fred Lindzey. I'd also like to thank Alice Outwater for her enthralling book *Water: A Natural History,* which was a great resource.

I would like to thank Lynn Nesbit and Susanna Porter for their enthusiasm, and I would like to thank the National Humanities Center, the MacDowell Colony, and the John Simon Guggenheim Foundation for their support.

I would like to thank my family, as always, for theirs.

Part 1

The Adirondacks are a group of mountains in northeastern New York State known for pristine woodlands and spectacular scenery. They occupy 500 to 600 square miles within the counties of Clinton, Essex, Franklin and Hamilton. The mountains consist of . . . gneiss, intrusive granite, and gabbro, and are geologically related to the Laurentian highlands of Canada. . . .

The mountains form the water-parting in the landscape between the Hudson and the St. Lawrence Rivers. The region was once covered by the Lawrentian glacier, whose gradual but powerful erosion produced the characteristic features of the area: scores of lakes and ponds, and many picturesque falls and rapids in the streams. It is a region rich in waterways. . . .

As well as scenic appeal, the region is known for its rich and various flora and fauna. Much of the area has been preserved . . . over 3,000,000 acres have been set aside to form the Adirondack Park . . . the wildlife within the region is extraordinarily vigorous and multitudinous. The region is heavily forested with spruce, pine and broad-leaved trees. The mountain peaks are usually rounded, and easily scaled. The vistas thus achieved, of mountain, lake, plateau and forest, are almost unequalled in any other part of the United States for scenic grandeur.

—Encyclopaedia Britannica, 1910

Chapter 1

The cabin was cool and dark, smelling of wood. Isabel set down her duffel bag inside the front door. Without looking at the unknown rooms on either side, she went straight down the dim hall to the door at the far end, a bright oblong of light. She pushed open the screen and stood looking out over the porch to the lake beyond.

It was late afternoon. The broad lake was still full of light, but across it, on the western shore, was a rising mass of shadow. The water was quiet, the reflections perfectly still: there, in silvery echoes, were the low wooded hills that ringed the lake, with the pure indigo sky above it.

Isabel heard her husband behind her, his footsteps hollow on the bare floorboards. When he reached her, she spoke without turning.

"This is beautiful." It was her first visit here; she had only been married to Paul since February, seven months.

"We like it," Paul said. He had come here every summer of his life, fifty-one years. He stood just behind Isabel, setting his hands on her shoulders. He was tall but light-boned, rangy and lean, without bulk. His hands on her were nearly weightless.

"We're letting the flies out," he said, and Isabel stepped obediently onto the porch, his hands awkwardly still on her.

The outer walls of Acorn Cabin were unpainted shingle, faded to silver gray from decades of Adirondack weather. Beyond the porch's rustic railing—peeled gnarly cedar—the ground sloped down mildly toward the water.

"Let's go to the lake," Isabel said. They had spent the day in the car, driving up from New York, and what she wanted now was air and light, open water. Exploration of the dark rooms of the cabin could wait.

Paul led the way down a narrow path through underbrush and young saplings. The air was dry and ferny and sweet. Through the trees the sight of water flickered intermittently, pale and calm. It was lost between branches, glimpsed again, glittering and wider, and then finally, as they turned a corner and arrived at the shore, the lake spread out before them, shimmering and complete. Down here at its edge the lake looked vast, its still-radiant surface immense and untouched. Around them was silence: the faint sibilance of air moving in the tree-tops, nothing more. It smelled of summer: trees, lake water, heat.

"This is heaven," Isabel said. Her voice, in the great openness around her, was small.

Paul put his arm around her. "Exactly," he said with satisfaction. "*Now* will you never leave me?"

This combination—warmth and absurdity—made Isabel laugh. She felt a surge of affection, then a flare of hope. *Maybe this will work.*

Hope was what Isabel was bringing to this marriage. It was nearly all she had: grief itself was a kind of death, it seemed. Two years of it had scoured her bare of other feelings. The time seemed past in which joy would rise easily to the surface of her heart and fill it. Grief had estab-lished itself at the center of her life, and though it no longer stormed through her, drenching and overwhelming, as it had at first, it was not gone. She still felt the grayness of her first husband's absence from the world, the silence everywhere without his voice. The pain at being un-able to tell him things: that she missed him. That she longed for him. That she still loved him. That she hated him for being gone.

It had not seemed that grief would ever leave, but after two years it had diminished, and she had determined, herself, to move on, to leave that gray landscape. What she felt for Paul was quieter than what she'd felt for Michael, but everything in her life seemed quieter. This kind of emotion—calm and muted—was what was left to her. She was forty-seven. All the other things—wildness and bliss and desperation, rage, the urgency of sex—lay behind her. She no longer expected them. What she aimed for now was loyalty and affection. Much of marriage was partnership; she didn't want to be old alone. When she was old she wanted someone with her whom she trusted, someone she knew. What she felt for Paul was a powerful tenderness, and she knew this would increase. Affection deepens over time and hardship; compassion strengthens with the years. What Isabel wanted was something quiet, durable, domestic. A backwater, somewhere safe. She was done with storms.

She leaned against Paul. She was still trying to learn his body, still teaching her own to expect it. There were moments when it still felt strange: too tall, too angular, for comfort. She tilted her head back against Paul's chest and looked straight up, at the great arch of sky.

"It's so clear," she said.

"Too clear, actually," Paul answered. "We're hoping for rain. There's a serious drought. It's hardly rained in months."

Isabel looked again, scanning the deep blue for a wisp of cloud, a skein of high mist, but there was nothing. The reaches overhead were empty. She liked Paul's knowing about the weather here, even when he was away.

"Did you come up here for the whole summer?" she asked. "When you were little?"

"Always a month, sometimes six weeks," Paul answered. "My mother would come up with me and Whit. My father came up for long weekends and the last couple of weeks in August. My grandparents were here for the whole summer. We stayed in Acorn, they stayed in the lodge."

Sweetwater Lodge was the original house, built by Paul's maternal great-grandparents in the 1890s. The three cabins—Acorn, Oyster and Whistle—had been built during the twenties for grown children. Over a century after the land was bought, the whole place—the houses and several hundred acres of land—was owned by a complicated family trust. Paul's mother and her two brothers each spent a summer month at the lodge, their children in the cottages. Just now Paul's parents, Douglas and Charlotte, were in the lodge; Paul and Isabel were to have Acorn for two weeks.

"Do you and Whitney share the cottage?" Isabel asked.

"No, it's mine unless he gets married. The rule is, you don't get a cabin until you're married. Until then you stay at the lodge."

Isabel had never met Paul's brother, Whitney. He lived in Wyoming, where he did something in the national parks. He hadn't been able to come to their wedding; a blizzard had closed the Laramie airport for three days. He was forty-five, unmarried. Isabel had wondered if he was gay, but it was a question she wasn't ready to ask: there was a faint chill in Paul's voice when he spoke of Whitney.

"And will Whit get married, do you think?" Isabel risked.

"Doubtful," Paul said, cool.

Probably gay, then, she thought. Maybe that was why Paul was so disapproving. "Does he come here often?"

"Not anymore," Paul said. "I guess the Adirondacks are small potatoes compared to the Bighorns."

"And Geordie?"

Geordie was Paul's son from his first marriage, his only child. Geordie was twenty-eight and lived in Vancouver, where he was a producer for the local television station. Isabel had met him only once, at their wedding.

Geordie was tall and lanky, like Paul, with a long face nearly identical to his father's: the same high cheekbones, the same ascetic hollows in the lean cheeks, the same wide, mobile mouth. Isabel had been so happy to meet him. He'd seemed so like another, earlier version of his father that she felt as though she'd been magically permitted to meet Paul as a young man. She'd stepped forward, beaming, to embrace this other, earlier Paul.

But Geordie would have none of it. He had leaned away from her embrace, his expression cool and distant. He barely put his arms around her; his touch was light and unwilling. He bowed ironically as she kissed his cheek. He scarcely met her eyes, and his gaze flicked away at once. Disappointed, Isabel stepped back and dropped her arms to her sides. What had his mother told him about her?

"As a matter of fact, this will be the first summer Geordie has missed," Paul said.

"Why isn't he coming?"

"He's been invited on a great rock-climbing trip. Apparently it was an offer he couldn't refuse."

Isabel wondered if Geordie's absence was because of her presence. She wondered whether Paul would tell her.

Isabel's own son, Ben, would not be coming up to the lake, either. He was working for a law firm in New York for the summer, and it was too long a trip for a weekend. Ben and Geordie had met at the wedding, too.

Isabel had hoped they'd become friends, but when she saw them stiffly shaking hands, their chins lifted warily, she saw they would not. It was too late to make a new family; everyone was too old. These two would never feel like brothers. They were genetic competitors from different herds.

Ben had been welcoming to Paul, at least, and he'd been kind when Isabel had first told him. They were in the apartment, in her bedroom. Isabel was sitting in the maple chair at her desk, Ben on her bed.

"I want you to meet someone," she said. It felt awkward to say this, like a confession. "Do you mind?" she asked, anxious. "Does it feel like a betrayal?"

Ben sat slouching, his knees splayed. His feet were tipped on their sides, soles facing each other.

"No." He shook his head, looking down at his running shoes. "I've thought about this. It'll be weird to see you with someone else, but I don't want you to be alone. You should be happy. You should have someone." He raised his head and looked at her. "Dad's gone."

At the wedding Ben had stayed near. Once, during the reception, when Paul put his arm around her, she felt Ben's gaze on her and turned. He smiled and silently lifted his glass, high and ceremonial.

Now Isabel and Paul stood side by side without touching. The lake was silent. Far out on the water some creature rose to the surface with a small *tock,* then fell away. Ripples moved swiftly away from the vanished presence. *Here is his center,* Isabel thought.

"Does it make you nervous, having me here?" she asked, teasing.

"Not so far," Paul said. "Should it? Is it dangerous?"

"Just that I'll know so much about you. You'll have nowhere to hide. I feel as though your whole life is here."

"That's sort of the point," Paul said. He reached up and smoothed her hair, clumsily, as though he were stroking a dog. "We're in this together now. I trust you." He smiled at her. "Do you want to go back and unpack, take the grand tour of the cabin?"

They turned from the lake and set off up the path through the trees.

Acorn Cabin was small and simple: a center hall with three tiny bedrooms on one side, a kitchen and bathroom on the other. The walls were unpainted wood the color of dark honey. The floors were bare, and the rooms were lit by ceiling bulbs.

"This is us," said Paul, opening the door to the bedroom closest to the lake. On either side of the window was a single bed, neatly made

up with a faded green bedspread. Between the beds stood a square table of unpeeled white birch; on the walls were flyspecked black-and-
white photographs of Adirondack views: flat lakes, rising mountains.

"Wonderful," said Isabel, looking around. The room felt clean; the
floor was swept, and the air held the faintly spicy smell of old wood.
"Was this your room when you were little?"

"Of course not," Paul said. "The grown-ups got the lake view. The
children got the impenetrable forest vistas."

The next room was smaller, with two bunk beds. A rush-bottomed
chair stood against the wall. The window looked into the deep woods.

"This was mine," Paul said. "No view, but since I was older, I got
the room closer to the view."

"There's nothing of you here," Isabel said, looking around. "Didn't
you have a panda or something? Wasn't there something you always
went to see when you first arrived?"

"Not inside," Paul said. "There are places like that out in the woods.
The tree where my hideout was. Where I used to ambush Whit."

"Why didn't you two share a room?" Isabel asked. "You make it
sound as though you were deadly enemies."

Paul shrugged, turning to leave. "Whit and I always had separate
rooms. We fought a lot; fighting was the way we played. We spent all
our time together, but it was strategic interaction, not fraternizing. War
was our business."

The spartan room next door was identical: the bare bunks, the slat-
backed chair. Isabel moved on to the kitchen, the largest room. It had
blurred linoleum on the floor and open shelves, full of cans. There was
a small electric stove, a deep porcelain sink, and an old high-legged refrigerator. The square wooden table had a metal top; around it stood
four high-backed chairs.

Isabel looked around at the room. "I can't picture Louisa here," she
said.

Louisa—formidable, opinionated, impatient—would have had something to say about this shadowy, antiquated setup. From what Isabel
had gathered, Louisa had something to say about everything. Louisa
had left Paul just as she was getting her Ph.D. in French literature at
Columbia University, after eighteen years of marriage. She had come
home after taking her orals and asked him to move out. She was
adamant, Paul told Isabel, there was no discussion. It had come as a

head-ringing blow to him: he had thought they were happy. But Louisa had been chillingly sure they were not. She now taught "Balzac and the Rise of the Nineteenth Century" at Barnard College.

Isabel had met her once, unexpectedly, at a party after she and Paul were married. Louisa walked up and stuck out her hand boldly, staring at Isabel with a fierce raptor's gaze. She was tall and lean and commanding, with short blackish-gray hair, rather elegant in a bluestocking way. Her eyes were brown, and the skin beneath them was stained dark. She wore a long smocklike dress, black stockings and dangling earrings.

"Ah," Louisa declared, with predatory relish, "the second Mrs. Tanqueray."

Isabel took the proffered hand out of reflexive courtesy. "Hello," she said limply. She felt Louisa's hard, angry knuckles. She could think of no retort.

"Who *was* the second Mrs. Tanqueray?" she asked Paul later. "What's it from?"

"Marquand? Oscar Wilde? I don't remember," Paul said, "but I think you're safe in assuming it's not a kindly reference."

"I sort of got that."

Louisa had smiled at her, baring her teeth. Isabel had felt the electrical charge given off by rival wives, the glow-in-the-dark signal coming from two bodies chosen by the same man. At that moment, when the two women stand face-to-face, the man has no role at all. His task is complete: he has produced these two giants. They are now huge and monumental, they have far outstripped him in size and energy. Anything may happen between them. He is tiny and powerless, shouting faintly from below as they step dangerously around each other on the hilltop.

Now Paul, in the kitchen, looked puzzled by her comment.

"Louisa? I don't know what she thought of it," he said. "We don't do much cooking here, just breakfast and some sandwiches. We always have dinner at the lodge. This isn't the heart of the household, the kitchen."

"What *is* the heart of the household?" Isabel asked.

"The lake," Paul said, as simply as he might name a lover.

Isabel thought again, *Maybe this will work.*

—

Isabel had known Paul when Michael was alive, though only slightly. They had seen each other at large parties, at Christmas buffets and museum openings; they had mutual friends, they all knew one another by sight. Paul had looked slightly bohemian with his bow ties, his round tortoiseshell glasses. His manner was offhand, nearly boyish, his gestures casual and unself-conscious.

But Isabel and Paul had never properly met, never spoken more than a few impersonal words until long after Michael had died, not until the afternoon when they found themselves in the waiting room at the eye doctor's.

Isabel was there to ask Dr. Lunet if there was something to be done about the way her eyes, willing partners of hers for so many years, were now refusing to perform their tasks. They focused only on objects at a distance, obstinately resisting making any sense at all of objects right in front of them. There were so many things Isabel had always taken for granted, taken as givens—the shape of her legs, the sight of her eyes, the expression on her face, the texture of her skin. But it seemed they were not givens. It seemed now that they had been merely loans, and were all to be taken away.

At Dr. Lunet's, Isabel gave her name to the receptionist and sat down. An appointment with Dr. Lunet was like an audience: he was tall and courtly, with a long, narrow skull, receding hair and thin, sensitive fingers. He wore immaculately pressed white lab coats over beautiful gray suits and quietly lustrous silk ties. His waiting room was hushed with mahogany and chintz. Isabel picked up a magazine and sat down on the sofa; across from her, a man and a woman sat in chairs.

"Excuse me," said the receptionist. She was a friendly young woman with full cheeks and hoop earrings. She held up an index card and spoke to the other woman.

The woman looked up, her mouth twitching impatiently. She was in her seventies and dressed for glamour. Her flimsy dead-brown hair was cut in a shoulder-length pageboy; her shoes and bag were shiny black alligator. Her nails gleamed scarlet.

"I'm sorry, but could you give me your name again, please?" the receptionist asked politely. "I'm having trouble finding your records."

The woman frowned. "Lipari," she said, vexed. "I've been coming here for years."

"I'm sure we have you," promised the girl. "Is it L-E-P-A-R-E?"

"Lipari," said the woman, crossing her thin legs. She spelled it out.

"Lipari," the receptionist said carefully, writing. "And could you give me your first name, please?"

"Countess," said the woman, pursing her mouth indignantly.

Isabel's eyes flicked up, and she met the gaze of the man sitting across from her. His face was immobile, but she saw hilarity in his eyes.

"Countess Lipari," the woman repeated, and snapped her bag shut. Isabel looked down again at her magazine.

When the countess had gone in, Isabel raised her eyes. The man shook his head.

"Wasn't that great?" he asked.

"Wonderful," said Isabel.

"I'm Paul Simmons, by the way," he said. "I think we've met."

"Duchess Green," Isabel said, "I think we have."

Paul cocked his head. "I actually hate to use my title," he said. "I never do."

"What is it?" Isabel asked.

"Mustang," said Paul.

Isabel liked him at once. They talked until she was called in to the doctor, who explained courteously that her condition was called presbyopia, and suggested glasses. When Paul called Isabel at her office the next day, she felt a little surge of pleasure when he spoke his name. But when he asked her to dinner, she hesitated.

It had been over a year since Michael had died, but she didn't yet want to be alone with another man. She went out to friends' houses, people she knew well. But she still felt wounded by what had happened, she was still vibrating and stunned by it, as though she had been rocked by a huge detonation. She felt separated from the rest of the race. The notion of another man as a possible partner seemed strange to her, and the thought of sex was alarming.

She asked Paul cautiously, "Would you call this a date that you're asking me on?"

"I'd call it whatever you want," Paul offered. "It's just dinner with me, in a restaurant. We can call it a meeting. A séance."

"Because I'm really not ready for a regular date," Isabel told him.

"Oh, well," Paul said reassuringly, "this isn't really a date. It's a subdate. Not a regular one. A preliminary episode. Absolutely no sex."

He made her laugh; she heard herself say yes. There was something guileless about Paul, something sweet and candid. He made her laugh, her defenses drop. And she knew it was time for this next step. Michael was gone.

Three days later, getting dressed for the dinner, Isabel felt differently. She had come home late from her office with barely time for a shower and none at all to wash her hair. Still dripping and damp, she came into the bedroom wrapped in a towel. The bedroom was small, its walls covered in narrow rose stripes. Isabel stood in front of her maple bureau. On it was a photograph of her parents, a silver-topped crystal jar of her grandmother's, a photograph of Ben at thirteen, and the glazed clay dinosaur he had made in third grade. There were no photographs of Michael: those were all stacked in a cardboard box on a high shelf in the hall closet.

Isabel began to dress quickly, avoiding the sight of herself in the mirror. She found a dress and put it on, wriggling to coax the long slide of the zipper up her back. From a lacquer box she took a short string of round silver beads. She set it around her neck, bowing her head to clasp it in back. She could feel the ends of her hair dripping against her wrists. She knew how her hair looked: dark and damp, hanging in wispy points. She knew how she looked, pale and serious, dark circles under her eyes. A widow.

What she was doing was absurd. Her eyes filled and she raised her head, blinking, then shook it rapidly. She lowered her hands, still holding the necklace. Michael had given it to her. The point of dressing up had always been for Michael; the point of going out had been to talk over the evening with him later. All this now was a sham; there was no use in pretending to be ready for a change. The change in her life had already come.

She laid down the necklace and set both hands on the bureau, spreading out her fingers as if she were about to speak. Ninth-grade Ben, his silky hair falling over his forehead, smiled shinily up at her, bright autumn foliage in the background. She was absolutely alone here. She lived alone. She stood without moving, looking down at the silver beads stretched out on the white cloth, framed by her two hands. She could hear herself breathe.

When Isabel reached the restaurant, Paul was waiting for her. The place was small and crowded. Paul sat at the end of the room, his back against the wall, his hands folded in front of him. When he saw her he stood, pushing at the table; its legs scraped shrilly on the floor. This was a mistake, she thought, and her heart sank.

"Hello," he said, making an odd gesture with his hand.

"Hello," Isabel answered, sliding down quickly into the other chair. She felt herself shrink away: she couldn't kiss him hello or even shake hands, she couldn't tolerate a touch. Their table was in the corner, and they sat at right angles. Isabel moved her legs away from his under the table.

Paul looked at her solemnly. "You look very elegant," he said.

"Thank you," said Isabel, who knew she did not.

"Would you like something to drink?" Paul asked. His chin was somehow stiff against his neck.

"A glass of white wine?"

It was a mistake. Why had she agreed? She should be at home right now, in bed with a book. Why was she here, and where was Michael? Why had he abandoned her to this?

Isabel waited for Paul to speak: the evening was his idea. But he seemed subdued and said nothing. They ordered and waited in silence for the drinks. When they arrived, Paul lifted his glass politely.

"Cheers," he said, nodding. Isabel dutifully lifted her glass. "Thank you for coming," Paul said. "I appreciate it."

Isabel smiled at him, despairing: he was going to be pompous.

After they ordered, Paul looked at her. "Isabel," he said. "With an 'A' or an 'O'?"

" 'A.' It's actually short for Isabela. It was my grandmother's name."

"Was she Italian?"

"Her mother was."

"Interesting," said Paul. "And her father?"

"A minister from Philadelphia. Presbyterian."

"More interesting. How did they meet?"

Paul's questions seemed conscientious, oppressive; Isabel struggled to respond.

"He was traveling in Italy, on the Grand Tour. They met in Rome, though she was actually Venetian."

Isabel had imagined the meeting: at a salon, an At Home like Isabel Archer's; or with friends, at the opera; or walking along raked gravel paths, among the cypresses in a garden, or in a long gallery hung with dark nineteenth-century paintings. Beatrice—blue-eyed and pale-skinned, her head held high, her silky red-blond Venetian hair twisted and pinned against her head—wearing a long full skirt, a black velvet ribbon against her alabaster throat. Thomas, Isabel's great-grandfather, in a black morning coat and striped trousers. Their feet slow on marble tiles. Isabel wondered what their first words to each other had been, the actual phrases. Impossible to know how people had talked in the past, what conversations had sounded like, when all that was left was the written word.

Whatever Thomas had said, it was what Beatrice wanted to hear. He had brought her back to Philadelphia, where they had five children. Isabel had always liked the idea of Beatrice's warm Italian blood mixing with Thomas's chill Scottish sort.

Paul smiled encouragingly, but Isabel was silent, the story sealed inside her. The effort of retrieving it, spreading it out for Paul's gaze, was too great. The story was from long ago. It was part of her past; she could not begin all over again.

The food arrived. Paul waited for a moment, then changed the subject. "So, Isabela," he said, digging a fork into the shell of an escargot, dragging out the oily curl. "Tell me about what you do."

"I work for an organization called Environmental Protection Resources."

"Ah," Paul said, nodding. "Do-gooders."

Isabel said nothing.

"Aren't you?" He looked up.

"We're an environmental group," Isabel said carefully. She knew people—men, mostly—who took offense at the word "environment," as though the idea of protecting the earth were a personal assault. She usually listened to these men in silence or changed the subject; rational discussion was out of the question, their responses were chemical. If Paul was one of them, that would be the end of this.

But apparently he was not. "Ah," he said, "I stand corrected." He smiled, but Isabel, who did not understand what he meant—was he in earnest? Or ironic?—did not smile back.

It was that way all evening. Paul was dutiful, Isabel silent and uncertain, unable to gather herself up to respond. She should not have come.

"And what do you do?" she asked as the main course arrived.

"I'm at something called the Stanford Trust," he said.

"What's that?" she asked politely.

"Do-gooders," he said. She glanced up at him, but he was looking down, and she wasn't sure if she was being rebuked or teased. After a moment she asked what they did.

"Medical research," he said, looking up. "Cancer. We're one of the best, actually. You'd have heard of us if you knew the field."

He spoke without arrogance, then smiled and fell silent. Isabel was struck by his courtesy, his kindliness: but she should not have come. She could not be part of these conversations, these gradual friendly incursions into another's life.

"They're doing amazing things now with heredity," Paul told her.

"Really?" Isabel asked. She lifted her water glass, nearly closing her eyes as she drank.

Afterward they stood outside on the sidewalk. It was cold; Isabel raised the collar of her coat and took out her gloves.

"Thank you very much for dinner," she said, smiling at Paul, now energized. She pulled on her gloves, ready to leave. Only ten blocks away, she could walk.

"I'll take you home," Paul said, lifting his hand for a cab. He wore a heavy wool overcoat, navy blue. He was very tall, taller than she had realized.

"I'll be all right," Isabel said, looking vaguely down the street. "I can walk."

"Let me drop you off," Paul said, determined.

"Really," Isabel said, "I'm fine."

Paul turned to look at her. "Why don't you want to share a cab with me?"

She couldn't answer him. "I didn't mean that. I just meant you don't have to."

"But I'd like to," Paul said, his arm still high, and a cab skidded to a stop beside them. The driver stared at them alarmingly. He was a Sikh, with fierce black eyes and a huge turban wrapped thickly around his head. Paul opened the door for her.

Five more minutes, Isabel told herself, climbing in. She slid to the far side of the seat, her hands in her pockets. Paul gave her address to the driver and leaned back. They set off in silence. Isabel looked out her window. Paul sat still, his back erect, his knees close together, his hands in his lap.

"I'm afraid this wasn't a success," he said.

"No, no," Isabel said guiltily. "Of course it was. I had a very nice time."

"Maybe you were right in the first place," Paul said. "Maybe it's too soon for you to go out."

Isabel was silent, startled. Had it been so obvious? But surely it hadn't been only her. Wasn't it Paul's fault as well? Hadn't he asked her too much too quickly? Hadn't his questions been relentless, intrusive? And there was something else besides the questions, some wordless, oppressive demand, for something she couldn't provide. Wasn't that true? Or was she wrong?

"Maybe that was it," she said. "I'm sorry if I wasn't much fun. It's still hard for me to—focus, sort of, on someone else."

Paul still spoke without looking at her. "Yes," he said. "That's the way it felt. As though you couldn't see me." His voice was thoughtful.

Isabel said nothing. It was true, she could hardly see Paul. But she could see no one. She never should have agreed to go out with him.

They drove rapidly through the darkened streets, the cab rattling dangerously. The driver seemed desperate to meet some unknown deadline, and the car barely paused at lights, cutting off other cars, hurtling finally up Park Avenue.

"Ah, we're going to die," Paul murmured solemnly as they veered diagonally into another lane at Seventy-third Street, just avoiding another cab. Isabel said nothing, waiting to get out. Five more blocks. They turned the corner onto her street, and the cab lurched to a halt before her building. She leaned over to Paul and put out her hand.

"Thank you so much," she said, but he was already opening his door to get out.

"I'll walk you to the door," he said.

He took her arm, clasping it above the elbow, as they crossed the sidewalk. His touch surprised her: gentle and courteous, somehow kind. At the front door he stopped.

"Thank you again," Isabel said.

"Don't keep saying that," Paul said. "I know you didn't have a good time. But please don't give up. There will be a moment when you emerge."

She looked at him. He was standing before her, his face tilted toward hers, his expression candid and serious. For the first time all evening, Isabel looked at Paul full in the face. His round glasses shone in the light from the lobby. His expression was steady and sweet. Isabel looked back at him. She felt warmth from him, tenderness. She could say nothing.

This was not what she had expected. They had understood the evening entirely differently. Anxiety rose in her. Had she been wrong? Had he not been demanding, not expected too much? Perhaps it was her fault after all.

Paul stood watching her. He had dropped his hand from her arm.

She could not bear him watching her like this, so steadily. "Good night," she said, and turned away. There was no doorman on duty at night, and she fumbled with the key, feeling Paul behind her. The door gave way, and she pushed through it away from him into the lobby. She heard the heavy door suck itself closed behind her, and she walked without looking back through the lobby to the elevator. She pushed the button and stood waiting, her back still to Paul, confused. She felt shame creeping into her. When the elevator arrived, she stepped inside, turning at last to face Paul.

He was still standing on the sidewalk, watching her. She could see his tall silhouette against the glass, motionless. She started to raise her hand to him, and the elevator door slid shut.

She felt the lift pulling her against gravity, she felt herself, her spirits, sliding downward as it rose. The evening had been a failure, her fault, not Paul's. He was right. She had been silent and inattentive. He had done his best, he had bought her dinner, asked her courteous questions. She had refused all he'd offered. What was the point of her behavior? She was ashamed. Why go out at all if you were going to be silent and unresponsive?

But she didn't want to go out at all, there was no point. Michael was still with her. She closed her eyes. The elevator slid up inside the darkened shaft, lifting her upward into the night. She felt grief approaching, Michael's absence. She couldn't support it, couldn't bear it, would not return to this—remembering, waking up to the cold wind in the darkened apartment. Hearing the silence. The gritty floor against her bare feet. She would not. She felt as though she were caught in a current, being carried toward the falls. The elevator stopped at her floor and the door opened.

Her apartment seemed suddenly small, expectant. The hall looked different somehow; the perspective of the rooms seemed altered. The place looked empty, the colors subtly drained of richness, depth. It was not the apartment where she and Michael had lived. She had been advised not to do anything right away, but she had sold that at once. She had never spent another night in that bedroom. She had slept in Ben's bed until they moved.

Isabel hung up her coat and turned out the hall light, leaving the apartment dark behind her. She went into the bedroom; she felt chilled. In her room she looked around for comfort at the rosy walls, the drawn curtains, the pale carpeting. Ben's gleeful ceramic dinosaur. But the room, the room was strange, secretive. All these things seemed to be waiting. Something beat against her heart.

What am I doing? She felt the risk of tears, real tears, not ones she could brush quickly away. Somehow Paul was mixed up in this. She saw his tall silhouette against the glass door. What was it? What had happened? Tears were imminent, and something rose up in her throat. She sat down on the bed, fighting. She felt it welling up, threatening. She would not let it come, she would not cry, would not. She would not go back into that grief, would not let it take her over.

everything was easier than subterranean. Once a toxic chemical plume entered the aquifer, deep in the mineral substrata where water spends much of its time, it was impossible to retrieve or neutralize, even to identify its source.

The morning after her dinner with Paul, Isabel came in to work early. The EPR offices were silent and the halls empty. Sitting down at her desk, Isabel opened her breakfast. It was not quite eight-thirty. Around her was the steady hum of New York City; inside the office it was quiet, nearly peaceful. Isabel unwrapped the buttery paper from her bagel, uncapped her milky coffee and took her first sip. The day stretched out before her.

She opened a report on the Mississippi Delta. River deltas were prime recipients of pollution. As it approached the sea, a big channel widened under the pressure of its accumulated water, creating ancillary channels and spreading sideways into the land around the main body. As it slowed and spread, it began to give up some of its buoyant burden, the shawl of upstream silt. Historically, this silt was rich and fertile; some of the best farmlands in the world were in deltas dense with organic muck. The arriving topsoil also reached the surrounding swamplands, creating huge and fecund breeding grounds for birds and fish. But the current runoff from agriculture was lethal, and the arriving silt was full of chemical toxins. Now the delta and swamplands were being poisoned, the languid waterways were full of death.

Isabel, reading about a plume of lethal chemicals, thought of molecules and their behavior, the way they moved and bonded. There was something else, too, in her consciousness, a small unquiet background presence, as though somewhere a burner was on, a telephone off the hook. She turned the pages slowly, underlining sentences, making notes in the margins. What was it, below the surface of her mind?

Soon after nine Netta Weisman arrived.

"Good morning," she said, taking off her gloves. "My God, it's cold out there. Whatever happened to global warming?" She unbuttoned her coat, brisk and energetic.

Netta had been at EPR almost since its inception. She was nearing sixty; her thick iron-gray hair was very short and cut on a stylish slant. She wore round black-rimmed glasses, a loose black pantsuit and low-heeled black shoes. Her EPR specialty was grasslands, and she was married to a bearded psychiatrist named Mitch. She was smart, practical and outspoken, also kind.

Chapter 2

The offices of Environmental Protection Resources were in a nineteenth-century cast-iron building in Tribeca. Stepping off the elevator each morning, Isabel arrived in EPR's airy two-story lobby: smooth white walls and gray tile floor. Three huge fernlike trees, in terra-cotta pots, stood in the light like natural deities, yearning gracefully upward toward the great windows.

EPR had renovated several stories of the old building, transforming them into clean, modern spaces. It was a point of pride that they'd used only organic materials in the construction: no synthetic fabrics, no toxic glues, no hidden carcinogens. Isabel believed that, at the moment you stepped off the elevator, your body understood this on some subtle physiological level. She believed that some part of you relaxed, relieved, as though you'd come inside from a hot wind.

EPR had been founded in the late 1960s by Wallace Outerbridge, a Wall Street lawyer and passionate outdoorsman. Watching the environment come under increasing assault, he'd gathered a group of friends to defend it. Their approach was not only idealistic but pragmatic: EPR sued whoever violated environmental laws. They sued anyone—international corporations, oil companies, nuclear power plants, cities, states, federal agencies. The stakes were large and the entities were powerful, so EPR was not always successful, but it often was, enough to make a serious difference, to make them feel that they were carrying the battle into the enemy's territory and, from time to time, forcing the unwilling enemy to retreat.

Isabel had worked at EPR for nearly thirteen years. She'd given it up during the four years in London, but EPR gave her the job back when she returned. It had saved her life after Michael died. Having another world to enter each day, one still intact, had been providential. And this seemed the essential task, protecting the earth. She could give herself up to it.

Isabel had begun at EPR as a volunteer, enthusiastic but untutored. Once involved, she took courses in environmental sciences—botany, biology, ecology. The natural world unfolded before her, intricate, beautiful in its logic and particularities, frighteningly fragile.

What seized Isabel's imagination was water, and the more she learned about it, the more marvelous it seemed. She loved its physical presence—limpid and protean. She loved its transparency, its lucidity, its radiance. Its subtlety, its benign potency, the fact that it was more essential than light to life. She loved the way it was always *in flux,* in complex and continual movement, through the landscape, the air, the oceans, through the depths of the earth, on its way from one place to another, one state to another. She loved the smooth synchrony of this process, the way it functioned effortlessly and endlessly: damp air rising as tingling vapor and piling into rain clouds, mist condensing on pine needles, snow driving onto bare peaks. It was like a mathematical formula—frugal and flawless.

She learned the patterns of water, its habits, the way it streamed continually across the surfaces of the natural world, flooding, flushing, scouring, carrying off waste and debris. The way it cleaned not only the landscape but itself: in a natural system, water purified itself. Water was always in the process of returning to its limpid, pristine, original self, a tendency Isabel found mysterious and oddly touching, an unexpected note of grace.

The more Isabel learned about natural hydrology, the more she admired it. She found the system itself beautiful, the way falling rainwater drained so smoothly into a stream, then the way the stream itself worked, carrying off waste from its banks by seasonal floods and disposing of it through swarming voracious microorganisms, plants, crayfish, shellfish. She loved the fact that all the riverine water of North America had once been filtered to pristine purity by vast beds of freshwater mussels, lining the bottoms of the waterways with their gliste[r] blue-black shells.

She loved the complexity of it, the way all the parts worke[d] gether: the way forests cooled the air, the way their leaves and ne[e] encouraged condensation so that more rain fell in a forest tha[n] open land. Isabel found this marvelous—a system that directed it[s] sources toward the greatest need. She loved the involvement of [crea-] tures: earthworms, in their slow sightless journeys, producing hu[mus,] the friable woodland soil that allowed water to seep down int[o the] earth. Animals, too: beavers, once numbering in the millions, we[re] great natural engineers. (Great in both senses: in the Miocen[e] beavers were seven feet long and their projects mighty.) M[ost] beavers had dammed streams across the country, producing pond[s,] bogs, wetlands that allowed water to pool and seep downward. O[n] western prairies, the great bison herds had made soft muddy wa[llows,] each a tiny swamp that cooled the air, encouraged condensatio[n,] allowed water to enter the earth. And humble gophers: the unim[agin-] ably populous prairie dogs created vast underground networks o[f tun-] nels that aerated the soil, making it porous and absorptive and all[owed] water to seep downward.

Seeping downward was the key, Isabel learned. Everything, all [na-] ture, depended on water seeping down, through soft earth, th[rough] bogs and swamps and marshes into the groundwater, then throu[gh fil-] tering layers of sand, shale, rock, down into the mineral deeps[, the] aquifer, the underground reservoir. The aquifer was the sou[rce of] freshwater springs, of ponds and lakes, and it was created over m[illions] of years by rainwater sinking into the earth. Deep in the miner[al] strata lay great bodies of water, cold and pure, unseen, locke[d in si-] lence. Far more valuable than oil or gold, these rich hidden [ode] lodes were the earth's real treasure.

This natural system, with its intricacy and flexibility and vig[or, gave] Isabel enormous pleasure. She loved the way it had worked o[nce. She] was passionately devoted to its protection now and she work[ed] for its future.

Isabel's specialty at EPR was effluent contamination, an activ[e field.] Pollution sources were many, and since water was always [moving,] seeping, leaching, percolating and drifting over vast distanc[es, they] were hard to control. Above-ground contamination was h[ard]

"Morning, Netta," said Isabel. "How's Mitch?" Netta's husband had the flu.

"Horrible," said Netta firmly. She sat down at her desk. "Mitch, sick, is really horrible. He never stops complaining. I brought him breakfast in bed this morning, which was very nice of me, and I listened to him complain for ten minutes, and then I couldn't stand it anymore. Thank God I have an office to come to." She shook her head and pushed her glasses up on the bridge of her nose. "I told him he's lucky he's not really sick, because if he complained any more, he'd have a divorce on his hands as well as a disease." She began leafing through the papers on her desk; she frowned. "And where is the answer to my last week's memo?" she asked rhetorically. "Do we have to wait until the entire state of Illinois is paved over before we do something about this?"

"Yes," said Isabel. She sipped the lukewarm dregs of her coffee.

Angela Wetherfield, the third person in their office, was late. Angela had been at EPR for two years. She was in her early thirties, a quiet, pale young woman with a cloud of light hair. She wore long dark skirts and neat leather lace-up shoes. She was from Seattle, a community so ecologically advanced that it bestowed on her a kind of aristocracy. Whenever a novel form of environmental regulation came up at EPR, people glanced at Angela. She might say quietly, "We started doing that in the seventies, I think." She made these announcements diffidently; she was rather shy. Angela was unmarried, lived alone and talked little about her private life.

Angela edited the newsletter that went to EPR members, who provided financial and political support. The newsletter reported on impending crises, current projects and past results, trying to create a sense of urgency but not despair.

That morning Angela hurried in, her coat swishing. She said a barely audible "Good morning," her pale eyebrows lifted as though in silent reproof at herself. She unbuttoned her coat, revealing a gray cardigan and a hunter-green skirt. She sat down on her rolling chair, pulling herself toward the desk. She took the top off her container of tea. The office was quiet then, the only sound the muffled plastic click of keyboards. After a few minutes Angela spoke.

"Isabel?" she asked, her voice high and tentative. "I wonder if you'd do a piece for the newsletter on the Waukegan Forest. They're trying to clear-cut it."

"The Waukegan Forest?" asked Isabel. "Again? I thought we'd stopped that."

"We did," said Angela. "Once. But the timber companies have a new strategy. They're trying to get it declassified as national parkland. It's been slipped into a bill to expand the highway system. We want the membership to write their congressmen."

"When do you need the article?"

"Tomorrow?" Angela's voice was questioning. "If that's possible? It doesn't have to be long."

"It's fine," said Isabel. This was a relief. "I can stay late. Can you give me the stuff on it?"

That morning Isabel had a meeting with some of the EPR lawyers, and at lunch she and Netta went to a Japanese restaurant. Throughout the day, while she sat in the meeting, walked down the sidewalk, unfolded her napkin at the wooden table, leaned forward to answer Netta, there were moments when Isabel felt as though she were watching herself. As though she were absent from her body, listening to her own voice. She was separate from something in herself. All day she sensed the undiscovered presence in the back of her mind. She did not move toward it.

After five the office began to quiet again. Netta left for the ailing Mitch, Angela, for her mysterious life. Isabel was alone, the only sounds now the rattle of her keyboard, the neutral hum of the computers and the faint, mad whine of the fluorescent lights.

Leafing through the folder, Isabel stopped at a photograph of a clear-cut mountainside. It looked like a battlefield, the long slope of desolate wasteland, giant torn-up stumps and jagged holes. The earth was gouged and rutted, plundered, ravaged. *Like Guernica,* she thought.

Isabel began to write, the dark letters springing magically into being on the luminescent screen.

Clear-cutting, she began, *is a kind of war on the environment. It brings about the destruction of one of our most powerful and beneficent natural systems— the forest.*

The forest provides enormous services to the environment. It prevents erosion of the soil, it lowers the temperature of the planet, it transforms harmful gases into oxygen and it shelters and protects wildlife. It also plays an essential part in the presence of water within the ecosystem.

Clear-cutting destroys the habitat, causes erosion, lessens the occurrence of rainfall and increases the occurrence of drought. As she wrote, Isabel thought of the silent northern forests at night. The great standing fir trees, guarding the shadows beneath them, leaning slightly with the wind and creaking as they moved, their branches shifting slowly. For no reason Isabel saw Paul's tall, motionless figure in the doorway of her building, his arms at his sides. She heard him say quietly, *Yes, that's how it felt. As though you couldn't see me.*

She stopped writing. *What is it I should do?* she thought. *Was it my fault?* She sat without moving in the silent office.

When she got home that night, it was nearly ten. Without turning on the lights, she went straight into her bedroom to look at the answering machine by her bed. There were no messages. She stood for a moment in the darkened room, still in her coat. This was it, the reason she had stayed late, this feeling of emptiness that now advanced. It had something to do with Paul. She felt a thin thread of shame. *Was it my fault?* She could not say exactly what might have been her fault. She could feel a trickle of remorse.

On the third evening Isabel called Paul. She sat on the bed while the phone rang, her head bowed. His machine answered, and she heard his voice. When he was through, she drew a breath and began.

"Paul, it's Isabel," she said firmly. "I wanted to tell you I was sorry about the other night." She paused. "I don't think I—" She stopped. "I'm sorry if it felt as though I couldn't see you." She paused again. "That's all. I'm sorry."

She hung up and sat still. It was strange to hear someone's voice, to hear it so quick and living, when the person was absent. Paul had sounded warm and cheerful, buoyant. She felt graced by his warmth. She felt lightened.

Late that night, nearly midnight, he called.

At the sound of his voice Isabel felt herself gather.

"Would you try again?" he asked.

The second dinner was entirely different.

This time Paul was easy, as he had been at Dr. Lunet's. Isabel watched him across the table. They were at a Vietnamese restaurant; the waitress was tiny, with high cheekbones and a long black braid hanging down her back. She smiled at them, nodding joyfully, as she set each plate before them, as though she had made the food herself.

"Why is she smiling like that?" Paul asked after the beaming waitress had left them. "Tell me why the Vietnamese want to come to America, and why are they nice to us when they get here?"

"A mystery," said Isabel. "Have you been to Vietnam?"

Paul shook his head.

"They say now it's really beautiful."

"Yes, I've heard that," Paul said. "Hard to imagine, isn't it? In my mind it's completely devastated. All my images of it are so terrible, bombs and mud and exploding bodies. Now all the pictures you see are green and peaceful. Beautiful temples and smiling people, all friendly to Americans. It's like a miracle."

"Forgiveness," Isabel said. "When does it come?"

"I suppose it depends on the act," said Paul.

"And on the person. People forgive extraordinary things. The parents of that girl in Kosovo who was raped and murdered by an American soldier: they forgave him. It was as though the act was so huge, so traumatic, that it went past the normal boundaries of behavior. The parents forgave him because they were human and he was human. It was too big. There was nothing left for them if they didn't forgive him, and there was no reason not to. Nothing would return the child. So the soldier became another bystander, sort of."

"Is there anyone you can't forgive?" asked Paul.

Isabel said nothing for a moment. "I try to forgive people," she said carefully. *But not Michael, not myself.*

Paul looked at her thoughtfully. "Revenge is not a useful occupation," he said.

"No," Isabel agreed.

Paul leaned forward, changing his tone. "I forgive everyone," he confided. "I don't care what people do." He gave a sweep of his hand. "Fine, fine, it's done, over. Next?" He looked up at Isabel, his face bright and expectant.

"What if the dry cleaner loses your suit?"

"Oh, well." He waved his hand again. "Assassination."

There was something loose and good-natured about Paul tonight, like a lanky adolescent. There was also an adolescent neediness, a fragility. As they left the restaurant, Paul held her coat for her. When she slipped into it, he stood still, holding her from behind, gently enfolding her shoulders, her arms, with himself. She felt him close around her; it seemed like tender pleading.

That was how it felt with Paul, tender pleading. And Isabel believed it was her responsibility to respond. The image she held of him, standing in the doorway that night, had opened him to her; it had revealed something larger and darker than she had understood. She could sense him whole now, his self expanding beyond that image, waiting, patient, responsive. This was who he was as a man. He was waiting for her.

They saw each other often after that and talked several times a day. Isabel told Netta about him at lunch.

"Good for you, Isabel," Netta said energetically, her mouth full, "the widow removes her weeds."

What Isabel dreaded was sex.

For sex had changed. It no longer glimmered before her, a pleasure, a haven. Now it was alarming, full of risk. She felt the anxieties of aging. She had liked her body well enough when she was younger: long rounded limbs, clear skin, a small waist. Now her skin was slackening, her belly set, her flesh heavier. What would Paul think? Perfect bodies were everywhere for comparison, stretched sinuously along the length of buses roaring up Madison Avenue, spread out across magazine pages, in bikinis, in underwear, entwined with muscular snakes, or not covered at all, merely artfully arranged. That was her competition.

There was also the fear of a stranger's body, strange flesh against her. And the mechanics—zippers, elbows, condoms. *How do you do condoms?* she wondered. She and Michael had never used them, being married and trusting before sex had become a lethal encounter. Did you talk about them, or was it all done in silence? Did you put them on together, or did the woman look politely away? (Men's sexual equipment was so mysterious in any case—it was so unlikely, that weird tumescence, the sudden emergence of a solid shaft out of those dangling scraps. What if women's breasts inflated and deflated like that?) And sex with a new partner was full of questions: which side to lie on, where to put your arm, the whole complicated process of accustomation.

But Isabel most feared disappointing Paul. She was afraid she would feel nothing. Since Michael's death, her body had become distant from her; it had turned cool and inert. But Paul didn't insist. He took her home after their dinners, movies, the opera, and left her at her door. He kissed her sometimes, chastely, sweetly, on the lips.

One night they were in a taxi after dinner, in the thick of an argument over the president's wife.

"How can you say that?" asked Isabel indignantly. "You're completely wrong."

"I'm not completely wrong," Paul said. "You are misreading the information."

The taxi arrived at her door.

"Oh, come upstairs and let me explain," Isabel said.

Standing on the sidewalk while Paul paid the driver, she wondered what she had done. In the elevator silence clamped down on them. Isabel turned to Paul.

"It's only a drink, you know," she said. "I'm only offering you a drink."

"I know that," Paul said, smiling at her. He had his hands in the pockets of his overcoat.

The apartment was preternaturally silent: it seemed never to have known sound. Isabel walked through the empty rooms, snapping on lights, trying to be brisk. She brought Paul a drink and sat down across from him. The argument seemed to have evaporated, and she could think of nothing to say.

"Thank you," said Paul as he took the drink. "Cheers." He raised his glass to her. They both sipped; there was a pause. Isabel wondered what would happen next.

"What would you like to have happen next?" Paul asked.

"I'm nervous about sex," Isabel told him.

"You know, I rather suspected that," Paul said. He smiled. "But what is it?"

"It makes me sick to my stomach," said Isabel.

"Perhaps we should avoid it, then," said Paul.

"I mean the idea of it."

Paul shook his head. "It doesn't have to happen until you want it."

"It might be never," Isabel said. "What if it were never?"

"It would be a shame," Paul said gently, "a waste."

"I don't want you to see me naked," Isabel said. "I'm too old."

"You don't think I'm old?" asked Paul. "I'm older than you are. We're in this together. I'll out-old you."

"It might not work," Isabel warned.

Paul shook his head. "Isabel, we'll do whatever you want. You're in charge. I'll wait as long as you like." He sat without moving in her big armchair, his glass held neatly in his lap.

It was a strange thing to hear. She had never heard a man sound so yielding, so tender.

If it isn't tonight, she thought, *it will be another night.*

It turned out to be all right. It wasn't wonderful, but it was wonderful in being all right. Isabel led him into her bedroom, and he put his arms gently around her. He held her quietly first, and she felt him a gentle presence, a balm, a comfort.

In bed Isabel hadn't frozen, she hadn't turned to stone or wept. She had been afraid of weeping. She had closed her eyes, let him move across her, do what he liked. Paul was a kind lover, quiet, attentive. It had seemed to work all right for him.

Isabel herself had cheated. Too anxious to let the flesh respond on its own, without any confidence in its ability, she had mimicked response. She tightened herself toward ecstasy, screwed her eyes shut and changed her breathing. Deceitfully, she gave out a crescendo of small wordless cries, drew her muscles into a final ecstatic knot, then collapsed.

When she opened her eyes, she saw Paul smiling down at her. She smiled back, closing her eyes blissfully. It was, she hoped, a small thing, a minor victimless crime. Kinder to Paul than truth, a relief to her.

Sex had not always been wonderful for Isabel. In the early days with Michael, it had been a splendid lustrous thing, endlessly renewable, endlessly pleasing, a mutual delight. But after Ben was born, things had slowly changed. Instead of a currency used freely, prodigious sums handed back and forth without accounting, instead of that early profligate trading, ledgers had been drawn up, lines ruled across the page, debits declared. There were withholdings: times when Isabel was too distracted for sex, too anxious about Ben; when there wasn't time, or she was too tired to feel anything, or she was angry. Early in their marriage, anger had often been part of sex, an invitation, a prelude, a powerful incitement. Some of their greatest sex had been fueled by rage, counteracting and reenacting it, duplicating the struggle, the overcoming, the surrender, the forgiveness, sex both displaying and obliterating the course of rage. Later on, though, rage had turned cold and internal. Michael became resentful, and if Isabel turned him away once, he turned her away three times. Sex became inexplicably political, a matter of intrigue and power. Later still, when Michael became so moody, sex had become darker, dangerous, tense and difficult.

So Paul was a relief. After that first time, he often spent the night in her apartment. Isabel expected nothing from the sex and never felt arousal. But she learned more and more to enjoy its tenderness, the animal comfort of being stroked. She felt grateful to Paul. It seemed that he had again offered her redemption, a chance at renewal.

When the doorbell rang that day, it was very early, not yet seven. Isabel was sitting dozily on the edge of her bed, and the sound ripped through the prespeech silence. She was still in her nightgown, thinking about her exercises, which she hated: twenty-five daily push-ups to ward off osteoporosis. She heard the demanding buzz and thought of the super. Only he would come up this early unannounced: no hot water, or the front elevator was broken. Isabel pulled on her old woolen bathrobe, looked unsuccessfully for slippers and padded barefoot to the door, tying the robe as she went.

Paul stood stiffly in the doorway. He was dressed and polished, his silk tie neatly knotted, his shirt gleaming. He held a long white florist's box and looked desperate.

"Oh," said Isabel, frightened by his expression.

"May I come in?" he asked, not moving.

"Of course," she said, stepping back. "What is it?"

He came inside and Isabel shut the door. His polished black shoes made her feet feel naked. She pulled her bathrobe tighter, reknotting the tie.

"These are for you," Paul said, unsmiling. He handed her the box. He seemed taller than usual.

"Thank you," said Isabel. She opened it: a jostling mass of long-stemmed white lilies, their narrow throats stained yellow with pollen. "How beautiful," she said, though it was hard to focus on the flowers; she felt surrounded by Paul's anxiety.

"And I have a question for you," Paul said. His back was ramrod, his chin high and tense. He folded his hands one over the other.

"Yes?" said Isabel. She felt alarmed, unready for whatever it was that made Paul so anxious. She smoothed her uncombed hair back from her face. She had not yet brushed her teeth and wondered about her breath.

Paul squared his shoulders. "Will you marry me?" He was frowning. "Please," he added, with unbearable dignity.

"Yes," said Isabel, to shut him up, put an end to this. "Yes."

"You will?" he asked. He took her hands, still clasping the lily box. His fingers were shaking, and by mistake he seized the folds of her bathrobe too.

Isabel nodded. "Yes," she said again; she meant it. She wanted widowhood behind her.

"Oh," Paul said. "Good." His face changed, filling with light and pleasure. "Oh, good," he repeated. He squeezed her hands, then took the florist's box from her and set it on the floor. He took her hands again, carefully, his touch now tender.

Chapter 3

Later, Isabel and Paul walked up to the lodge, taking the trail through the woods. By then the evening sun was lying in broad bands against the tree trunks. Walking, they moved in and out of shadow, and Isabel felt shade suddenly cool against her legs, then the secret warmth of the sun distant on her skin.

The trail led to the sweeping circle of driveway before the front door; trees stood in green masses around the house. Sweetwater Lodge was large and handsome, rustic, gray-shingled, with small-paned windows and a sloping roof that swooped up at the bottom, like a pagoda's. Shallow granite steps led to the broad front door, which was dark-paneled oak. On either side was a casual stand of waist-high ferns.

Paul pushed open the heavy door. Inside, the hall was high-ceilinged and dim, with wood-paneled walls. A huge stone fireplace was swept clean and empty. On the rough-hewn mantelpiece was a round hammered copper tray, dull and unpolished. The house was cool and silent.

"Hello?" Paul called.

"Out here," a man answered.

Paul led Isabel through the high-ceilinged living room, dim and vast, with dark walls and exposed beams. Here was another huge fireplace, made of slabs of granite. Over it hung an enormous rack of moose antlers. Sofas, covered in threadbare damask and skirted with heavy fringe, were flanked by giant humped armchairs. The walls were hung with dim Adirondack scenes—men in canoes on open water; views of undulating hills; a startled buck in a forest clearing.

High overhead hung a huge white trumpeter swan, his powerful wings open wide. His long, straight neck was stretched out toward his destination, his black legs and feet tucked close against his body. His feathers, darkened with age, held a quiet shimmer; the soft pale curves of his chest caught the light.

Across the room, French doors opened out onto the porch. This had a stone floor and a broad, open view down to the lake. A row of rustic wooden rocking chairs faced the water. Paul's parents were sitting side by side, drinks in their hands. Paul's father stood when they appeared.

"Here they are," he said jovially. "Hello, Isabel." He stepped forward, nodding, courtly and welcoming. Douglas Simmons was in his early seventies, lean and rickety, with wild white hair and seamed pink cheeks. His eyes were a faded blue, the color nearly gone.

"Hello, Mr. Simmons," Isabel said. She held out her hand to him. "It's so nice to be here."

" 'Douglas,' please," he said, shaking hands and blinking pleasantly.

Isabel turned to Paul's mother. "Hello, Mrs. Simmons."

Charlotte Simmons was tall and lanky, with pale skin and an imperial nose. Her dark reddish-brown hair, going gray, was set in neat short curls. She was wearing checked pants, and her long legs were stretched out in front of her, her crossed feet set comfortably on a wooden stool.

"I'm not getting up," she announced, waving her glass, as if the announcement nullified her bad manners.

"Please don't," Isabel said. She leaned down to kiss her new mother-in-law. Charlotte lifted her cheek; it was soft and dry.

"It's just beautiful here," Isabel said, looking around.

"Well, it's a funny old place," Douglas said comfortably, pleased. "We're used to it. What can I get you?"

Paul and Isabel settled into chairs with their drinks. All of them faced the lake, as if watching a movie.

"How was the trip?" Douglas asked, eyes on the water.

"About eight hours," Paul said.

"Not too bad," Douglas said, jostling the ice in his glass. "You know, we used to take the train up," he told Isabel. "When Paul was little, we took the train to Utica, then drove from there."

"I loved the train," declared Charlotte, as though she had been challenged on this. "The train was heaven. You put your trunks on the baggage car and you were all set. You had meals in the dining cars. You could play games." She looked at Isabel. "We used to play cards and checkers. You could do anything. It used to take a day and a half, before the big highways went in."

"It sounds lovely," said Isabel. "I love trains."

"Trains were the first great populist solution," Douglas said. "Before trains, only the rich could afford to travel. You know what Lord Rothschild said in the eighteen thirties, when the idea of trains was raised in Parliament." He paused. "He spoke against it. He said"—Douglas affected an English accent—"it would only encourage the lower classes to move about needlessly." He smiled at this outrageousness. "But you know, he was right. Not about 'needlessly,' but it's exactly what's happened. Everyone began to travel. Cars made it even easier, but you know, easy travel has changed the world."

Douglas spoke with a kind of faded and elegant conviction: the words seemed ones he had spoken many times before. This was something he took pleasure in, like running his hand over a worn tapestry. The others listened in silence; they knew all this. This was Douglas's territory, a region he had years ago declared his own. The ideas here were tamed, under his command.

Isabel wondered what he meant by changing the world but did not ask. His declaration seemed to have pumped the air from the space around them.

"Paul and Whit hitchhiked when they were older," Charlotte said. "Bored by the train. Have you met Whitney?"

"Not yet," said Isabel.

"You'll *love* Whit," declared Charlotte, "he's divine. *Nowadays,*" she went on, "of course, you wouldn't let your children hitchhike, it's all serial killers out there. But then things weren't so dangerous. I used to think of hitchhiking myself." She waved her hand. "There you'd be. By the side of the road, the world before you. A dashing roadster grinding to a halt. The spray of gravel. Adventure ahead."

Paul snorted. "You'd have had Edwards drive along behind you. The chauffeur," he explained to Isabel, then turned back to his mother. "In case you didn't get a ride soon enough."

"I often thought about hitchhiking," said Charlotte, ignoring him. "So romantic."

"If there was one thing hitchhiking was not, it was romantic," said Paul, looking out at the lake. "One time I stood in the rain outside Poughkeepsie for two and a half hours. For some reason, people don't want to stop for you in the rain, when you really want them to. It's one of those inverse relationships—the more you want someone to stop, the more they don't want to. God, I was cold." He shook his head, reminiscing. "I swore that day I would never hitchhike again."

"And did you?" asked Isabel.

Paul shook his head again. "Never."

"But why did you do it to begin with?" she asked.

There was a pause.

"Well, there were no more trains by then," said Paul. "Driving was the only way. And it was during the time of Fiscal Responsibility. The older generation of Simmonses had decided that the younger generation should be denied vehicular transport in order to simulate real life, which was meant to be difficult. Meanwhile, the Simmons household moved eight hours away, so that we were basically homeless unless we managed to make our way three hundred miles across country."

"You had beds," said Charlotte. She lifted her chin. "In the apartment."

"No meals," said Paul. "No food."

"You had beds," said Charlotte, and drank from her glass.

The lake was quiet, and the shimmer on its surface was beginning to turn silver, the air darkening into evening. Flickering silhouettes began to swoop above the water, darting and twisting through the air.

"Swallows are out late," Charlotte observed.

"Those aren't swallows," Paul said, "they're bats."

"Swallows," Charlotte said, watching them.

"They're not," said Paul. "Swallows don't fly like that. And swallows don't come out at twilight. Those are bats."

There was a silence. The creatures flittered restlessly over the lake.

"Your mother," said Douglas, "has her own sources of information. Sometimes her opinions match those of the general public, sometimes they don't." Paul said nothing. "Isabel? Freshen your drink?"

"He's still cross about the hitchhiking," Charlotte observed, not looking at her son. "I'd like another, please, Douglas." She held up her empty glass.

Isabel was drinking only soda water, out of caution. She wanted her head perfectly clear. She was trying to understand Paul's parents, and it was like trying to learn a foreign language.

The first time she had met them, she and Paul had gone down to Charleston, South Carolina, where the Simmonses spent the winter. They had a tiny eighteenth-century house: narrow staircases, wide floorboards, wood-paneled walls. That evening they all sat outside on a terrace filled with geraniums.

"You're getting married in *February*? In *New York*?" Charlotte's voice was disbelieving, faintly outraged, as though she was personally offended. "But it's so inconvenient. No one's in New York in February."

Charlotte seemed to Isabel brutal in an atavistic way, casual and thoughtless, utterly amoral, like a crocodile. Douglas was affable, apparently unaware of everything: his wife's thoughtlessness, his son's resentment, the currents that swirled around him. But this, Isabel decided, was impossible. His imperviousness must be strategy, not reality.

"When's Whit getting here?" asked Paul when his father came back with the drinks.

"Tomorrow," Douglas said, handing Charlotte her glass.

"Late-ish," Charlotte added.

"I didn't know Whitney was coming," Isabel said to Paul, surprised. He nodded without speaking, and Isabel felt again as though she were in the middle of some esoteric game, the rules of which could be learned only through observation.

The four of them sat on the porch watching the air darken over the lake, the black creatures skittering.

Charlotte spoke suddenly into the silence. "You'll love Whit," she repeated with authority, "he's divine." She drained her glass, tilting it so that the ice slid against her lips. She stood up. "Dinner."

A massive dark table stretched the length of the dining room; the four of them sat at a small round table at one end of it. On the walls black wrought-iron sconces held dim candle-shaped bulbs; on the table were four candles. The rest of the high-ceilinged room was shadowy, near darkness.

Douglas unfolded his napkin. "What about Moose Lake tomorrow?"

"We should wait for Whit to do that," Charlotte said at once. "He loves Moose Lake."

"Whit loves all the lakes," Douglas observed. "We won't be able to go anywhere, then." He smiled at Isabel.

"Well, not Moose," Charlotte said decisively. She put her elbows grandly on the table and clasped her hands like a duchess. "Anyway, we don't know what the weather will do."

"It hasn't rained since April," Douglas said. "I think we can hazard a guess."

The door behind them swung open, and a short gray-haired woman came in holding a tureen. She had a small pleasant face with full cheeks and light eyes. She wore a white apron over a white turtleneck and jeans.

"Hello, Miriam," Paul said.

"Paul," Miriam said, nodding at him. She was courteous but reserved.

"You haven't met my wife yet," Paul said. "Isabel, this is Miriam Hall, who runs our lives for us."

"Hello, Miriam," Isabel said, smiling at her.

"Hello," Miriam said, nodding again, not quite smiling. She gave Isabel a watchful look. Isabel wondered if she should stand and shake hands, but it would be awkward, with Miriam carrying the tureen. Isabel hesitated; the moment passed.

Miriam spoke to Charlotte. "Do you want this beside you, Mrs. Simmons, or shall I pass it?"

"I'll serve it, Miriam, thank you, just put it down here."

"Miriam," Douglas said, "tell us what Eddie thinks about the drought. Anything new?"

Miriam shook her head slightly. "Nothing in the forecast. There are a couple of fires."

"Near here?" Charlotte asked.

"North of here," Miriam said. "Hamilton County."

"I wouldn't worry," Charlotte said, "we never have them here. Never been a fire here."

Miriam did not answer but stood waiting in the doorway.

"Thank you, Miriam," Charlotte said again, and Miriam turned to go.

When the swinging door closed behind her, Douglas said, "I don't like hearing about fires. It's awfully dry here. These mountains would go up in a moment."

Charlotte shook her head. "These woods have stood here for hundreds of years, for *eons,* without burning."

"Surely not eons," Douglas said mildly. He drank from his wineglass. "That reminds me. Eddie says the boathouse needs reshingling."

"Pass me your bowl," Charlotte told Isabel. "Eddie is Miriam's husband."

"How much?" said Paul to Douglas.

"Eight thousand," said Douglas.

"Holy smokes," said Paul. "Do we have that much in the trust?"

"We can have," said Douglas, "if we take it away from something else. Or we could put on cheaper shingles. Asphalt or whatever. Or we could just tear the whole thing down."

Charlotte passed Isabel's bowl back. "Now give me yours," she said to Paul.

"And put the boats where?" asked Paul.

"We could put up something more modest," said Douglas. "Use aluminum siding instead of cedar shakes."

"We could tear the whole house down and put in a double-wide trailer," suggested Paul.

"It may come to that," said Douglas.

"Just so I don't have to see it," Charlotte said. "Don't do it until I'm dead." She put a careful ladleful of soup into Paul's bowl and glanced up at Isabel. "I used to think everything was getting better year by year. I thought we were improving things." She set the bowl on Paul's plate. "Now I know it's getting worse. I just don't want to be there when it all happens."

Yes, thought Isabel, *it must shift at some point. When you're in your twenties, when you first encounter the world, you think that persuading everyone to agree with you is just a matter of explaining things properly.*

She had thought it would be simple—how could people *not* want to rescue their beautiful green planet, how could they not want to honor its innocence, its wild splendor? She had been certain that the natural world had been put at risk merely through ignorance, inadvertence. She'd thought the errors would be easily reversed. Now she saw the struggle as endless, her opponents fixed and relentless, the battle joined. She herself felt fixed and relentless: she would never stop.

"You don't want to see all *what* happen?" Paul asked his mother. "You act as though there'll be some apocalyptic moment when the world is suddenly overrun by bad taste."

"I'm not talking about bad taste, Paul," Charlotte said. "I mean everything." She gestured with her chin. "Pollution. Politics. It's all going to hell."

Paul shrugged. "Things move back and forth across the political spectrum like a pendulum. It's a bad time now for the environment, but things will shift. They always do. They'll shift in ways we don't imagine."

"You think someday the Republicans will start protecting the environment?" asked Isabel.

They all looked at her.

"Are you a Democrat?" Charlotte asked.

"Yes," Isabel said into the sudden silence. She wondered if she would be asked to leave.

"Good," said Charlotte, pleased. "So am I, and so is Whit. It's Paul and Douglas who have no vision."

"Perhaps," Paul suggested, "we have a different *sort* of vision."

"So you do," said Charlotte. "Impaired." She gave a short cackle.

"Isabel's not only a Democrat," said Paul proudly, "she works for an environmental group."

"Good for you," Douglas said, nodding at her. "Courage of your convictions."

"I send 'em money," Charlotte confided. "Support what they do. Don't go on the marches."

"Money is great," Isabel said inanely.

"Of course, Daddy sends the other side money, too," Paul said. "More than Mother does."

"You don't know how much money I send," Charlotte informed him.

"Good soup," Douglas said. The soup was cream of carrot, pumpkin-colored, thick and velvety.

"It is, isn't it," said Charlotte. "I think Miriam has been taking lessons."

"That means she'll quit," Douglas said. "Someone will snap her up."

"If she quits, I quit," Charlotte declared. She picked up the small porcelain bell by her water glass and rang it. When Miriam came through, Charlotte said, "That soup's very good, Miriam. Have you been taking lessons? You're not getting ready to leave us, are you?"

Miriam smiled, leaning over to pick up the tureen. "Thank you." She moved quietly; she was wearing sneakers, Isabel saw. She wondered when the last time a cook here had worn a uniform and a deferential manner. Maybe it had never been like that, maybe in this part of the country no one was deferential. It was clear that Miriam was very sure of who she was; she gave not the remotest hint of servility. To the contrary, she seemed almost cool. She served the rest of the meal—poached fish—without speaking.

After dinner they moved to the huge living room for coffee. Charlotte sank into the corner of a long brown sofa, and Isabel settled gingerly beside her. The men sat in the overstuffed armchairs, ancient, faintly moth-eaten. All the furniture looked ponderous and immovable, as though it had been designed for giants in another era.

"Now tell me again about Geordie," Charlotte said to Paul. "Why isn't he coming?"

"He was invited to go rock climbing," Paul said. "It was somewhere he's always wanted to go, in the Canadian Rockies. With a group of really good climbers."

"Don't know why he can't go rock climbing in this country." Charlotte spoke to the coffeepot. "Sugar?" she asked Isabel.

"He does climb in this country," Paul said. "He just doesn't climb *only* in this country."

Douglas shook his head slowly and looked at Isabel. "In my day, after you graduated from college, you got a job in the training department of a bank. After that, any mountain climbing you did was done during vacation." He smiled, raising his eyebrows ironically. "Nowadays, everyone seems to put the vacation first. Before the training program."

Isabel could see that she would have to learn these smiles.

"Geordie's not putting his vacation before his job," Paul said. He picked up the demitasse cup and saucer. "This is his vacation. He's taking it to go rock climbing. He actually has a good job, as I've told you, and he's doing very well." He was leaning back in his chair, away from his parents. He stirred the tiny cup.

Douglas said nothing. He took a sip of coffee and looked at Charlotte.

"Whit didn't go to a training program at a bank," she observed.

"Well, neither did I," said Paul, irritated. "Neither of us did, and it was a very good thing, as a matter of fact. You think I'd have been better off at a bank? My college roommate went into the training program at Morgan Guaranty thirty years ago, and now he's stranded. No job. They don't care. Banks don't keep you on anymore. They throw you out to make way for younger blood. Now what's he going to do? He's fifty-two years old."

"There are other places besides Morgan Guaranty," Douglas observed.

"Right," said Paul energetically, "and Whit and I didn't choose them." He was gaining heat as his father turned cool. "I went into publishing, and it seemed like a good place to go at the time. And it *was* a good place then. I had twenty great years in publishing, and then the rules changed and it wasn't a great place to be, and I left." He set his cup and saucer on his crossed knee. "Do you think I made a bad choice? What's your point, Daddy?"

Douglas did not answer. He looked over at Charlotte. "Nothing for you to get so steamed up about," he said, and raised his coffee cup.

Charlotte said nothing, her eyebrows raised as though she was considering something, her mouth set. Outside, a wind moved among the dark trees; they heard it faintly, as though from underwater. Isabel waited. No one spoke.

At last Paul leaned forward and set his cup on the table. "Well," he said briskly, "it's getting late. We had a long drive up. I think we'll head back."

Obediently Isabel stood. "Good night, Mrs. Simmons," she said, "Douglas. It's so great to be here."

Charlotte looked up, her back straight. "Good night, Isabel," she said. "Glad to have you here. Another Democrat."

Douglas stood, nodding courteously. "Good night, Isabel. See you tomorrow."

Paul and Isabel walked back through the woods. Paul went first, holding the flashlight in one hand and Isabel's hand in the other. They did not speak in the whispering dark. Several times Isabel tripped over roots or rocks. The path, smooth in the afternoon sunlight, was suprisingly complicated now.

At the cabin door Paul turned on the light. The hall sprang into visibility: long and shadowy, the doorways black rectangles. The air smelled damp and woody.

In their bedroom Isabel undressed quickly and slid into the narrow bed, shivering at the cold sheets. Her skin turned to gooseflesh. Paul clambered carefully in beside her. The bed was not really big enough for two, but she was glad for the warmth. They lay with their arms around each other. She shivered, still chilled. The shaggy blankets were heavy but not yet comforting.

"Hold on," Paul said against her hair. "You'll warm up in a few minutes."

"I know," said Isabel, "but right now I'm so cold." A gust overtook her, and she trembled violently. Paul tightened his arms. Isabel burrowed closer to his chest, pressing herself against him. His skin was stretched tight over his breastbones. She could feel the life beneath it, the thrumming of his heart.

Isabel thought of the evening, of Paul's parents: Douglas, turning disapprovingly away from his son; Charlotte, raising her eyebrows at his words. Handsome and implacable, like a pair of raptors. So chilly, so unreachable. If she were to fall in love with Paul, she thought, it would happen here, with his parents, simply to redress the balance.

"I love you," she told Paul firmly, her teeth chattering.

—

In the morning Paul and Isabel sat on their own porch, plates in their laps. The cool air was fresh against their faces. Below them the lake reflected the sky, pure and pale. There was no wind.

"I thought we'd take a picnic to Wicconet," Paul said.

Isabel nodded. "Fine," she said. She was in his hands here: lake, islands, family, all were unknown to her.

After breakfast Isabel did the dishes while Paul fixed lunch. Humming, he made sandwiches, wrapped them and packed everything carefully into a knapsack: bottles on the bottom, oranges next, then the sandwiches. He was clearly practiced at this.

When the pack was full, Paul turned and slid his arms through the straps. He settled the light load onto his shoulders.

"You asked what it was I looked forward to, coming up here? This is it. This moment, starting out for the day." He paused, tilting his head, diffident. "I hope you like it?"

"I do," Isabel promised, though she didn't know yet what starting out meant. "Of course I do." She did love the landscape, the long sweeps of forested hillside, the silent gleaming lakes. She was glad to be here.

The boathouse was beyond the lodge. They took the path that ran through the woods, then through a brushy meadow, stretching along the shore. Looking up toward the house, Isabel saw Paul's parents sitting motionless on the porch. Isabel lifted her arm to wave, and they both waved back at once. Paul, ahead of her, strode on without looking. He seemed not to know they were there.

"There are your parents," Isabel said, but he did not turn. "On the porch," she added. Now uncertain, she looked up at the house again. The Simmonses sat watching them. At the far side of the meadow, the trees closed in again. Isabel waved once more just as she stepped into the woods after Paul. The Simmonses waved back. What *were* the rules of this game, she thought, and how would she know when she'd learned them?

The boathouse was a much smaller version of the lodge, gray-shingled, with swooping eaves. Inside, the unpainted wooden walls and floors held a hollow, echoey silence. The wall on the lake side was open to the water; down the middle of the room and on each flanking side was a set of boat racks, like bunk beds, rising up to the ceiling. The boats were stacked in tiers.

"When I was little, all these racks were full," Paul said. Now there were only a few canoes scattered among the racks, a windsurfer and a mahogany motorboat tied inside the building. The water came inside, a tidy walled bay.

"That's my parents' canoe, the *Elsinore*," Paul said, pointing, "and that's Whit's, the *Weetie*. This one's mine, the *Panama*." He laid his hand on its long green flank, giving it a single slow pat. "Want to help me get her in the water?"

They each took an end. Hefting it, Isabel was surprised by the boat's lightness. They slid it sideways off the rack, then turned it over awkwardly in midair. Paul moved backward, Isabel following. They carried the canoe to the edge of the dock and lowered it into the motionless water. It floated easily on the calm surface, buoyant, all ungainliness gone. Its curved ribs and narrow thwarts were varnished wood, a translucent honey color, like the clean skeleton of a sea creature.

Paul crouched and held the bow while Isabel climbed in. The canoe gave sickeningly beneath her foot and Isabel paused, holding Paul's hand, balancing before the second step. She sat in the bow, spreading her feet, settling her weight.

"Ready?" Paul asked, and climbed into the stern.

He showed her how to paddle, how to push the wooden tip cleanly into the water, thrusting it down and away, then digging deep into the water, twisting it smoothly as she brought it out.

"It should make no sound," he said, and Isabel tried to slip the blade in silently. It was heavier than it looked, and the gesture not as simple. She overbalanced, leaning heavily forward and back, rocking to right herself.

"Stroke evenly," Paul told her, from behind. "We should have a rhythm. Don't worry about steering. I'll steer." She tried to stroke steadily, in time with Paul, though he was behind her.

They quickly left the shore behind. Isabel turned once, to see how far they'd come: the lodge and boathouse were already distant, barely distinguishable among the trees. She turned back to face the smooth crystalline waterscape.

"I came across a muskrat out here years ago," Paul said behind her. His voice carried easily across the water. "I don't know what he was doing so far out; usually they swim along the shore. I could see the big 'V' he was making, his wake, but not his face, and I tried to creep up on whatever it was. I came up right behind him. When he heard me finally, he turned around to look at me. I was so close I could see his whiskers dripping. The water on them was silver. His eyes were black and bright. When he saw me, he dove under, but the water was so clear I could still see him. I followed him for a little while, and then he went deeper and I lost him. But every time I come out here, I think of him and look for him." He laughed. "It was twenty years ago. Thirty."

Isabel looked out across the calm water, searching for the flash of silver on a bristly muzzle. She loved this: the light on the water, the cool air, the sense of beginning, the animals living in this world.

She wished Ben were coming up, he would love all this. Michael would have, too: the quiet boat, the lapping water, the clear light. Sometimes she felt his presence strongly, as though he were there, watching, not angry, not mournful, just there, aware, a part of things. At times the feeling was so vivid that she found herself turning her head to look for him. She was shocked again by the knowledge that he was not; he was nowhere. This never seemed completely true.

After his death, she had thought about Michael all the time. He was in her mind every moment, during every conversation, at work, while she was laughing, in the subway going home, while she was alone in the apartment: all the time a part of her was with Michael, shocked continually, reminded that he was gone. Over and over she learned that he was gone. He was nowhere on earth. It seemed too large to assimilate, a problem her mind could not solve.

At night she dreamed about Michael, not narratives but specific moments. She dreamed that he took her in his arms, not in a romanticized abstract way but exactly as he had held her. She could smell him, his chest, the rich draft of his armpits; she could feel the collarbones at the top of his chest. She could feel his arms around her. When she woke from these dreams, she was shocked again: he was gone.

The sun on the lake was not yet high, and the light still fell in a morning slant. Ahead, the shoreline seemed uninterrupted, a dense mass of green, but as they moved deeper into the lake, islands began to detach themselves from more distant shores.

"That's where we're going," Paul said, behind her. "On the left. That's Wicconet."

Isabel lifted her paddle. Silver drops of water slid down the shaft and onto her arm. Her skin tightened at the water's touch. She set the blade back down in the water, feeling the heavy pull against her stroke. Ahead, the island began slowly to take shape against the flat sheet of lake. It was low, and long feathery grass grew along its shore.

They drew closer, skimming through the green shallows. In the clear water below were mossy brown rocks, a few narrow translucent fish flickering among them. By now the sun was nearly overhead.

"What are they?" Isabel asked.

"Trout," said Paul. "These are young ones."

She was pleased to be here, she thought, in this cool beautiful place, with a man who was so comfortable here. They stopped paddling and drifted smoothly into shore. Along its edge the rocks were subtly striated. Fine horizontal runes recorded the lowering of the lake, the presence of the drought.

Once on the shore, they spread out lunch on the grass. The lodge and the boathouse were now invisible; the lake looked virgin, undiscovered.

Isabel unwrapped her sandwich. "I thought your parents were coming with us."

"Nope," he answered.

Isabel looked at him. Surely they had all talked, the night before, about a shared excursion? But Paul was closely addressing his sandwich and did not look up. Was there a *froideur* because of the unpleasant discussion of careers? Or had that been a normal conversation?

"We'll see my parents later," he said. "I wanted to take you on your maiden voyage alone. Get you your sea legs." He smiled at her.

"I like your mother," Isabel said experimentally, wondering if it was true.

"Unbelievable," Paul said dryly, "but kind of you to say so."

"No, I do," said Isabel more firmly, trying to convince herself. "We're going to be friends."

"Good luck," said Paul. He took a bite of his sandwich. "Were you friends with Michael's mother?"

Isabel was silent for a moment. She thought of Theresa's broad powerful face, her scornful, challenging gaze. The heavy lines from nose to mouth, like the Red Queen's. Theresa at the funeral in her navy blue suit, her coarse iron-gray hair swept back in a thick bun. She had come over to Isabel in the big featureless basement of the church, where the reception had been. Long tables stacked with food. People standing in little groups, talking in low voices. The airless room. Theresa's heels clicked sickeningly against the concrete floor. She stopped before Isabel, who was talking to someone else. Isabel knew, of course, that Theresa was there. Theresa stood still, waiting for Isabel to turn. When she did, Theresa spoke with precision.

"I never thought he should marry you," she said. "I told him not to." Her eyes were bold and contemptuous. Isabel had no answer for her, and after a moment Theresa turned and walked away, her heels clicking. She carried a dark handbag with sharp corners, and her skirt was creased where she had sat on it during the service.

Isabel answered Paul slowly. "No," she said. "We weren't friends. I don't want that to happen again."

Paul smiled at her. "Ma's all right. She's just impossible, that's all. But your plan is noble." He crumpled his sandwich wrapping into a small springy ball and dropped it into the knapsack. He took out the oranges, handing Isabel one. They began to peel off the skin in hunks; the smell of citrus bloomed in the still air. Above them, high up, a hawk wheeled lightly in the empty sky, shifting from wing to wing.

"It's not noble," Isabel said. "It's part of my job."

"How do you mean?" asked Paul.

"When you get married, you each have to connect with the other's family. It's your job to do that, to make a bond. It's hard, because families are like tribes. You already have a family, with its own language and foods and customs, and now you're being asked to adopt someone else's. So you instinctively resist them all, especially the mother-in-law. She's too powerful: she's your husband's first allegiance, his first love. She seems like a threat, so it's natural to treat her as an enemy. That's what I did with Michael's mother without realizing it, and it was a mistake." Isabel paused, still tugging at her orange. "I should have made an alliance with her."

"You declared war?"

"Not exactly. At least not deliberately, but I didn't make her my friend," said Isabel. She was piling pieces of peel into a tipsy stack. "I was very young when I married Michael. Theresa was a formidable woman, and she frightened me. I thought I had to keep my distance so she didn't undermine my marriage somehow. I didn't want her near me. So if she called and I answered the phone, I handed it to Michael right away. I never called her; it was always Michael. And once, when we were staying with her in Chicago, she invited me to have lunch with her alone. I made an excuse not to. Now I can't believe the way I behaved." Isabel shook her head at the memory of herself, timid, self-absorbed. "Of course, she never suggested it again. She's a woman who holds grudges. And I think she didn't want Michael to marry at all. She was probably relieved to find a reason to wash her hands of me. Michael was her only child; I don't think anyone would have been good enough for him."

"Her husband died?"

"Her husband died when Michael was ten." Isabel began to pull apart the inner sections of her orange. Juice ran down her fingers. "So she and I were never friends, and that was terrible in the end. It meant that when things got bad with Michael, I never called her. I never asked for help, I never wanted to admit to her that anything was wrong. It meant I was completely alone with him. And Theresa might have helped. At least she'd have known, afterward, that she'd done what she could. After Michael died, she and I didn't speak. We could have helped each other then, too, if we'd been friends." She set the separated orange crescents in a neat pile on top of the peels. "It was a huge mistake. I'd never let that happen again. Families are crucial allies. And things go wrong, there are always crises. You need them then."

Far out on the lake a gust of wind skidded across the water's surface, turning it to sudden glitter. Where they sat, among the crushed grass and bracken, the air was still and hot.

Paul shook his head. "You think about things in a way I never would," he said.

"It's how I see them," Isabel answered. Delicately she split a crescent in two and took a bite. "So now that I've married you, I have to make friends with your mother. With your whole family."

"Good luck," Paul said, grinning. "I've never managed it."

"Don't be ridiculous," Isabel said. "Of course you have. You're just thinking of irritations. And you're friends with Whit, anyway."

"How, exactly," Paul asked, "would you define 'friends'?"

"You're friends with your brother. Aren't you?"

Paul cocked his head. "We're brothers, not friends," he said. "It's different."

Isabel waited, but Paul said nothing more. He ate the last of his orange and wiped his hands on the long grass. He leaned back on one elbow, looking out at the lake, squinting against the brightness.

Siblings were always complicated, thought Isabel. There was always that fine, durable thread of rivalry, the memory of terrible feuds. A child pushed out of the bathtub or into a closet; the moments of fear, humiliation, powerlessness. She remembered the time Sam had locked her in the cellar and turned out the light. How she had screamed, how she had hated him. Standing on the top step in the dark, her parents' old painting clothes hanging on the wall over her like draperies of doom, banging on the rattly door, wild with rage. She had planned to kill her brother with a hammer. Remembering it, she still felt the distant shadow of that fury, the outrage. Sam lived in Seattle now, and they seldom saw each other. They talked every other month or so. She'd say they loved each other, but what had it meant, that hatred, set beside the love? It was much more powerful than anything she'd felt for him since.

When Isabel was finished eating, she lay back beside Paul on the sweet grass. The scent of bracken rose up. Isabel closed her eyes and felt the sun blazing against her eyelids. It was hot these days, fierce, as the protective ozone layer thinned. She felt the sun sizzling, millions of miles away in the empty sky, burning grimly. She thought of the ozone layer like a pale drifting shawl, light, evanescent, cool.

Isabel put her hands at her sides, and Paul's hand closed over hers. They lay in silence, the moist earth at their backs, the sun on their faces. The island was quiet, the only sounds birdcalls and the gentle lapping of tiny waves against the shore.

Paul spoke without moving. "You never talk about Michael."

Isabel said nothing. She hated hearing his name spoken like this, unexpectedly. "No," she said, and then, unwillingly, "Do you want me to?"

There was a silence.

"I want you to feel you can," Paul said carefully. "I don't want you to feel constrained."

"Thank you," said Isabel, and squeezed his hand. She dreaded talking about Michael with anyone but Ben. She did not open her eyes.

Paul spoke again. "I guess I do want you to," he said. "It seems he was such a big part of your life that, if you never talk about him, I feel as though there's a big part of you I don't know."

Now Isabel opened her eyes. She took her hand from his, holding it over her forehead, shading her eyes. "I don't mean to keep things from you," she said. "But it's hard to talk about him." Actually, speaking the words was nearly unbearable. The thought of going back into it was like descending into a tomb, black and dank. "You know what happened. What do you want me to say?"

"Nothing," said Paul flatly. "I don't want you to say anything."

He was hurt, then. After a pause Isabel said, "I'll talk about it if you want."

"No," Paul said. He turned on his side, toward her, his feet in hiking boots set one on top of the other. He stroked her hand. "Not unless you want to. I don't mean to force you. I just don't want you to think you can't talk about him in front of me, that it would bother me. You needn't shield me, I mean."

"Thank you," Isabel said, uncomfortable. She hadn't been thinking of shielding Paul; perhaps she should have. She now felt ungenerous. "Thank you," she said again. She could not talk about Michael, could not reenter that clammy blackness. She was trying to move forward; it was why she had married Paul. Going back into that dreadful darkness where Michael was, taking someone else with her, having to hear his reactions while her own echoed through her head, trying to respond to him, would be more than she could stand.

After a while Paul squeezed her hand and let it go, rolling onto his back and folding his hands on his chest. Isabel understood that she was refusing him something. She felt a thin coil of resentment at him, for making her feel mean-spirited.

Later, Paul sat up. "Want to take a walk?" His voice was cool and impersonal.

Isabel stood at once, offering amends. But Paul had turned distant, and they walked the faint path along the shore, circling the island, in silence. Back at the canoe they packed up and set off again.

The afternoon had slipped away, and the sun had shifted. The sky now held great piled mountains of cloud, high and radiant. The air had turned cooler, and as they set out in the *Panama,* a small wind zigzagged across the surface of the lake. The trip back seemed longer to Isabel. As they paddled steadily toward the boathouse, it seemed not to grow larger.

When they finally reached the shore, gliding in silently across the still water, the whole surface of the lake was in shadow, the light falling only on the wooded slopes above the lake, on its eastern shore. Paul and Isabel clambered onto the dock and lifted *The Panama* out, dripping and heavy. They settled the canoe on its rack, the paddles in the thwarts.

As they started up the path through the woods, Paul took the right-hand fork.

"Are we going up to the lodge?" Isabel asked, confused.

"Whit ought to be here by now," Paul said without turning.

Walking up through the meadow, Isabel could see three people on the porch. No one spoke while Paul and Isabel mounted the wooden steps. When Isabel reached the top step, Douglas stood politely, as did another man who stepped forward to greet them.

Chapter 4

"Whit," Paul said as his brother moved toward them.

The two looked disconcertingly alike, the differences between them subtle. Whit was slightly taller, perhaps more solid. The planes of his face were tauter, and his skin seemed burnished.

"Paul," Whit said, and they clapped each other's shoulders, grinning. "Good to see you."

Paul turned. "You haven't met Isabel." He stepped back to stand beside her. "My wife."

Whit smiled. His eyes were blue, like Paul's, but remarkably bright.

"Hello," she said, holding out her hand.

"Hello," said Whit. "Isabel What?" His fingers were rough against her skin.

"Isabel Simmons," she said, smiling, "what did you think it would be?"

"Could have been anything," Whit said. "So you've taken his name."

"It's your name, too," Charlotte reminded him.

Isabel nodded without speaking. It was like looking at the sun. She wanted to move away.

"I'm sorry I missed your wedding," Whit said. He spoke slowly, with a trace of a drawl in the consonants.

"I told Paul not to get married in February." Charlotte rattled the ice in her glass, triumphant.

"I did my best to get there," Whit apologized. "We had a whiteout. Horizontal snow for three days straight. No one could get in. I tried to get someone to fly me out. Those pilots in Laramie fly in anything, but they wouldn't even answer the phone during that storm." He shook his head and smiled. "I was thinking of you." He was still looking at Isabel.

Isabel said politely, "We were sorry you couldn't come."

"Next time," he promised.

Charlotte laughed. "Next time she gets married?"

"Next time you ask me," Whit said to Isabel, with a brief nod, like a bow.

"Speaking of next time," Charlotte said, and held up her glass.

Douglas stood to take it and said to Isabel, "Whit was just telling us about one of his projects. You know he's a conservation biologist." He turned to his younger son. "That's right, isn't it? That's what you're called?"

Whit nodded. "By some people," he said easily, smiling. His manner was different from Paul's; he seemed tolerant, comfortable with himself, with the world.

This was the first Isabel had heard that Whit was a scientist. From Paul's description, she had imagined some sort of mountain bum, a nature lover who ambled about fixing trails. She wondered why Paul had been so vague; or had she not been paying attention? She no longer wondered if Whit was gay.

Douglas left to refill Charlotte's glass, and Paul and Isabel sat down. Isabel took the chair at the end of the row.

"Now," Charlotte said, "go on about the mountain lions. So interesting."

"We're doing a study of them at the university," Whit said. "It's been going on for a number of years. It's pretty slow work, partly because of the nature of the study—we're trying to track a particular population over a prolonged period—and partly because lions are hard to observe. They're solitary, they travel a lot over long distances, and their habitat is pretty rough. It's not like watching chickens in a pen."

"And what is it you're trying to learn about them?" asked Charlotte, frowning to show attentiveness.

"Everything we can. How they interact with each other, the way they live, what they eat, what their territories are, how far they travel, when they move around, when they see other lions. When they breed. Patterns of behavior. Basic things."

"And what do you find?" Douglas asked, reappearing. "Are they thriving?"

"I wouldn't say thriving. They're struggling, like all the animals we study. Shrinking habitat. Climatic shifts. Rising temperatures, extreme weather, drought: everything's affected."

Charlotte accepted the drink from Douglas. "I always think lions are so exciting," she said.

Whit nodded. "They can be just that."

The way he spoke—laconic, spare—implied something more than was said. Isabel wondered what sort of excitement the lions provided; the notion of this remained in the air.

"No," said Charlotte loftily, "I mean real lions."

"These are real lions," Whit observed.

"Well, when I say 'lion,' I mean an African lion," said Charlotte. "With that big mane. So regal."

"There are actually a number of names for the American lion," Whit said mildly. "Cougar, mountain lion, puma. Catamount. Panther, painter. I like puma, myself, but a lot of people out west just call them lions. We have lion dogs out there, and lion hunters. When we say 'lion,' we mean the native animal."

"But the ones here are smaller, aren't they?" Charlotte asked. She swirled the ice in her glass.

"You're being a geographical snob, Ma," Paul said. "You're being Afrocentric."

"What are you talking about?" Charlotte said crossly. "I'm not being anything of the sort."

"It sounds a little that way," Douglas said, smiling pacifically at his wife. She didn't answer, and Douglas turned to Whit. "Why don't you tell us a bit about the lions you're studying."

Whit began to talk. Isabel, listening to his voice, looked out into the evening. The lake below was darkening slowly, sinking into night. The wide stretch of water was, mysteriously, paler than the velvety forests overlooking it: the lake's calm surface was still reflecting the last wide pallor of the sky. In the canyon, the lion moved quietly, invisible against the dun-colored sand, the soft clouds of sagebrush, the tawny maze of tumbled boulders.

The lion ranges alone, moving steadily across the upland meadows, through scattered woodland, along the high canyon rim, down its steep sides, into its wild and broken bowl. He watches everything. On soft padded feet he slips over the ground without stopping or pausing. He is searching for prey.

The long-legged mule deer, their coats dark and velvety, move across the hill together, in a loose shifting herd. They step delicately through the trees. Their matte-brown pelts—dark along the back and head, pale on the chest and belly—are perfectly camouflaged among the broken shadows, the silhouettes of trunks, the scumble of underbrush. The deer make no sound on their narrow cloven hooves. They lower their heads to browse on the short grasses; suddenly they raise their heads again, stop chewing and freeze, wary and restless. They look this way, then that, their dark eyes wide, intent, watchful. Their long ears swivel, vigilant: any moment may bring death. But just now they see nothing, hear nothing. They see no creeping shadow; the small breeze carries no predator's scent. The only sound, the only movement, comes from this breeze, which shifts lightly in the leaves. After a moment the deer drop their heads again to the ground and graze. They take a quiet step forward, then another; they flick their short tails. The flick is dangerous, an eye-catching flutter in the broad, motionless landscape.

The lion, moving down the canyon wall, sees the flicker in the glade below. He stops, his gaze fixed on the deer. The end of his heavy tail, just above the grass, gives a twitch. His eyes widen intently, becoming entirely round. In a human gaze, this wide-openness means innocence; in a lion's, assassination.

The lion moves carefully now, with precision. His long, lean body lowers, melting close to the ground. He slinks through the brush, supple and silky, his movements fluid. His padded feet muffle the sound of his steps. He must creep unseen close to his prey: these deer are fleet, and they would easily outrun him. Success—his life—depends on his sudden apparition, on one dextrous leap, perfect and fatal. An adult deer is a dangerous target, tall, strong, fast. It can kick and trample an attacker, and an injured lion cannot hunt. He must eat once a week, and a lion who can't hunt will quickly starve. Efficiency is crucial. The more risks the lion takes, the more energy he expends, and the more injuries he sustains, the sooner he will die.

The lion chooses his prey with care. The ideal animal is young, straying from the herd, close to the broken shadows of the brush. An animal ignorant and unseasoned, slow to bolt, easily overpowered.

The lion creeps downwind toward the herd without sound. He has chosen a target. He works his way invisibly across the landscape, through the scattered brush, nearer and nearer the herd. His wide gaze is fixed on the animal, his muscles are taut. Everything in him is focused and intent. Adrenalin floods through him. His blood vessels have expanded, and in the big cavity of his chest his heart is thundering. He is now lost, deep in the dream world of the kill; there is nothing else in him now but that. His yellow eyes are round and rapt as a demon's. The closer he gets, the more slowly he moves, stealing inch by inch through the dwindling cover. His breathing is shallow, his body has lengthened and lowered. His ears are flattened. He does not blink.

The young deer takes another step, raises his head and looks around the glade. The lion freezes, erasing himself among the sandy scrub. The deer looks away, flicks his tail casually, lowers his long neck again. The lion flows soundlessly toward the animal, his tawny belly sweeping the tops of the dry grasses. Behind the last bush he gathers himself, bunching his hindquarters in a final rapid shuffle, balancing, preparing for the spring.

The lion explodes up out of the brush in a swift enveloping leap onto the animal. Mouth wide in a crimson snarl, ears flat, the rampant lion throws himself onto the withers and shoulders of his prey. His great hooked claws are extended, his heavy paws crushing. The lion's weight and the shock of the assault throw the slighter animal off balance. The panicked deer staggers; he crashes down, his legs thrashing. The lion's curved claws lock the deer into immobility, a close and fatal embrace.

The first bite is high on the animal's neck, penetrating the slender muscles at the back of the skull. The lion's teeth close in alternate alignment with the prey's vertebrae. Next is the killing bite: the smooth white teeth sever the spinal cord, ending consciousness, bringing down over the deer the swift blanket of death.

In that first instant of skirmishing commotion, the rest of the deer have fled. They float into the air, rising and falling in high, alarmed bounds through the trees. The glade is now empty; the sound of them

dies away. The crouching lion, his eyes glaring, drags off the warm car-
cass. His tail thrashes heavily against the dry ground like a muscular
snake. He steps slowly backward, tugging the deadweight toward cover.
What he wants is a rocky overhang, a tree with low, sweeping branches.
The velvety fur of the deer rucks up against the stones, ruffling against
the rough earth. Its dark liquid eyes are still open but dulling now.

When Whit finished speaking, there was silence. The lake and sky
were at last turning black. Finally Douglas spoke.

"Boy," he said, and shook his head. "That's something, Whit. Pretty
terrifying, actually."

"Ah, the Lion Man," Paul said, his voice light and ironic.

Charlotte stood abruptly. "Dinner," she said, and led the way back
inside.

They sat again at the round table, which seemed smaller now, more
brightly lit. Charlotte sat between her two sons, Isabel between Douglas and Whit. Miriam brought in a platter, offering it first to Charlotte.

"Miriam's been studying, we think," Charlotte said. "Haven't you,
Miriam? You get better every year."

Whit must have greeted Miriam earlier; now he only smiled at her
and helped himself to the chicken: smooth white slivers with crackle-
brown skin. "This looks great," he said.

Miriam smiled but said nothing.

Now that he was not looking at her, Isabel could examine his face.
His eyebrows were different from Paul's, and his mouth, more supple,
had a different slant. His story about the lions, the kill, had changed
the evening. Isabel felt somehow alight.

Charlotte helped herself to mashed potatoes, handed the bowl on
and sat up straight. "Now, Whit," she said. "Tell us what's going on at
the university."

"Not much that's new," Whit answered. He took the bowl from
Charlotte. On his wrist, beneath the shirt cuff, were fine golden hairs.

"But where are you in the department?" asked Charlotte.

"Where I always am, Ma," he answered cheerfully. "Lowly tenured
professor of environmental biology, specializing in large carnivores."
He smiled at her. "No change."

"And what about your plans?" she said. Charlotte was drunk, Isabel
realized. She spoke with the irascible single-mindedness that alcohol
confers. "We want to hear what your *plans* are."

"My plans," Whit repeated good-naturedly. "Hiking, canoeing, maybe a little camping."

Charlotte, unamused, took a swallow of her drink. "Funny."

"I don't mean to be flip," Whit said. "I really don't have other plans. My plan is to be here for two weeks and go back to Wyoming. That's it."

Two weeks, Isabel thought.

His face was nearly the same shape as Paul's. The eyes were different, and the skin.

"That's a plan," Paul observed, nodding.

Charlotte knitted her brows. "But what about long-term?" she asked. "For the future?"

Whit shook his head. "Only the future knows."

"He won't tell us," Charlotte said, looking around the table.

"Ma, he has told us," Paul said peaceably. "He doesn't have any plans."

"I think we can let Whit tell us what he has to say," Charlotte said.

There was a silence, then Whit smiled kindly at his mother. "If I come up with any plans, I'll let you know," he said. He began to eat.

"I'd like another drink," Charlotte said, and Douglas rose to take her glass.

Whit turned to Isabel. "Have you been here before?"

"Never," she said. "It's incredibly beautiful." She kept herself from saying more, afraid of gushing.

"But have you spent any time in the mountains before? Are you a hiker or a canoer?" He looked at Paul. "Have you brought us an outdoorswoman?"

"Pretty much," Paul said proudly. "She's a rider. She hikes. Today she learned to canoe. She does just about everything."

"A rider?"

"She grew up around horses," Paul said.

"One horse," Isabel amended. "I had a backyard horse."

"Best kind," Whit said, and turned to Paul. "You should bring her out to Wyoming. We'll go riding."

"I'd love it," Isabel said simply.

Douglas reappeared with Charlotte's drink. He handed it to her and sat down. Charlotte leaned forward.

"We still haven't heard your long-term plans, Whit," she said.

Whit shook his head patiently. "I don't have any. I am where I'm going to be."

"But then where do you go from there?" asked Charlotte impatiently. "What's the next step?"

"It's not like the army, Ma," Whit said. "I'm not trying to be a general."

"But you must be trying to be *something*."

"Not in the way you mean," Whit said. "I'm probably where I'm going to be. I'm pretty happy there. It suits me." Whit seemed to absorb tension, dissolve it.

Charlotte did not move. She looked at him, waiting.

Whit sighed. "Okay. I'm going to stay in Wyoming. I'm never moving back east. I'm never going to law school. Never going to be a banker. I'm forty-five years old."

Charlotte looked at Douglas. "Still time," she said, obstinate. "Could still change his mind. Get out of Wherever, Wyoming. Get a job at Columbia Presbyterian."

"Ma, you know I'm not that kind of doctor," Whit said. "The only place I can do what I do is where I am. There are no large carnivores in Manhattan. Or at least not ones I want to study."

Charlotte sipped from her drink and frowned. "Did you put water in this?" she asked Douglas. "It's too weak. Water *ruins* Scotch."

"Where are we headed tomorrow?" Paul asked Whit. "Shall we do Moose or Pemmican?"

"Did you put water in this?" Charlotte demanded again.

"You know me better than that," Douglas said. He turned to Paul. "I vote Moose." Charlotte glared at him, but he looked pleasantly at the others.

"Pemmican," said Paul, "just to be ornery."

"Pemmican," Charlotte declared, setting the offending drink down on the table.

"Which would you rather?" Whit asked Isabel. "Moose Island is farther, but they're both portages."

"Moose," Isabel said without thinking, then felt disloyal.

"Moose it is," Whit said. "My favorite hike."

Charlotte took another sip. "This tastes like pure water," she said. "I'd like another one, with some Scotch in it."

Without looking at her, Douglas stood up. "I am feeling the hour," he said to the others. "I'm ready to go up. As my father used to say,

'There are worms to eat and eggs to lay.' Good night, all." He gave the table a nod, not including Charlotte, who eyed him sullenly. He turned to her. "Coming?"

Charlotte stared at him for a contentious moment, then stood, swaying slightly. "Good night," she said with exaggerated dignity, and stalked past him. Douglas nodded at them all again and followed her.

The others said good night. When Charlotte reached the doorway, Paul called, " 'Night, Ma."

Without turning, Charlotte said, "I'm not coming canoeing with you tomorrow. Don't feel up to it."

No one answered. The other three sat listening to Douglas and Charlotte slowly mount the front stairs. Miriam pushed through from the kitchen, stopping when she saw them still at the table.

"That was a great dinner, Miriam, thanks," Paul said, standing. Miriam nodded, beginning to clear. Paul turned to Whit. "Scrabble?"

Whit nodded and looked at Isabel. "A family addiction," he explained.

They sat in a shadowy corner of the living room at an old wooden card table. An iron floor lamp held a battered honey-colored shade over them. The house around them was silent. Paul opened the Scrabble board and slid the tiles onto it with a slithery rush. They drew to go first; Isabel won elegantly, with an "X."

"Will your mother really not come with us tomorrow?" she asked, picking up the rest of her letters.

"Of course she will," Paul said. "She just wasn't getting enough attention tonight. She likes attention. And she doesn't think either one of us has done quite well enough with our careers. She gets reminded of that each time she sees us. She wants to hear that Whit is going to see the error of his ways, move back east and become what she calls a real doctor. She wants me to go to Harvard Business School."

Whit shook his head, examining his letters. "Not going to happen."

Paul set his letters in order on his tray. "These are winners," he told Whit. "You're in trouble."

Whit cocked his head, raised his eyebrows and grinned.

"Were you always the quieter one," Isabel asked him, "or was it living in Wyoming that did it?"

"He wasn't allowed to talk, growing up," Paul said. "I only allowed him four words a day."

"It was tough," Whit said.

"That's three," Paul said.

To Paul, Isabel said, "Didn't you tell me he worked for the National Park System?"

"I told you he worked in the parks," Paul said. He was frowning at his letters.

Isabel turned to Whit. "How did you end up in Wyoming?"

"While I was in college, I went up to Alaska one summer," he answered. "I worked as a camping guide along Prince William Sound. That was when I got interested in being a naturalist. I changed schools and got my B.S. in Texas, in the wildlife program. Then I got my master's in wildlife ecology at Utah State. I worked on coyotes and then on badgers. After I got that degree, I went out to Oregon and worked for Fish and Wildlife. I did a survey of pelagic birds on an island off the coast, where they breed and nest. Then I started my Ph.D. on mountain lions at Oregon State. That took six years. After that I drifted around a bit, teaching here and there, and wound up in Laramie." He smiled at her. "Where things are pretty good."

"You teach?"

Whit nodded. "And I rustle up funding for projects, then I identify students for them. When they're set up, I go out with the students into the field to supervise. I spend a few weeks with each one."

"Catching and tagging mountain lions," said Isabel.

He nodded again. "There are other projects, but that's a long-term one."

"You go out on horseback?"

"Mostly. We go out with dogs. It's mostly best to go on horseback, but there are some places you can't get to on a horse, and you have to go on foot." He looked at her appraisingly. "So you're a rider."

Isabel nodded. Horses had been her first love, the passion of her childhood, her early adolescence. Her little chestnut mare, Chappie, had died at the age of thirty-one in the small field behind her parents' house in Bedford Hills. Isabel hadn't ridden in years, but the language of horses is not lost. To speak it now with Whit would be returning to a beloved childhood tongue.

Chappie had been the center of Isabel's world: the silky brown face turned toward the barn door in the mornings, the urgent sound from the back of the mare's throat as Isabel measured out the grain. The sleek hardness of Chappie's glossy back in the summertime, her thick halo of fur in the winter. Her grass-scented breath.

"Do you have your own horse?" she asked Whit.

He shook his head. "Not now. I used to."

"What kind?"

"Quarter horse–Appaloosa cross. Most of the horses you see out there are quarter horses. I got mine when he was two, and he died at twenty-three. But now I spend more time in town. I borrow horses from the houndsmen." He looked up at her. "I believe it's your move."

Isabel wanted to ask more. She wanted to know what kind of hounds they used, what it was like to find a lion.

She imagined the scene: it was just before dawn, and the trees were beginning to show against the sky. High up in the branches was a dense blurred silhouette. Below the tree, the big rangy hounds in a milling crowd, their bugling cries. Heads up, looking into the branches. A tracker dismounting, the horse sidestepping quickly, snorting in alarm. All the horses nervous, smelling the lion.

Isabel, drawn to the scene, felt Paul's silent disapproval beside her. Instead of talking, she looked down at her row of letters. She had ended up with an unpromising group, despite the dashing beginning: XEETPSU. She studied them at length, shifted them back and forth, sighed, frowned and finally laid out five letters on the double-word score in the center: UPSET.

"A poor beginning," she said.

"Twenty-four," said Paul, writing down the score.

"Modest," said Whit, "not poor."

It was his turn next, and after a moment he began carefully to set down his own letters. His fingernails were clipped straight across, his hands very clean. He set an "R" beneath Isabel's "T." One neat letter after another was placed in a line to make TREMORS, a long perpendicular ladder that opened up the lower regions of the board.

Part 2

Chapter 5

In the mid-1970s, when Isabel graduated from Ann Arbor and moved to New York, it seemed as though life in the metropolis was merely a continuation of life in the college town. It seemed that being young and liberal placed you at the center of the universe.

In Michigan the students had dominated everything. They were responsible for the dramatic activities—the raucous rallies, the midnight demonstrations on the quad, the sit-ins, the heated editorials. There were occupations of the administration buildings, chains and padlocks around the dean's doors, strident student voices issuing nonnegotiable demands from megaphones. There was the electrifying idea of political potency, the heady notion that the students could *make* nonnegotiable demands, not only in the university but in the nation. There was the idea that the students themselves—untrained, inexperienced—had triumphed, simply through energy and determination and inventiveness, over the whole vast entrenched empire of the military, with all its multiple branched and layered enterprises: civilian misinformation, covert forces, corporate contracts, intransigent generals. There was the possibility that the students themselves were partly responsible for ending the grisly war in Vietnam. The night Johnson announced his decision not to run for another term, everyone went out and danced on the quad in the darkness, celebrating their own success.

Then there was their appearance. They were so exotic—so beautiful, they thought—so vivid and extreme. They stood out so boldly against the rest of the world. The short-short skirts and the loose long hair, the suede pants and beaded vests, the luxuriant swinging fringe. Thonged sandals, bare feet, high boots. Long legs; legs were everywhere. Everyone was suddenly thin; breasts were out. And everyone was suddenly ethnic, in handwoven clothes, embroidered tunics, braided leather, heavy tarnished brass buckles. They were a new tribe.

Then there were the things this generation had discovered. The delirious overwhelming music, which was louder than any music ever had been before, the primal bass line pounding like a furnace beneath the wild cries of the electric guitars, the raucous, soulful vocals, the shaggy, anguished, screaming singers. There was the exhilarating dancing, the endless delirious suggestive motion. And of course there were drugs: the sweet claustrophobic inhalations of marijuana, the slow wild ballooning of sensations inside the brain. And sex.

All those things seemed absolutely owned by Isabel's generation, created by them. No previous generation had even thought of these things. Certainly no other generation had been as liberated or as powerful. Before them, everything had been run by older people: men in stiff-brimmed hats, women in gloves. Before, rules had governed the world. Now young people were in charge: radical, impassioned, barefoot. Now it seemed there were no rules; young people could challenge anything. Being young and American, at that moment, conferred a sense of supreme entitlement.

In New York Isabel found an apartment and a job. The apartment was on Eighteenth Street, far west, in a pleasant, shabby, low-skyline section of the city. The neighborhood was quiet and the inhabitants mostly Puerto Rican. On warm evenings people sat on stoops outside their houses along the broad avenues; the gentle rattle of Spanish hung in the air.

Isabel's apartment was a narrow railroad flat, a fourth-floor walk-up in a run-down brownstone. It consisted of two long, thin rooms, the first a sort of entrance hall with a row of kitchen appliances along one wall, flanked by a bathroom and a closet. The second room was a step down from the first, described in the ad as a "sunken living room." It held Isabel's foldout sofa bed, a small desk and two faded thrift-shop chairs. The windows looked out over an untended yard into the spindly branches of an ailanthus tree. Above her was the roof, and in the mornings pigeons congregated overhead, walking in circles and cooing sociably.

Isabel worked for a Democratic city councilman, Jonathan Dudley, who was running for Congress. Dudley was a rising New York star, young, intelligent and photogenic, with a high rounded forehead and silky light brown hair that he wore rather long. He was famously rich; his grandmother was an Astor, and his beautiful young wife, Belinda, was on the best-dressed list. Dudley was also surprisingly shy, though full of a vivid energy. He was the magnetic center of the office: when he walked in, everyone's posture improved. He was a conscientious worker and impeccably liberal, as though to make up for being an Astor. He was a friend of the Kennedys and a dove on Vietnam. He supported gay rights, the environment, education and aid to the elderly. His staff worshiped him.

The Dudley office was a string of shabby rooms on East Fifty-eighth Street, cramped and chaotic. Telephones rang constantly, and all surfaces were stacked with piles of papers and worn green files. There was a full-time staff of eight and a varying number of part-timers. Isabel, full-time, sat at a Formica-topped table facing the front door. Her official job was head of the volunteers, but she was also the receptionist, greeting constituents, colleagues, volunteers and friends, as well as UPS, the telephone repairman, and the electrician.

Despite Dudley's fabled wealth, there never seemed to be quite enough money to run the office. The rooms were small, the walls scuffed, the floors dingy. Isabel's salary barely paid her rent; she didn't care. No one there cared about salary. They were all in their twenties, all liberal, all idealists. The men were there for the politics, the women for the energy. They all wanted to work in just this sort of place, one driven by principle and belief, one with just such a vivid and glittering vision of the future. They all believed that Jonathan Dudley would become president. They all believed that the country was being overtaken by a gradual, sweeping, irresistible current of liberalism. They all thought that everything they wanted was lying before them.

That summer Isabel felt she was at the center of the world, with her life spreading out like an open field. She thought it would always be like this, endless, fertile, rolling. It seemed as though everything was hers, not for the taking but for the doing. It seemed as though she and her friends could achieve the things they aspired to, that life would go on revealing itself as interesting and varied and wonderful. What she wanted was to make things better in the world, and it was clear that this was possible.

This was the summer Isabel met Michael. They were at a party in Greenwich Village, someone's summer sublet, upstairs in a town house, a series of narrow high-ceilinged rooms. The living room walls were covered with bookshelves jammed tightly with paperbacks. On the floor was a thin red-striped rug that kept rucking up underfoot. There was no air-conditioning, and the night was hot and steamy. The windows were open, and noises from the street drifted in: groaning thunder from passing buses, occasional sirens. The sound of conversation rose to blot out that of the city.

Isabel and Michael stood in the hall near the kitchen, drinking white wine out of thin plastic glasses. Michael was standing beneath a ceiling light, and the illumination spilled down over his face. He had a hawk's bony nose, thick dark eyebrows and a generous mouth. He was very tall and thin, wide-shouldered, big-boned.

They stood talking, nearly shouting, against the noise of the party. Isabel's neck and shoulders were bare, and her skin was damp with the heat. Her silk top clung.

Michael asked what she did, and when Isabel told him, he shook his head.

"Dudley'll lose the election," he said.

"He will not," Isabel said.

Michael nodded affably.

"Why do you say that?" Isabel asked, and added teasingly, "What do you know?"

"I'm at the Columbia School of Journalism," he said modestly. "Nearly a journalist."

Michael's manner was beguiling. He was serious about what he said, he believed absolutely in it, but at the same time he gave you leave to laugh. He relished absurdity. He brimmed with energy; it seemed that if touched, he would give off glancing sparks, little licks of lightning.

"But why do you think he's going to lose?" Isabel asked.

Michael smiled at her. "I have a theory."

"Well, it's wrong," Isabel said, smiling back.

"Tell me why," said Michael, leaning down to listen.

The party was crowded and the hall narrow, and each time someone passed, Michael and Isabel were pressed against each other. Isabel explained, speaking into Michael's ear, which he had set politely by her mouth. She found his closeness distracting, the intimacy of the ear, with its tender spiraling convolutions. Michael's eyes were cast down in concentration as Isabel talked, and she had the sense that his whole body, his entire consciousness, was focused on her words. She was aware, too, that with each word, her breath moved across the delicate whorls of tissue. When she had finished, Michael raised his head and nodded.

"We need to talk," he said. He looked around and frowned, as though he had just noticed the noise, the throng. Now Michael spoke into Isabel's ear, and she felt his breath. "Let's get out of here," he said, and took firm hold of her upper arm, propelling her gently toward the door. She felt his fingers on her skin.

Out on the landing, Michael—not letting go of her arm—said urgently, "Come on," and they clattered down the three flights of stairs toward the darkened street, as though making a dangerous escape. There was something slightly wild about Michael, something glittering and unpredictable. Isabel liked that.

Over dinner he told her his story. He was from outside Chicago, an only child. His father had died when he was ten, his mother had not remarried. He had gone east to boarding school and college, and was now in his second year in the master's program at Columbia. He was writing a long piece about New York City politics; he was completely absorbed by them. He explained his theory about Dudley.

"He's a dinosaur," he told Isabel.

"He is not," Isabel answered, indignant. "What do you mean?"

"He's about to become obsolete. The time of the patrician politician is over. The country is becoming populist, the voters are turning against rich people from Harvard. They're going to want a self-made man from a blue-collar background. They want leaders who reflect the common man, not the elite. Entitlement is losing ground; in ten years people who went to boarding school will be saying they went to high school instead of to Groton. A privileged background will be something you disguise."

"Oh, no," said Isabel, shaking her head. "There's a long tradition in America of patrician leaders. Thomas Jefferson, Teddy Roosevelt,

FDR. Look at John Lindsay and JFK. People love glamourous patricians."

"JFK was not patrician," Michael said.

"But people thought he was. He went to Harvard," Isabel said. "Anyway, people love the fact that Dudley has money. They love his fabulous family, the huge old mansions. They love that picture of his grandmother on opening night at the opera: seventy-five years old, in her white ermine stole and the diamond tiara. The articles *always* include that picture. The press *loves* Jonathan."

Michael shook his head. "The tide is turning," he said. "I promise you. The day of the WASP is over. *Finito.* For two hundred years this country assumed that New England elitists should run the country. It's changing. Sorry," he said kindly, "but your team is about to lose." A small candle guttered on the white cloth between them. Michael's cheekbones were high, like a Tartar's.

"What do you mean, my team? It's yours, too," Isabel said. "You're in this, too."

Michael shook his head again. "I'm Jewish," he said, and for the first time his voice sounded complicated. Isabel hesitated before she answered.

"Well," she said, picking up her glass, "so what? You're still from Lake Forest: you're from privilege, not from hunger. You're not immune. Lawrenceville, Williams, Columbia—you'd have a hard time calling yourself blue-collar and self-made."

"But," Michael said triumphantly, "I'm not going to run for office. I don't have to prove anything. I'm safe." The tension had gone from his voice. "You, however, are in trouble. When you're struggling to get elected to your local school board, you'll be begging for populist validation. You'll be asking me to be photographed with you, wearing my yarmulke. You'll be eating out of my hand."

"Probably," said Isabel, laughing.

It turned out that Michael had theories about everything, and what he liked to do was explain them. Enthusiasm lit him up. He wanted to go overseas as a correspondent, he told Isabel. He wanted to run the Paris office of *The New York Times*. He wanted to write about Europe and communist Russia, the Middle East and China. He wanted to reveal everything, to explain the politics and philosophy of other places. He wanted to be the nation's observer, to translate the world for

America. There was hardly enough time for everything Michael wanted to do; it seemed he wanted to start right then, that minute, before coffee. Listening to him, Isabel felt the pull of his current.

"That's a rough sketch of me," he told her. "Now tell me everything about you. Where did you grow up?"

"The northern tip of Westchester," she said, "a place called Bedford Hills. Very leafy and rural. My father's a minister, my mother's in the garden club. I went to elementary school there, then to boarding school outside Philadelphia, and then I broke all the family traditions and went to college in the Midwest. It was a nice, boring middle-class upbringing. Like yours."

Michael smiled and tilted his head without answering.

After dinner they went out into the summer night. Michael stopped a cab and Isabel slid inside, wondering if he was coming with her.

"What's your address?" Michael asked, and gave it to the driver. He leaned in the window to speak, putting his hand on the roof of the cab. The gesture—resting his hand easily on someone else's property— seemed to Isabel masterful, in the way that men were masterful, using the physical world in the way that suited them. Isabel looked out at his body, bending slightly; she could feel her own body, aware of his. She hoped he would come with her. He slid in beside her and closed the door.

"I'll take you home," he told her, then he added suddenly, attentively, "If that's all right?"

Isabel nodded, wondering what her apartment looked like. Had she made the bed? If the sofa bed was unmade and open, the room was filled with chaos. And had she left scattered clothes and shoes everywhere as she'd dressed for the party? It was entirely possible; in fact, it was probable. She wondered if this revealed the flaws of her character in some important way.

Michael paid for the taxi, and Isabel led him up her four flights of stairs. She was aware of him behind her on the steps, she heard his breathing as she unlocked the door. They stepped inside and she turned on the light: a complete mess, just as she'd feared. The sofa bed stood open in the middle of the room, the rumpled sheets littered with clothes, belts, scarves, abandoned underwear. Shoes lay scattered on the rug.

"It looks like a crime scene," Isabel said ruefully.

Behind her, Michael took hold of her upper arms. She felt a long, cool awakening thrill.

"Isabel," he whispered, "Isabel." He put his mouth at the nape of her neck and she stopped moving.

Much later, when they rose to the surface, when they stopped moving and opened their eyes, still breathing long breaths, they were lying aslant, their heads at the foot of the bed. The sheets were twisted into ropes, the pillows on the floor. Isabel leaned off the bed to get them as though leaning from a boat. They rearranged themselves on the bed, stretching out leg to leg, Michael's hand on Isabel's bare hip. The air conditioner hummed loudly, took a breath, shifted gears and went on more quietly. They talked in the dark, looking sightlessly up at the ceiling. They turned to each other, they stroked each other's damp skin slowly, then urgently, they went to sleep and woke up and touched each other again and slept again until it was dawn. In the early light Michael's skin was warm and honey-colored.

"You," Isabel said, setting a finger on the curve of his eyebrow, "are perfect." Hearing the words, she was embarrassed. She had not meant to say that; she had meant to say only that she liked his skin.

"You," said Michael, and he set his mouth against her throat; she closed her eyes. He took her wrists and raised them above her head, holding them together with one hand. He looked down at her, his face close.

"You," he whispered, "make me crazy."

That morning she was late for work. After Michael left, Isabel moved slowly, as though underwater. When she finally set out, her hair slicked, still wet from the shower, there were dark circles shimmering beneath her eyes. She had hardly slept. Well, sex was so much more valuable than sleep. You could sleep anytime.

On the subway she stood holding the greasy pole, dazed, sated, barely aware of the jolts, of the bodies crowding around her. Her own body felt battered and stiff. *Well used,* she thought.

When she reached the office, Elena, a pretty blond girl from Boston, was already at her table. Isabel sat down and uncapped her cup of coffee.

"I'm sorry I'm late," she said.

"It's okay," Elena said. "It's a slow morning." She looked at Isabel. "Are you all right?"

"I'm fine," Isabel said, and heard herself add, "I'm in love."

That summer she could not get enough of Michael. She was dazzled. She longed for his presence. At work she spoke his name whenever she could. "Michael has a theory about that," she told anyone who would listen. Everything he said was interesting to her; she memorized his life like a new language.

She learned that Michael had gone to summer camp on the Upper Peninsula and won prizes for woodcraft and canoeing. "So did everyone else," he told Isabel. "It was an unwritten rule." Michael's first girlfriend was named Kathy. They went steady for two months in eighth grade and almost never spoke, communicating entirely through third parties. When Michael was small, his family had a tan cocker spaniel called Harrods. At fifteen Michael had lost a front tooth in a football game, and the tooth he now had was false. He tapped on it with his index finger to show her. It looked like the other one, but she now knew it was not. Isabel felt as if she were being trusted with the esoteric knowledge of a new religion.

In ninth grade Michael had wanted to be a doctor. "I had a microscope," he said. "I used to put things under it and stare at them. I was being scientific, and the only scientific person I knew was the doctor. I could see myself in a white coat, with a stethoscope around my neck, telling people what the facts were."

"You're still doing that," Isabel told him, "you just don't have the stethoscope."

"Should I get one?" he asked. "For credibility?"

Michael's childhood bedroom had a sloping roof and dormer windows. After he'd grown to full height, he could straighten up only when he was standing in front of the window. "The rest of the time I had to stand like this," he said, tilting his head to one side. "So I used to walk around the house like that. It drove my mother crazy. I'd tell her I was doing it to save time, because I'd just have to tilt my head again as soon as I got to my room."

They were at Isabel's, cooking dinner. They stood side by side, he at the stove, she over the sink. There was no counter space, so Isabel used the sink to work in.

"What did your street look like, where you grew up?" Isabel asked him. "I have to visualize it."

"Small white houses and little squares of lawn. Each house had a driveway leading past it to a one-car garage and a small yard in back. Some houses had a tree in front; ours did not." He glanced at her. "This may come as a disappointment to you. You may have thought Lake Forest was all big brick mansions and huge lawns, but you would be wrong. We, for example, did not live in the brick-mansion district. We chose instead the not very exclusive, pretty inexpensive district."

"Very sensible," said Isabel. "What did your father do?"

"Worked for an insurance company," Michael said. But something had changed, and he had turned careful. His voice was complicated again. Hearing the change in his voice, Isabel said nothing more. She was rinsing pieces of chicken, holding them under the cold stream of water.

Michael said, abruptly, "My father changed our name."

"What was it before?" asked Isabel.

"Greenberg," Michael said. "He moved to this country right before the war and dropped the '-berg.' He thought it would be better for business. Better for the family: a new world, a new life. A lot of people did that then."

Michael was stirring sliced potatoes in a pan on the stove. The heat was beginning to rise, the pale slivers to turn soft and translucent.

"What did your mother think about it?" Isabel asked. She turned off the water and blotted the chicken dry.

"I don't know what my mother thought. She won't talk about it. If the subject comes up, she shakes her head and waves her hand"— Michael gave a brisk decapitating gesture with the spatula—"as though it's over and there's no point in discussing it."

Isabel shook dry green flecks of tarragon onto the chicken, rubbing them into the damp skin.

"It seems painful for you to talk about this," she said.

"About what?" Michael asked. "Being Jewish?" The word held a small charge.

"I don't know what it is," Isabel said, slowly, "but there's something. I hate it when you sound in pain, so I sort of don't want you to talk about whatever it is that does that. But I don't want you to think I don't want to hear it. I want to hear whatever you want to tell me."

Michael shrugged. "You want to hear about being Jewish? When I was at Lawrenceville, freshman year, my roommate came in one afternoon. He said, 'Hey, Green, you're not Jewish, are you? Someone bet me a dollar that you were, but I said you weren't. You aren't, are you?' "

Isabel drew in her breath. "What did you say?"

"I said, 'No, I'm not Jewish.' I said it just like that, as though he was crazy."

"God," Isabel said.

"A dollar." He shook the steaming pan.

"What a horrible kid," said Isabel.

Michael shook his head. "Actually, he wasn't. He was actually a nice kid. He had no idea what he was saying; he thought he was defending me." He paused. "What bothered me most was that I never knew what my father would have said about what I'd done. I never knew if he'd have thought I said the right thing—I mean, wasn't that the whole fucking point of changing our name? And of not going to temple? Dropping the religion? Why had he changed the name if he didn't want us to seem not Jewish? If he didn't want me to say straight out, 'No, we're not Jewish'? He'd done everything he could for us not to be Jewish. Wasn't I meant to blend in with the goyim?" Michael paused again. "But I also thought maybe my father would have been disappointed by what I'd said. We were safe here in America. There was no holocaust in Chicago, it was all over. He might have felt that I'd betrayed him, us, our family, our whole tribe."

Steam rolled from the pan, and the oil began to sizzle.

"Do you remember him much, your father?" Isabel asked.

"Of course I remember him. I was ten when he died. I remember him very well." He frowned, stirring the simmering mass. Isabel turned and put her lips against his neck.

As the summer wore on, it seemed to everyone—at least everyone on his staff—that Dudley would win. His opponent, Frank Pulio, was a blue-collar conservative. He was dark and scowling, with an overhanging brow. In the office, behind Dudley's back, they called Pulio "Cro-Magnon Man." His manner was confrontational. "Let's be clear about this," Pulio would say, pounding his fist into his palm. He was tough on crime and taxes, but mostly his strategy was to remind the voters of Dudley's inexperience.

The press loved Dudley: he gave excellent quotes, and he was photogenic. So was his clear-skinned blond wife, with her dimples and pointed chin, her tailored linen suits, the exotic whiff of luxury she gave off. For his campaign, Dudley rented a bus from an elegant French restaurant. Gold Edwardian lettering on a deep green ground said RESTAURANT LUTÈCE. Dudley stood on its steps, pipe in his teeth, smiling and waving as he was carried slowly through the streets.

Dudley talked with passion and conviction about education, the environment, drug rehabilitation: all the things that mattered. How could he lose?

Chapter 6

In August, Isabel took Michael out to Bedford Hills for the weekend to meet her parents.

On Friday evening she stood waiting in Grand Central Station by the newsstand on the lower level. The stand was brightly lit, a patchwork of magazines on the walls, stacks of newspapers on the floor. The ceiling was low and dark. Watching the approaching crowd for Michael, Isabel drew in a shallow, unwilling breath. The air felt warm, already used.

A flood of people, faces damp with heat, moved steadily past her toward the trains, spreading through the dim underground spaces like water. The center of the crowd was constant, but along the edges people slipped loose, hurrying ahead. A man in a gray suit passed Isabel, his shirt open, his tie loosened. He broke into a ponderous, heavy-footed run, his briefcase hanging at the end of his arm like an anchor. A portly woman in a creased turquoise dress surged forward, jostling against a teenage boy in wide-bottomed jeans that dragged along the gritty floor. The pace was swift and relentless. The trains did not wait.

Heroic, Isabel thought, *the human tide.* They had all come flooding forth that morning, pushing in the other direction through these same dim hallways, urgent and determined, striding toward jobs, the day, the task. Now, just as urgent, just as determined, they were heading back toward evening, to a particular haven, somewhere north, beyond the city limits, somewhere holding a meal, darkness, peace. Some greenery, more sky.

Michael arrived suddenly, appearing at her side.

"You're here," she said, vastly pleased. His presence obliterated everything: the hustling people, their heroism, the shadowy station, the used air. She could smell him.

"So are you." He kissed her briefly: she tasted his mouth. It was astonishing that this should be permitted, she thought.

They moved into the crowd, shuffling beneath an archway down into the station's deep airless interior. People hurried along the narrow platform past conductors in blue-black uniforms. By the tracks the atmosphere was urgent, imminent. Within the cramped tunnel, sounds echoed and boomed: footsteps, shouts, machines. The train lay stretched out along the walkway, panting mechanically as it prepared for departure, giving off a cold mineral stench.

Isabel and Michael found seats and sat down. Michael looked around at the faded rattletrap car. The plush on the seats had been worn away by strange bodies, the paint was chipped. Sticky black grime lay deep in every corner; the floors were filthy.

"How old are these trains?" Michael asked. He pushed back against his seat, which gave uncertainly. The red plastic cover on his armrest was torn, revealing limp beige stuffing.

"Ancient," Isabel said. "My father says these engines still have cowcatchers in front, that there are arrows still stuck in the seats. This line hasn't been changed over to electricity yet."

"What does it run on now? Steam?"

"I don't know," Isabel said. "Hamsters, maybe?"

"And why hasn't it changed over?" Michael asked, curious.

"There's some political wrangle involving the government and the utilities and—who? I can't remember," Isabel said. "Ask my father. He'll tell you the whole story. The trains to Connecticut were changed ages ago, they're all fast and clean and perfect."

"I have a theory about these utilities," Michael announced. "They're a sort of hybrid between capitalism and socialism. It's really interesting." He again looked around at the car, now proprietary. Behind them a man heaved a bag up on the overhead rack, then thudded into a seat. Michael's eyes narrowed, considering everything he saw as subject matter.

Isabel smiled to herself, liking the way he was engaged by things.

"What is it?" he asked. He slid sideways toward her, crossing the division between their seats, and set his head next to hers.

"You see the world differently from the way I do," she told him. "It's fun."

Michael picked up her hand. "How do I see it?"

"Like a chessboard. You see everything as governed by abstractions: politics and economics, religion and history."

"Yes, well, but that's the way it is," Michael said. "That's the correct way."

"But I don't see it like that. I see one big conflict—a big continuing struggle that goes back and forth between liberal and conservative, I guess—and then I think everything else is personal."

"What do you mean, 'personal'?"

"I think people are run by emotions. I think they feel one way instinctively, and that decides their responses to everything."

"You think facts make no difference to people? The power of reason means nothing?"

Isabel nodded. "More or less. I think people take a position and then find the facts that will support it. You can't persuade anyone to change his point of view because of facts; people only listen to the facts they want to hear. They find ways to discount everything else. They say, 'Yes, but—' and then they ignore whatever it is you've said and they start on something new. Or they say, 'You can find statistics to support anything you want.' Or something like that. People ignore anything that counters their chosen position. In psychology it's called cognitive dissonance theory: you only want to learn things that will support your position, and you avoid other information. Anyway," Isabel finished, "I think the world is dominated by emotions, and you think it's dominated by abstractions."

"But what about economics?" Michael asked. "What about politics?"

"I don't know," Isabel said. "What about them?"

"Don't they matter to you?"

Isabel shook her head and started to laugh. "I'm sorry, but they don't."

"*What?*" Michael asked, grinning. "Does it frustrate you that they matter to me?"

"I love it," said Isabel. "It's like a foreign language, and I love the fact that you speak it so fluently. You give me a new way of seeing things. It makes me feel that between the two of us we're covering everything. It's actually very comforting."

Michael reached up and stroked her hair back from her forehead. "Does it bother you that we're so perfectly acting out sexual stereotypes?" he asked. "Me for reasoning, you emotion?"

"Sorry," Isabel said again, "not at all."

Isabel loved talking with Michael. She admired him because she loved him; she loved him because she admired him. She found everything he did interesting, remarkable.

The train started unobtrusively, easing lightly forward without a sound. It seemed uncommitted, as though it might stop again shortly, but instead it kept on, smoothly building up speed, sliding through the labyrinth of lightless tunnels.

Michael opened his newspaper, and Isabel felt him relax, slipping comfortably into its depths. Her own book lay unopened on her lap. She stared peacefully into the black mirror of the window beside her, at her own muted reflection resting lightly on the rough stone walls beyond. The train hurried beneath the streets, clicking and shifting, making its hidden way northward. Isabel closed her eyes, swaying with the shuttling movements of the car. It was comforting to be carried swiftly and safely toward a destination. Beside her, Michael closed the paper, then opened it again. Suddenly the sound of the wheels changed as the train rose triumphantly, angling swiftly up past walls of blank concrete siding into the mild light of the summer evening.

Out in the open the train rattled, rapid and staccato, through the urban landscape. They were uptown now. Over by the river, clusters of tall modern buildings towered over low nineteenth-century roofs, reflecting the reddening gleams of the setting sun. The buildings were of dark red brick, with bright squares of primary colors scattered down their sides. Perpendicular rows of balconies stood out along the walls. But the balconies were crammed with objects, stuffed like closets with things set helter-skelter, exposed to the elements and the passersby. No one sat on them enjoying the sunset; leisure and comfort did not prevail over these buildings. These were the East Harlem projects; their dark looming silhouettes signaled poverty.

Watching the tall shafts slowly shifting as the train passed by, Isabel felt the familiar current of guilt and anxiety. The question seemed to be what it was that you were meant to do for the world, how much you were meant to feel. If you let the misery of the world flood in on you, press its full weight against you, you'd have no choice: you'd give your life up to it. And if you didn't let in all the misery of the world, how much did you keep out? Whose misery did you reject?

Isabel's father, Randall, was an Episcopalian minister. This had made Isabel feel secure when she was little. She knew that what her father did was right. She heard respect in people's voices when they said, "Oh, your father's a minister!" She felt her father's certainty when he spoke from the chancel or at someone's doorstep. His words carried a deep sense of calm.

As a child, Isabel loved the look of her father in his black robes, the way he moved in them. She loved the crisp radiant strip of white collar above the black shirt, the mysterious flow of the swinging black folds. She loved the breathing silence of the church when the two of them were in it alone. She trusted her father's relationship between the material world and the spiritual one. She felt protected by her father's presence.

In college, Isabel began to withdraw from both her father and his religion. At Ann Arbor it was fashionable to challenge everything, to view all institutions as hypocritical. Isabel did not want to be her father's creature, and she began to question her father's attitudes. Why should she not? She told herself that her father, like all the others— politicians, generals, businessmen—was hypocritical.

In the summer before her junior year, late one evening she told him so. Isabel's mother had gone to bed, and Isabel and her father were alone in his shabby library at the back of the house. Isabel, in cutoffs and a tank top, sat on the rumpled plush sofa. She was barefoot, and her long hair hung down her back. She held a bottle of beer, something she had never done so boldly, in front of her father. But that was what she wanted that night, to challenge him.

Isabel tucked her dirty bare feet underneath her. "You chose a rich community," she told Randall scornfully. "It's easy being here in Bedford. All your parishioners belong to the Bedford Golf and Tennis Club!"

Randall listened courteously. He was sitting in his low, faded armchair, and the light from the floor lamp spilled down onto his scalp. As

Isabel talked, she saw that her father's hair was thinning, his skin showing pinkly through it, and this made her angrier, for some reason, more indignant.

Randall held a tall glass of water on the table by his chair. He sat looking at it, waiting for Isabel to finish. She could see his mouth pursing patiently as he listened, the small outward flex of his lips.

"There are people starving in Appalachia," Isabel told him. "Everyone in Bedford is rich. Why didn't you go somewhere you could help people who actually needed it? The only help people here need is with their golf swings."

She was pleased with that. She sat waiting triumphantly.

Randall said nothing for a moment, waiting for her to go on. When she did not, he answered. "What you say is partly true."

Isabel raised her eyebrows ironically and lifted the bottle to her mouth.

"What you say is partly true," Randall repeated. He folded his hands on his small round stomach. "I do have an easy parish, and most of my parishioners are comfortably off. So most of what I offer them is spiritual solace. But that's what I'm trained to do, Isabel: offer spiritual solace. Everyone needs that, no matter how much money they have. People here suffer terminal illnesses, they feel as much heartbreak and fear and despair here as they do anywhere else." Randall drank from his glass.

"But as you know, I work in other places, too, not just in Bedford. And, as you know, there's a church network. We work with much poorer parishes, sharing resources. You know about Saint Mark's food and clothing drives. You know about the Midnight Run to New York. We do a lot for poorer places, and one of my responsibilities is to share our resources with places that have less." He paused.

Isabel did know all of this, of course. As a child she had gone with her father to deliver bags of food, piles of clothes. She knew he'd founded the Midnight Run, taking food and clothing to homeless people in the city. She frowned heavily at her beer bottle and dug at the label with a fingernail, trying to peel it off.

"But it's certainly true," Randall went on, "that this place is comfortable. If I'd been alone, I might have made a different choice. But I wasn't alone, I had a family. I didn't think it was fair to ask my wife and children to live in a poor community. There were some things about a life like that which I didn't mind for myself but I didn't want for them. And I'm sure self-interest plays a part, too, it usually does." He paused again to drink from his glass. "But this community means a lot to me. I'm glad we live here, and I feel I'm accomplishing things. There are wonderful people here who have given me a lot. And there's work to be done wherever you are. I'm happy to do it here. I wouldn't change what I've done."

He looked up at her. The light caught in his tangled eyebrows.

"The thing is, Bella—you do what you can. Whatever it is you can do, you do. You don't blame yourself, and don't blame other people, for not doing more. You choose something and you do it, whatever it is." He stopped and sat calmly.

Isabel was silent, angrily turning the beer bottle in her hand. She could think of nothing to say and felt ashamed. Before his clarity, her own accusations seemed small-minded. She felt the misery of the world beating against her; she felt guilt, her own shortcomings, beating against her, too. Surely she should be giving her own life to this, as her father had. What sort of person was she that she could not? It was she who was the hypocrite.

At twenty-two, out of college, Isabel had stopped blaming her father for the way he led his life, though she still hadn't decided how she should lead hers. Reminders of the world's misery brought pangs of anxiety and shame. What was enough? How did you decide what work was yours? How could you do enough?

Now the brick towers began to recede. No longer boldly silhouetted against the river, they subsided into the patchwork cityscape to the south. Isabel sent a silent message to the people in the projects. *We're doing what we can,* she promised. She thought of Dudley's programs, of everyone's commitment and determination. *Things will get better,* she told them fervently, *trust us.*

As the train flowed north, the buildings grew fewer and farther apart. The skyline lowered. The East River was steady and reflective, the calm roseate sky widening over it. Everything about a train was comforting, Isabel thought: the rocking motion, the steady clicking rhythm, the landscape speeding pleasantly past. The knowledge that, even still and passive, you were moving purposefully toward something.

Isabel thought ahead to Bedford Hills. By the time they reached it, the sky would be darkening. Over the sloping roofs of the station house, the trees would be green and cool. Beyond the station was the row of small shops: the picture framer, the Italian delicatessen, the struggling thrift shop. Above the stores was a hill, and beyond that were green meadows, long driveways, fireflies.

Her parents' white clapboard farmhouse was in a hollow beside a narrow dirt road. An old stone wall ran along the road, a rusting iron gate set into it, facing the front door. Flagstones, nearly hidden by encroaching grass, made a path from the gate to the unused entrance. Shading the house was a pair of giant sugar maples—wedding trees, the Pierces were told, planted 150 years earlier. The driveway passed the house on the right, turning behind it to the small garage, tucked beneath a vast and somber hemlock. Behind the house was the big garden, bounded by a split-rail fence. Years ago this had been the paddock for Isabel's horse, who had grazed it down to scrubby grass and weeds. Now it was divided into lush rectangles by mown grass walks. The wide flower borders were full of sword-leaved iris, fragrant lilies, voluptuous drifts of roses. Daylilies thrust their fiery heads up like arrows from the leaves' soft mass.

Leaning against the train window, watching the sky begin to fade, Isabel wondered if there would be enough light to see the garden when they arrived. Even in the dark, the lilies held a silvery shine, and the garden gave off a rich nocturnal fragrance.

Her mother would be in the lighted kitchen, and as they walked in through the dusk, they would see her through the window, standing at the stove, dish towel tucked around her waist. Isabel's mother was short, and thick through the middle. Her dry, feathery brown hair was graying, and reading glasses hung on a chain against her sloped bosom. As she moved about the kitchen, she hummed, and sometimes she sang part of a song out loud, repeating the same phrase over and over with long silences between. Coming in from the car, they might hear her singing. The air would be cool, and as the kitchen door opened on them, her mother would turn, smiling. "Here you are," she would say, pleased.

Isabel looked now at Michael, who was frowning, deeply engrossed in the paper.

"Are you worried about meeting my parents?" she asked him.

Michael looked up at her. "Should I be?"

"No," she said. "Absolutely not. My mother will love you."

"Your father won't?"

"No, of course he will," Isabel said. "He's just not as demonstrative. He'll love you, too."

"Then why did you bring it up?"

"Just that I thought you might be worried, and you shouldn't be." She looked out the window again.

"They won't care that I'm Jewish."

"I've already told you they don't," Isabel said. "That doesn't bother them at all."

"Even your father the Episcopalian minister."

"My father isn't a bigot. And he loves talking theological theory," Isabel said. "He's thrilled at the idea of talking about religion with you. He'll expect you to be an expert on Judaism. That's the biggest risk you run, is not knowing enough about religious theory."

Michael folded up the newspaper. "Well, I'm not an expert, so I just may disappoint your father." His face had not lightened from the frown he had worn for the paper. His tone did not match Isabel's; it was oddly hard, challenging. "And I have to warn you," he went on, "that just because we're going to Bedford to meet your parents and everything is going to be so wonderful, it doesn't mean that we're going to buzz right out to Chicago to meet my mother."

"Okay," Isabel said, hurt. She wondered what he meant.

"Because my mother will eat you alive, and it's not an encounter I'm looking forward to with any pleasure."

"That's encouraging," Isabel said. She rolled her eyes, trying to make him laugh.

Michael looked at her and then away. "I'm exaggerating," he said. "But my mother can be a little overbearing."

"I'm sure we'll get along," Isabel said.

"Yeah," Michael said. He leaned back against the seat and closed his eyes. His hands rested on the newspaper in his lap. He began to speak without opening his eyes. "You know my father killed himself?"

Isabel stared at him. "I didn't know that."

Michael opened his eyes. "He shot himself."

"Michael," Isabel said. She felt breathless. "I'm so sorry."

"Yeah," Michael said. "Thanks. It was a long time ago." He looked away from her, straight ahead.

"Why are you telling me now?" Isabel asked.

"I don't know," Michael said. "I guess it's because we're going off to meet your wonderful parents who are so great, and who live in this beautiful house in the beautiful countryside, and your father's a minister and your mother's a gardener, and they're going to love me and everything is so charming and perfect. It's a slightly different picture from what I have to offer." He gave an ironic smile. "Full disclosure, I guess." He held up his hands, palms out.

"Michael, I'm so sorry," Isabel said again. "I had no idea."

"No, why would you?"

"Was it unexpected, your father?" she asked.

"To me? Yes," Michael said. "My mother knew."

The train slid to a stop, and the door at the end of the car opened with a pneumatic gasp. The conductor thrust his head in.

"Val-halla," he said, his voice booming out, nasal, singsong, "Val-halla." He closed the door.

Isabel waited, but Michael said nothing else. "How did it happen?"

"It was in the late afternoon," Michael said. "It was dark outside, it was winter. The tenth of December. I'd come back from school and I was upstairs in my room. I was lying on the rug, playing with an airplane. I was lying on my side and looking in at the cockpit of a fighter plane and getting the pilot ready for takeoff. I was making a revving-the-engines noise, and I heard the sound of the gun. I remember being confused by the two noises, the one I was making and the one outside, and thinking for a minute that I had made the one outside. I was looking in at the pilot and the controls when I heard my mother scream downstairs. She was right underneath me, in the living room. I remember thinking as soon as I heard my mother scream that the noise had been outside, somewhere else, so it had nothing to do with us. We were inside, where it was safe.

"My mother screamed, and then she called for me to come downstairs. And for a little while, maybe it was only a few seconds but it seemed like a long time, I didn't answer and I didn't move, I just lay there on the floor because I didn't want the next thing to happen. I didn't want whatever it was to begin.

"My mother came to the bottom of the stairs and called me again, and this time her voice frightened me and I got up. I went to the top of the stairs. She was standing with her hand on the banister. She said,

'Go out and see what's happened to your father.' I stood at the top of the stairs looking at her, and it was as though everything darkened.

"It was night outside, and the garage had suddenly become a place I couldn't bear to go into. I didn't want to see what had happened to my father, to see whatever it was that had brought up this voice from my mother, this face looking up at me from the bottom of the stairs. And then she said it again, and I couldn't stand hearing her voice, the way it sounded, so I went down and she told me again to go out to the garage. That's where she said he had gone."

"She made you go alone?" asked Isabel.

Michael nodded. "She couldn't stand to do it herself. It wasn't that she wanted me to be the one, it was that she couldn't do it but she had to know."

"So you found him?"

Michael nodded again.

The conductor had returned and was now making his way down the aisle. His heavy black jacket was unbuttoned over his vest, showing a row of brass buttons. Most of the passengers had already given him their tickets, and he walked slowly past the seats, clicking his metal puncher. "Tickets," he said, his voice resonant, "tickets." He passed them. The door behind them opened with a sigh, then closed.

"The light was on in the garage. My father was lying in the middle of the floor," Michael said. "He had backed the car outside to give himself the whole space. Underneath him was a big oil stain, like the shape of a continent. I remember seeing that and telling myself that this was all right, that he had been standing up when the shot went off, that he didn't lie down on the oil spill, so that by the time he fell on it, he didn't feel it because he was dead, but at the same time I was trying to believe he wasn't dead—he was lying there right in front of me, there was nothing else he could be, but I was trying to believe he wasn't, I was trying to find some explanation for the way he was lying, sprawled on the floor with the gun next to him, all that dark blood flooding from his head, spreading across the concrete, blotting out the oil stain. I couldn't really look at his head, I couldn't look straight at it. It wasn't like a head."

"God," Isabel said quietly.

"I knew my mother was waiting for me in the house. She had stopped screaming, and I knew she was standing in the kitchen, waiting for me to come back. I didn't move, I didn't know what to do. I stood there and tried to work out how my father was still alive, somewhere else, that this wasn't him, or that it was him but it was a trick, that he was alive and he would stand up somehow, in some way I hadn't yet understood, and while I was thinking and trying to work it out, the blood was moving, pulsing out, pooling in a circle around him.

"I was putting off going back inside. I could picture the three wooden steps leading up to the back porch, and the bristly worn-down brown mat outside the kitchen door. The mat made me sick to my stomach. I couldn't imagine myself walking up those three steps, then stepping on the mat, opening the storm door. I couldn't see how I could do it. And inside the house my mother was quiet, waiting for me."

"How terrible," Isabel said.

Michael was staring straight ahead, as though waiting for something. "Yes," he said simply. "Terrible."

"I'm so sorry," she said. "It must have been so hard on you both. And hard on you, being the only child."

Michael shrugged. "I can't say."

"How did your mother stand it?"

"She's a powerful woman," Michael said. "At first she was stunned. Afterward she was furious. I think rage took her over, really forever, because he'd walked out on her. He'd had the last word. And it also changed things for us financially; we had to move to a smaller house. That was when she went to work for the Art Institute. She used to say, 'You must never let this happen to your family, Michael.' Or 'You're the man of the house now, Michael, remember that.' And she'd give me this meaningful look. It would terrify me when she said that, as though a huge collar were settling around my neck. I'd want to bolt. But at the same time I felt so sorry for her because I knew she couldn't bolt. This was her life."

The conductor pushed the door open and called into the slowing car, "Hawthorne next, Hawthorne," then he closed the door.

Isabel reached up to stroke Michael's temple. She could see his eyelashes against his cheek. He leaned his head slightly into her hand, but the movement was an acknowledgment of her touch, not a request for support. He sat without moving, patient.

Other people's lives, she thought. *Like canyons revealed, these fearful, shocking gorges.* The story he had told her seemed an outrage. Isabel wanted to refuse it, protest it.

But she could see from Michael's silence, his stillness, that he had passed beyond those feelings. He no longer protested this; he had absorbed it. It was something he owned, a sadness that was part of him.

Isabel said nothing more.

It would stay in your mind forever, she thought. The sound of the gunshot so insultingly close. The sense of missing it by seconds. The waste of life. The sense of guilt. *How could his mother endure this, how could she bear up? How could you ever forgive yourself?*

Chapter 7

Isabel felt honored to be told about Michael's father, to be permitted to know such a wound, trusted enough to approach it. She was certain she could heal it. That was the point, wasn't it, of being in love? Wasn't that the point of love itself—that it could change lives? Though in those early days, their life together didn't seem to need changing: it was good. She could feel Michael beating along beside her like a winging bird, strong and adventurous, his eyes on the horizon.

Michael's graduation from Columbia took place in early May. It was held in two parts, a smaller school ceremony on Wednesday and the large, full-university ceremony on Saturday. Michael's mother could not come to the smaller ceremony but flew in late on Friday night. The next morning she and Michael had breakfast together, near Michael's apartment. Afterward they walked to the Columbia campus, where Isabel met Theresa for the first time.

It was a cool day, the sky overcast, the breeze damp. Isabel, who had dressed for sun, shivered slightly and rubbed her bare arms. She was at 116th Street, standing at the entrance to the campus from Broadway, watching for Michael and his mother. Isabel was eager to meet Theresa: they were already allies, partners, in a way, weren't they? She was full of hopeful expectation.

At the same time Isabel felt diffident, aware of the disadvantage of coming late, joining people who have already met, eaten a meal, without you. They have made an alliance, formed a whole, you are an awkward addition.

The crowd on the sidewalk was full of graduating students, conspicuous in their rented medieval gowns, against the casual urban squalor of upper Broadway. It was a moment of revelation: the presence of the academy revealed within the larger world. The faces above the somber robes were buoyant.

There was Michael; Isabel raised her hand and smiled. Michael smiled back, and Isabel's gaze slid to the woman beside him. Theresa's eyes were already on Isabel.

Theresa looked nothing like her son. She was short, and there was a heaviness about her, though she was not fat. She moved with dignity, very erect. Her face was handsome, with a broad forehead and large features. She held her head high, and her thick graying hair was drawn back from her face in a bun. Her eyes were large and dark; their gaze was powerful, not friendly.

"Hello," Isabel called out as they came up to her. She ignored Michael familiarly and put her hand out directly to his mother. "I'm Isabel Pierce. It's so nice to meet you, Mrs. Green." Her voice, in her own ears, sounded oddly loud.

"Very nice to meet you," Theresa said flatly. Her handshake was strong and dry, like a man's. Theresa withdrew her hand and looked up at Michael, as though the next move must come from him.

"Isn't this exciting? Aren't we proud of him?" asked Isabel: Michael was to be celebrated. Not only was he about to graduate, but he had won the Beadling Prize for reporting at the earlier ceremony.

But Isabel's enthusiasm was not returned. Theresa frowned faintly and nodded without speaking. Isabel wondered if she had been too eager, too proprietary.

"I've saved some seats," Isabel said, changing the subject. She had left her sweater spread across two chairs in hopes that, civilization being at its peak at this place and moment, the sweater would not only not be stolen but that its claim would be respected.

"Good move," Michael said to her and nodded. "Great." But his eyes slid past her; he seemed distracted. Theresa, her chin high and queenly, said nothing and looked away. Isabel wondered now if it had been a poor idea to save the seats. Was she being presumptuous, taking charge? Or maybe she shouldn't have mentioned it, as though she were asking for praise. As a possible daughter-in-law, should she appear subservient? She remembered a Chinese memoir in which a young bride, moving into her mother-in-law's household, had to make "the full kowtow" before the older woman: prostration with arms outstretched, head down, forehead touching the floor. Was this what Theresa would require?

Nothing more was said about the seats. They joined the crowd, moving along in the crush. It was too crowded, too public, to talk.

The ceremony was held outside, on the huge open rectangle of the campus, six blocks long. The four sides were big neoclassical buildings, their friezes carved with great names: Homer, Demosthenes, Voltaire, Shakespeare. The open space was filled with folding chairs, all facing the wide steps of Low Library at the north end. In the first rows sat the undergraduates, facing the podium. The graduate schools were behind and above the podium, on the steps, facing the lawn and the audience.

The seats Isabel had found were near the front. They were still empty, the sweater spread, making its claim.

"Well, okay," Michael said. "I've got to go. I'll see you afterward. I'll meet you back here." He ducked his head and put his hand awkwardly up to the back of his neck. Isabel would have liked to step close and give him a pat for reassurance, but in Theresa's stern presence she did not dare touch him. Michael gave a sheepish grin, and his eyelids fluttered slightly.

"Good luck," said Isabel, though there was nothing he needed luck for now.

"Good luck," Theresa murmured.

"Thanks." Michael strode off into the crowd. Moving, he lost his awkwardness.

Around them, the throng milled. The mood was festive, no one was still. Everyone was shifting, moving somewhere else, waving, searching for seats, looking for friends. The steady stream filled the broad central aisle.

When Michael had gone, Isabel and Theresa sat down awkwardly. The chairs were very close, the two women nearly touching. Theresa set her purse beneath her seat and opened the program. She began to read it with great attention, staring down as though memorizing it.

Isabel opened her program but only glanced at it. She looked vaguely around at the flood of strangers, wondering if Theresa would talk to her.

When she and Michael had first talked about his mother's visit, Isabel admitted that she was nervous. "You told me once your mother would eat me alive."

"Yes, well, I was exaggerating," Michael said. "She won't do that."

There was a pause.

"What will happen?" Isabel asked. "What will she do?"

Michael shook his head. "She will love you." But he said this in an odd comic way, wagging his head and smiling, so it was clear that this was not really the truth.

"What is it she'll hate about me?" asked Isabel. "I need to know. That I'm a shiksa?"

"No," said Michael. "She doesn't really care about that."

"Then what is it?"

"That you breathe in and breathe out," Michael said.

"*So* great to hear this," Isabel said.

"Can't help it," Michael said, grinning.

Isabel could see that Michael's grin was partly to comfort her and partly gleeful satisfaction. She could see that a tiny part of Michael enjoyed this opposition, liked the idea of his powerful, dangerous mother on guard against the world.

"She feels a little threatened around my girlfriends," Michael explained. He put his arm tightly about Isabel. "But you know, it will be okay. You are fabulous. She'll just have to learn that. And she will." He kissed Isabel's head firmly, and she felt comforted, and she forgave Michael his smugness: who would not bask in such powerful love? And she understood Theresa's fierceness: who, having been deserted so violently, so suddenly and cruelly, would not be vigilant about another departure? But still, Isabel was anxious about the meeting: how would they become allies?

Now, sitting beside her, Isabel noticed Theresa's clothes: a prim striped suit, navy and white, the skirt modestly covering her knees. Isabel was abruptly conscious of her own thighs, mostly bared by her short skirt. Her legs seemed suddenly to occupy her whole frame of vision. At home, standing in front of the mirror, the length of the dress had seemed perfect; now, seated, it was wholly wrong. It was a dress she'd loved until this moment: sleek and tailored, made of rose-colored linen. Now it seemed shamefully short. Her thighs looked wide and pale next to the proper navy-and-white stripes.

Isabel determinedly raised her eyes from her mesmerizing legs. She would make this go well.

"I'm so glad to finally meet you," she told Theresa. "I've heard so much about you."

"Have you?" Theresa answered, looking up from her program. She looked at Isabel, cool and curious. "What have you heard?"

It was not the friendly response Isabel had expected. "Well," she said, gathering herself. "About what you do, and—" She considered but could not bring herself to say "what a great mom you are." Theresa would never believe that. Or would she? Maybe all mothers thought they were great no matter what they'd done. Isabel didn't risk it. "Well, Michael told me a lot about his childhood," she finished vaguely, then, worried that this suggested the suicide, she hurried on. "And I'm so interested in what you do, working at the Art Institute."

"Are you?" Theresa asked without smiling. "Are you interested in art?"

"Well, yes," Isabel said, flustered. Wasn't that a given? Wasn't everyone educated interested in art? Would she have to prove it—would Theresa test her? Could Isabel remember anything from History of Art 101? Was François Boucher seventeenth or eighteenth century?

Isabel was unnerved by Theresa's manner and looked away, considering what to say next. She wondered if Theresa would ask her about herself. Was she interested in where she came from or what she did?

Isabel had left the world of politics. Dudley had lost the election, as Michael predicted, though Isabel told Michael his dinosaur theory had nothing to do with it. "Dudley was running against an established incumbent," she said. "The odds were always against him." But privately Isabel was proud of Michael's astuteness, his eccentric theory.

Dudley had reduced his staff after the election, and Isabel was doing temp work to pay the rent. She had also begun to volunteer at an environmental organization. She was ready to tell Theresa about this, how vital the issues were, but Theresa had gone back to scrutinizing the speakers' names. And Isabel did not dare ask Theresa what she did— fund-raising, wasn't it?—because she had already mentioned how interested she was by it and couldn't now ask what it was. Isabel frowned in frustration: how had she managed to get off to such a bad start with Michael's mother, despite her intentions?

The wide aisle beside them was still crammed with people. The chairs up on the steps had begun to fill up with the graduate schools. Isabel realized that Michael's class had taken its place, sitting in a solid bloc to the right of the podium. She scanned the rows for his face.

"There's Michael," she said, leaning toward Theresa, raising her hand to wave. Theresa looked where Isabel pointed but said nothing. It seemed that waving was beneath her dignity. After a moment she asked the air, "What's taking them so long, I wonder?" Her voice held a trace of asperity. Isabel, feeling somehow responsible, said she didn't know, and they fell once more into silence. Isabel could feel the heat given off by Theresa's solid form. Theresa looked about calmly, her face immobile. Gradually the aisle next to them began to clear. The undergraduates in front of them settled down and stopped talking. Music started up, and there was a collective sense of imminence. The crowd quieted, becoming attentive, anticipatory.

In this new silence Theresa leaned close to Isabel, spoke invasively into her ear: "You've heard about his breakdown?" she asked.

Isabel turned and stared at her. For a moment she rejected the sentence. She refused it. She also understood that this was not possible, that she could not refuse it. She felt herself fixed and frozen by Theresa's black stare, and chilled by the terrible word. *All right,* she thought, *all right,* she'd take it, but then what?

She was too chilled by it to answer, but it seemed imperative, staring into Theresa's pitiless eyes, that she respond at once. She did not know how. The unseen orchestra began to play an introductory piece with a strong marching beat.

Isabel had not heard about Michael's breakdown.

With the freezing words still in her ears, looking into Theresa's eyes, she realized that there had been something, that she had known about *something*. She understood now that this was what it had been, a breakdown. But the thought was terrifying.

There was still the problem of how to answer Theresa. Isabel felt she was being challenged, that her answer was important. If she said no, she admitted ignorance and risked being dismissed by Theresa as insignificant. But if she said yes, Theresa might simply nod and turn away, saying nothing more, and Isabel needed to hear what Theresa had to say next. But would it be disloyal to Michael for Isabel to hear things from his mother that he had chosen not to tell her himself?

Theresa still watched her, her expression impassive, but Isabel sensed in her a kind of greed.

"I knew there was something," Isabel said finally. "When was it?"

"His first year in college," Theresa said. "He was hospitalized for six weeks." She paused. "The locked ward."

Isabel could feel her heart pounding, not only at the news but at what Theresa so clearly meant by it: for Isabel to be frightened.

"Hospitalized," Isabel repeated. Theresa had succeeded. She thought of heavy windowless doors, straitjackets, attendants in soft-soled shoes. Drugs closing down the mind. Electric-shock treatments.

Theresa nodded. "McLean," she said.

Isabel nodded, too. Her breath felt strange in her throat. It was not just the word, not just the information. It was also Theresa's breathing closeness, the fixity of her gaze.

McLean was the psychiatric branch of Massachusetts General Hospital; it was a standing joke to say that someone was taking a vacation there. Did this fact make Michael's situation better or worse? It meant it was serious. Six weeks: really serious. Isabel wondered again if she had to believe this. Could it possibly not be true?

The music began in earnest: a college band full of bright brass and the rattle of drums. Behind them was a sense of gathering; ahead, on the steps, faces looked toward the rear. Isabel turned, to escape Theresa. At the far end was a close mass of sober robes and mortarboards, the matte black relieved by the bright hoods and vestments of the degrees, wide bands of scarlet, cobalt, purple. The group began a slow swaying march. Theresa turned, too, her gaze interested, as though looking at something on the far horizon.

Isabel watched the procession, trying to remember. What was it that she knew? What was it exactly that Michael had said? It had been at dinner one night, with friends, at a restaurant. A comment about mental health: what had it been? Someone said something to Michael, grinning, about being sane. Michael had laughed.

"Right. How would I know?" he said obligingly, and everyone else laughed, too, pleased. There had been an odd moment of excitement surrounding his remark, both knowing and protective. Isabel had not wanted to inquire in front of his friends, but later, in bed, she asked.

She referred to it elliptically; she found she didn't want to say the words "mental health" to him. But he knew at once.

"I had a bad time in college," he told her. Isabel was on her back, looking up at him. He was on his side next to her, cradling his head on his hand. "Bad bad," he said gently. "Really bad." She had looked up at him and he had looked directly back.

She had not asked what that meant. Right then she had not wanted to know more. Instead she had reached up and stroked his neck, and then other things had happened and they had stopped talking. When Isabel thought about it later, she reminded herself that she knew lots of people who'd had bad times in college. "Breakdowns" were how these times would be described by other people. In Ann Arbor, her friend Jeff had ended up in the emergency room on a bad acid trip, and then was held in a psychiatric ward. For how long? Weeks or months? She had gone to visit him once or twice: he had a large pleasant room with a window covered unobtrusively with metal bars. Jeff usually wore grimy turtlenecks and ratty jeans, but there he was wearing brand-new wide-wale corduroys and a knit wool shirt. He noticed her look. "My parents sent me all this stuff," he told her with an ironic smile, as though the new clothes were absurd. During her visit he had stayed sitting, had hardly moved. His eyelids were heavy, nearly closed. He talked slowly and loudly, and when he laughed, it was all on one note. He told Isabel he was writing a lot of poetry; he was amazingly productive. Usually it took him months to write a poem cycle, but there he had finished one already. He seemed smug and self-satisfied about this. Everything he said made sense but seemed entirely false.

The Columbia faculty strode past, smiling in a public manner. They were mostly men, mostly white, mostly middle-aged and bespectacled, a phalanx of black swaying robes. They filed up the steps and took their places behind the podium. The weather was increasingly uncertain, the sky full of moving clouds. Isabel pulled her sweater around her shoulders.

The president of the university stepped up to the podium and smiled at the crowd. He cleared his throat, the microphone whined horridly and he began his speech. Theresa now leaned away from Isabel, cocking her head to listen. Apparently she had said all she intended to say. She settled into her seat with great attentiveness.

No one had known if Jeff was crazy or whether the psychiatrists had overreacted to the drug trip. Maybe he really had been crazy before the acid, Isabel thought, and no one had noticed. Jeff was a lit major, very smart and famously subversive. Irony was his worldview. Before the acid trip he had once invited Isabel to his apartment, on Valentine's Day, to watch him shoot up on heroin. He told her it was a ritual she'd enjoy: the most intimate form of self-love. Isabel went, out of loyalty and horrified fascination. She watched Jeff tug a rubber leash around his arm and snap his dirty fingertip against the bulging vein. He had talked the whole time, fast and excited, eager as a lover, yearning to set the needle into the tender blue river. That, Isabel thought now, remembering that dangerous undercurrent, was crazy. Michael was not like that.

The president was identifying the groups of graduates. "The School of Nursing," he said, pointing to the students behind him, and the group, all women, clapped proudly for their school. The audience joined in. "The School of Engineering," the president said, turning to his left. There was no clapping, and after a moment there was an undercurrent of laughter. People craned in their seats to see. On the far left, over the heads of the students, a fleet of paper airplanes, twenty or thirty, climbed and swooped erratically through the air. They went straight up, then dove down in crazy loops and spirals, vanishing among the engineers, who grinned at their own antics: mad scientists.

What was mad? In college you didn't know if your friends were crazy or not; all behavior seemed acceptable. It often seemed to grown-ups, the authorities, that students were crazy when everyone else—their friends, their peers—knew they were fine. But now Isabel thought maybe the grown-ups had been right. College was unstructured; no one looked after you, no one noticed. No one was in charge. You could choose to skip classes, to stay in your room for weeks. You could choose not to sleep or eat. You could choose to take drugs, get high, nod off, hallucinate. How normal was that?

But up to a point, it was. College students tended toward extreme behavior. How would you know if a friend had lost mental control? Who decided? It always seemed that your obligation as a friend was to protect someone from the grown-ups. But you never really knew about anyone else. What had happened to Jeff? Isabel wondered guiltily. She'd heard he was in San Francisco making independent movies. But was he all right? Had she been a good friend, had she paid attention, done everything she could? What could you do for someone who was going crazy? She had a panicky feeling, saw him spiraling into darkness, out of control.

The president introduced the first speaker and stepped back, relinquishing his place.

"Ladies and gentlemen," the speaker began, smiling benignly at them. He was a black man, thin and graceful, with close grizzled hair. "It is my pleasure"—he paused—"and my honor"—he smiled again— "to speak today at this great university."

Isabel tried to concentrate. *You know about his breakdown.*

She could ask Theresa about none of this. Saying anything at all to Theresa felt dangerous. Theresa was staring up at the speaker. He had taken hold of the podium and leaned confidentially close, gesturing with long fingers. ". . . intellectual challenge," he was saying, and then something about the long row to hoe.

Isabel looked over at Michael. He was in the back, partially blocked by other faces. He turned, and she could see his entire face, his long sweet face, his beaky nose, his dark thick-lashed eyes. He was looking in her direction, and she smiled, but he made no response.

Isabel set her feet on the chair rung beneath her, bracing herself. What was it about graduation speeches? So ponderous, everyone so honored to be asked to speak, so flattered to be the object of attention. But of course they weren't; the object of attention was the graduates. The speeches were only laborious markers, attempts at gravitas.

Isabel shifted, keeping herself carefully away from Theresa. She did not want her skin to brush against the older woman's. Theresa must feel threatened, she thought. Isabel was coming too close to the prize. Theresa must be afraid that Michael wanted to marry her. Theresa was right. Isabel and Michael had talked often about the future, which seemed a place they would inhabit together. Isabel assumed they would marry.

You know about his breakdown. The words gave Isabel a small horrid thrill. She wondered if a breakdown had genetic implications. Was she supposed to ask medical questions about heredity? And was madness in fact hereditary, or was that nineteenth-century gossip?

Isabel knew that Michael was not mad. He was a brilliant journalist about to graduate with honors. She'd known him for nearly a year, and he was sane. He had moods, but most people did. And anyone could sink into a depression; college was a time when people did that. Michael was fine. He had already been offered jobs by three major newspapers. He was completely fine, he was wonderful. Looking down, he saw her then, and his face lightened. He smiled at her. The sky began to spit rain, tiny drops misting from the clouds, which had now spread completely across the sky.

Isabel had lost track of the speakers, the speeches. The president stepped back to the podium and began to confer the degrees. There were too many students for each one to come up individually, so the president solemnly graduated each school in turn. "The School of Nursing," he intoned, and turned to look at them. Those students stood, received applause and sank down again, graduated. "The School of Journalism," the president said. Isabel could see Michael over the heads of the others. He was smiling. The audience clapped. Michael's head disappeared, the students sank back down into their seats, and it was over.

Isabel, still clapping hard, looked at Theresa to see if they could share at least this, the triumph of the beloved. But apparently they could not. Theresa did not return her look, and when the clapping died, she reached down for her purse and began to search in it. She drew out a new box of cough drops, which she carefully unwrapped, the paper rustling loudly. She lifted out a dark brown gelatinous oval and tucked it into her mouth. She put the box back and snapped her purse shut. She lifted her chin, craning her head to watch the president finish naming the schools, as though she needed to see him in order to hear him, and as though she had never met the young woman seated next to her.

Chapter 8

Michael's mother stayed in town for several days after graduation. The three of them went out together: to a play, museums, meals. Theresa was polite to Isabel, reserved, but now pleasant. Michael seemed unaware of any tension. He acted cheerful but distracted, as though his bright, clear self were faintly muffled. He was casually affectionate with his mother, and teased her about being overprotective.

"Don't worry, Mom," he told her. "If I end up moving to Miami, I'll call you every day. I'll call you every hour if you want. Is that what you want?"

But Theresa did not smile at this. She looked away, displeased. Isabel wondered if it was her own presence that caused the coolness. She was very careful with Theresa, trying to be unassuming.

Much of their conversation was about Michael's future. He had decided not to stay in the city; coming straight from graduate school, he would not be offered a job at a big New York publication. Staying here would mean working for a small paper, or working freelance, which he didn't want to do. Instead he would start out elsewhere, choosing one of what he described as the "more exciting job in the less exciting city" options. He'd received offers from newspapers in Baltimore, Miami and Boston and was trying to choose among them. The discussions made Isabel uncomfortable, since she had no place in them.

"You don't want to go to Miami, Michael," she told him. "Miami's awful. All flash and crime."

Theresa gave her a brief level look, reminding Isabel that her opinions on this were irrelevant.

"What's wrong with Miami?" Michael asked, apparently unaware of his mother's look. "Miami is actually a very interesting place. It's one of the few really international communities in this country. Politically it's very complex."

Isabel, stung, looked down at her plate and did not answer.

At times Theresa softened. They went to a Bonnard retrospective at the Metropolitan, where Theresa stood in front of one large painting without speaking. Michael came up next to her, his hands in his pockets, and shook his head.

"I don't get it," he said, visibly bored. "I know this is my lack, but I just don't see why this is important. It's pretty, but it's dull."

Theresa turned to Isabel, smiling at her. "We can't let him get away with that. *You* don't think it's boring, do you?"

Isabel, pleased to be asked, shook her head.

"It's so rich, Michael," Theresa scolded. "How can you call Miami complex and interesting and this painting dull? How can you not have a response to it? It's *sumptuous*. Bonnard created a whole sumptuous world with color in a way no one had really used it before. And it's not just color, it's also narrative: this is a room you can walk into, a room you *long* to walk into. You yearn to be in that room, sitting on that sofa, looking out that window. Your whole life would be different if you were there. How can you stand there like a lump and say it's boring?" Theresa, laughing, shook her head and looked at Isabel, inviting collusion. "You can't take him anywhere," she said to Isabel, and her face was lit up with affection and good humor, and Isabel laughed out loud, and so did Michael, and then so did Theresa. At that moment, standing in the high-ceilinged marble room, it felt as though they were all friends.

But these flashes were rare. During most of Theresa's visit, she spoke little to Isabel and looked at her seldom. Her presence was inhibiting, even when Michael and Isabel were alone together at night. Isabel said nothing to Michael about the breakdown, waiting until Theresa had left them fully.

On Monday she left, and that evening Isabel and Michael went to a small Chinese restaurant near his apartment. They walked along upper Broadway without speaking. It had turned suddenly warm, and the sidewalks were full of people moving through the spring evening. Upper Broadway was a rich ethnic mix, skins of all color, polyglot, casual, everyone in jeans and T-shirts, sneakers. It was impossible to tell the delivery boys from the Ph.D. students, and of course someone might be both. The dark-skinned boy who delivered your pizza might be a scholarship student paying his rent.

Michael walked with long ebullient strides, his head high. His mood was expansive, but Isabel was quiet. She watched the sidewalk, thinking about what she was going to say. Once Michael threw his arm around her, and she walked close to him briefly. But she did not adjust her steps to his, which made the embrace awkward, and he dropped his arm. This pleased Isabel, because she did not feel close to Michael and was preparing herself for hostility.

The more she thought about Theresa's behavior, the angrier she became. It was outrageous, Theresa whispering about the breakdown as the audience went silent. It had been a declaration of war. And what did it mean? *Was* Michael crazy? Isabel felt both attacked and duped, frustrated and wary.

In the restaurant they sat at a tiny table against the side wall. A young Chinese waiter with a wide blank face and a shock of blue-black hair came over to them. He wore a white shirt and black pants, a dish towel wrapped around his waist. He put down two battered plastic menus, poured water in their glasses and left.

Isabel drank, not looking at Michael. She was trying to think of how to begin. He picked up his menu and studied it.

"I'm not going to have moo shu pork," he announced. "I always have that, and tonight I'm going to have something different."

Isabel glanced down at the menu. "Why change?" she asked shortly. "If you know you like it."

She felt that somehow Michael was to blame for Theresa's coolness, or that he should apologize for it or praise Isabel for being so good-natured. At the very least he should acknowledge it. But Isabel didn't want to criticize Michael's mother. She wasn't sure how this conversation should go, or how she wanted it to go.

She did want to know more about the breakdown. And she wanted to know what would happen to the two of them, though this was a question she couldn't ask. The thing was, she wouldn't really need to know about the breakdown, and about Michael's past, if she were not included in his future, and this made her even more unhappy.

Michael snapped the menu closed and put it down. "Well," he said decisively, "because I'm ready for a change." He folded his arms on the table and looked at Isabel. "That's where I am. Heading for change. Ta-da."

Isabel looked at him, then back at the menu of incomprehensible Chinese characters. "Well, clearly," she said. "Where will you go? Since you're definitely leaving the Big City." She could not resist a faintly scornful tone.

"Oh, New York," Michael said dismissively. Isabel could see that he'd already left it. "People in New York are totally provincial," he said. "They can only see New York. They think it's the imperial city."

"Well, it is," Isabel said stubbornly.

"But remember, I grew up in Chicago. I didn't grow up worshiping New York. Anyway, there is no imperial city in America," Michael went on expansively. "The continent is too wide, and the culture is too diverse, too layered, it has too many admixtures."

This was exactly the sort of thing that was irritating about Michael, Isabel thought, that he came up with words like "admixtures."

"America's too big to have one place that's the center of everything." Michael was warming to his subject. "The United States is larger than the continent of Europe: imagine claiming that Paris was the center of England, or Rome of Germany. The thing is that there are more vital centers in America than New Yorkers want to believe. And if you live here, it's easy to forget what's going on elsewhere."

"You're just trying to find reasons to leave," said Isabel.

"Of course I am," Michael said. "What do you think I should do, drag myself around in sackcloth and ashes, moaning, because I have to leave the center of the world? That would be really sensible."

This was another irritating thing about Michael, that he was so quick and flexible during an argument, that he could maneuver so easily. That he didn't mind accusations; he accepted them. Also that he was so sensible.

"Okay, fine," Isabel said. "So what are your thoughts on all this?"

"Well, I like Boston a lot," Michael said, turning serious, "and the *Globe* is a great paper. But the job they offered is the least interesting of the three. Also I kind of already know Boston, because of Williams. Boston was the metropolis for me, for four years, and I'd like to go somewhere else."

"Miami, then?" asked Isabel, making a face. Miami was detestable, she thought, so vulgar and articifial, all that glaring sunlight and thousands of old rich people buying condominiums and playing golf. The beaches lined with hideous high-rises, the waters fouled by motorboats.

"Well, I'm actually tempted by Baltimore," Michael said. "The *Star* is a really good paper. It has a long tradition of great writers."

"And Baltimore?" Isabel asked sardonically. "What does it have a long tradition of?" The city seemed to her unspeakably dreary, deadly and dull. But all of these places seemed dreary and dull; she hated talking about them. And what was she doing in this conversation, anyway, listening to Michael smugly reviewing his choices, choosing some wonderful place to go off to without her.

"Well. For one thing, my plan is that wherever I go now will be temporary. I hope I'll be back in New York in a few years, having won my spurs, and get the Big Job here. Then I'll be here for a while, until, I hope, I can go to Europe and manage one of the bureaus there. But right now here's what I want to know. Which place do you like the best?" Michael asked.

She looked up; he had leaned forward and was watching her attentively. "What do you mean?" she asked warily. "Which place do I like best for you?"

"No. Which place would *you* rather go to?" Michael asked. His look was serious and sweet.

Isabel was prepared for an argument, but it looked now as though something very different was about to happen. It seemed important that she learn about Michael's breakdown quickly, now, before the conversation went in the direction it seemed to be going. Shouldn't she know what she was getting into? Wasn't that fair? Necessary?

But it did not seem possible. Everything sounded different now, and she could not change the subject and talk about something else, and she could not look away from Michael's eyes.

The waiter appeared. "Ready to order?" He flipped through his order pad.

"I'll have this chicken," Isabel said, pointing to something.

"Moo shu pork," Michael said, and Isabel began to laugh.

"I thought you were changing?" she said when the waiter had gone.

"I forgot what I was going to say," Michael said, "I'm concentrating on something else." He looked abashed, his eyelids fluttering as they did when he was nervous, and Isabel stopped laughing. Michael had become somehow fragile. The atmosphere between them held importance, a kind of fear, and Isabel could feel that they were hovering on the brink of something. She felt anxiety herself and opened her mouth to speak but said nothing. Her heart beginning to pound, her hands and feet growing cold. She drank from her water glass; Michael looked down at his mat. He folded his hands on the table, lacing his fingers together.

"Bel," he said, and at the sound of his voice, Isabel felt her breath change.

"Yes," she said, and now everything seemed preordained. They had gotten onto some sort of track, and there was no longer any chance of digression, they were headed somewhere unavoidably.

"I want you," Michael said, the words sounding immensely difficult, "I mean, will you, to marry me." He was nodding as he spoke, and pausing between the words, and looking at her as if he were in shock. As he spoke the words, they seemed to go powerfully into the world, each one of them enormous, separate, impossible to connect with anything else. Isabel was looking into Michael's eyes, but she was also aware that his fingers were white at the tips, that he was crushing his hands tightly together as he spoke, and this knowledge, of his tense, fierce hands, was part of her response, as well as his gaze, which seemed earnest and loving but also terrified, and she was also aware of the restaurant around them, it seemed amazing that they were in this public place, and there were people around them, quite nearby, who were talking and laughing, a part of this completely private moment between them that was also encompassing the universe.

When Michael finished his sentence, Isabel found herself looking at his mouth, which seemed to tremble slightly. She did not want it to tremble, and it seemed that something immense was sweeping over both of them, something frightening and joyful and brave, and as part of that, she nodded quickly and said, "Yes. I will."

When the waiter came back with their loaded plates, they were leaning toward each other across the table. They had seized each other's hands, and the waiter stood still, waiting for them to move.

After dinner they walked home, now comfortably in step, their arms locked around each other. It was not late, and the streets were full of people idling through the warm night. Summer was in the air, and school was over for the year. They walked down Broadway, with its narrow islands lined with battered city benches. Already some old people were sitting on the benches, settled in, watching the passersby, the traffic roaring past. Overhead the stunted trees were starting to leaf out, struggling to perform the annual miracle of spring in the city.

"Do you think those people ever go anywhere else?" Isabel asked Michael. "Do they have children who come and bring them dinner, or is this it, sitting on the bench at Broadway and a Hundred and Fourteenth Street? Is this their only diversion?"

"It's not so terrible," Michael said. "They all look clean and well dressed. They're not homeless or hungry or anything. They all have rent-controlled apartments."

"It is terrible," Isabel insisted. "Broadway is not a park. It's a little strip surrounded by traffic." A police car raced past them, siren wailing, light circling fast and crazy. "It's terrible here."

Michael hugged her closer, knocking her hip with his. "Okay," he said. "We'll retire to somewhere else. Miami."

She laughed. She still had to ask about the breakdown, but it had now receded. It was now out near the horizon somewhere, and up close was Michael.

They had decided on Baltimore, and now the city seemed a fascinating place. It was now full of history, and charm, and lovely old unspoiled buildings, brick and brownstone, wrought-iron streetlamps, flagstone sidewalks. The countryside was very near; real rolling farmland. Isabel would be able to ride. The city was having a renaissance in the arts; all sorts of interesting things were happening. Isabel would find something fascinating to do, maybe in a whole new field. It had become a city that she could not wait to move to, a new frontier. Even the name seemed different. Now it had a warm glow, rich and antique: *Baltimore*. It had depth and charm, it rolled beautifully off the tongue.

They spent the night at Michael's apartment. He lived in a cramped series of rooms on 110th Street that he shared with two other graduate students. Michael's housecleaning skills were minimal; in fact, so was his awareness of dirt. The kitchen was so anciently, appallingly filthy, the grease so deeply and permanently embedded on every surface, that Isabel refused to cook in it. When they spent nights there, they went out for meals. Michael's bedroom was small and messy, its space mostly taken up by the double bed and the TV. Dirty clothes collected peacefully on the floor until Michael, in heroic and infrequent spasms, swept everything into a bag and took it to the Laundromat.

That evening Michael and Isabel lay on the unmade bed, their arms around each other. They watched the news and talked about their plans, but all the time Isabel knew what she had to ask Michael. After the late news Michael stood and turned off the TV and started to undress. Isabel drew in her breath and began.

It all felt different now. Before she had felt self-protective, challenging and accusatory. She had been prepared for animosity, battle, but that had changed. Now Isabel felt that anything threatening him was something she needed to understand so she could ward it off.

"Your mother told me about your breakdown," she said in a rush. Michael was standing with his back to her, unbuttoning his shirt, facing a chair already covered with clothes.

"She did," Michael said, and sighed. He turned to look at her. "That was kind of her. What did she tell you, exactly?"

"That you were in McLean for six weeks," said Isabel bravely. "The locked ward."

Michael sighed again. "Sounds pretty terrifying, doesn't it. I don't actually think it was six weeks, I think it was more like four. But it was McLean. And the door onto the ward was locked. That's true."

Isabel waited. She watched him. "So what happened?"

Michael closed his eyes, then opened them. He took off his shirt and turned to throw it on the chair. His shoulder blades sprang out sharply against his skin. He turned back to Isabel. "It's hard to describe, but it's—I was depressed. It's hard to describe depression. It's something that takes over your life. It's like something shutting out the sky. It closes you down." He was frowning now. Pain had entered his face, and he talked slowly. "I got more and more unable to do anything. A sort of paralysis takes over your consciousness, a weight on your mind. I went to fewer and fewer classes. I sat in my room more and more of the time. Finally I couldn't leave my room. I couldn't go to classes. I couldn't go to meals. At the end I couldn't get dressed. I couldn't even sit up in bed."

There was a silence.

"Why couldn't you sit up?" Isabel asked, her voice small.

"It was too frightening."

"Frightening?" asked Isabel. She was trying to imagine it. She wanted to understand everything that had happened to Michael. "What was frightening about it?"

"It's hard to explain now. But everything was too risky. It was risky sitting up, moving all the parts of my body so radically. I knew if I did sit up, everything would be different, it would all be changed, and that was too dangerous. Everything would be in a different place. Just finding my socks was too much for me. They might be in different places; one might be under the bed, too far away. Everything is full of risk when you're in that state. Fear permeates everything. Your heart starts to pound at the idea of doing anything. The smallest movement is terrifying. Any change. There is no decision you can make."

He sat down on the bed next to Isabel. She stroked his bare arm and he smiled at her.

"But fear of what?" she asked. "Was it physical fear?"

Michael shook his head. "Not exactly. It's not specific. It's just fear, terror. Everything is terrifying. The world around you, the air, is permeated by terror. Your pulse races, you can't breathe properly. You can't talk or move."

"And then what happened? Did someone call a doctor?"

"My roommate finally reported me to health services. They sent a nurse over, and by then I wouldn't open my eyes or move. I heard her when she came, but I had an idea that it was all part of something else, a sort of plot of some kind—and of course that was right, it was a plot of some kind—so I didn't answer her or move. So they sent me to McLean. Strapped into an ambulance."

"Oh, Michael," said Isabel, stroking his skin gently. His voice gave off the echo of pain; she could feel that it had taken him over.

"Do you want to know the rest?"

She said nothing, letting him decide.

"They kept me there. I was on drugs. Every few hours someone would come in and give me more pills and stand there while I took them. They kept me nearly unconscious. I don't remember very much of it, but I do remember feeling that it was an incredible relief, not being in charge. It was a relief knowing that I could do nothing, I didn't have to do anything. People came in to check on me all the time. I hated having them there sometimes, but I also loved it. The nurses gave me baths. I remember crying because I was so scared of being bathed. The idea of moving into the bathroom, of starting the loud water. But they did it very gently, and I wasn't hurt, nothing happened. My mother came to see me a few times. I saw a therapist every day. After a while I felt better, and finally they let me go. I made up the classes in summer school. I saw a therapist for months. After about six months I stopped taking the medications, and now I'm fine. It was four years ago."

Isabel rubbed her hand gently back and forth on his shoulder. "Do they know why it happened?"

Michael shrugged. "Depression is inscrutable. No one knows when it will hit or why. Often it attacks when things are going well. I had just been told that my thesis would be in the honors program. Who knows?"

Isabel waited a moment. "And your father?"

"I guess that had something to do with it," Michael said, nodding. "You can imagine what the shrinks said when they heard about that. You can hear them breathing hard, the little yips of excitement as they pick up the scent."

Michael was sitting on the edge of the bed, his elbows on his thighs, his head bowed. His long, beautiful back was turned to Isabel, and as she listened, she continued to stroke the smooth skin of his shoulder.

She thought of him—brave, vital Michael, full of energy and strength—lying curled up in his darkened room, speechless, helpless with fear, unable to sit up or speak. This stayed with Isabel afterward as a cautionary reminder. She felt that her task was to prevent this from happening again.

And her memory of that evening, when Michael proposed to her and they agreed that their lives from then on would be joined, always included the two moments—the first at the restaurant, Michael, his face alight, leaning toward her across the tiny table, confusing the words of his stupendous question, when he seemed powerful and open, charged with vitality and tenderness, a moment quick with possibility and life. Then there was this other, later moment, when Michael sat turned away from her on the bed, his back exposed, talking about fear, his voice revealing the memory of that black enveloping paralysis. And in that second moment he seemed still and closed, helpless.

Part 3

A mixed hardwood forest, of conifer and broad-leafed deciduous trees, will show stubborn resistance to mild and even repeated drought. The extensive root system works as a vast vascular network, reaching deep into the ground, tapping into the distant recesses of the watershed.

In drought conditions both persistent and severe, however, the trees are unable to reach the reserves, as the water level falls below the deepest, most searching roots. Then the tree's normal methods of survival are interrupted.

The leaves shrivel, turning dry and weightless. The tips curl, the green edges roll inward. Sometimes they fall. Transpiration halts, closing down the natural cooling system. The production of insect repellents ceases, which leaves the tree prone to infestation. As the water table continues to fall, the grip of the roots in the dry earth becomes less potent.

During a prolonged and dangerous drought, the entire forest stands dry and enfeebled, its normal capabilities for survival deeply compromised.

"Eye on the Forest," Isabel Green,
EPR Newsletter, Spring Issue

Chapter 9

The next morning, after breakfast, Paul and Isabel set out for the boathouse, walking up through the woods. The early air was cool and fresh, sweet with balsam.

They arrived first and were already on the dock, settling the *Panama* in the water, when they heard the others. Voices were muted; it was too early for talk. The lake was quiet, too, the only sounds the gentle wooden *thunks* of canoes being taken down from the racks, the footsteps on the hollow floor, the slow sloshing as a canoe slid gently onto the glassy water.

Paul and Isabel, in the *Panama,* hovered off the dock, waiting for the others. Mist hung in translucent clouds over the lake. When the other canoes were in, they all set off, sliding quickly across the lake. There was no sound now but the liquid dip of paddles, a woody creak as a shaft touched the side of a canoe. Isabel was in the bow, the flat silver surface ahead of her. She could feel Paul's movements behind her. Each time she sank her paddle into the water, she felt him do the same. She tried to keep the swing of her arm steady and rhythmic, in synchrony with his.

On her right she began hearing the sounds of another canoe. The *Weetie* was pulling slowly abreast of the *Panama*.

Paul called out, "We're not racing."

"Neither am I." Whit grinned at them. "Sorry. Don't mean to pass you. Can't help myself." His sleeves were rolled up, and when he dipped his paddle, a long muscle jumped along his forearm. He moved steadily ahead.

"No racing, you two," Douglas called from behind, "or we'll never catch up."

"We're not racing," Paul answered. "Whit's showing off."

Whit did not turn but raised his paddle in a friendly salute. Then the paddle rose and fell in the water.

This time they made straight up the lake, past Wicconet, past the other islands looming mysteriously through the mist. As the morning wore on, the mist evaporated, turning the lake crystalline, the islands jewel-like. When Isabel raised her paddle, she smelled the sweet greeny scent of fresh water. After the first hour, her arms began to tire. The trip was much longer than yesterday's, and she began switching sides, from right to left, then back. She felt Paul accommodating her movements.

"Stop paddling if you want," he told her. His voice was quiet, his offer confidential. "I'll keep us going. Take a break."

"Thanks," Isabel said. She laid her paddle flat across the canoe in front of her, resting her arms. She felt the long thrust of Paul's stroke, propelling them forward in a smooth skid across the water. It was a luxury to sit still.

She had slept little the night before. When they had gone back to Acorn after dinner, Paul had suggested that they push their two beds together into a makeshift double. The new arrangement had a high, hard double ridge down the center, with a low, hammocky hollow on each side. The interleaved sheets and blankets pulled easily apart, and there was the risk of the two beds sliding away from each other during any sort of activity. Isabel thought the arrangement unsatisfactory.

In bed they both lay reading. Paul was on his back, his book propped on his chest. Isabel, who liked strong light, lay on her side, holding her book directly under the dim circle from the bedside lamp. Her back was to Paul. When she heard him turn off his light, she stopped reading but did not move. She was hoping he would not shift toward her.

He leaned across to her. "Good night," he said mildly. He was only going to kiss her, then, and go to sleep.

She was relieved, but as she turned, her book slid to the floor. Isabel felt a flash of irritation: at the ridiculous bed, at having to turn so awkwardly, at having her book land facedown, pages bent.

"Good night," Isabel said, and kissed Paul's dry lips briefly. "I'm going to read a bit more, if you don't mind."

"I don't mind," Paul said. He smiled at her and moved closer, pressing himself against her back, one arm thrown over her shoulder, holding her snugly against him. Isabel leaned away from Paul, toward the lamp. Paul's arm lay on her shoulder. As he fell asleep, his limb turned heavier.

When she closed her book and turned out the light, Paul's arm was still holding her fast. She slid down into her hammocky side of the bed. In his sleep, Paul felt her movement and reflexively clasped her tighter, pulling her toward the raised metal ridge. As he relaxed, his arm turned weighty and inert again.

Isabel lay motionless, waiting for him to shift—weren't people meant to toss in their sleep? He did not stir, his breaths were long and peaceful, his arm fixed onto her shoulders. Isabel tried shifting herself, hoping that Paul would stir in response, drawing his arm away. But each time she moved, his arm clenched and stiffened, grasping her more tightly.

Claustrophobia swept over her like a hot wave. She slid out from beneath him, disengaging his fingers from her shoulder. Paul's deep breaths paused, then stilled. He was now silent, partially awake. His hand patted clumsily at the sheet, groping for her, but she was standing on the cold floor beside the bed.

"Where are you?" he asked, his voice thick with sleep. "Don't leave me."

"I'm right here," Isabel said, beyond his reach. "I'm just going to the bathroom. I'll be right back."

"Mm," said Paul, unawake. He rolled over, and his breathing steadied. Isabel picked up her book and left the room quickly, as though escaping. The cabin was full of silence and shadows. In the next bedroom, Paul's, she turned on the light by the bed. She climbed into the bottom bunk, pulled up the coarse blanket and opened her book.

She was now wholly awake, and the night sounds were vivid. A cricket just outside the window trilled one high, liquid, musical note again and again. The pages of her book gave a papery scrape as she turned them, the blanket rustling thickly when she changed position. She moved carefully; all sounds seemed loud in the deep forest silence.

She was aware of the dry woods sweeping up the gentle hillsides, rising in the darkness to the mountains. She heard mosquitoes drifting against the screen, she heard the heavy thump of moths. She could feel the night passing, the hours moving on. Outside the trees moved, branches shifting heavily. She was alone in this vast nocturnal world. Inside the cabin there was silence. There was no sleep in her. She felt herself racing, her blood thrumming, poised and ready.

It was much later—she had nearly finished her book and was afraid to look at the window for fear it would be graying with dawn—when her eyelids began to lower: sleep was finally relenting. She crept back into the darkened bedroom and climbed into her side of the bed. The sheets were cold and crumpled, and Paul was now on the far side, facing the wall. Isabel tucked herself into a ball and pulled up the covers.

Paul took a long sleeping breath and gave a sigh. "You're back."

"Yes," Isabel said. She wondered what he knew, whether he thought only moments had elapsed and she'd just been in the bathroom, or that she'd been absent for hours.

Now, in the sunlight out on the lake, Isabel felt slightly hallucinatory from the lack of sleep. The world seemed strange and remote, seen through the scrim of fatigue. She felt one beat behind the day.

As they neared the head of the lake, they could see Whit sitting on the shore beside the *Weetie*. He was wearing hiking shorts. His arms were deeply tanned, but his legs were oddly pale. He smiled at Isabel as they closed in. "How are you doing?" he asked. His voice was quiet, the sound carrying across the flat green water.

"Okay," she said, adding loyally, "Paul's doing most of the work."

Paul pivoted the *Panama* and they slid in sideways. Whit held out his hand to Isabel. Climbing out, she felt his fingers on her hand and wrist.

"Thanks," she said, not looking at him. When he let go, she could still feel his touch, like an imprint.

Douglas and Charlotte drew up behind them, paddling comfortably in unison.

"Hi ho," Charlotte said cheerfully. A fisherman's hat was slanted rakishly over her bright dark eyes.

Paul pulled the *Panama* out of the water in one long, smooth tug, hoisting it up onto the shore. He flipped the canoe over and lifted up one end, positioning himself underneath it.

"Ready?" he asked Isabel. She ducked inside the canoe behind him and straightened, hoisting the narrow arc over her head. The world became hollow and dark. The inside of the canoe smelled like the lake, liquid and green. Trickles of water found the top of her head, her shoulders. All she could see ahead was Paul's back and tanned legs; to the side she saw tree trunks. Paul began walking; she followed, trusting and blind. They walked along a wooded path that twisted among the trees. The canoe had seemed light in the water, but now it was weighty. Isabel shifted her hands.

"Only a little farther," Paul said.

At the end of the path the trunks thinned, giving way to lake, another wide waterscape. Paul stopped at the shore, and they lifted the *Panama* up, twisted it and dropped it gently into the water.

"Welcome to Moose Lake," Whit said. He was already in the *Weetie,* drifting.

Douglas and Charlotte appeared, their canoe bumping slightly against the trees. They lowered it at the water's edge.

"That portage is always longer than I remember," Charlotte announced.

"They all are," Douglas said, and Charlotte laughed her odd bark.

They set off on the new lake, which was wider than their own. The three canoes were abreast, and Charlotte turned to Isabel.

"How are you doing?" she asked kindly. "This is a long trip for a beginner."

"I'm all right," Isabel answered, pleased to be asked.

"I always ache on the first day," Charlotte confided. "Blisters. What about you, Whit? You don't paddle out there, do you?"

"He doesn't need to paddle," Paul said. "Whit's a Mountain Man. He pulls trees out of the ground with his bare hands."

"What about you?" Charlotte asked Paul. "You in good shape?"

"I'm never tired, Ma," Paul said. "I just never am. I'm always fit."

"Go to one of those gyms?" Charlotte asked. "Do those excercise classes?"

"No, Ma," Paul said. "Can you see me in a leotard?"

Charlotte barked. "I thought maybe the weight-lifting part. You know your father's friend Jack Hansley has a 'personal trainer.' " She made this sound absurd, and everyone laughed.

"As opposed to an impersonal trainer," Paul said. "Someone who never remembers your name."

"A personal trainer," Douglas said thoughtfully. "I think I'd like a personal hygienist to help me floss my teeth."

"Don't be disgusting," Charlotte said. "We don't want to hear about your teeth."

"My teeth are not disgusting," Douglas declared stoutly. Charlotte did not answer.

It was another half hour to Moose Island. They saw it long before they reached it. The island was higher than the others, pine-tipped in the center, with grassy bluffs along the shore. When they arrived, they tethered the canoes and clambered ashore. A trail led up the bluffs, and at the top was a wild meadow full of long, summer-dry grass.

They settled down in a semicircle, facing the lake and the low mountains beyond. Charlotte knelt and began unpacking her knapsack. She wore a striped polo shirt and faded khaki hiking shorts, quite long. Her socks were neatly turned down over her ankles; blue veins twisted up her legs. She took out a tin plate and began setting sandwiches on it. Everyone began opening knapsacks; each had carried a share of the lunch.

"Miriam made these sandwiches," Charlotte said, arranging them. "They should be bloody good, after all her fancy lessons."

"Did you find out if she really has taken lessons?" Paul asked. "We can't lose Miriam."

"There's something going on. There always is," Charlotte said vaguely. The lunch was now spread out on the flattened grass: a thermos of soup, a plate of sandwiches, fruit, cookies, bottled water and fruit juice.

"What are these sandwiches?" Douglas asked, leaning over the plate.

"Nightingales' tongues. Something like that," Charlotte said. She had taken one and was sitting comfortably on the ground, elbows around her knees.

"What I have for lunch every day," Paul said. "Don't you?" he asked Whit.

"Most days," Whit said.

"What *do* you eat for lunch?" Charlotte asked Whit.

"Bologna sandwiches," Whit said.

"*Bologna,*" said Charlotte, making a face. "Whit, that's disgusting. It's perfectly revolting."

"Good, though," Whit said to Isabel.

"What do you do all day?" Isabel asked him. It seemed safer to talk to him now, in the sunlight, with the others around.

"It depends on what's going on," Whit said. "Some days I'm in the classroom. But I spend a lot of time out in the field with graduate students. In the woods tracking bears, in the canyons watching lions, things like that. I visit each student, reviewing methods and talking about whatever problems they're having. That's really the best time for me, being out in the field." He laughed briefly. "Maybe the worst time for the students, having me looking over their shoulders. Observing them observing."

"Bears? Your students study bears?" asked Charlotte. She passed around a tin plate of raw carrots.

"Large carnivores are my specialty." Whit bowed, introducing himself. "Bears, mountain lions, wolves. Of course there are students who choose other areas: large herbivores, riparian ecosystems."

About his work Whit talked in a measured drawl, his language precise. Isabel found this unexpectedly charming, the careful academic terminology so deeply at odds with the rancher's drawl. So at odds with the wilderness itself, the antithesis of the academy.

"We have bears," Charlotte said. "I guess that's the only large predator we have here. Isn't it?"

"Actually, there's some evidence that mountain lions are returning to the Adirondacks," Whit said. "They were here a hundred years ago, and there have been a lot of unconfirmed sightings recently."

"Well, *that* should be exciting," said Charlotte. "It'll keep the tourists on their toes."

"They aren't usually dangerous to humans," Whit said. "Most animals aren't unless they're threatened."

"Grizzlies?" said Douglas. "I thought grizzlies were dangerous."

"Well, grizzlies," Whit agreed. "You're right, grizzlies are always in a bad mood. Most fatal encounters in wilderness areas involve grizzlies."

"And what happens?" Paul asked.

"Mostly it's wildlife photographers," Whit said. "They all want the great shot and they go too close. All animals feel threatened by humans, and the closer you are, the more threatening you are. But wildlife photographers feel they're like the press during wartime. They think they have special rules and they can come in as close as they like. The bears don't agree. The bears think rules are rules. The photographers are human beings, and if they pass a certain point, the bears will kill them. That's their rule, and they follow it."

They were eating now, sitting in the long grass, the lake spread out before them.

"Well, why doesn't anyone tell the photographers that?" Charlotte demanded. "It's ridiculous."

Whit shrugged. "The photographers don't want to know. And they're in wilderness areas; they can do what they want. That's sort of the point."

"They sound like fools," Charlotte said disapprovingly.

"Well, you wouldn't obey any rules, Ma," Paul said. "If you were out hiking, you'd do whatever you wanted to do. If someone tried to tell you what to do, you'd have them fired."

Charlotte began to laugh. "Hate rules," she said, looking at Isabel and shaking her head.

"Imagine Ma," Paul said to Whit, "arguing with the rangers."

Everyone laughed at the thought of Charlotte at bay on a steep trail, scathing, irate, ordering rangers out of the path, hungry grizzlies waiting around the corner.

"Have to call in the choppers," Whit said, grinning. "Be the only way." He raised his thermos and took a long swallow of water. A ripple moved down his throat.

"I remember the time you boys saw the bear," Douglas said. His hair, in the sun, was brilliant white, and his skin, visible through it, was nearly translucent. *He's old,* Isabel thought, surprised, touched.

"A bear and two cubs," Douglas said. He smiled at the memory, but his sons said nothing. He turned to Paul. "Remember?"

"Yup," Paul said, but something rigid had come into his face. He looked out over the lake.

"You two were so excited," Douglas went on. "Where was it, Granite Peak?"

"It was Granite Peak," Paul said, "the long slope before the summit."

"I forget what it was you did. What was it? When you told us about it, of course it was all over by then and you were safe, but it was pretty scary to hear about." Douglas smiled at Isabel.

"It was a mother and her cubs, that's why it was so dangerous," Paul said. He turned to Isabel. "We didn't know about the cubs, which is why we acted so dumb. We were out hiking, and we saw the bear kind of ambling around the meadow. She was nuzzling among the rocks, turning them over for beetles, and eating blueberries from the bushes. She was pretty far away from us, or at least that was how it felt. We just kept going on up the trail. It also felt as though, while we were on the trail, we were safe, as though the trail itself was out of bounds for her. A safety zone. Human territory."

Whit grinned.

Paul continued, "So we just kept on going up the trail, and pretty soon she was behind us, way off to the left. Then we looked around and she was coming after us. She was coming at a dead run, galloping over those rocks and hummocks. Her head was up and she was fixed on us, she was coming for us. And all of a sudden she wasn't far away at all, that distance meant nothing. And the trail! Christ!" Paul yelped. "It was just a little piece of trodden earth. A safety zone!"

"What did you do?" asked Isabel.

"Ha!" Charlotte chortled. They were all laughing now. "What do you think they did?"

"We ran," Whit said.

"We ran so fast," Paul said, shaking his head. "I've never run so fast."

"But it was the girl," Charlotte said. "That was the problem."

No one spoke.

"What girl?" Isabel asked.

"Paul had some girl up for the weekend," Douglas told her. "It was long before your time. Years ago. You were only in your twenties, you boys."

"She ran just as fast as we did," Paul said. He bit into his sandwich, squinting into the sun.

"What happened?" Isabel asked him. "You haven't told me about this."

"He has a dark past," Charlotte told her. "You're going to have to pry these things out of him."

"Nothing happened," Paul said. "We all ran up the mountain faster than the bear did, though obviously she could have caught us if she'd wanted. Bears can run as fast as racehorses. When we got up to the next plateau, we could feel that she wasn't following us, so we slowed down and looked. She'd gone straight on across the meadow to her two cubs, who were playing around near where we'd been. They were behind some bushes, which was why we hadn't seen them. When she stopped, we stopped, and we sat down on the rocks and waited for them to leave. It was a big meadow, and there were a lot of rocks for her to turn over, but we didn't move for hours, until they'd finally left. Then we gave it another half hour to make sure they were gone. We went down the mountain without speaking; we were sweating with fear. I was listening so hard, coming down that path afterward, that I heard every sound, every twig. The next day my eyes ached from watching."

"And who was the girl?" Isabel asked.

There was a pause.

"Just a girl," Paul said. "A girl from New York. I never saw her again, after that weekend."

"She didn't make the grade," Charlotte said bossily to Isabel, sounding pleased. "Have some fruit."

Isabel chose a plum with a pallid bloom across its smooth purple skin. She bit through the thin surface, wondering what had happened with the girl that caused this silence, so much later. She tried to remember how you were in your early twenties. You weren't quite as fragile as a teenager, you'd made some connections and broken them, you were still struggling to learn how it all worked, the thing between people. You were still mystified by passion and joy and anger, incapable of making order out of the wild and flaming landscape you were stumbling through.

In her early twenties Isabel was already married to Michael. On one of her birthdays he'd taken her out to dinner and given her a gold pin and they'd quarreled terribly. At the end of the meal they'd sat in furious silence waiting for the check, and on the cab ride home they'd sat without speaking, looking out separate windows. What had the fight been about?

That night Isabel had slept on the living room sofa and wept into the big square red velvet pillow and planned to leave her husband. (It was before Ben, when she'd still believed that she could leave. After Ben was born, she'd felt knitted into Michael in some final and absolute way. It was something that had only partly to do with love, something that gave her no choice.)

She had wept that her marriage was over so soon. She wept because she loved her husband. She wondered where she would spend the summer now that she was single, and who would get the David Hockney print they'd bought together, and whether tears would stain velvet, which should not get wet, she knew.

Early in the gray part of the next morning, Michael had come into the living room to find her. Their quilt was wrapped around him like a monk's robe, and his head was penitentially low. He climbed over the back of the sofa, rolling carefully down to lie beside her. "I'm sorry," he said, and he put his face next to hers and slid his bare arms around her shoulders.

All those fights, all those rampageous evenings full of rage and self-righteousness, absolute determination, all those arguments and declarations, those appalling revelations, all those risings and leavings of the room, sleeping separately on sofas and in guest rooms, all those great dark preludes to the sudden and absolute reversals deep in the middle of the night or at dawn, the plunge back into amity, bliss.

Isabel could not remember what any of their fights had been about. She still felt knitted into Michael; she still missed him. She wished he were here with her, sitting on this island with the man who seemed to be her husband, listening to his family talk.

After lunch they stretched themselves out on the dry grass, replete, indolent. Isabel remembered a line from a poem—what was it? *The lion of contentment / has placed a warm, heavy paw on my chest.* Isabel felt the paw's benign weight pressing against her. It was midafternoon, the dead dull bottom of the day. The sun beat down and the air shimmered. The insects chanted their high mad harmonies.

"Me for a nap," Douglas said. He was lying flat on his back, his arms at his sides. With his long straight nose and pearly skin, his eyes closed, he looked like a marble crusader carved on a tomb.

"You make that idea seem very pleasant," Charlotte said. She lay down stiffly beside him and pulled her hat over her face. "Good night," she said from beneath it.

"Let's go for a walk," Paul said to Isabel. "We can swim if you like."

"I don't have a suit," Isabel said.

"We don't wear them here," Paul said. Beyond him Whit lay on his back, gazing at the sky. "Want to come?" Paul asked him, but Whit shook his head.

They picked their way along a faint trail that led downhill through the trees. The cove was on the other side of the island, small and sheltered, the trees coming thickly right down to the water. A large gray rock rose up from the lake forty feet from the shore.

Paul and Isabel stood in the trees to undress. Isabel pulled her shirt over her head and felt the breeze meet her bare skin. Under the trees it was shady. Gooseflesh rippled up her arms, her nipples tightened. Paul, ahead of her, was already wading into the water, his buttocks glowing eggshell white. When the water reached his thighs, he threw himself into a shallow dive, his body breaking the surface with a long splash. He came up facing Isabel, grinning, his face dripping.

"It's great," he said. His voice across the water was low and intimate. "Come on."

Isabel waded in. The lake bottom was soft and blurry between her toes, the water cold against her calves, colder still as it rose icily against her thighs. Before it could invade further, she hurled herself deliberately into it. She came up next to Paul, the shock tingling through her.

"It is great," she said. Her body felt spangled.

"Let's go out to the rock," Paul said, heading off.

They were in deep, the bottom dropping off suddenly. Isabel felt nothing but water beneath her. Spreading out her arms, surrounded by the transparent green surge, she felt deliciously bold. The water touched her everywhere. She stretched out her legs, feeling the strength of her kicks, the strokes of her arms.

The rock, sloping out of the lake, was shaped like a whale, dappled with lichen. They clambered out onto its rough surface and settled in the sun, facing the island, their knees held in their clasped arms. Their smooth, streaming limbs were radiant against the gray lichen of the rock, the dark water below.

"This is lovely," Isabel said, closing her eyes. "I've never sat naked in the sun before." She was beginning to dry; she could feel the water tingling off.

"You've been running with the wrong crowd," Paul said. "You've been deprived." He glanced at her. "Actually, I've been deprived: you look very nice like that."

"Thank you," Isabel said, her eyes still shut. She opened them to see a dragonfly glinting near the rock, flicking toward them over the water. It lit near them, green and gemlike, suddenly motionless, its wings shimmering.

"Tell me about the girl," Isabel said, looking at the dragonfly.

"What girl?" Paul said, but the air tightened.

"The girl with the bear," Isabel said.

Paul shrugged, squinting toward the shore. "Nothing to tell. She came up that weekend and it didn't work out. I never saw her again."

"What was her name?"

"Her name," said Paul, "was Marilyn Hornby."

Isabel waited, but he said nothing more. Carefully she lay down on the rock, trying not to scrape herself on the rough surface. She lifted her chin and faced the sky: a high veil of clouds was forming, loose wisps against the deep blue. She rested her arms at her sides and closed her eyes.

What were the things you did not want to tell your spouse? Was it different for a second marriage? Had Paul already told Louisa about Marilyn Hornby? There had been something comforting about telling Michael old horrors—the time the girls in ninth grade wrote her a letter listing the flaws in her character—because, however dreadful the story was, the fact that she was telling it made her the survivor, the hero. Both proved, by their complicity, by their present happiness, that those things had no more power. But maybe Paul had already told that story and didn't need to neutralize its poison again. Or maybe he had never told it; maybe it was still too venomous to approach.

What were the things you would tell no one? The things that had been done to you that were too humiliating ever to relive, or things you had done to someone else, things for which you could never forgive yourself. What Isabel never wanted to talk about was Michael's death; she would never forgive herself that.

"Christ," Paul said suddenly, cross, his voice raised. "You can't come out here, Whitney. We're here. You said you didn't want to come."

Isabel opened her eyes and raised her head. On the shore she saw Whitney turning, going back into the shadows.

"Sorry," he called, disappearing.

Isabel felt her skin tightening as the breeze moved across it. He had seen her. She pressed her knees together. There was a pulse between her legs. Her husband sat beside her, frowning, his long pale limbs sprawled out on the rock.

They waited, and when Whit was long gone, they swam in together, breasting the tiny wavelets and wading up the shore. When they got out, the air seemed cold, even in the sun. Isabel, shivering, shook herself to dry off. She wondered where Whit was—was he swimming alone, on the other side of the island? She thought of his smooth body moving through the green surge, his strong legs. The thought rose up in her mind and she flung it away, trying to shake it off like the drops of lake water.

"Do you ever bring towels?" Isabel asked as they dressed. She pulled on her underpants, the thin fabric clinging to her wet skin.

Paul shook his head. "Against the rules."

"I thought this place was so simple and rustic," said Isabel. "Casual. But I've never seen so many rules."

"It's a totalitarian state," Paul agreed. "But it's about to fall, like all totalitarian states. It will collapse in the next generation."

"What will happen?" Isabel sat down on a rock to put on her socks.

"Everything will break down. Whit hardly ever comes here, so he won't want a full share of the place. Two of my cousins live in California, and they won't want one. I can't afford to buy everyone out. No one wants to sell to a developer, but no one wants to give up the shares for nothing, either."

"Whit wouldn't sell to a developer, would he?"

Paul shrugged. "Why would he want this place? He lives out west, he has no children. It's too big for a single person."

"But he might get married. He might have children," Isabel said.

"Possible but unlikely," said Paul. "He had some woman out there for years. We never met her. I don't know what happened, but it never worked out. Now I don't think he'll get married. So what would he do with this place?"

"Why would a developer want it? There's nothing here," said Isabel.

"Some genius would put up time-share condos along the lake," Paul said. "Clear-cut thirty acres and put in a golf course. Any land can be developed. And even if it failed, if the condos didn't sell, it would be too late, the land would still be ruined." Paul finished tying his shoelaces with a definitive tug. "That's why we need you in the family, to help sort all this out."

"Me?" asked Isabel.

"You're going to make friends with everyone, remember?" Paul said. "You're going to forge alliances."

"I'm going to make friends with everyone. That's different from sorting everything out."

In fact, she was liking Paul's family more and more, peacemaking Douglas, kind and laconic Whit, outrageous Charlotte. But the idea of negotiating among them, dealing with inheritance and property rights, running the lodge for Paul's unfriendly son, hiring Miriam's successor and reshingling the roof, was daunting.

"Still, you'll have to do it," Paul said gleefully, patting her shoulder. "I'll be dead or drooling down my chin, and you'll be in charge."

"That won't be for decades," Isabel told him. "By the time you're dead, you'll have sorted everything out yourself."

"With your help," Paul said. "You're much better at these things than I am. People skills, isn't that what you delightful feminists like to call them?"

They were now dressed, and Paul started off, then stopped and turned back to her. Light came down onto his face, filtered through the leaves.

"I want you to know how happy it makes me, having you here," he said.

"I'm happy being here," said Isabel. It was true.

He turned and went on through the dappled shade. She followed. The woods were quiet in the afternoon heat.

After a few minutes Isabel spoke. "Tell me about the bears here."

"The only ones we have are black bears," said Paul reassuringly. "They're the least dangerous kind. They're small and not usually aggressive. They run away from humans, unless you have the good sense to separate a mother from her cubs. I don't think they swim out to islands, if that's what you're worried about. I've never seen one on an island. But I promise to take personal responsibility for protecting you from any bear we find."

"Thank you," said Isabel. "What about Marilyn What's-her-name? You didn't protect her."

"Marilyn What's-her-name," said Paul firmly, "did not need my protection." The path here was barely readable.

When they came back up onto the bluff, Charlotte and Douglas were still motionless in the sun.

"I'm awake," Charlotte said without stirring. Her hat covered her face. "What time is it?"

"Three o'clock," said Paul. "You don't have to move. We have another half an hour before we should leave."

"Where's Whit?" she asked.

"I don't know," Paul said.

"Thought he was with you."

Paul snorted. "He came over and spied on us while we were swimming," he said irritably. "I told him to go away, and I don't know where he went."

Charlotte took the hat from her face. "You sound like sixth-graders," she said. "What? Came and spied on you."

Paul did not answer.

Douglas gave a long wavering sigh, his eyes still shut. "I suppose I have to get up," he said.

"Only if you want to come home," said Charlotte. "Here's Whit."

Whit was coming up the hill, his hair wet, his shirt stuck to him in dark patches.

"Where'd you swim?" asked Paul.

"The other side of the point," said Whit. "Sorry I barged in on you. I didn't see anyone as I came into the cove, and I thought you'd gone somewhere else." He looked at Isabel. "Sorry."

"It's all right," she said. He had seen her.

On the trip home the canoes stretched out at a distance along the lake, widely separated. Whit was again in the lead. As she paddled, Isabel watched him moving along before her, his movements steady. His reflection rode glimmering beneath him, broken by bars of fluid silver. The sky darkened with clouds and the air was cooling. The water was now a somber gray-blue, its surface beginning to fret and quicken with ripples. On the second lake they paddled faster, against the possibility of rain.

Chapter 10

The rain held off. Each afternoon, along the western side of the lake, masses of cumulus clouds collected in spectacular drifts. Stately billows piled up sumptuously, shining against the setting sun. The baroque outlines glowed gold, fringed with radiance, as if the clouds themselves gave off light. The interiors were rich and ominous, with deep somber shadows, as though what lay within were not merely the absence of light but its opposite.

Each evening at the lodge the five of them sat on the porch overlooking the lake. Each evening they watched the clouds building to fiery crescendoes before darkness set in. Each evening there was the hope of rain, but the clouds gave off only rays of streaming light. Beneath the evening splendor the rolling forestland lay parched. The soft woodland paths gave off puffs of smoky dust underfoot; the tips of leaves were dry and curled.

Each day there was another expedition: a canoe trip, a hike in the woods. The groups varied. Sometimes Douglas and Charlotte stayed home, once Douglas came without Charlotte, occasionally Whit went off by himself. The one constant was Paul and Isabel, who were always together. Isabel, living alone for the last two years, had become accustomed to solitude. Now she found herself thinking of it longingly—lunch on the porch by herself, walking alone through the woods. It seemed churlish and unsociable to suggest this, unwifely.

On the days when she and Paul went out by themselves, or with Douglas and Charlotte, Isabel found herself edgy, oddly conscious of the time, ready to turn back from the start. One day she glanced at her watch in the middle of the lake; it was half past two. Why was she checking the time? There was nothing to hurry for, no reason to get back. She addressed herself to the moment: the blue lake ahead, the rhythmic stroke of the paddle. Later she found herself glancing again at her watch—2:38.

On Tuesday of their second week, Paul and Isabel and Whit hiked up Alumet, one of the highest local mountains. None of these was very high—Whit called them all foothills, which irritated Paul—but Alumet was some distance away, and the climb made a good day's walk.

The three of them set out after breakfast on the path along the lake, walking single-file through the woodland sunlight. Paul was first, Isabel next, Whit last. They walked easily along the flat, their strides loose and lengthy, the air morning-fresh. In the shadowy upper branches, birds called. A small downy woodpecker, its bold black-and-white barred suit capped nattily with red, followed them for a while. It flickered silently from tree to tree, lighting on a lichen-mottled trunk, dodging shyly behind it and then, invisible, sending a modest rattle into the woods. A veery, hidden deep in the interior, gave its melodic liquid call, a spiral of descending glissandos.

At first the path ran straight and level, parallel to the lakeshore, but after half an hour's walk it struck off at an angle, away from the lake, moving up onto the slopes of the first low hills. As they climbed, their steps slowed. It was late morning, and the air was hot and dry even in the deep shade. The woods here were mixed, and the maples, birches and oaks made radiant patches of green light among the somber conifers. The woods turned gradually to pine; the shade deepened, the path softened and the air grew tangy. The slope grew steeper, and the path began slanting in switchbacks, long traverses with hairpin turns. They leaned forward with each step, their bodies canted to stay upright. Isabel could feel the tendons at the backs of her legs. Sometimes she took hold of a narrow tree trunk to pull herself up the slope. She began to glow with heat and sweat. She felt her heart expanding, its rhythm speeding up, her whole body taking part. She liked this feeling of awakening, each step a victory over slope and height. She could feel Whit walking behind her.

The summit appeared without warning; the woods grew thickly right up to the top. Isabel realized they had arrived when she saw the four corners of the fire tower, its straight lines smooth and strict among the trunks.

"Here we are," Paul said, pleased. He stood beside the tower, hands on his hips.

A weathered sign announced: ALUMET FIRE TOWER. NO TRESPASSING. PROPERTY OF THE FORESTRY DEPARTMENT. A wide staircase, nearly a ladder, went up one side. The steps were much steeper than the hillside, almost vertical. The three of them climbed up it, past the tree trunks and the bare interior branches, past the leafy, aromatic upper branches, coming out finally into the open. At the top was a small square balcony with a railing; they were suddenly in the middle of the bright sky. They moved about, looking out in different directions, leaning into the view, smiling, exhilarated by the space.

They ate lunch sitting on the splintery wooden floor, gazing out over the treetops. It was the first view they'd had all day, the green waves of densely wooded hills stretching toward the far horizon. The air softened with distance, and the mountains were faintly blue where they met the sky. Along the farthest crests the silhouettes blurred and melted, subtle, smoky, into the surrounding air.

It was silent except for the faint sibilance of air sweeping through empty space. Over the next hilltop a buzzard swung slowly in wide circles, his long dark wings outstretched on an unseen breeze. Isabel felt the sun against her legs.

"You have to admit," Paul said to Whit, "this is great."

Whit nodded. "Great for bark eaters."

Paul laughed. " 'Adirondack' means 'eater of bark,' " he told Isabel. "It was what the Iroquois called the Algonquin. Or vice versa, it's not clear. But it was derisive, whoever said it." He looked back at Whit. "But you know this is great. Great as the Rockies," he insisted. "Must be."

Whit looked out across the gentle green undulations. "What I like about Wyoming," he said, "isn't just the distance. It's the emptiness. This view right here is great, and it's sort of mine in a way a western view will never be. I feel connected to it. But it feels closed in here. There are too many trees for me." He paused. "There's something about open spaces."

Hearing him, Isabel saw the great empty sand-colored reaches, the high burnt-brown mesas. Badlands, prairies, deserts. Low curving bare hills. The vast sky and the silence.

Paul said nothing for a moment, then repeated, " 'Too many trees,' " and Isabel could feel his resentment.

"Only for me," said Whit, courteous. "Everyone has their own view. But emptiness does something for me. It changes things." He paused. "It makes everything serious. Open space around something makes it powerful. In open space you become serious yourself."

Paul raised his eyebrows. "Air," he said. "You like air."

Whit shrugged. "I guess I'm not explaining this very well."

They sat silently, then Isabel asked Whit solemnly, "Would you call your point of view 'west-o-centric'?"

"Maybe," he said, grinning. "Occidental orientation. The West is where I live. I'm there for a reason, I guess."

"And is that the reason?" Isabel asked, curious. "Because of the way it looks?"

Whit nodded. "You could say that."

The buzzard shifted gracefully and began to make wide circles in the other direction, tilting darkly against the deep blue. White bands glimmered dimly along the underside of his wings.

"Interesting," said Isabel. "Most people don't choose a place to live on aesthetic grounds, do they? No one in New York does."

"What do you mean by that?" asked Paul.

"I mean no one would claim that New York is beautiful, or move there for the way it looks. You live there for other reasons," Isabel said.

"Why do we have to trash New York just because Wyoming is so great?" Paul asked.

"I'm not—" Isabel began, but Paul interrupted.

"I happen to love New York," he declared. "I think it's a great city. It's incredibly beautiful as well as incredibly ugly, and it's probably more alive than any other city on the planet."

"True," Whit said.

Isabel said nothing, chastened. She was also confused: how had she managed to take sides against Paul? But somehow she had, and she put her hand lightly on Paul's knee in apology. The skin felt dry beneath her fingers. At her touch Paul looked up, his eyes unfriendly. She smiled, but his expression did not change, and after a moment she took back her hand. She looked out again across the green waves of hills.

"Who uses this tower?" she asked to change the subject. "Have you ever seen a forest ranger up here watching for smoke?"

"Actually, this is the summer we ought to," Paul said, "the worst drought anyone can remember, plus those two fires up in Hamilton County. But no, I don't think I've ever seen a lookout here. I remember when we were little, we weren't allowed to climb up to this platform, for some kind of official reason. Don't you remember, Whit? Maybe there were fire watchers here then."

"The Forestry Department has changed its fire policy since these towers were built," Whit said.

"Right," Paul said. "They just let fires burn now, don't they?"

"Well," Whit said, "fires are seen now as part of the big plan. They do a lot of useful things in a forest. They get rid of deadwood and fungus, open up the ground to sunlight. That makes for new growth, which is forage for animals. Some trees need very high temperatures to germinate, so they can't reproduce without fires. And fires select for fire-resistant species, since they kill off the trees that are susceptible. But for decades the idea was to prevent them altogether, so now the forests are choked with flammable wood. The idea is that the whole continent is starved for fire."

Starved for fire. Isabel thought of the wide land, its great standing forests silent and gray, the floor brown with dead needles, dense with underbrush, the forest corridors silent. Sleeping Beauty waiting for the flame.

She squinted through the wooden railings out at the distant hills. She was looking, she knew, the way you search, fascinated, for what you dread—the curved fin rising among the sifting waves—uneasy that your looking might somehow call it into being. She scanned the ridges for the first faint plume, loose and transparent still, a filmy presence drifting mildly above the trees it would later devour.

"The other point of view," Isabel said, "is that we should still prevent forest fires because we've interfered so much with the natural system."

"How do you mean?" Paul sounded challenging.

"We've destroyed the fire controls. We've drained the swamps and paved the meadows, killed the animals that were part of the water system. We've channelized the rivers, put in storm drains and cut down forests. So there are fewer wetlands, fewer ponds and fewer streams to stop fires from spreading. Global warming is causing droughts and making the weather more extreme. So the trees are parched and ready to burn, and the winds are high and dangerous. We've created a sort of fire factory. Now, once they start, forest fires just keep burning. The winds drive them on, there's nothing to stop them."

Paul put his hand on her shoulder. *"Apocalypse Now,"* he said cheerfully to Whit, "that's my sweetie. Always looking on the bright side." He shook his head at Isabel.

He was laughing, being funny and gentle. Isabel smiled at him: she was being too earnest, as always. But what she'd said was true.

After lunch they climbed down the ladderlike stairs and began the walk back. Now they leaned backward, their strides loose; the slope urged them toward hurtling recklessness. The woods, in the afternoon heat, were quiet, the birds still. The only sound was their steady footsteps along the path. Once they climbed down into a deep ravine to cross a narrow brown stream that clucked and murmured. Isabel, looking up, thought she saw movement, a shadowy form up along the ridgeline.

"What do you think about the mountain lions, Whit? Are they really moving back here?"

"Hard to say whether they're here or not, without finding a track or a kill." He looked around appraisingly. The tree trunks stood in close ranks, gradually obscuring the distance. The ground beneath them was deep and soft. "It's prime territory for lion. There're a lot of deer here. There's no reason for them not to be moving back."

As they went on, Isabel thought of the lion, deep in the shadows, silent, his round eyes upon them. Moving among the pines, head low, weight shifting from shoulder to shoulder with each step.

At the end of the day, nearly back, they walked again along their own lake. The light was low and slanting. Whit was in the lead, and when he reached the fork in the path between the lodge and the cottages, he stopped and turned.

"See you later," he said, lifting his hand. He was standing in the clearing on the edge of the gravel drive, in the strong late afternoon glow, and beyond him the open space was lit up. A lock of hair had fallen across his forehead, shading his eyes. It glinted in the sun.

Paul nodded. "Bye," he said. Isabel smiled at Whit, and he went on.

They turned onto the path to Acorn. This was in dense shadow, branches meeting closely overhead. Isabel followed Paul into the trees, blinking against the darkness. The small dim rooms in the cabin seemed gloomy and airless, like a punishment. She drew in a breath and Paul turned at once.

"What is it?" he asked.

"Nothing," Isabel said, surprised he was listening so carefully, vexed at herself for being so loud.

That evening the clouds along the hills were dark and sulfurous, steaming, shot with red. The sky slowly gave up its light, dimming gradually. The five of them sat on the porch watching. At dinnertime, when they made their way inside, the lighted dining room seemed bright. Isabel blinked in the doorway.

"It's getting dark earlier now," Paul said, drawing out her chair. "It's funny how noticeable it is. It's only a week since we got here, and already it feels different. The nights are drawing in, the earth is starting to tilt."

Isabel smiled at him as she sat down. "Thanks." She was pleased by Paul's courtesy, and she liked the way his mind worked. She loved that phrase—"the nights are drawing in"—with its grand sweep, its sense of terrestrial purpose. The ample, leisured summer evenings would be drawing in, each one deeper, until, in the middle of the dark night of winter, at the moment of the year's fulcrum, the celestial shift would take place. Then the evenings would begin to open out again, expanding toward spring, spreading themselves quietly through the garden, out to the meadow, down to the shore, along the horizon, along the lip of the broad, hospitable earth.

Douglas was beside Isabel at the table. He settled himself down, ceremonially putting his drink on the table, napkin in his lap. He looked around and cleared his throat in a preparatory way.

"I'd like to make a little toast," he said. "A Philadelphia toast; I'm not going to rise. I'd like to toast Isabel." He nodded at her. "On the occasion of her first visit here." He looked at the others and lifted his glass.

"Why, thank you, Douglas," Isabel said, touched.

"We're pleased to have you here and in the family." He took a ritual sip of his drink. Everyone lifted glasses, smiling at Isabel, who nodded, smiling back.

"Now that you're an initiate," Douglas said, "what do you think of it?" He made a gesture that took in everything: the house, the people, the mountains beyond.

Isabel was struck by his kindness. It was oddly comforting to be named, recognized.

"Thank you, Douglas," she said again. "I love it here. I love the hikes, and I loved my first portage. I even loved the paddling, though Paul did most of it—"

"Not true," Paul said loyally.

"—so I didn't actually even get tired. But I really just love it. It's all beautiful," Isabel said.

"Well, we're fond of it," Charlotte said briskly. "Of course it isn't everyone's taste. Too rustic for some, too wild. A lot of people want *golf.*" She grimaced on the last word, and the others laughed.

"Which, of course, you and Dad play," Paul observed.

"Only in the winter," Charlotte said reprovingly. "Only in Charleston. Never here."

"It would be difficult here," Paul said, "since there's no course." He was teasing his mother. It was Douglas, with his kind toast, thought Isabel, who had started this current of affection.

"You a golfer, Isabel?" Douglas asked. Miriam appeared with a platter of fish fillets, pleasingly blackened.

"I'm not," Isabel said. "My parents aren't, and I never got started."

Douglas nodded approvingly. "Very wise. A terrible waste of time."

"You love it," Charlotte informed him. She helped herself to the fish.

"Terrible waste," Douglas repeated, and smiled at Isabel.

"Is this local, Miriam?" Charlotte asked.

Miriam shook her head. "They bring it in from somewhere else. Idaho, I think."

"Idaho," Charlotte said, and looked around the table. "Wouldn't you think we could raise our own fish right here?" She looked back at Miriam. "What's so great about Idaho?"

"No pollution," Paul said. He passed a dish of broccoli along to Whit. "No acid rain."

"We've pretty much stopped the acid rain around here," Douglas said. "We had it, but we've cleaned it up."

"Actually, acid rain was sort of caused by the Clean Air Act," Isabel said.

Charlotte stopped chewing. "What!"

Isabel nodded. "Well, sort of. Unintended consequences. What happened was, smokestack industries were discharging two kinds of particulates, one large, one small. The act required that the big ones be filtered out, which they were. What no one realized was that the big ones were mostly alkaline and the small ones were mostly acid—sulfur and nitrogen oxides. Together, they'd neutralized each other. They'd done a lot of other bad things, but they hadn't caused acid rain. Alone, the small acidic ones went into the airstream and bombarded the Northeast. And that's how we got acid rain."

Douglas shook his head. "These environmental movements," he said.

"Uh-oh, here we go," Paul said, resigned. "Here we go."

"Well," Douglas said, "I know you like to make fun of this, Paul, but really, environmental laws can be too strict. They're often impractical."

"How do you mean, impractical?" asked Isabel. She felt herself tightening.

"The thing is," Douglas said, "everyone wants a clean environment, but at the same time everyone wants cars and computers and electric lights and plastic containers. These things come at a cost. Environmentalists don't want to pay for them."

"There are other sources of energy," Isabel said. She'd heard these arguments often, and they were wrong. "There are sources that don't cause global warming."

"Global warming," Douglas said, seizing on it. "That's something that hasn't really been proven as fact."

"Actually, most scientists feel it has. And many of the predictions they made twenty years ago are coming true: the temperatures are rising, the weather is increasingly erratic, storms are more dangerous, we're having droughts and floods, cyclones and tornadoes where they've never been. High constant winds. Disaster areas across the globe. It's all happening."

Isabel paused: listing these things reanimated her fears, her sense of the whole planet tipping silently toward a kind of death. This made her feel panicky and irrational, and she tried for a return to reason. "There are other sources of energy we could use," she repeated.

"But they aren't practical," Douglas said. He smiled at her again, patronizingly. "They just aren't practical. Solar heat!" He gave a little dismissive snort. "Now, Isabel, I'm just as environmentally concerned as the next fellow, but you see, I'm practical. This is a big country, and it needs energy. We have to have it."

"Solar heat actually is practical," Isabel said. "Reagan stopped the government support of its development because the oil and gas industry felt threatened. But even if it weren't, it's still not practical to poison the environment. Pollution places a huge financial burden on public health. Cancer and asthma are on the rise, and they're both directly linked to pollution. It's really not practical to damage public health to protect the profits of private corporations."

She could hear herself talking faster, her voice rising. She was turning shrill. She was lecturing, but she could not help it. Here was a chance to convince the other side, and it was so crucial, so urgent.

"The health costs of these businesses are huge, but they don't count as operating expenses because the polluting companies aren't held responsible. The government and the taxpayers pay the cost financially in taxes, and physically with their bodies. People sicken, they die." The last sentence was melodramatic, she knew. She couldn't help herself.

Douglas shook his head. "You know, Isabel, every advance has its price. Nineteenth-century textile mills, for example, were very dangerous places. There were a lot of industrial accidents, but we needed textiles. What we did was make the process safer. We didn't stop producing textiles. You can't stop progress." He sounded reasonable and paternal. "That's something we have to learn. And you have to balance things: saving a little tree frog from extinction shouldn't necessarily prevent the expansion of an airport. We can't just quit every time we see that progress is going to make for changes. You can't stop progress."

What always happened in discussions like this was that Isabel could not go on. Listening to these arguments gave her a profound sense of disjunction. Beyond the words she could feel the presence of the whole doomed beautiful world, spinning silently through deep space, dying. She could feel the rivers being poisoned, running silver with mercury; the air thickening with lethal smog; the soil turning toxic. Insects and animals dying out, children born deformed, women infertile. Allergies, asthma, cancer. There was no end to it.

With all this swarming in her mind, she would listen to someone explaining, with great certainty, as though logic were on his side, why everything should continue as it was—why tons of nuclear waste should be dumped regularly into the North Sea, why the eardrums of whales should be shattered routinely by the navy's sonic blasts. Why the destruction of the planet was not inevitable but necessary, part of progress.

She could make no bridge between the two. She could not answer in the same tone, even the same language. Instead she turned frantic with fear and sorrow, felt her mind tip toward a kind of frenzy. She wanted to reach out and grab lapels, to cry into faces, to shout out the truth so that it would be indelibly known. To plead, *Don't you see?*

Isabel said nothing. She drew in a deep careful breath and lifted her fork.

It was Charlotte who spoke. "Well, I'd take the side of the tree frog against the airport," she declared. "I can tell you that. No question." She looked at her husband and said sternly, "Douglas, you have no idea what you're talking about, tree frogs."

"I know just as much about tree frogs," Douglas said testily, "as you do."

Charlotte tapped her finger on the table. "The point is," she said, "the point is that we have an expert here." She nodded toward Isabel. "Isabel knows all about tree frogs. Don't you?"

"Some," Isabel said, admitting, "they aren't my specialty."

Charlotte nodded again, as though her point had been proved. "And everything *is* being poisoned," she said to Douglas. "You know there used to be more birds here than there are now. More fish and more animals. They're dying."

"Because of the Clean Air Act," Douglas said facetiously, "as we've just heard."

But Whit shook his head. "No, no," he said amiably to his father, "we're not letting you get away with that. It's the factories."

"The fact is," Douglas said, "that you can't stop progress. You just can't do it."

"Actually," Whit said, "progress isn't always unstoppable. Sometimes we do stop it. When it suits us."

"What do you mean?" Douglas asked.

"Chemical warfare, for example," said Whit. "It was banned after World War One because it was inhumane. It always seemed strange to me: isn't war inhumane by definition? Its only purpose is to kill people. Weapons are designed to cause death. So why is one form more inhumane than others? And if we can agree to ban one form of war, why not the rest? Why not just have virtual war, or something symbolic, a football game or chess? But still, we stopped the use of chemical gases, which had been a huge military enterprise."

"It was a political reaction, banning chemical gases," said Douglas stiffly. "A political response to the worst war known to man. Now, of course, these madmen in the Middle East are developing illegal weapons, chemicals, gases, anything. They don't care what we ban."

"But Douglas, everything is a political reaction," Charlotte told him. "Everything. People are political."

"Charlotte," Douglas said, "making these pronouncements of yours doesn't clear things up."

"Douglas," Charlotte answered, "you make pronouncements, too. You think yours clear things up, but they're just your opinions. You only think my pronouncements don't clear things up because they disagree with yours." She spoke with energy but without rancor, and the others began to laugh.

Douglas looked resigned and shook his head. "Never marry a headstrong woman," he said to Whit.

"But it's fun, isn't it?" Isabel asked Douglas, trying to woo him back. "Being married to one?"

Douglas smiled kindly at her, and she felt forgiven.

"Of course it's fun," Charlotte said. "He'd die of boredom if I had nothing to say."

"Difficult to imagine," Douglas said to the air.

"Actually, Isabel would rather have no progress at all and no pollution," Paul said. "She'd be happy if we all still lived in caves." Everyone looked at Isabel. "She's a Luddite."

"It's true, I am a Luddite," Isabel admitted. She could not tell if Paul's tone was mildly scornful or lightly affectionate.

"But Luddites are good," Whit said. "We need Luddites as counterweights. To redress the balance."

"I don't want balance," Charlotte said. "Hate balance. What I want is extremes. Which reminds me, I'd like another drink, please. The extreme sort." She leaned back in her chair, her glass held up, and Douglas rose to take it.

For the rest of the evening Isabel said little, listening to the talk but not joining in. At first she'd felt welcomed by Douglas's toast, accepted, but that had changed with the uncomfortable conversation. Now she felt oppressed by his attitude, so rigid and intolerant: it was exactly what was responsible for the devastation of the environment. But she also felt ashamed of her own response, which had been unyielding, just as rigid and intolerant as his. Inappropriate for dinner conversation with her parents-in-law or anyone else. She had not responded with courtesy to the courtesy shown her. She'd damaged the circle of intimacy Douglas had created. Where was her social grace, that would permit everyone to have his or her own view?

During the rest of dinner she could see the others being careful. They kept a polite distance from her, from any risky subject. She felt ripples still spreading away from the black stone of anger she had thrown, but how could she not cry out? How could people not see the urgency? She could not reconcile the two: polite conversation, the death of the planet.

She had failed, though, here at this table. This thought began a miserable slide downward as she remembered other failures, times when she had felt disgrace afterward. The time when young Ben had picked up a whole platter of spaghetti—everyone's dinner—and hoisted it jauntily on one hand, pretending to be a waiter, and it had slid off his palm onto the kitchen floor and shattered. Isabel had yelled at him for being cocky and careless. At the sound of her angry voice, his face had frozen, stricken, as though she'd slapped him, and her heart had smote her. That moment rose up at her always. And then the rest, the great cluster of failures around Michael, all the things she could not bear to consider.

So Isabel sat listening, looking attentively from person to person as each spoke, the low blue flame of anxiety burning steadily inside her. Whit, beside her, seemed a friendly presence, though he didn't speak to her again. Toward the end of the meal she passed him a plate, and as he took it, he gave her a smile so kind, so deeply *intended,* so accepting, so complete, that Isabel felt her eyes suddenly, surprisingly, fill.

By the end of the evening she felt as though the family had undergone a subtle realignment, or maybe it was her own understanding that had shifted. She'd been surprised that Charlotte had taken her side, and that her mother-in-law could be generous and funny, unexpectedly wise. Isabel had been surprised, too, that it was Whit who had rescued her from the awful conversation, not Paul. Somehow she had managed again to alienate Paul, who avoided her eyes. At the end of the evening, when the tear in the social fabric had been restored, she hoped, by the interweavings of conversation and simply by time passing civilly, that she had been forgiven by the rest of the family, reaccepted on some visceral level—even Douglas had given her a kiss good night. She felt forgiven by everyone but Paul, who was still aloof.

When they left, walking back through the woods, Isabel shivered. She rubbed her arms, which rippled with gooseflesh. A cool damp wind was surging through the treetops, the branches swaying overhead.

"Going to rain," Paul said from behind her.

Chapter 11

The next day was cloudy and sullen, the air damp and oppressive. Rain threatened. In the dull morning light, the cabin seemed somehow darker, the walls closer, the corners more shadowy. The dim ceiling bulbs gave a useless glow.

Isabel and Paul had breakfast inside at the small kitchen table. Its top was covered in a stained gray sheet metal, folded around the corners like cloth, its surface dry and grainy, unpleasant to the touch.

Isabel gingerly put down her plate, trying not to scrape the metal with her fingers. Paul brought over his milk and cereal. His long-sleeved shirt hung loose over his jeans, and the unbuttoned sleeves flopped at his wrists. He pulled out a chair with his foot and sat on it diagonally, a leg on either side of one corner.

Isabel folded her fingers around the mug for warmth. The chill was insidious. "So what do you do here on rainy days?" she asked.

"Go to town," Paul said. He began to eat.

"Will everyone go?"

Paul shook his head. "Not my parents," he said. "Probably just Whit and us." A grain of cereal was stuck to his upper lip, and it rode rhythmically as he spoke.

Isabel nodded, squinting against the steam from her mug.

In midmorning the three of them set off, crammed into the front of the pickup truck. Isabel had been given the shopping lists. This was a mark of trust, she knew, from Charlotte: things to get from the super-market for Miriam, from the drugstore for Charlotte and from the hardware store for Eddie. Whit drove. Isabel sat between him and Paul, her feet on the hump in the middle, her knees modestly close together.

As they started down the drive, Whit lowered his window, setting his arm out. Cold air rushed in and Isabel shivered.

"Would you mind rolling up that window?" Paul asked politely. "My wife is getting cold."

My wife, Isabel thought.

"Already doing that," Whit said. The window was sliding up; he had felt her shiver, too. Isabel was shoulder to shoulder, hip to hip, with them both.

It had begun to rain. When the first light taps began against the windshield, Paul said, "Finally."

The taps came harder, and Whit turned on the wipers. The trees turned black and gleaming, the branches dripped. The narrow dirt roads became rough and slippery beneath their wheels. The wind tossed through the woods. Young trees and shrubs crowded alongside the road, and wet black branches slapped at them.

After half an hour Whit bore left at a fork onto another dirt track curving on through the dark trees.

"Where are you going?" Paul asked, frowning.

"Casco Corners," Whit answered.

"Thank you," said Paul sarcastically. "But why the long way?"

"Better road," Whit answered.

Paul said nothing. The rain was heavier now. Whit set the windshield wipers a notch faster; they whipped back and forth in a manic arc. A bushy sapling laden with rain, blown sideways, cracked hard against the windshield, making them all flinch. Cold air crept into the cab from the outside, small icy whispers curling up from beneath the seat. Isabel began to shiver again. The heater was in the middle of the dashboard; Whit reached out as Paul did, and their hands touched.

"Sorry," said Paul, drawing back.

It was Whit who turned on the heat. A hot baking smell rose from the floor, and Isabel began to relax. She realized she'd been clenched and rigid in a long motionless shiver. The dry heat was a relief. No one spoke until they reached the village.

Downtown Casco Corners was a haphazard cluster of shabby two-story buildings, now streaked and darkened with rain. The Bait and Tackle stood beyond a muddy parking lot churned with tire tracks. The Family Barber shared premises with D. H. Neary, chiropractor. The diner, with rusting chrome trim, stood next to a gas station offering AHI brand, self-serve only. Across from the diner was the hardware store, which had cracked fake redbrick walls. It had no sign, but the front window was a surrealist collage of dusty tools and gadgets crammed on top of one another.

Whit parked outside, the engine idling.

"Okay," he said. "Shall we stay together or split up? One of us could stay here for the hardware, and the other two go out to the mall and do the supermarket and drugstore. We could meet back at the diner for lunch."

Isabel waited for her husband to answer.

"Or we can do everything together," Whit said after a moment. "We're not in a hurry."

"There's no point in doing everything together," Paul said. "It's inefficient."

There was another pause.

Whit said politely, "How shall we split up."

Paul gave his own thigh two brisk pats, for decision. "I'm the one who talked to Eddie," he said. "I'm the one who knows what he needs for that engine. I'll do the hardware stuff. Isabel has the food list, so you two do the rest."

"All right," Whit said.

Paul opened his door and cold air swarmed into the cab. "See you at the diner," he said, already turning away, lowering his head against the rain. The wind whipped at his hair, at the cracked yellow slicker.

"Bye," Isabel called, but he was gone, striding quickly across the broken sidewalk, his shoulders hunched under the jacket. As he walked, he pulled the hood up over his head.

The rain was coming down harder, driven by the wind. Whit notched the wipers up again. The blades whined, slapping back and forth.

When Paul left, Isabel moved over slightly, but her thigh was still close to Whit's. They were still lightly touching.

At the end of the block was a traffic light. A support cable had broken, and the light box drooped heavily in the center of the intersection, off-kilter, swaying slightly in the pelting rain.

"Where's the mall?" Isabel asked. She had made her hands into fists against the cold; now she rubbed them lightly together, warming them.

"Just outside town," Whit said. The swaying light turned green, and they started off slowly. The streets were slick. Rain bounced against the pavement. They passed Golden Rule Auto Sales, a row of used cars lined up along the road, noses out, like hopeful animals at a shelter. The placard in each windshield had an exclamation point after the price, as though the number itself were a revelation: $695! $795! Beyond Golden Rule, the town gave way to abandoned pastures, fenced with sagging barbed wire. Weeds and red cedar were taking over the fields. In the rain, the tall ragged grass was dun-colored.

They're leaving town together, thought Isabel. The phrase appeared in her head. The windshield wipers slapped back and forth, hard. The heater was on full blast, and the air in the cab was turning warm and steamy.

"Why have you never married?" she asked. She was looking straight ahead. The rain was sluicing down, sliding heavily down the windows and across the windshield in sheets.

"I had never met you," Whit said.

He did not look at her. He turned the wheel hard, and the truck swerved from the road, jouncing onto a dirt turnoff, then stopping abruptly. Whit turned off the engine; they sat without speaking. A wire fence edged the field next to them, its black lines rising slackly to the tilted metal posts. There were no other cars. When the engine quieted, the only sound was the rain, drumming on the roof of the cab, pouring its opaque curtain over the windshield and windows. Isabel felt the warmth from his thigh. She could not bear to turn toward him. She waited for him to touch her. She was aware of every part of her body, as though it were lit up on a screen.

Whit picked up her two hands, white from being clenched. He rubbed them between his. His hands were large and hard and warm.

"You're freezing," he said gently. His voice was quiet.

"Yes," she said.

"You'd have a hard time in Wyoming."

Isabel looked straight at him for the first time. "Yes," she said.

His face was solace. The way his eyes were set, deep under the shelving of his brows and wide apart; the long broad slope of his lips. The gentleness of his gaze. She would have liked to drink his face, to take it in.

As he warmed her fists, his hands grazed the tops of her thighs, and she shivered.

"What will we do?" she asked.

"What do you want?" he asked.

"Touch my face," she said.

She closed her eyes. For a moment there was nothing, and she was afraid. Anything, right now, might be the wrong thing to do.

She felt his hand move slowly over her face. He stroked the different parts carefully, as though he were blind, first discovering the slope of her cheek, then the shallow arch of her brows, and finally she felt him touch her lips, very lightly.

His touch felt like healing. Isabel lifted her chin, tilting her head back. She was trembling. She opened her eyes. He was looking at her, and she took a breath.

"We can't go on," she said. She moved her face away. "If we go on, we can never go back."

Whit dropped his hands. "We can only go on," he said, "if we're going to." He waited. There was a silence. What was between them was filling the space around them. It was becoming real. "Would you leave him?"

" 'Would I' or 'will I'?" she asked. After a moment she shook her head.

"I take that back," she said. "I'm not asking you that. But you can't ask me that, either. We can't play dares, asking each other how far we'd go. We should—" She stopped.

But this was worse, the notion that there was anything at all that she and Whit should do together, that they should collaborate, have a plan. She shook her head again.

"There's nothing we should do," she said.

The night before, coming back from the lodge after dinner, Paul had been silent and remote. Isabel was still echoing with chagrin over her argument with Douglas, and she thought Paul was angry at her because of it. Defensive, Isabel fell silent, too, and they undressed without speaking, stepping past each other politely, moving through the small dim rooms as though they were alone.

Paul was in bed reading when Isabel climbed in. She settled into the hammocky dip on her side, facing away from Paul. She spoke over her shoulder. "I'm going to sleep over here, if you don't mind," she said, her voice cool. "When I try to sleep closer to you, the covers keep pulling apart, and I end up caught in the middle and cold."

Paul was lying on his back, his book resting on his chest. He did not answer, and Isabel twisted to look at him, prepared for hostility. Paul's eyes on her were steady and patient. They were not what she'd expected.

"All right," Paul said quietly. "I don't want you to be caught in the middle and cold." He reached out and smoothed the hair away from her forehead.

His touch seemed strange to her, and she felt an impulse to shift her head away from his hand. But she held herself still, looking back at him. His eyes did not change.

Guilty at her impulse, she asked less coolly, "Do you mind?"

Paul went on stroking her hair, her forehead. The room was very quiet, and she could hear the modest rustle of the sheet against Paul's arm as he stroked her. The only light came from the small bedside lamps with the age-stained shades; pools of shadow claimed the corners. There was another silence. He looked into her eyes.

"Are you leaving me?" he asked lightly.

At the words she had felt her heart surge. Somehow the question angered her. "No," she said, hoping the anger wasn't in her voice. "I'm just staying on my side of the bed."

"I hope you're not leaving me," Paul went on, his voice very low, "because that would break my heart."

As he had said these words, such terrible ones, Isabel felt in him a waste of sadness, an expanse of soft darkness engulfing him, and she felt her anger toward him dissolve.

"I'm not," she said gently, "I'm not." She had felt a surge of warmth, a swelling of what she hoped was love, though she hoped he would not lean toward her and take her in his arms. His hand kept moving across her forehead, his fingers kept brushing against her skin. She had waited without moving, meeting his gentle, unbearable gaze.

Now, in the truck, Whit watched her.

"Then what should we do?" he asked.

Isabel set her hands on her knees, taking herself back. She looked at the windshield. Steam was beginning to mist it over. The curtain of rain had been keeping them invisible to the world; now the world was becoming invisible to them.

"This won't get better," she said.

"Do you want me to leave?" Whit asked. "I can leave tomorrow."

She looked at him: leave?

"Has this happened to you before?" she asked.

He shook his head slowly, holding her in his gaze.

"Not like this," he said. "I've had women in my life, sometimes for a long time, but it hasn't been like this. I didn't know this could happen. Has it happened to you before?"

"With my husband. My first husband," she corrected herself. "Michael. I thought it wouldn't again."

"It didn't happen with Paul?"

Isabel looked at him. "If it had, I wouldn't be here with you." They were not touching now. She sat apart from him, her knees tightly pressed together, her hands tucked between them. Whit sat half sideways, leaning against the door, watching her.

"My brother's wife," he said.

"I know," she said.

"Do you love him?" he asked.

She hesitated. "I don't not love him."

"If you love him, if you're happy with him, that's the end of it," Whit said. "Just tell me."

"And if it's not?" she answered. "What do we do?"

He looked at her without answering. She thought of his hand on her face.

"We need to know each other better," he said. "Before we know what to do."

"And we do that now?" Isabel asked. "We get to know each other better here? In front of Paul? In your parents' house?"

He looked down, then back at her. "What else do you suggest?"

It was already too late to go back, she could see that. They had established an alliance now, a secret, a pact. They had become conspirators, even if they never spoke or touched again: this conversation itself was treason. Now their eyes would always meet, they would always have things to say to each other privately, later. They had made the connection. And they had done irreversible damage: the membrane that contains two people in a marriage, that holds them there in privacy, that seals the treaty of loyalty and intimacy, had been pierced and destroyed.

"What else can we do?" Whit repeated.

Isabel shook her head.

"Isabel," Whit said. He said it as though for the first time, and she looked at him. "A beautiful name."

Outside, the rain pounded against the roof. The windshield was entirely opaque.

"Why couldn't we have met before?" Isabel asked.

"I should have come to the wedding," Whit said.

She laughed ruefully. "Worse."

They studied each other's faces.

"I don't want to give you up," Whit said.

"You don't have me," Isabel told him.

"In a way I do." Whit looked down at his hands. "I feel as though we do have each other." He looked up at her. "You have me, if you want me," he said.

They looked at each other without moving.

"What happens next is up to you," Whit said. "It's not my decision, it's yours."

If she were to leave Paul?

Isabel saw Paul's silhouette from that first evening, standing on the sidewalk outside her door, dark and silent, aware. She thought of him in the cabin the night before, in the bedroom, asking if she was leaving him, his voice so gentle and patient.

"I can't leave him," she told Whit. "How could I? I've promised. We're saving each other's lives."

Whit nodded slowly. "No, then." He looked down at his hands again. There was a long silence.

"Two marriages," Isabel said despairingly, and what she was continually dreading, trying always to evade, came rising up: Michael's face, the last evening.

"I can't do it again," Isabel said. She tried to keep her voice even. Michael's face. She felt the wave inside her, threatening to rise.

" 'Again'? " Whit asked her. "But you didn't leave him, your first husband?"

"I told him I was leaving," Isabel said. She had told no one this. "I never would have."

Hearing the words spoken aloud was dreadful, and the wave rose up inside her and broke in her chest. Isabel put her hands over her face. She felt Whit's arms around her and she wept.

"Shhh," he said. He stroked her hair, holding her closely. "Shhh," he said, "shhh."

The relief of being held: like sinking into sleep. She had not been held this way since Michael's death. She and Ben had held each other many times, but Isabel was Ben's comforter, his parent. With Ben she had never let go, and with Paul she had never wept.

Being held this way was a luxury, and Isabel gave herself up to it, letting go as though stepping off a mountain, loosing herself into the air and allowing gravity to take charge. Yielding to grief and solace, she wept and was held.

The sobs were long and exhausting. Over and over they drained her of breath. Whit held her. "Shhh," he whispered. "Shhh." He rocked her, his head against hers. "Shhh."

When there was nothing more in her chest, Isabel pulled away. She sighed lengthily, her breath still uneven, and rubbed her eyes. Her head felt swollen and dull, her face smeared and damp. She smiled weakly at Whit and shook her head.

"You see," she said, "you wouldn't want me. You see what it's like."

"I can see you're in trouble."

"More than trouble," Isabel said. "I'm trapped. I can't get out of this."

Whit shook his head. "I don't believe it. You'll find your way out."

"Why do you think so?"

"Because you're strong," Whit told her. "You won't give up."

Isabel sighed again and rubbed her eyes. "I like hearing you say that," she said. "I like hearing the words."

"Isabel," Whit said, "don't blame yourself."

Isabel looked at him. The notion stretched before her, a landscape of relief. "How can I not?" she asked.

"Don't blame yourself," he said again. "It's over."

But Isabel shook her head and took a deep breath. "We should get going," she said. "Paul will worry."

Whit nodded and cleared the windshield, his hand making bright liquid arcs in the blank gray. He leaned back to wipe the rear window. Isabel watched him: she now knew his limbs, how his arms felt.

Whit started the engine. Isabel moved to the passenger's seat, and he looked over at her.

"I'm glad I know you." He reached out and touched her cheek, stroking gently with the backs of his fingers.

Isabel leaned hard against his hand. "We know each other now," she said. "That's something."

"A lot."

"Yes," she said. "I'll know you're there."

"I'm here." Whit smiled and put his hand back on the wheel. Isabel turned, too; they both faced ahead into the watery landscape. She could feel the touch of his hand against her cheek, tender, alive.

Chapter 12

The mall appeared suddenly, a row of low flat-roofed buildings among the rainy fields. In front was a wide parking lot, mostly empty, the blacktop puddled with water. The supermarket was flanked by smaller shops: the dry cleaner, the drugstore with a fluid pink RX glistening in the window. A few cars were clustered near the supermarket entrance.

They parked, and Whit reached behind the seat for their slickers. Isabel twisted the rearview mirror to see her face. Her eyes were liquid and brilliant, veined with scarlet, her eyelids swollen. She wondered how long it would take for her to look normal. By the time she saw Paul?

The world was visible again through the windshield. A woman in a blue jacket opened the door to the drugstore. The earth was trundling along, and other people were in the offing.

Whit handed her a slicker. "You look fine," he told her. "Great."

Awkwardly Isabel pulled on the stiff slicker. She got out the shopping lists, Charlotte's token of trust, and smoothed them open on her knee.

"The lists," Whit said.

"Here's yours." Isabel handed it to him.

"Thanks," he said. "So. All set?"

She nodded, looking at him. Neither moved. Next to them a car door slammed, an engine started with a cluttery roar.

"Here we go, then," Whit said, and they each opened the door and stepped separately into the rain.

Isabel pulled up her hood as she got out. The slicker, found that morning in a closet, was much too big for her. Isabel wondered if it had belonged to the giantess Louisa, if the clammy air in the sleeves had been there since Louisa had last worn it. She wondered if Louisa had ever had an affair—was that why she had left Paul?

The sleeves hung drowningly over her hands, and the huge hood sloped claustrophobically around her face, narrowing her vision to a sliver. She'd lost sight of Whit at once. She could see only a few yards ahead, the blinkered view, she thought, the straight and narrow.

The rain was letting up, but the wind blew in sudden swirling gusts. Isabel began to run, splashing flatly through the pools, sending up ragged sprays of water.

At the supermarket entrance she stopped, sheltered by the over-hang, and pushed back the hood so she could see. A row of rusting carts stood jammed into one another. Isabel tugged one free and pushed it toward the electric door. The cart's rear wheel shimmied, pulling to one side. She set her weight against it, forcing it straight. The door threw itself open.

The store was low-ceilinged and small, with only two checkout counters. At the nearest stood a heavy teenage girl in a turquoise sweater, her long dark hair in oily ringlets. She leaned against the cash register, frowning at her fingernails—black talons fanned before her plump face.

The place had an odd unsavory smell. Isabel turned in to the pro-duce aisle, past a bank of pale iceberg lettuce, the bright orange of car-rots. Isabel walked slowly, the wheel shuddering. She was looking for the meat department.

What was she doing?

Touch my face. She could still feel the touch of his skin on hers, and it could ruin everything. It was contraband. It could poison her life. What was it she wanted?

She passed rows of pallid tomatoes, mealy, flavor-free, in their nar-row plastic baskets. Who bought these things? Only people who had never tasted them—but how many new buyers would there be?

She thought of the night before, Paul's question. He had laid his book down when she spoke. His head was propped against the headboard, his chin pressed into his chest. The patient look in his eyes, the sadness around him like a dark mist. *It would break my heart.*

She thought of Michael's face the last night.

She felt sickened. What kind of person was she? She was married to Paul.

Perhaps grief was to blame. Grief was disruptive and unpredictable. Perhaps it was responsible for her behavior. But wasn't she moving past grief? Wasn't she putting all this behind her, the irrational wilderness of grief? She was moving on, to become reliable, dependable, kind. That was why she had married Paul—she was reconnecting.

At the aisle's end, beyond the papery-skinned onions and the dusty brown potatoes, was the meat counter. "Three roasting chickens," Miriam had written in rounded letters. Isabel wondered exactly what a roasting chicken was. She hoped there was a butcher to ask. But why did she not know this elementary fact about cooking?

For she had been a cook. She had cooked with delight during much of her marriage to Michael, during all of Ben's childhood. Cooking had been an offering of love; it was one of the womanly skills. She had loved giving dinner parties. For guests she'd made *boeuf en daube, vitello tonnato.* For her family she'd made bread, pasta, soups. Birthday cakes, fancifully trimmed, names and decorations traced on gorgeous waves of icing. Meals had interested her.

When had it stopped? When Ben left for school? Michael had always traveled, and when Ben left, Isabel was often alone. In London she had cooked little—she had felt so strange there, so alien. Dinner had lost its place in the day, cooking had lost its interest. And the era of cooking seemed over somehow. She remembered asking a friend once, at a dinner party, if she'd made the soup. Her friend sighed. "No," she said, "but doesn't everybody know I can cook?" Isabel could cook. She had cooked. It was like going to college; she had her degree.

After Michael died, she had stopped absolutely. Food had lost its usefulness: life itself had lost. Isabel did not even consider cooking for herself; she made scrambled eggs for supper or heated something frozen. It was as though her mind had been wiped clean of all earlier knowledge, as though all those luscious creations—*saucisson de fois de volaille en croute,* chestnut-stuffed goose, homemade mayonnaise—had existed in someone else's life. She could not imagine making them now; it was like speaking Finnish. Her cooking for Paul was simple and uninspired: risotto, hamburger, salad. He didn't seem to mind. He cared little about food and could never remember a meal.

Isabel stood over the rows of packaged meats, hoping to see something labeled "roasting chicken."

She wondered if Paul would sense something. Would it show? Was her face still swollen? The wall was paneled in wavery mirror; she looked in it. Her face seemed more normal, though the eyes were still narrowed, the lids puffy.

She felt something hanging about her, a kind of floating stain.

She had never had an affair during her marriage to Michael, though there had been times when she'd thought of it. Late in the evening, dancing at a party, she'd felt the upswelling surge of the night, of alcohol, of the body, the delicious possibility of sex.

At work there had been times when she'd looked forward to seeing a certain man, when she'd been aware that his eyes fell on her in a particular way, that he listened attentively to her in meetings. She remembered being with one of these men in an elevator: Donny Welner, the sleeves of his striped shirt rolled up on his arms, his tight curly hair close against his elegant skull. He looked at her as she got on, and as they slid upward, he smiled. She smiled back and felt the floor rising beneath them, felt the lift of possibility.

But it was only for a moment; an affair was unthinkable. Not only did she love Michael, but he was fragile in such a serious way; an affair would have put more at risk than her marriage.

Isabel scanned the poultry and frowned: she could not bring back the wrong kind of chicken. She pushed the service button on the mirrored wall, hoping the panel would slide open on a kindly white-haired man, patient, courteous, ready to explain.

Waiting, she inspected a large bird, livid-skinned, its legs pressed tightly against the massive chest. Wasn't that the right size for roasting? Roasting turkeys were large. But wasn't the rule that the bigger a bird was, the older it was and the tougher? Though maybe that was no longer true now that birds were factory-bred, pumped with hormones and steroids. Their brains were addled by continuous lights and crowded cages, their feed full of antibiotics and pulverized animal bones. It didn't bear thinking about, animals bred for food. Their lives were misery.

When she first learned about factory farming, Isabel gave up meat. A private, unambiguous act, she'd thought, but she'd been wrong. People took it personally, as a rebuke. Michael had been furious. He called her a sanctimonious knee-jerk liberal. "But look," Isabel had begged. "Just look at the pictures. Michael, look at what they do to the animals."

But Michael wouldn't look at anything. He'd called her manipulative, and they'd fought. For a while Isabel had made two different kinds of meals, one with meat and one without, but that meant Ben had to take sides, which made him miserable, and finally Isabel gave it up. She put out of her head the images she'd seen, the struggling, wild-eyed animals. It was them or her husband. That had been just before they'd gone to London.

Looking back, she could see the pattern, how Michael's rages had built in series. Now she could see those awful years in London. Each time Michael turned dark, Isabel turned frantic. Each time, she longed for it to be over, for him to return to her. Each time he did, she'd been certain it was for good.

She looked at the motionless panel on the wall. Maybe there was no butcher on duty. She pressed the button again.

Suddenly she felt the eerie certainty that Paul was behind her, that he had arrived from the hardware store and was walking toward her. She turned guiltily to see the silhouette of an approaching man. But it was a stranger, a thin hatchet-faced man with a two-day beard, wearing stained khaki pants and lace-up work boots with worn crepe soles. He was stepping oddly, on his toes, carrying a six-pack of beer. When Isabel turned, he met her eyes, then looked away.

Was this what she was going to do? Have guilty hallucinations?

Isabel looked back at the small carcasses. Everything was packaged to conceal its origins, the limbs in smooth mounds on absorbent tissue, wiped clean of the abattoir. In other countries butchery was more straightforward. She remembered seeing, in Mexico, a pig's head on a slab, the mouth jovially open, a thick frill of white lashes across the closed eye. A whole lamb hanging from tied hind feet; the neat black cloven hooves, blunt innocent muzzle, soft pale fleece. The gamboling creature from children's rhymes, emptied of life.

Are you leaving me?

She could not leave Paul.

And she barely knew Whitney. This small business of the flesh, of the body—merely the touch of his hand on her cheek, his arms around her while she cried—this meant nothing, didn't it? The body was a tramp, a slut, it would respond to anything. It would heat up suddenly with lust, blood flooding through tissue, liquids flowing, heart pounding at any old caress. Wasn't that right? Didn't this mean nothing? Or did it mean everything? What if it meant everything? Because it was what she longed for, this touch.

She couldn't stay with Paul if she was going to act like this. If she was going to long for another man.

It might mean everything that she felt this way. Because it was unfair to Paul for her to feel this way. She would have to leave him.

This is absurd, she thought, *you don't leave your husband because of a single moment of sexual yearning. These come to everyone, you pass them by. You don't leave your husband for them.*

Why do you leave your husband? What are the reasons?

And it wasn't a single moment of yearning. He had held her while she cried.

The mirrored panel jarred open on a huge solid woman in a blue smock with a white puckered shower cap covering her hair. She wore heavy brown eye shadow and dangling earrings. She had a short upper lip and pendulous cheeks. Her look was ominous. She did not speak.

"Hello," Isabel said, awkward at such naked malevolence. "I need three roasting chickens, but I don't see where—"

"Right there," said the woman vengefully, pointing to the top row. She turned as she slid the panel closed, her massive blue shoulder blocking the narrowing opening until the mirror stretched again along the wall without interruption.

Isabel picked up the chickens. How was it that rudeness had become so nationally endemic, so central to American self-respect? Part of salespeople's jobs seemed to require boisterous uncivility toward the customer, but why? How did it serve capitalism? Or anything?

The chickens were heavy in her hand, sinisterly damp. The creases of the plastic wrap held scarlet pools. Isabel put them in her cart, wiping her hand on her jeans.

No, she would have to leave Paul. She would have to. She could feel Whit's hand on her face.

She looked at her list: paper towels, tarragon, Lysol. She was now in paper goods, staring at the towers of bulging white packages. What was she looking for? This plenitude stunned you. Isabel stared at the bright labels. Napkins, Kleenex, what was it?

"Hi," someone said behind her, and she turned. At the sight of Whit's face, her heart rose up, and this frightened her. This was how it would be, then?

"Hi," she said. She wondered if she was blushing. This was a public place: everyone here would know Whit and his family. They would know the truck that had been parked off the road in the rain. The man in the stained khakis would know Eddie. Everything they did here would be noted.

"How're you coming?" Whit asked.

"Almost finished," she said. "If you want to find some tarragon, I'll meet you at the checkout."

Whit nodded and turned away.

They would always be in public, their voices would always have to be neutral. They would never be alone together again, it was as simple as that. Why would Isabel be alone with her brother-in-law? Without her husband? It would not happen. They would never talk again, and the thought of this was like learning that the sky would always be overcast. There was nothing to look forward to.

She thought of telling her father she was leaving Paul. She imagined his face. She imagined telling Ben.

She scanned the shelves: paper towels. She took down a plump pair, airy inside their plastic bubble, and started back, leaning against the cart's determined list.

Whit was waiting at the checkout counter. They stood without speaking while the girl with the black talons rang them up. Without looking at them, she slid their things across the sensor panel with a lazy, practiced hand, her long nails clicking against the glass. She looked up at the cash register.

"Thirty-seven eighteen," she said in a bored voice and turned her head to check the clock.

Whit paid and picked up the bags. The rain was coming down hard again.

Inside the truck the rain folded down around them, sealing them off once more. They set the bags behind the seat, and Whitney turned to her, and they looked at each other in silence. These were the last moments they would have like this.

His eyebrows were like Paul's, the same long curve. It was the eyes that were different, the hollows deeper, more wide-set. And there was a heft to Whit. A kind of weight at the core. Comparisons are odious, her father said, and certainly it was odious to compare your husband to his brother. How was it that you decided between things? What were the ways besides comparisons?

Whit raised her hand to his mouth and kissed it. "I'm glad I know you," he said again.

Isabel nodded. She felt his mouth on her hand.

Whit set her hand back on her leg, relinquishing her, and turned to start the engine.

The windshield wipers began their brainless sweep. Outside, the rain beat the landscape into hazy gray shapes. They drove slowly; the road was slippery, and water sluiced across it, flaring up suddenly from the wheels. They did not speak again.

At the diner, Paul was already in a booth. He looked up when they came in, and Isabel saw irritation on his face at the sight of them.

Did they look like a couple, somehow, coming in the door together? Now guilt rose up in her. Her chest seemed small.

Isabel slid in next to Paul. "Hi."

"You guys have been awhile," Paul said.

He seemed cool, or was she imagining this?

"What happened?" he asked.

Isabel and Whit spoke at once.

"They didn't have any roasting chickens," Isabel said. "They had to do some up fresh for me."

Whitney said, "We had more things to get than you did. We should have known we'd keep you waiting."

They hadn't contradicted each other; it was the way they both spoke, so quickly, and with such force.

And she'd lied. She never lied. Why hadn't she told Paul she couldn't find the chickens, the truth? The first thing she'd said to her husband was a lie.

There was a silence.

"Sorry," Isabel added. "For keeping you waiting."

Paul nodded and said nothing.

"Have you ordered?" Isabel asked Paul. Her slicker felt stifling, and she unzipped it.

"No," Paul said. "I waited for you."

"I'm sorry you had to wait," Isabel said again. She made herself pat his knee. He looked away; he was going to sulk.

Whit raised his hand for the waitress. She was in her sixties, short and thin, with straight graying hair parted on the side. She had thick glasses, a friendly smile.

"What can I get you folks?" she asked. She picked up Isabel's glass and filled it from a metal pitcher. She poured from the side instead of the spout, and the water sloshed out haphazardly.

"A cheeseburger, rare," Paul announced, "french fries and coffee."

"Right," the waitress said, nodding. She filled Whit's glass.

When she left, they sat in silence. Isabel could feel Paul's unfriendliness beside her. She drank from her glass.

"Why do they always pour from the side of pitchers?" she asked. "Why not use the spout?"

Paul shrugged and looked away. Whit shook his head. "I don't know," he said into the silence.

Isabel looked out the window and tried again. "This is some rain," she said.

"It's not nearly enough," Paul said shortly. "We need days of slow rain, not this fast, heavy stuff." He looked outside. "And it's letting up again."

Chastened, Isabel said nothing.

"We've had a bad year out west, too," Whit said. "Very little rain. I wish we had some of this out there."

"Might it be raining there now?" asked Isabel.

Whit shook his head. "Not likely. We don't get much in the summer. A few thunderstorms, that's all. We get rain mostly in the fall and the spring. Snow in the winter. Summers are dry."

Paul looked at him. "How does that affect the lions?"

His tone was faintly challenging, and Isabel was reminded of Charlotte.

Whit looked at him mildly. "Just as you might imagine. In a drought there's less water for everyone, so everyone's stressed, up and down the food chain." He picked up his water glass. "Makes me want to have a drink." He smiled.

Paul did not smile back. "Does that make it harder to get funding if there's less going on?"

"There isn't less going on in the field if there's a drought," Whit said. "There's always something going on." His tone was still mild. "What makes it hard to get funding is the climate in Washington, not the climate in Laramie. But you already know that."

Paul did not answer. He set his lips together, looked down at the table, then up again. "So," he said, "water or no water, you'll be scrambling up and down the canyons in the dirt."

Isabel had never seen this before, Paul picking a fight.

Whit set his elbows on the table and folded his arms. "I wonder what you mean by that," he said.

Paul stared at him. "Well," he said. "That's what you do. Isn't it?"

"You're beginning to sound like Ma," Whit said.

The waitress came toward them, walking rapidly under her precarious burden: three cups of coffee carried in an uneasy triangle. She slid them on the table, the dark liquid slopping into the saucers.

"There you go," she said.

"Thank you," Isabel said. The men said nothing. The waitress nodded cheerfully and went off, her soft-soled shoes squeaking.

"Thank you," Paul said to Whit.

"What's your point?" Whit asked.

"Maybe Ma has a point," Paul suggested. "You're forty-five and still scrambling around in the dirt."

Whit looked at Paul steadily. The color along his cheekbones suddenly heightened. "Interesting way to put it," he said.

"You say it yourself," Paul said. "What kind of life is it?"

"I happen to like what I do," Whit said. "Is it all I'll ever do? Maybe not. Maybe I'll make some changes sometime, come in from the field. But I'm not ashamed of what I do." He took a sip of his coffee. "Anyway, what do you care? Why describe it that way? I could say you're working for a two-bit operation in a field that doesn't interest you in the least. I could ask why you do that."

Now Paul's face tightened. "It's actually not a 'two-bit operation,' " he said stiffly.

"I'm sure it's not," Whit went on, "and even if it were, I wouldn't call it that, because you're my brother, and I wouldn't insult you. Also, it would be none of my business."

The waitress appeared again, laden and cheerful.

"Could only manage two this time," she said, putting down platters of food in front of Paul and Isabel. "Married folks first," she said brightly to Whit. "Be right back."

There was silence.

Isabel picked up a french fry and took a delicate bite. Under the table her legs were crossed, her feet tucked beneath her, under her seat.

Whit was sitting inches away, and she could feel the heat given off by his body. She could still feel his hand on her cheek.

Chapter 13

On the way back from town no one spoke. The rain had stopped, though the sky was still overcast. Isabel, in the middle again, kept herself narrow, trying not to touch the body on either side. Whit, beside her, was like stone.

When they left the paved road, the truck slowed, bumping and sliding over the slippery surface, the ruts still slick with rain. Whit drove soberly; sprays of muddy water sloshed heavily on either side.

It was late when they got back. Whitney pulled up outside Acorn; Paul opened his door before the truck stopped. He got out without looking at his brother.

"See you later," he said from outside the truck.

"Thanks for driving," Isabel said, climbing out after him. She did not look back.

"Yup," Whitney answered, "see you at dinner."

The rains had darkened the day, and as the truck pulled off, its red taillights gleamed in the dull air. It seemed already like evening.

The cabin was dark and chilly. Isabel turned on the lights, but the rooms were still shadowy, and gloom gathered in the corners.

"Want some tea?" She picked up the heavy kettle.

"No," Paul said, heading down the hall. Isabel filled the kettle and set it on the burner. She sat down to wait. There was no sound from the bedroom.

The awakening kettle made a series of watery clucks, then a plume of thickening steam rose from its spout. Isabel picked it up by the heavy coil of wire wrapped around the handle. As she did so, a red flash bit into her: her fingers turned suddenly brilliant with pain.

She dropped the kettle with a rackety clang, sucking in her breath. She turned on the tap and put her hand into the icy stream. The cold moved into the burn, numbing it. Isabel turned her hand back and forth under the water, feeling the coolness sweep into her fingers.

Paul appeared in the doorway, his face forbidding. "What happened?" he asked.

"I burned my hand," Isabel said.

"How?"

Isabel gestured with her chin. "I picked up the kettle."

"Bare-handed?"

"I thought—" It sounded stupid now. "I thought the coil would be cool."

"You picked up a boiling kettle and thought the metal handle wouldn't be hot?" Paul demanded.

Isabel said nothing.

"Metal is a conductor of heat," Paul said. "That's why kettles are made of it."

Isabel turned her hand beneath the water.

"I'll see if there's any ointment," Paul said. He sounded annoyed. "We may have to go up to the lodge."

"I don't need ointment," Isabel said. "It's not serious." She took her hand from the water; at once the red glow stormed back, and she replaced it. She heard Paul's footsteps in the hall.

She didn't want ointment, didn't want to take her hand from the cool rush of water. When she was little, you were told not to put your burn under cold water, which you longed to do. Instead you were told to smear on ointment, grit your teeth and let it throb. Now the theory had changed. Now you were told no ointment, only cold water: all these theories were set forth with such authority.

Paul came back with a crinkled tube of ointment. It was old and stiff, and most of the lettering was flaked away. Isabel wondered what generation it was from, what century. Could ointment go bad?

"Here," Paul said shortly, unscrewing the top.

Obediently Isabel took her hand from the water. Pain flooded back in at once, but she held her hand out toward her husband. He squeezed a thick yellow worm onto her palm.

"Rub that in," he commanded.

"It hurts," Isabel said, wincing.

"Hold it up," Paul said, screwing the top back on the mangled tube. "Up. Up in the air." He raised his own hand to show her, palm out. Isabel held up her hand like a child asking a question. They faced each other, hands raised, as though making a ceremonial vow. Isabel's hand began to throb.

"Ow," she said apologetically, and moved it back under the water. She looked back at him. "Thanks."

"You're not supposed to put it under water," Paul said disapprovingly.

"I think it's changed," Isabel said. "I think now you are." The water felt blessed, and she turned her hand under it again.

Paul left the room.

When her hand felt better, Isabel turned on the kettle. When it steamed a second time, she gingerly picked it up, wrapped in potholders, and awkwardly poured the boiling water into her mug. The gesture, so inconsequential minutes ago, now seemed perilous: the lethal heat so close to her wounded flesh. The water darkened in her mug with the infusion. She sat down, waiting for it to cool.

Around her the cabin was silent. It was growing dark outside. Isabel's hand pulsed. She rested her elbow on the table, hand raised. She listened for Paul; she heard nothing. She wondered where he was, what he was doing. She pictured him lying on the bed, his hands clasped behind his head, looking up at the ceiling, thinking. She hoped he was reading. She blew on the tea. She hoped he was not thinking.

She wondered why he was so angry. Was it part of the continual simmer between the brothers, did this happen regularly? Or was it because of her and Whit, whatever it was? The complicity between them was like a bold line across a landscape, dividing everything into before and after. Guilt had entered her consciousness: though they had done nothing, they had become a couple.

She wondered if she was acting guilty. What would she be doing normally, if nothing had happened? She'd be in the bedroom with Paul, clear-eyed, companionable. Not sitting alone in the kitchen, her burned hand held in the air. She blew on her tea again. If nothing had happened, she'd go in and ask what the matter was. She'd soothe him, offer solace. She took a cautious sip.

When she had finished the tea, she set the mug in the sink. Her hand was better, the ache a low subterranean beat, but she still held it high, as though asking for truce. There was still no sound from the bedroom; perhaps Paul was asleep. Rainy days—the air pressure, wasn't it soporific? Isabel went quietly down the hall for her book. She would take a bath while he slept.

But Paul was not asleep. He lay stretched out on the bed reading. He looked at her as she came in.

"I'm going to take a bath," she announced.

Paul did not answer. His face was closed and remote.

Suddenly the sight of him, stretched out with his shoes loutishly on, and his behavior—his lassitude, the hostile cock of his head—angered Isabel. Why should he be so angry? Why should he take out his anger on her in such sullen silence? Without speaking, she took her book from the bedside table. She went into the bathroom and shut the door, relieved to be alone.

The bathtub was huge and ancient, claw-footed white porcelain with tea-colored stains around the drain. She set in the rubber stopper, heavy, dense as stone, and turned on both spigots. The water coughed and clanked noisily up through the pipes, then, blasting and spitting, it thundered into the tub. Isabel undressed and stood naked, shivering in the chilly air. She held out her good hand, testing the water. She was impatient with Paul's adolescent sulkiness, his continual hostility toward Whit.

When the tub was half full, Isabel climbed in, her skin goosepimpling at the sudden heat. The water was transparent, faintly bluegreen against the white sides. It was blissfully hot; steam rose from the surface. Isabel picked up her book, setting her elbows on either edge of the tub. Now the cabin was full of deep silence.

Isabel stared at her book and read the same impossibly long sentence over and over. She was trying Proust for the third time, trying to sink with him into the vast reaches of memory, trying to let his past move into her and obliterate her own present. She had loved the earlier parts of the book, the "Combray" section, so rich and so funny, but she had reached "Swann in Love," and it was troubling and painful. The elegant Swann, who had been so self-possessed and effective, sophisticated and intelligent, was now revealing himself as lethally stupid, craven, obsessively and self-destructively in love with the monstrous Odette. Isabel could hardly bear to witness his self-inflicted torture. She found her mind sliding away from the painful scenes of Swann, miserable and abject, and the contemptible Odette, so callous and self-absorbed, so indifferent to his pain.

The only sound in the cabin was the faint liquid slosh of the water when she moved. Isabel raised her eyes from the page. And then, alone in the silence, she found herself unwillingly remembering her own past, sliding helplessly down into that troubling well, moving inescapably to that last night, Michael's, which was also unbearable, because she certainly should have known what was happening, she should have understood that he was in pain, she should have done something, and for the second time that day Isabel began to cry, the tears slipping silently down her damp face to lose themselves in the water surrounding her body.

Later, Paul knocked loudly on the door. "We should leave in about twenty minutes."

Isabel's voice was by then steady. "Be right out."

They walked up to the lodge in the semidarkness. The sky was still overcast, the air chilly. Isabel wore a sweater. The woods were damp, and they walked along the driveway instead of the path. They did not speak. Paul's footsteps on the gravel sounded heavy and relentless.

At the lodge the others were in the living room. Charlotte and Douglas were on the big sofa, Whit by the fireplace. Coming in, Isabel looked at Whit, then away. He now seemed a central presence; it was difficult not to look at him. What would normal be?

"What a ghastly day," Charlotte said, holding up her glass in welcome.

Douglas stood politely. "I hear you got some rain in Casco," he said. "It barely sprinkled here. I hope we get some more tomorrow."

"It was gloomy all day today, I don't want it to rain tomorrow," Charlotte said. "It can rain while we're not here. Or at night. While we're awake, it should be good weather. Anyway, come and have a drink. Tomorrow's supposed to be clear again, blue skies and in the eighties."

She leaned back expansively. "It's too damp on the porch," she went on. "I hate hearing the water drip off the eaves. I always think it's running down the back of my neck. We can have a fire. What do you think?"

"I'll make it," Whit said, getting up. He knelt at the hearth and began crumpling newspaper in his big hands. It was safer for Isabel now, his back turned.

Douglas stood. "What can I get you, Isabel?"

"I'll do it," Paul said, moving to the drinks tray. "What does Eddie say about the rain?"

"Says it's not enough," Douglas answered. "Where it did rain, it was too hard, apparently. He says the ground is so dry, this may just run off."

"But it was damp and gloomy all day," Charlotte complained again. "Not enough rain to help and not enough sun to use." She made a face.

Douglas sat down again. "Anyway," he went on, "it didn't go near those two fires up north, and now there's another one to the east."

"When it's this dry, the water evaporates before it has a chance to soak in," Whit said. "And if we get any wind, it'll make it worse."

"Impending disaster," Charlotte said, waving her hand. "So," she said to Isabel, "you've been to Casco. What do you think of our metropolis?"

"I liked it," Isabel said. "I thought it was sweet."

"Sweet!" Charlotte threw back her head and laughed throatily. "That's not a word I'd have chosen. Seedy, maybe. You sure you went to Casco? Where did you really take her, Whit?"

There was a moment's silence. Whit was stacking logs, his back still to the others.

"We went to Casco," Paul said, bringing over their drinks. "Isabel liked it. She has a very appreciative nature."

"Unlike me, you mean," Charlotte said. "You're probably right. I find Casco Corners a bit dreary," she told Isabel. "Of course, I'm fond of it, too, but that's because I've been coming here since the age of one."

"Like us," said Paul, but Charlotte ignored him.

"We, on the other hand, went nowhere today," she went on. "We slept all day. We got up for lunch and then we took naps afterward. We only just got up now. But what did you all do in Casco? Tell us everything that happened. You've been out in the world."

There was a silence, then Paul and Isabel spoke at once.

"Paul went to the hardware store," Isabel said.

"Isabel and Whitney went to the mall," Paul said.

"You all split up?" Charlotte said. "You sent your wife off with your brother?"

In the silence there was the brief abrasive sound of a match being struck, the swift hiss as it lit. Whit set the flame in the twisted papers, where it flared, running lightly along the edges. He straightened and turned back to the room.

"Why would he not?" he asked. "We're grown-ups."

The fire had caught. Behind him rose a dense stream of smoke, and a low yellow flame sprang up among the logs, flickering brightly.

Charlotte took a long swallow from her glass.

"I've always liked Casco," Paul said, and from his tone Isabel took heart. He seemed to be emerging from his black mood and turning sociable. "When I was little, I wanted to work at the gas station there. It seemed really big-time—being tanned and greasy and solitary and in charge of all those important things, fuel and lubrication and tires. Using the air hose. Looking at oil. Incalculably glamorous."

"But you did it, didn't you?" Charlotte asked. "Didn't you work there one summer?"

"That was Whitney," Paul said.

"Oh, yes," Charlotte said, unembarassed. "I knew it was one of you. It's a good thing I only had two children." She swirled the cubes in her glass, which was nearly empty.

"And how was it, working there?" Isabel asked Whit.

"Not incalculably glamorous." He smiled; for a moment they smiled openly at each other. "Definitely not that."

"What about you, Isabel?" Douglas asked. "Was there a girl's equivalent of the gas-station fantasy?"

"Waitressing," Isabel said. "I thought waitresses were so cool: those little ruffled aprons and the neat dresses. The squeaky white shoes and the little pads and pencils. Bringing food, bringing people what they wanted."

"And did you live out the fantasy?" Douglas asked. "Always a dangerous thing to do."

"I did. I worked at Friendly's one summer," Isabel said. "Also not glamorous. We were on our feet for eight hours at a stretch, and I learned why they had those squeaky shoes. We counted every step. We knew how many steps it was to the pickup counter and to the ice machine. I spent a lot of time cleaning up after little kids. Mothers would come in and just turn them loose. They wouldn't say anything, either, when they left, they wouldn't apologize or thank us, they'd just walk away from this giant battlefield: french fries all over the floor, ketchup smears, torn-up napkins, spilled drinks, dripped ice cream."

"But the aprons?" Douglas asked.

"The aprons were cute," Isabel told him, relieved at his friendliness.

"The first rule of adult life," Douglas said. "The perception of power is different from the wielding of it."

"Power," Isabel said, "is not what that seemed like."

Charlotte was trying to catch Douglas's eye. Twice she lifted her empty glass and set it on the coffee table, and finally she pushed the glass toward him. "Could I have another drink, Douglas?" she asked.

Douglas rose, and there was silence until he returned.

Charlotte looked at the others. "Dreadful service you get here." She took the drink from her husband. "Thank you."

"What about you?" Isabel asked Douglas. "Did you get a job like that?"

Douglas shook his head. "When I was growing up, children didn't have separate lives. I did whatever my parents did in the summer. We went to Cape Cod and I hung around." He lifted an eyebrow. "Grim, eh? Imagine an adolescent today spending the summer with his parents."

"We spent our summers with you," Paul said.

"And?" Charlotte asked. "Did it damage you?"

"That's not the point," Douglas said mildly. Charlotte shrugged.

They moved in to dinner. Charlotte turned expansive when Miriam appeared. "Miriam," she said, "Isabel's just had her first trip to Casco Corners. She thinks it's sweet."

Miriam's gaze shifted to Isabel.

"I liked it," Isabel said, now embarrassed by her own word. "I like small communities. It's a real place. Everyone knows everyone else."

Miriam smiled privately. "That's right," she said. "Everyone knows everyone else."

Isabel thought of the hatchet-faced man in the supermarket. Had Miriam heard something already? But there was nothing to hear. She and

Whit had done nothing in front of the hatchet-faced man or anyone else; there was nothing to know. Only the matter of the twenty minutes in the truck, parked along the road. Only the matter of Whit holding her in his arms while she wept; only the words they had spoken. She did not look at him.

"You know everyone and everything that goes on, right, Miriam?" Douglas said jovially. "Even though we're an hour away. Miriam knows everything."

Miriam shrugged. "Not too much goes on around here," she said, frowning. "But what does happen, I guess we know about." She set the soup in front of Charlotte and pushed back through the swinging door.

"You see," Charlotte said, instructional. "It's no good running off to Casco Corners to misbehave. The word will follow you right back home." She set the ladle into the tureen. "Douglas, hand me Isabel's bowl, will you?"

"I don't know if summer people are watched as closely as the year-rounders," Douglas said.

"Are they not!" Charlotte said energetically, ladling soup. "Remember the time the—who was it? Years ago. Those people in the stone house up near the point. She was having an affair with someone else's husband, and they used to meet in Casco Corners in a parking lot. Helen Simpson. And all the help knew it, and they all told us, so then everyone knew it. It was a terrible scandal. Remember that?" She shook her head and handed the bowl back. "When I first heard about it, I wouldn't believe it. That's just talk, I said, just gossip." She made a disparaging gesture and laughed. "And I was right, it *was* gossip. But it was also true. Oh, it was terrible. It got so no one would have either one of the couples at a party. There were scenes: someone walking out of someone else's dining room. Accusations. Shouts. That sort of thing."

"And what happened?" asked Isabel. "Did the marriages break up?"

"You know, I don't remember," Charlotte said. "Isn't that strange? I can't remember what happened. Those things seem so vivid at the time, you don't think you'll ever forget something, and then it just blurs, things grow over it, moss, sort of, and then it's gone. The Simpsons sold the house years ago. I don't remember what happened to the marriage."

They began sipping the soup.

"The Longs had that house after the Simpsons," Charlotte said, looking up suddenly.

Douglas snorted and shook his head. "Clement Long," he said.

Charlotte began to laugh. "Remember the time you boys took Claire Long out in the sailboat at night, and you were becalmed, and at three o'clock in the morning her father called your father and demanded that she be brought back?"

"I was angry," Douglas said reminiscently.

"Who were you angry at?" Paul asked. He poured himself more wine. "Him or us?"

"Primarily him," said Douglas, "though I'm sure I passed it along to you. He could just as well have gone out himself in his own damn motorboat. There were three of you in the boat. Claire was perfectly safe."

"Waiting for the wind to come up," Charlotte said. "Claire Long was a pretty girl. Didn't one of you go out with her?"

"I had to go all over the damn lake in the dark to find you," Douglas said, still indignant. "Took me nearly an hour, because of course you didn't have a light. I had to stumble on to you. Boy, was I mad."

Charlotte finished her soup and set her spoon down. "I don't blame him for calling you," she said, putting her elbows on the table and setting her clasped hands under her chin in a queenly way. "Something could have happened. They could have capsized, been hanging on to the boat for hours. We were responsible, in a way."

"In what way?" Douglas asked.

"She'd left from our house," Charlotte said. "She was under our protection. It was like that girl with the bear."

"Marilyn Hornby," Isabel said, without intending to. The others looked at her.

"That's the one," Charlotte said. "What if something had happened to her? She was staying with us."

"If something had happened to Marilyn Hornby, it would have happened to us, too," Whit said. "I don't think the bear would have chosen just her. We all would have been bear food."

"You'd have protected her from the bear, wouldn't you," said Paul.

Whit looked at him. "So would you."

"Me?" Paul raised his hands. "Why would I have protected her?"

Whit said nothing, and Charlotte looked from one to the other. "What's going on?" she asked.

Whit shook his head and looked down at his plate. Paul poured himself more wine.

Douglas cleared his throat. "I think the boys are working some things out, as they say, from years ago," he told Charlotte.

"We're discussing them," Paul said. "I don't know if they can actually be worked out. These particular things."

Whit did not look at him. The kitchen door opened on Miriam.

"Delicious," Charlotte said absentmindedly, and Isabel nodded in agreement. Miriam began silently to clear. No one spoke. When Miriam had left, Charlotte cocked her head to one side.

"I'd like to know what's going on here," she said, looking at Whit. "I feel like someone in a murder play. Agatha Christie. What? Everyone knows something I don't. Motives, alibis."

Whit shrugged. "Ask Paul," he said. "He started it."

"I don't think so," Paul said. "I don't think it's fair to say that I started all this."

"Fine," Whit said abruptly. He did not look at Paul. "Then you didn't." He stood up. "Actually, I'm kind of done in. All that rain has deadened my brain. I think I'll hit the hay."

"Before coffee?" Charlotte asked.

Whit nodded and pushed his chair neatly under the table. Paul stood and looked at him.

"What is it?" Whit asked.

"Where are you going?" Paul asked. His voice was belligerent and strange.

"I just said," Whit told him. "I'm going to bed."

"But where?" Paul asked.

There was a long silence. Whit stared at Paul. Isabel could feel Paul next to her. He was trembling; she wondered if he'd had too much wine.

Whit looked down, then back up at Paul. "Look," he said slowly, "don't blame me for that. It wasn't my idea."

"What wasn't your idea?" Paul asked, his voice full of fury. "It wasn't your plan to spend the night with my girlfriend?"

There was a pause.

"That's not exactly what happened," Whit said.

"Well, what exactly did happen?" Paul said.

"I won't tell you exactly what happened."

"But you were in bed together," Paul told him.

Whit paused, then nodded. "Sort of."

"You fuck," Paul said.

Charlotte rapped her knuckles on the table. "Now, look, you two," she said, peremptory. "I don't want talk like this at my table. I won't have that language."

"You don't want us to use these words," Paul said, "but you don't mind if we act them out."

Douglas stood up. "Paul and Whitney," he said firmly, "whatever this is about, you keep it between yourselves. This is not the time or place to discuss it. I want you to drop it. You can take it up another time, between yourselves, but this is inappropriate." There was a pause. "Now. Would anyone else like coffee? Isabel?"

Isabel shook her head.

"Charlotte?" Douglas asked.

"Yes, please," Charlotte said. Douglas gave a little bow and vanished into the kitchen.

Whit turned from the table. "Good night."

Paul, still standing, looked down at Isabel. "You are making my life a misery," he said distinctly.

There was a moment of silence.

"I hope that's not true, Paul," Charlotte said. "I hope your life is not a misery." She sounded stern, as though she could order Paul not to believe what he'd just said.

Paul ignored his mother. He stared down at Isabel. "Tell me that you are not," he said, his voice terrible.

Isabel stood and said to Charlotte, "Good night. We're going back to the cabin."

"Are we?" Paul asked. He swayed slightly.

"I am," Isabel said. "Come with me."

Chapter 14

They used flashlights going back to the cabin, making their slow way through the trees in the dark. The lights shifted fluidly over the rough bark, the rusty needles on the path. Around them the woods were black and quiet. Watching Paul's steps ahead of her, Isabel saw they were hammering, angry, but unstumbling. He was still lit by rage, though maybe now more sober. They did not speak on the way.

Inside the cabin Paul closed the door behind her, shutting out the night's cool dampness. The door made a quiet thud and the latch clicked home. The air in the cabin was close. Paul turned to face Isabel.

"What are you doing?" he asked.

He had been waiting to ask this.

He was standing too close, he was dense and pressing. He had never before seemed threatening. Isabel stepped back; she could feel him towering. His body seemed hard and unwelcoming, his arms muscular, jostling. The cabin offered her no refuge, these small bare rooms with their shadowy corners. He stood waiting for her to answer.

"Am I making your life a misery?" asked Isabel.

"Do you think you are not?" he asked. His eyes were fixed on her, his gaze was ravenous. It was now filled with fury, but its fixity and desperation reminded her horribly of the day when he stood outside her apartment, holding the box of lilies.

"Why did you marry me?" he asked.

She stared at his face: the deep parenthetical lines from nose to mouth, the delicate whorl at the inner corner of his eyebrows. She had come to know him. He was wounded, her fault. What she should do was step forward and take his face in her hands. She did not move.

"I've made a mistake," she said.

Unbearably, he misunderstood. "With Whitney?"

"No." She shook her head. "I shouldn't have married," she said. "It was unfair to you. I'm sorry."

He had begun to breathe deeply, his mouth closed. The sound was loud in the confined space. His chest rose and fell strangely. "Do you want us to separate?" He spoke very slowly. "Is that what you want?"

Isabel looked straight at him. "It was a mistake for us to marry." She spoke steadily. She had said it again, the words now existed in the world. She could feel the movement starting up around her, the great mass of rock breaking loose, surrounding her, beginning to carry her down the slope.

Paul watched her. She could hear him breathing. He was further away from her now; there was distance between them.

Isabel shook her head. "I'm so sorry," she said. "Paul." She moved away and sat down at the table. "I didn't mean for this to happen."

Paul laughed unkindly. "Presumably not."

Isabel folded her hands meekly. "What would you like me to do now?"

Paul turned away from her and walked down the hall. At the end of it he stopped and came back to stand near her. "I want you to leave. To-morrow."

She hadn't considered this. "Well," she said. "Of course. If that's what you want."

"Unless you'd rather leave now."

She could see that fury filled him, and she wondered again if she was safe here.

"Now?" she said. "It would be difficult."

What did he want? She thought of the dark woods outside. The car was his. Did he want her to walk? Carrying her suitcase?

"Yes, it would," Paul said coldly.

He hates me, Isabel thought, sickened. "Where would I go?" she asked, standing up.

"*Have* you anywhere to go?" he asked.

"What do you mean?" she asked, then realized that he meant Whit. Paul imagined that she and Whit had a plan, a future. What Paul imagined was worse than what had actually happened, but what had actually happened was not to be explained. "No," she told him. "I have nowhere to go."

She would have to find a new apartment; she never should have given up her old one. A wasteland of arrangements lay before her, problems over money.

"Would you like some tea?" she asked. She needed a task. She took down the box of tea and turned to Paul, who did not answer. He was still standing by the chair, his hand on its back. He was staring at her. His face looked drained and hollow. She waited.

He shook his head. "No."

He would refuse anything she offered him now, she could see that. Beneath his eyes the skin was bluish. *At this age we start showing what we feel,* she thought. *A twenty-year-old shows only fresh young skin no matter what happens, but for us, things show in our skin, in our faces. When we feel pain.* She felt a rush of tenderness for Paul, with his drained gray face. Tenderness, affection—it felt very like love. What was it, if it was not love, and why could she not make it into love? Why could she not make her feelings do as she wished? They were her own. But she could not. The feeling, whatever it was, rose up in her chest, weakened, then withered.

She turned to the tea. She felt him watching her. She waited for the kettle to boil, her back to him. Cracking sounds came from the burner as it heated up.

"How can you do this?" Paul asked her. His voice was rising. He had not finished with her.

She would not turn. In the dim light she watched the metal coils turn from lead to dull red, the concentric circles incandescent beneath the kettle.

"I don't mean to," she answered.

"How can you just announce you're leaving?"

She said nothing. Steam appeared, a stream of mist in the kitchen's dimness. Lofting toward the ceiling, it reminded her suddenly of Michael.

She saw him in the doorway of the little kitchen in London, the plume of steam. What was the moment? She could remember only his face, lit up and happy, the steam drifting between them. She'd been at the stove, and he'd come in from work excited about something. When Michael was happy, he was ebullient, exuberant. "Turkey!" That was it. "We're going to Turkey!" he'd announced. "We're going to find out everything about the Ottoman Empire. This young Turk is going to investigate all the old ones!" Michael's face radiant through the steam.

Isabel turned back to Paul. "I'm sorry," she said again.

"Don't tell me that," Paul said angrily. *"Don't go on telling me you're sorry."*

Isabel shook her head. She took a tea bag from the box. The scent, delicate, aromatic, bloomed in the dull air.

"It's not you," she said. "It's me. I wasn't ready to get married."

"I see that," Paul said. He crossed his arms.

"I never should have done it."

"Stop it," he said, his voice loud.

She felt again his size, the rage in his body. She shifted slightly away from him.

The water was boiling now with a lisping hiss. Isabel took the kettle off the burner and filled her mug. The warm vapor rose around her face. She sat down at the table.

Paul stood over her chair. "What's amazing to me," he said, "is that you'd have the unbelievably poor taste and judgment to behave like this here, at this place, in front of my family."

"Behave like what?" Isabel asked guiltily. "What do you think I've done, Paul? I haven't done anything."

"You've announced that you want a divorce—you don't think that's anything? And Whit," Paul went on angrily. "It's just what he did before."

"Before?" Isabel asked.

"With the famous Marilyn Hornby," Paul said bitterly.

"What happened with the famous Marilyn Hornby?"

Paul pulled out a chair and sat down. "You want to know?" he asked. "Okay. I'll tell you. That year we were all up here, staying at the lodge. I'd met this girl in New York at the beginning of the summer. I didn't know her well at all. I'd only met her once, but I liked her, and I invited her up for a week."

Whit had been without a girlfriend, so from the start, they were a threesome. Marilyn had long, silky blond hair and light blue eyes. Her upper lip was short, so that her mouth was often, enchantingly, slightly open. She was very tan and very long-legged, with narrow fingers and toes.

The three of them sat up each night after dinner, playing cards or sitting on the porch in the dark. When they went out in the canoe, Marilyn sat in the middle, Whit in the bow, Paul in the stern. Paul watched her. She wore cutoffs that came to the top of her thighs, a T-shirt that kept riding up over her back. He could see the smooth vertebrae rising up against her skin, which was supple and gleaming. He watched her back; she kept on leaning forward, talking to Whit. In the beginning Paul talked to them, too, he was part of the conversation. After they set off, Marilyn trailed her hand in the water and squealed. "It's freezing," she said, her voice high.

"It's not that cold," Paul answered. He was excited by her excitement, by the energy coursing through the air. But she said nothing back. "Wait till we throw you in," he said boldly. "Then you'll see how cold it is." The promise of violence, submission.

But Marilyn did not answer him, and after a while he realized that she was not talking to him. She answered only Whit. From then on he watched her in silence, and he saw that all her movements were directed not at him but at Whit.

It was after this that they had gone on the hike up the mountain and been chased by the bear.

When they came down, when they finally stopped, gasping, on a lower trail, Marilyn leaned against a tree trunk and closed her eyes.

"God. I thought we were going to die." She was breathing loudly.

"We might have," Whit said.

Marilyn opened her eyes. "But you would have saved me. Wouldn't you?" She was looking at Whit. The question was so blatant, so naked, that Paul felt his face turn stiff.

In the middle of the next night Paul found himself awake, suddenly brought to consciousness by something, a commotion of some sort. As he groggily sat up, got out of bed, he heard the sounds of struggle: footsteps, hisses, turmoil. He went out into the hall in his pajamas. His parents' door opened and Douglas appeared.

Whit and Marilyn Hornby were in the hall, entangled with each other. Marilyn's honey-colored hair was tossed and disordered. Her bathrobe had slid off one shoulder, and her neck was exposed. Her nightgown strap was pulled down over a bare round shoulder, polished, shocking. Her bathrobe cord was untied, and she was barefoot. Whit was wearing only his pajama bottoms, loose and faded; his torso was bare.

As Paul and Douglas drew closer, Whit and Marilyn stopped struggling and pulled apart, fierce and staring. Charlotte stood in her bedroom doorway, her face startled and sleep-swollen.

"What's going on here?" Douglas asked. He stood forbiddingly before them. At that time Douglas was in his early fifties, his prime. At work he had become chief operating offer at the bank, at home he was the head of the household. These were children breaking rules. He disapproved of all this, the temerity, the unseemliness of this midnight struggle, and he was outraged by such a rank whiff of his child's sexuality. He stood in his bathrobe, frowning, taking charge. Charlotte, beside him, held her dark blue robe closed at the throat. Her hand clutching her throat, her staring face, the long robe all gave her a tragic look.

Douglas raised his voice. "What's going on here, Whitney?"

No one answered. Whit and Marilyn stared furiously at each other. Violence was in the air between them.

"Whitney?" Douglas repeated.

"Nothing," Whit said, not looking at him.

"All right then," Douglas said. "I think everyone can go back to their rooms. And I don't want to hear any more noise tonight from anyone."

Marilyn whirled, her mouth pursed, her eyes slitted. She pulled her bathrobe up over her shoulder and strode into her room, loudly shutting her door. Charlotte went back into the bedroom, but Douglas stood with his arms crossed, magisterial, admonitory, watching Paul and Whit.

Paul stood in the hall staring at his brother's face, yearning for him like a lover. He felt himself pulsing. He could see the rounded point of Whit's chin, the place where his own fisted hand would meet it, the ridge of hard knuckle snapping the chin up into the air, perfectly, forever. His hands longed for this, they tingled at his sides.

Whit would not look at him. He turned, under his father's watchful stare, and went back down the hall to his room. Neither would Paul look at Douglas, who stood waiting; he turned and went back to his room and shut the door. In the dark he stood still, staring straight ahead.

He saw Marilyn's smooth beautiful face, the slightly parted lips opening into that intimate space, the shining teeth, the mobile tongue. He saw the lean suntanned toes, the polished shoulder. He heard again the struggle outside his door. Whit's hand had bared the shoulder. Whit's arms had been around her. He heard a sound in the room and, after a moment, realized that it was himself. He was panting. His own mouth was open, and he was panting with rage. He made his way through the dark to his bed and sat down. His heart was pounding. He felt as though his body had opened up to the black night, as though he had become huge and dark and murderous, like the miles of woods around him. He could not get back into bed. He could hear every noise in the world, the smallest sound. He could not think of what to do.

The next morning, when he came into the dining room, his mother said loudly, "Good morning, Paul." She gave him a formal nod. When Whit arrived, then Marilyn, she did the same. Whit still would not look at Paul. Paul thought of beating him. He thought of each blow. Marilyn's face was sullen and closed. She ate her toast carefully, chewing slowly, her eyes down. During the meal Douglas and Charlotte talked briskly to each other. None of the others spoke.

Afterward Marilyn went out onto the porch, and Paul followed her. She stood sulkily before the railing, staring out at the lake, her arms folded over her chest. Her lips were pressed together, pouty. The line of her cheek to her chin was straight and perfect, and her hair fanned out across her back. She was beautiful. Paul hated her.

"What's up?" he asked.

"I want to leave," she said, not looking at him. It was Thursday; the plan had been for her to stay till Saturday.

"I'll take you to the train," Paul said.

It was a two-hour drive; they did not speak once. At the station he carried her suitcase to the platform. The suitcase was metallic blue, hard and big, and it bumped against his shins. He stood with her on the platform, squinting toward the train. The station seemed abandoned; they were the only people waiting. Marilyn smoothed her hair back down over her shoulders and looked at her shoes.

Paul thought of her narrow tanned toes. He put his hands in his pockets. He hated her. He thought of what he would say to her as she left; he considered final remarks. He wanted something ironic and crushing, unanswerable. He stared into the distance, willing the train's arrival. He wondered if they were saving lunch for him at the lodge; he'd forgotten to ask. Marilyn smoothed her hair back again, sliding the silky mass between her first and second fingers, then tossed it over her shoulders and frowned at the tracks.

The train arrived quietly, without announcement. It slowed, then halted neatly beside them. An opened doorway stopped right in front of Marilyn.

Paul turned, his hands still in his pockets. It was the moment for his speech. He opened his mouth to destroy her.

Marilyn seized her bag with both hands and wrestled it onto the train. She jumped on behind it and turned back to Paul. "Thank you very much," she said coldly.

It was his moment.

"Good-bye," Paul said.

Marilyn pushed through into the passenger car. The door closed behind her, and then the train started up smoothly and she was gone.

Paul stopped.

"And then what?" Isabel asked him.

"Nothing," Paul said. "I never saw her again."

"But what happened with Whit?"

"What do you mean?"

"What did he say about it?"

"We never talked about it."

Isabel stared at him. "Never?"

He shook his head.

"How could you not?"

"What should I ask him?" Paul asked, raising his voice, suddenly furious again. *"What do you suggest? 'Did you screw my date? How could you do such a thing?' "* He stared coldly at Isabel. "What good would it do to ask him about it?"

"No, nothing," Isabel said. "I'm just surprised you never discussed it."

"Well," Paul said, belligerent, "we never have. Once, Whitney started to say something about her, that she was a jerk, something like that. I told him to shut up." Paul rubbed his hands on his thighs. "He'd had a chance to be on my side, and that was in the middle of that night. It was a little too easy for him to take my side later."

Isabel said nothing. He was too angry.

Paul went on. "My brother moved in on my girlfriend in our house, right in front of me, in front of everyone. What is there to talk about? I don't want to know any more about it. I don't want to know what happened between him and her." He stood up, pushing the chair back from the table. "Or between him and you."

"Paul," Isabel said. "Nothing happened between me and Whitney." The words were like stones in her mouth.

"Goddamn you," Paul said.

"Paul."

"Don't say anything," Paul warned. "Don't tell me. I don't want to know about it. I know something happened between you and Whitney."

"You're wrong," Isabel told him. "I don't know what you're thinking, but you're wrong." Her face felt hot.

"Don't," Paul said dangerously.

There was a silence.

"What do you want me to do?" Isabel asked.

"Stay away from me," Paul said. He walked back down the hall, and at the door to their room, he turned. "Come and get your things out now. I don't want you sleeping in here."

Isabel set down her mug and walked to the bedroom. He stood at the door like a guard. She went to the bureau and opened the drawer. "Do you want me to pack?" she asked. She kept her voice quiet.

"No. Just take what you need tonight and get away from me." He was tight with rage. She could feel him, furious, behind her. She took her nightgown from the closet, a sweater, her book. She felt humiliated, as he intended. If she forgot something, would she be allowed back for it later? Paul's brow was thunderous. He was waiting for a reason to attack her.

Isabel tucked her things into a bundle, and holding it against her chest like a refugee, she walked to the door. "I think that's everything," she said. "Good night."

He didn't answer. His face was terrible.

"I'm sorry," she repeated, stricken. She felt again the rush of tenderness. Useless: it was she who was causing this.

"Get out," he said.

She stepped past him quickly.

Behind her she heard Paul moving roughly about, dragging the beds apart. She went into the farthest room—Whit's—and shut the door behind her. The door was flimsy, one thin board, with no lock. She was surprised to have looked for one—was she afraid of Paul? She thought of his presence, too heated, too close, in the hall. She wondered how far his anger would take him. She undressed quickly, trying to make no noise. When she was settled in the bunk, she listened again. She could hear Paul. The cabin was tiny; she could hear his every creak in the bedsprings. She heard him roll angrily over, she heard him turn, turn back. In a little while she heard him click on the light, and she waited to see if he was getting up, if he was coming to her. But he did not. He must be reading. She heard him go into the bathroom, then back to his room. She heard him shut the door.

Isabel lay still in the dark. She did not try to read: Swann and Odette would drive her mad tonight. She lay still and waited. She knew what was coming.

Part 4

Chapter 15

In Baltimore Michael and Isabel lived on a quiet residential street lined with tall sycamores. The softly mottled trunks, the high green shade, the dry rustling leaves gave off an air of peace. Their house stood in the middle of the block, a tall brownstone with white marble front steps. Michael and Isabel had two floors: more than they needed, but the rents in Baltimore were low. Why should they not have what lay within their reach? Life seemed casually munificent, and plenty a given. It seemed they were entitled to happiness.

The rooms in the house were large, with high ceilings and an air of benign decrepitude. In the mornings sun came through the tall windows in slanting shafts; motes of dust hung motionless and radiant. Behind the house was a small green yard where, each spring, a magnolia tree put forth bruised pink blossoms. Almost as soon as they arrived, Isabel became pregnant.

Michael had been hired at the *Star* by the metro editor, Link Caulfield. Caulfield started Michael off on the rookie's beat with "cops and obits" and watched his progress, moving him next to reporting on a suburban county and finally to the treasured city hall assignment.

Isabel was happy there because she saw that Michael was happy. She saw that he liked every part of what he did. He liked making the rounds of the police stations, coming to know the sergeants on duty, scanning that day's collection of strange activities—a naked man in a top hat on a rooftop, reading loudly from the Bible; a car stuck tight in a narrow alley. He liked writing the obituaries, learning the intricacies of Baltimore families, their placement within the city's history. He liked driving around Arundel County, covering 4-H shows and library fund-raisers.

He liked the city of Baltimore, its mixture of populism and aristocracy, maritime and agricultural history; its ancient glory as a great deep-water port, its faded splendor, its troubling racial undercurrents, the gentle grandeur of its eighteenth-century buildings. He liked the exuberant stretch of bright water at the heart of the city. He liked the eccentric landmark of downtown Baltimore: a tall brick bell tower with an impeccable artistic lineage—Venetian Renaissance—topped by a giant Bromo-Seltzer sign.

Isabel could see that Michael found all this energizing. She watched him open himself to the new life, spreading himself out to embrace it. He liked the other reporters, liked the sense of curiosity they all shared, the need to reveal, explain, bear witness; he liked the deadpan humor in the city room, the steady urgency of deadlines. In the mornings, when he arrived at the big brick *Star* building, he jogged up the wide stone steps two or three at a time. He was surging up toward the day. He could not wait to start.

Michael told her aboout the city room and the reporters. He sat next to Bobby Klausman, a smart, slow-talking southerner with a high forehead and a dense mat of brown curls. Link Caulfield had an office down the hall. The city room and everyone in it were overseen by Jess Haughton, the assistant day editor.

Haughton was short and pear-shaped, with sloping shoulders and a high waist. He wore ballooning white shirts, and his pants rode high, clasped by a narrow belt set at his widest point, the apex of his belly. His small face was set with two deep parallel frown lines, and he was fussy and outraged, like a chicken. Haughton was in charge of layout and cared only about space on the page.

"What's the budget? What's the budget?" He talked fast, in a high, irritable staccato. "How many inches?"

"I could tell Haughton I was breaking a story on the president dealing drugs," Michael told Isabel one evening, "and all he'd say"—Michael drew himself up and his voice turned shrill—"is 'How many inches?' "

Michael was in the bathroom doorway. Isabel's back was turned to him; she was shaving her legs, with one foot set in the sink. Her leg was covered in a thin layer of creamy white foam, like frosting.

"What's he like?" she asked, looking at him in the mirror.

Michael stretched his chin in the air, thinking. "Testy," he said, "but not mean. He's found one thing to focus on, and that's all he thinks about. That's the way he lives his life. I like him."

Isabel leaned forward, over her swelling belly. It was beginning to change her axis, her center of gravity.

"Is he married?" Isabel asked.

"Hard to imagine him married. He's a little odd," Michael said. "He keeps a feather duster on his desk."

Isabel looked up at him in the mirror. "A what?" she asked.

"You know." Michael flicked his wrist.

"A feather duster?" Isabel repeated, delighted. "What does he do with it?"

"Dusts the typewriters," Michael said. "It's like a nervous tic. He does it when he's under pressure. First he does his own typewriter, and then, if things get worse, he goes around the whole city room and dusts everyone's typewriter, all the reporters'." He pursed his mouth and whisked his hand back and forth.

Isabel bent again over her leg. "What do the reporters do when he comes by?" She drew the razor up the inside of her calf in a long, smooth stroke, revealing a swath of immaculate skin. The smell of soap was fresh and faintly tart.

"No one says anything," Michael said. "Klausman frowns and stares down at his story as though he's thinking up the end of the sentence. No one looks at Haughton, they don't look at each other, they don't look up at all. It's like a spiritual visitation. When he's gone, they start typing again. No one mentions it. The first time he did it, I thought he'd gone crazy."

"And now you don't?" She raised her eyebrows in the mirror.

Michael shrugged. "Haughton's good at what he does. He's been there for years. He just likes to dust, that's all. Nothing strange about that." His voice turned loud and official, like a sportscaster's. "When the going gets tough, Haughton gets dusting." He watched Isabel exposing new paths of skin in the creamy foam. "But you can understand that. You're a girl. Isn't that what you girls like to do?"

"*Love* dusting," Isabel agreed. "Can't get enough dusting."

"Which is what's so adorable about you all," Michael said.

Isabel made small deft strokes around her anklebone, and a drop of dark blood bloomed. "Still," she said mildly, "he sounds a little crazy to me."

"Maybe," Michael said. "But who am I to call people crazy?"

Isabel set the tip of her finger against the bone and held it for a moment. When she lifted her finger, the drop swelled slowly, deep purple-red, shining. She turned on the water to rinse it away. Beneath its stream, the blood vanished, but when the water stopped, a reminiscent veil spread out across her skin.

Late one afternoon Isabel visited Michael in his office. She walked down the long second-floor hallway, a rubbery brown floor smelling of chalk. At the far end was the city room, and Isabel heard the racket of typewriters and voices. In the doorway she stopped.

The room was medium-size and filled with desks. At most of them sat men at typewriters, papers adrift beside them. On one side of the room was a short man in shirtsleeves, his desk facing in toward the room. He was standing imperiously before it, hands on his hips, and looking right at Isabel. Would it be rude for her to look for the feather duster? Too obvious? She looked away, searching for Michael. He was at a desk across the room, his back to her. He was on the telephone, and the sight of him produced an aural connection; she could suddenly hear his voice among the others.

"Was there anyone else there?" he asked. "All right." He was writing on a pad. "Yes. Yes, thank you very much."

Isabel began to thread her way through the desks toward him; a middle-aged man was making his own way toward her.

Link Caulfield was lean and balding, with leathery dry skin and pouched, watchful blue eyes. He wore a striped shirt with the sleeves rolled up over his elbows. His metal-rimmed glasses were stuck up at the top of his forehead. He walked with his hands in his pockets, his manner proprietary. She smiled at him. As they drew close, he stopped, his eyes narrowing.

"Mrs. Green?" he asked.

"I am Isabel Green," Isabel said, and at once Caulfield's manner changed and his expression turned charming. He drew his feet ceremonially together and dipped his head in a tiny bow.

"Link Caulfield," he said, and Isabel saw in his shift to sudden attentiveness, his smiling courtesy, the reflection of Michael's success.

"We're very glad," Link Caulfield went on, "to have your husband here with us."

"He's very glad to be here," Isabel said, smiling back. She gave a little dip of her own head: they were both saluting Michael. As she smiled, she could feel Michael's presence across the room. She could see him talking into the phone, the set of his shoulders urgent, intent; he was tapping his pen against his paper. She could feel his quicksilver current, his energy; she knew Caulfield could feel it, too. She could not wait to reach him, her husband.

And Michael, hearing her voice, turned and saw Isabel among the sweaty men at their desks, in the dingy office. Isabel in her red dress, her hair loose on her shoulders, stood smiling at him, and Michael smiled back. Isabel could see the delight in his look, the same delight she felt.

When Ben was born, Michael fell suddenly into fatherhood. It was an unexpected ecstatic plummet, bringing out a kind of joy that was new to him.

One evening when Ben was not yet a year old, Isabel carried the baby into their bedroom. Michael was on the bed; he held out his hands, and Isabel set Ben on his father's lap. Ben was naked and damp from his bath. He stood excitedly on Michael's knees, his starfish fingers seizing his father's hands. He stamped unsteadily, leaning against Michael's grasp, hiccupping with pleasure.

"Hup! Hup!" Michael said. "Go, Ben!"

Ben kicked out boldly, his gestures loose and uncoordinated: he was learning his body. His fair silky hair stood up in waves. His milky skin showed a fine blue tracery of veins beneath. The smooth curve of his belly sloped down to the tiny bobbing peanut at its base. Ben marched and cheered, his toes sliding and clutching at his father's knees.

"Go, Ben," Michael said encouragingly. In a different voice, he said to Isabel, "I can't believe we've done this. We've made a new human being. All his blood is going through the veins in the right direction, his belly is doing exactly what a belly's meant to do. We made him, but we don't know how. It works. And he even has a soul. I can't believe it."

Ben kicked out giddily, staggered, lurched sideways, but Michael's hands held him upright. Ben laughed deep in his throat, a rich liquid gurgle.

"Believe it," Isabel told Michael.

It was soon afterward that Michael received the promotion to the city hall beat. His apprenticeship over, he had been awarded what he wanted: the turmoil of city politics.

Isabel thought that the two things—Ben and the promotion—would knit Michael into a kind of safety. How could they not? He now had an existence beyond himself, approbation and a task.

Safety for Michael was what Isabel wanted. There had been periods of alarm: by now she had seen Michael's black moods. In fact, she'd seen them from the beginning without understanding what they were. She'd thought they were merely tension, part of the way people were, the way life was.

The first time, they were at Isabel's apartment. She woke up to find Michael immobile beside her. He was so still that she thought he was asleep, but then she saw his eyes were open. He was watching the ceiling. His presence seemed hard and clenched, and when Isabel spoke, he abruptly got out of bed. He had to leave early, he said without looking at her. He got out of bed quickly, jerking the sheet back roughly, and began to dress. Isabel, hurt and baffled, went into the bathroom to brush her teeth. When she came back out, Michael was gone. The heavy front door was shut.

Disbelieving, Isabel wrapped a towel around herself and stepped out onto the grimy linoleum of the landing. She heard footsteps clattering down. She leaned into the stairwell and called out his name.

The footsteps stopped. There was a brief silence.

"What is it?" he shouted back angrily.

Staring down, Isabel could see only his hand on the metal railing. There was nothing she could say, wearing only a towel and shouting down into the dark stairwell.

That mood lasted two days. Michael had been angry at everything, angriest of all, it seemed, at her. But it had been only a bad mood, not madness, Isabel was certain of that. It was true that while the mood was in full sway, Michael was unreachable, but afterward it was completely over. And the moods didn't happen often. Still, Isabel wanted them to stop altogether, and as Michael grew more certain of his success and abilities, more settled into happiness, she believed they would.

When Michael got the promotion, he called her at once from the office. "Local kid makes good," he said. "I'm on city hall."

He spoke quietly—he was at his desk—but Isabel could hear elation in his voice.

"Fantastic!" she said. "When did you hear?"

Michael told her about being called in to see Caulfield, the honor of it—his was one of the briefest apprenticeships in the paper's history—the talk of the next step. Isabel could hear excitement. There might have been something else, something blurred and somber, something lower on the emotional scale, but Isabel did not hear it. Or she did not want to hear it.

Michael went on at his usual rapid pace, leaving early for work, eager, intent. But as the weeks went by, something seemed to be slowing him down. Isabel realized that he was staying in bed longer in the mornings; some days he was nearly late for work. He seemed preoccupied, tense and short-tempered. It was the stress of the new job, Isabel thought; she assumed it would pass.

One morning she woke to find him staring upward, his gaze fixed and distant. His body touched hers nowhere. He lay without moving.

"What's wrong?"

Michael lay still, frowning and intent. It seemed as though this body belonged to someone else. He was inside it but unconnected. The sheets lay over him like a shroud.

Isabel waited for him to speak, for something to happen in the silence of the room. There was the distant sound of cars, the quiet rustle of the breeze moving the window shade. The thought came to her that she was alone. She began to be afraid.

She drew an uneasy breath to repeat her question and heard a faint sound from Michael, a tiny moist parting as he opened his lips to speak. Isabel waited. Still he did not look at her. The room was completely silent again. Then Michael's lips closed, and he very slightly shook his head.

Isabel rose up on one elbow, leaning over him.

"Michael?" she said. "What is it?"

He did not turn. He still watched the ceiling, or something between himself and the ceiling. It took him a long moment to respond, as though he were rising up through fathoms of dark water to reach her voice. It seemed an immense effort.

"Nothing," he said finally.

He lay without moving until Isabel got out of bed, saying, "Well, it's time to get up." Then he slowly sat up on the edge of the bed, his bare back to her, his head lowered. His hands were set on the rumpled bedclothes as though he was about to push himself off, into the current of the day, though he did not. He stayed on the bed. He had taken on some sort of cargo, some unspeakable ballast.

Isabel said nothing more. She left the room, hoping that, alone, he would gather himself, make the necessary effort.

When he came downstairs, his footsteps sounded casual, hurried, somehow intentionally sloppy. He left without eating.

The city council was in session then, and Michael was covering it. At issue was a plan to develop the harbor as a tourist attraction, to tear down the old unused industrial buildings and put up modern ones, to make the wharf into a stylized theme-park environment.

One evening they sat at dinner. Isabel was eating; Michael was not. She had begun to ignore certain things about his behavior: the strange artificial way he talked sometimes, as though trying to convince himself of what he said. The way he moved in the mornings, as if underwater. The way he had nearly stopped eating. The stiffness that seemed to be creeping into him, the fact that nothing seemed funny to him. Isabel ignored these things because she did not know what to do about them. The fact that they existed made discussing them with Michael more and more impossible. She ignored them because they frightened her. They had appeared mysteriously, and she hoped they would disappear the same way.

Michael cut a bite from his hamburger and set down his fork. The pink meat lay bloody on the plate.

"They don't know what they want," Michael said. "None of them. It's like herding cats."

"Isn't it a good idea, tearing down the wharf?" Isabel said diffidently. "I mean, there actually isn't much shipping here anymore, is there?"

"None," Michael said, "but the people who represent the industry don't want to let go of anything. Basically, nobody wants anyone else to get anything. Everyone's afraid that they'll lose out." He pushed his fork angrily into the lima beans.

Isabel went on eating, her eyes lowered. It seemed risky to talk, or to meet Michael's gaze.

"Christ, Haughton," Michael said suddenly. "I can't believe a guy waving a chicken wing around is in charge of my articles."

"Is it actually chicken feathers?" Isabel asked, trying to change the subject. "I wonder where he got it. You can't buy them like that anymore, they're all synthetic."

Michael stared at her. "I don't actually give a fuck what kind of feathers they are," he said. "Nor does it matter."

"I thought you liked Haughton," Isabel said meekly.

It had been a mistake, the attempt to distract him. She took another bite. She had no plan. What she hoped was that if she acted as though everything were all right, if she ignored Michael's mood, she would be able to coax him, soothe him, into a better one.

"Haughton is a fat-bottomed little jerk," Michael said.

"I thought you liked him," Isabel repeated, frightened by his ferocity. "I thought you said he knew a lot."

"Are you the expert on my job?" he asked coldly. "Are you going to tell me what I like?"

Isabel did not answer.

"Are you the expert on my job now?" He spoke softly and insultingly. Sickened, Isabel stood and picked up her plate. She turned to carry it to the sink. But this, apparently, was worse.

"Don't you walk away from me," Michael said, leaning toward her, his voice poisonous and terrible, and Isabel stopped in midstep, her back to him. She stood, waiting for what came next: *"Don't you ever walk away from me."* Isabel, holding the dirty plate in her hand, began to cry.

She learned that for Michael, the most dangerous times were moments of achievement, when he felt others' expectations rise. When Michael had finished a piece that was challenging and important, when he'd worked hard on something, shaped and smoothed it, then turned it in, that was when the blackness rose up through Michael's mind, curdling and nauseating.

It was having the piece seen by others, being exposed through it and then judged by it. It became horribly clear to him how unsuccessful the work was, how deeply flawed, how impossible correcting it, achieving anything better, would be. The thought of having the work read, revealing his inadequacies in this way, was unbearable, mortifying. It was like being flayed.

When this happened, nothing could convince Michael that the new work was anything but failure. The reminders of all other work he'd done—successful, effective—only showed how excruciatingly far he had fallen.

One night he called from the office.

"I'm going to be working late," he told Isabel. He spoke loudly, brusquely, as though he had to raise his voice to make her hear. A bad sign.

"All right," Isabel said. "What time do you think you'll get home?"

"I don't know," Michael said irritably. "I have no idea. That's what I'm telling you."

"I didn't know if you wanted me to keep anything for you for dinner," Isabel said.

"No," Michael said, and hung up.

It was late when he came in. Isabel was asleep and woke to hear Michael moving around in the bedroom, not quietly.

"Michael?" she said, raising her head. She felt groggy and slow. The bedroom was dimly lit, and she saw a dark figure at the bureau.

"Obviously," Michael said, not lowering his voice. He emptied the coins from his pocket onto the plate on the bureau with a challenging clang.

Isabel's mouth felt thick, and her eyes were heavy. She was confused by sleep, and by his manner. He did not turn to look at her.

"What time is it?" she asked. Her eyes closed.

"What time is it," Michael repeated, as though this was a stupid question. "Quarter past twelve."

In his voice there was trouble, and Isabel struggled toward wakefulness, clarity. "What's wrong?" she asked.

"What's *wrong*?" Michael said. Now he turned to look at her. "Nothing's *wrong*. Why do you think something's *wrong*?" The light came from the open door behind him, and she could not see his face but could feel him staring angrily at her.

"I don't know," she said, confused.

"Can I not work late—which I told you I was doing—and then come home late, as planned, without getting accused of something being wrong?" Michael asked slowly and unkindly.

"I didn't accuse you of anything," Isabel said.

"Oh, excuse me," Michael said. "I beg your pardon. You're right, of course. You didn't accuse me. You simply implied through your language, your manner and your line of questioning that something was wrong with the fact that I stayed late at work and now am home."

Isabel sat up in bed. Her eyes were adjusting, and she could see him more clearly, standing by the bureau. She could see his shape, his white shirt, but his face was obscured by gloom, as though her husband's face was gone and what was there was unknown to her. She could feel his own darkness radiating toward her. She could feel him hating her triumphantly.

The black moods came over him like monsoons, devastating, blotting out everything else. There was no other weather while these held sway. There was no way out of them but through the high murderous winds, the pelting rains, the rising moiling floods. They went on for weeks. Isabel could feel Michael trapped in his own darkness, she could expect nothing from him. She learned to stay down, out of his way.

The moods were kept at home. Michael was terrified of losing control, letting them slide into public view. He was never late for work, nor did he miss a deadline: those lapses felt fatal. He kept absolute rules for himself, containing the misery at home. He turned on Isabel.

Afterward, when the torment was over, he and Isabel picked their way through the silent ruins, trying to restore the world.

In the living room, where Isabel had slept on the sofa, Michael appeared one morning before dawn. The light was gray and muted. Isabel woke up—she had barely slept—to see Michael over the back of the sofa, his hair stiff and spiky. His face looked creased and miserable. Isabel waited, alert, bracing herself. The night had been a battlefield. She didn't know what he wanted now.

Michael climbed in next to her, wrapping himself and the blanket around her. She smelled his rich early morning smell, his skin, his hair. He was back.

"I'm so sorry," Michael said into her neck, moving his whole body around hers. "I was horrible to you. I'm sorry."

They lay together on the sofa. He pulled the blanket up over their heads, darkening the room above them, muffling and blotting out the rest of the world, creating a shadowy private space.

"I love you," he whispered soberly. From upstairs came Ben's early morning sounds, the liquid trills and questions. Isabel lay still, unwilling to leave the newly discovered tenderness. Michael held her against him. "Please," he said, "never leave me."

Each time Michael returned to Isabel and the two of them reached the other side of the storm, their rediscovery of each other was so tender, so profound, that it seemed they had reached a new place. Each time they felt they had learned something important, something crucial and altering. It seemed they would never again descend to those black depths.

The fights and terrible scenes connected them almost more than the peaceful times. Afterward Michael was shaken by what had happened. He became repentant, tender, devoted. He carried Ben around the room on his shoulders and made him scream with joy. He cupped Isabel's face in his hands. "You're my lifeline," he told her, his voice subdued.

Afterward Isabel understood that Michael was helpless in his moods, overtaken by them. She began to understand that she could help him, and it seemed that this was her task.

Besides, the moods did not come often. There were months and months between them, sometimes a year or more. The rest of the time—most of the time—he was fine, and when Michael was fine, he was wonderful.

Chapter 16

Michael was a success at the *Star*.

He was a confident and imaginative writer, and his articles began to attract attention. His series on two Baltimore neighborhoods, one white, one black, won a national award for the paper, and Michael began receiving calls from other publications. By then, after four years there, Michael felt ready to leave the *Star*. He was ready to be wooed to New York, ready to listen to offers from the glossy weekly magazine *Bulletin*.

Bulletin was then run by its founder, Enoch Patterson, who was lean and silver-haired, in his seventies, with blazing blue eyes and wild white eyebrows. He made a point of interviewing every writer the magazine hired. Famously crusty, he was known for difficult questions. He liked throwing people off balance.

When Michael came into his office, Patterson sat waiting behind his desk.

"Michael Green?" His tone was peremptory. "Sit down," he said, not getting up. He leaned back in his tilting leather chair and looked at Michael, pursing his thin lips judiciously.

"I hear you're from Chicago, Mr. Green," he finally said, his voice severe.

"That's right," Michael said politely.

"Then I must congratulate you, Mr. Green," Patterson said, bowing his head slightly. He paused for pride to well up at the coming compliment. "You have one of the most corrupt political machines in the country."

"Thank you, sir," Michael answered at once. "*And* we have the nation's slaughterhouse. We're not just corrupt but brutal."

There was a silence. Michael's reply was too good-natured to be impertinent, but it was a near miss.

Enoch Patterson looked out at Michael from beneath his eyebrows. "I see," he said.

At that moment in his life Michael was ready for anything. He felt himself anyone's equal. When he was reaching for something, he was at his most confident, and *Bulletin* wanted brash young men.

Bulletin's offices were in a sleek, reflective, glass-walled skyscraper on West Forty-eighth Street. The magazine had a staff of several hundred people, bureaus on five continents and an international edition. Michael bought two very expensive suits, and his posture improved.

At *Bulletin* the writers were divided into two categories: leg men and word men. (There were no women writers then. At *Bulletin,* women were researchers.) The leg men were travelers, nomads, adventurers. They received phone calls, grabbed their briefcases and went straight from the office to the airport, boarding midnight flights for Saigon, Moscow, Somalia. They came back with tired eyes and stubbled cheeks; they told about filing reports from near-vacant hotels, the stutter of sniper fire in the background, the sumptuous boom of mortars exploding in the empty swimming pool, hotel foundations rocking with the shock. The leg men were surrounded by an aura of impenetrable glamour; they were buccaneers, heroes.

The word men were the editors. They stayed in New York during faraway revolutions. Once or twice a year they went on carefully planned trips to the overseas bureaus, departing at convenient times and staying in comfortable hotels. The word men held no glamour in the physical world, but in the intellectual world they ruled supreme. They had complete control over the leg men's stories. They could shorten, cut, radically alter or simply expunge. They could do whatever they wanted. Their risks were philosophical, intellectual; their powers were absolute.

Privately each group looked down on the other. The leg men called the editors "the suits" and "the ivory power." They made slighting comments about virility.

Even more privately each group envied the other.

Michael was hired as a word man. On his first day at *Bulletin* he called Isabel from his new office. He spoke in a low, important voice: "Pundit here. What would you like explained?"

Michael called the leg men "testosterone brains."

"They can't write," he told Isabel, "so instead they get on planes and go wherever people are killing each other. It's sad, really."

Each Friday the magazine was put to bed, and on those nights Michael came home late, exalted, feeling as though the entire world and its discontents had been put to rights, all its issues identified and explained. Each week a wilderness of sprawling, disorderly growth sprang up all over the globe; each week the staff of *Bulletin* stepped forward, rolled up their sleeves and took it on. They pruned, mowed and clipped the shoots into an orderly and recognizable pattern. Michael had become part of something large and effective.

With the move to the magazine came a raise, and Michael and Isabel, dazzled by what seemed like riches, decided to buy an apartment. It would be an investment. They planned to be in New York for the rest of their lives, to have another child (in fact, they had already begun trying), and they wanted to settle. Buying an apartment felt like a step into the adult world.

It was February when they went out looking, with a real estate agent called Pat. She was in her fifties, with short, coarse blond hair and a gaunt face, deep lines in her cheeks. Her arms and legs were bone-thin; Isabel wondered if she was ill. She wore a bright red wool coat as if to distract from her thinness.

That day, by the time they reached the apartment on Riverside Drive, they had seen six others. Isabel and Michael were tiring from the preceding series of disappointments: the chopped-up, impossibly small rooms, exorbitant prices, unacceptably awful locations. When they arrived at the Riverside apartment, Pat opened the door and stood aside to let them through.

Isabel went first into the silent rooms. Light flooded through an archway in the front hall; she walked through it into the empty living room.

The windows were tall, and a soft aqueous radiance shimmered in long bands across the dusty floor. The sky filled the view; it seemed there was nothing between the room and California. Even in February, on that dull, early darkening day, light filled the room. Isabel walked to the window. Below, across Riverside Drive, the wide swift river spread out, a sheet of water coursing mysteriously past. Isabel watched it, the strange combination of movement and constancy. She had never lived by water before. *What a luxury,* she thought, *to have this dreaming steady current, wide and powerful, the dark water always there beyond the window, infinite.* It seemed a sign, a widening of possibilities.

Michael came and stood close behind her. She could feel his warmth and turned to look at him, smiling.

"What?" he asked her, nearly whispering.

"The river," she said, whispering back, and he touched her shoulder.

Their footsteps echoed against the bare walls. The last inhabitants had been there for years, decades. Against the dingy painted walls were ghostly *pentimenti,* silhouettes of furniture, paintings, reminders of earlier lives. The wooden floors were lusterless, the windows misted with grime, but the walls were thick and the ceilings high. Isabel walked through counting closets and bathrooms. The river stayed in her mind, wide and blank, a sheet of light.

There were two bedrooms across the hall from the master. It was the smallest that drew Isabel, and as she approached it, she felt herself gathering. In the doorway she stood still.

The room was square, with two windows. Winter light flooded in, laying radiant rectangles on the dusty foor. The windows gave onto an empty courtyard far below; at a distance was another wall, washed with sun. It was quiet there; Isabel could barely hear the street. She stepped into a slanting rectangle of light and felt the room around her luminous with promise.

Her next child would be a daughter. In that quiet room Isabel closed her eyes and held herself suspended, apart from the world. She let longing pool up in her. She heard Michael come in behind her and turned.

"Nice," he murmured, as though he too could feel the promise of the room, could feel it inhabited. He touched her hair.

When they'd seen the rest of the apartment, Isabel and Michael went back to the living room with Pat.

"What do you think they'll take?" Michael asked Pat. He cleared his throat with nervousness: he had never bought an apartment before.

The smile left Pat's face. "The asking price," she said, indulgence gone. "Riverside never goes down."

They paid the asking with a flourish of ignorant bravado. It was much more money than they had or could afford, though they wouldn't realize this until later, when they were struggling with a mortgage. They would nearly have to sell it several times, but now, knowing none of this, feeling powerful and fortunate, they took it. They wanted the height, the light, the water. They wanted the third bedroom, the second child. This would be their haven, the place their life would take place. They believed things would unfold gracefully and reasonably before them, that they had control over their lives.

At that time Michael's depressions were not discussed. When they were absent, discussion did not seem possible. It was too frightening, too terrible, when things were calm, to call up the specter of that howling torment. Michael resisted discussion absolutely, so to raise the issue was to return to that fury. Isabel could not bring herself to cast them back into it; it was better to leave it, to live in the day.

When the moods appeared, no discussion was possible. Then nothing was possible but battening down and holding on until it was over: eyes tightly shut, teeth clenched, head bent. Then they were both powerless.

The fall after they moved to New York, when Ben entered preschool, Isabel started working at EPR. In those first years she was a volunteer, going in only in the mornings, but as Ben's days grew longer, so did hers, and by the time he was in school full-time, she was at work full-time.

One evening when she and Michael were in the kitchen making dinner, she said, "I can see why men are the way they are." She was at the sink. She turned on the water, filling a saucepan to boil potatoes.

"I think I'm going to leave that one alone," Michael said. "I'm not even going to ask which particular male component we're talking about."

"I mean the way men don't ever want to talk about anything serious," Isabel said. She turned off the water.

"I beg your pardon," Michael said. He stood at the counter peeling carrots. Damp orange curls rose at each stroke. "I sense an implied slur. We talk about serious things; who would discuss world peace if we didn't?"

"I mean the real things," Isabel said. She set the saucepan on a burner. "Domestic peace. Family issues."

"Family issues," Michael said. "I see."

"What I mean is," Isabel said, "if you're at the office, all that recedes. You don't have to think about it. You're away. Why bring it up? There you are at your desk, you have meetings to go to, phone calls to make." She shrugged. "Now I get it. We can *both* be men. When I'm there, I don't want to think about difficult things any more than you do." She walked to the refrigerator.

Michael had rolled up his shirtsleeves. As she passed, Isabel gave his back a friendly stroke. She did not want him to think she was on the verge of raising difficult issues, the very issues he did not want to discuss; nor, at the end of a long day filled with EPR business, did she. She did not want to ask Michael if he had seen the therapist that morning, as he'd promised, or if he was taking the pills. She could not actually bear the thought of asking.

"Interesting," Michael said. He straightened, the peeler in one hand, a bright slither of carrot in it. "So we should have let women have jobs all along. Given you the vote, everything."

"Gotten us out of the house," Isabel agreed, taking a bag of new potatoes from the fridge drawer. "Given us something else to think about besides *kirche kuchen kinder.* Because if we're going to think about them, you're going to have to talk about them."

"Whereas if you have a job," Michael said, "you'll want to talk about—"

"Saving the earth," Isabel said. She poured the new potatoes into the colander, careful not to bruise their thin skins. "The important stuff."

"Well, and there you have it," Michael said agreeably. "Works out perfectly."

Isabel's job saved her. When things at home were good, the job was a stimulating addition. When things at home were bad, the job was a shelter for her sanity. Work was rational, professional, collegial. There she was unthreatened by the fierce and secret eruptions—unnamed and undiscussed—that swept through her home life. And the issues: it was a relief for Isabel to be part of something so large and public.

All this was salvation. Isabel entered into this world fervently, as though converting to a new religion. She learned the litany: toxic plumes and cellular mutations, subterranean leaching, riparian ecosystems, tall-grass prairie, biodiversity. She learned about political strategies, mineral rights and grandfathering, depletion allowances and clear-cutting. She memorized chemical formulae, quoted names and dates and legislation. The more she understood, the larger and more frightening the risks seemed. The earth felt increasingly frail and imperiled, its protection essential. The more she learned, the more determined, more fervent, she became. The worse Michael's moods became, the more dedicated to her cause Isabel became. There were things here she could do to help.

For she had begun to believe that there was not so much she could do to help Michael. In New York, after much resistance, she had persuaded him to see a doctor. They found both a therapist and a psychopharmacologist, and for a short time Isabel thought that the burden was off her shoulders, that the experts would solve the problem. At first Michael saw both doctors, who devised a program for him: sessions twice a week and medication. Small bottles appeared in the medicine cabinet. Michael took something to raise his serotonin level, whatever that was, which magically neutralized the black tide. That year was without episodes, and during that time Isabel felt safe.

But Michael began to complain of side effects: there was nausea, and waning libido, and then the therapist moved away. The psychiatrist they found to take his place, Dr. Rifkin, a short balding man with glasses and bad breath, would not work with the psychopharmacologist. Dr. Rifkin worked alone, and he wanted to try something new. "We'll get it right," he kept telling Michael. Michael took things alone, then in combination and in different dosages. The medications worked for a while and then did not, or they worked but the side effects were intolerable. Michael began to complain about the doctor, and the way he described the man to Isabel—acerbic, heavy-breathing, forgetful—made her heart sink. Michael didn't want treatment; he didn't want to believe he needed it.

One morning, looking in the medicine cabinet, she noticed his bottle of pills. It seemed that the level was unchanging—was it perpetually full? She quietly took down the bottle to look at the label, her body realizing before her mind did that this was a violation of trust.

As she held up the bottle, she could hear Michael in the next room, getting dressed. She read the prescription date, the number of pills. She felt a sinking, a grieving. She understood that the problem had not been solved. She understood that this was how their life would be.

Chapter 17

In those years, when Ben was still young enough to be walked down the block to meet the bus, it was Isabel, usually, who walked him. In theory she and Michael alternated, but EPR started its day earlier than *Bulletin,* and Isabel liked the brief, companionable walk with Ben.

One cold February day when Ben was in fourth grade, Isabel stood with him on the corner of West End Avenue. The sky was low and gray, a dense cottony ceiling. The air moved in from the river, damp and chilly. To the north the traffic crested over a little rise and streamed steadily toward them, lines of cars, vans, taxis, all heading into the day. Isabel faced uptown, shoulders hunched against the cold, watching for the yellow school bus. The wind gusted and swirled, scattering bits of bright trash from the gutter and cartwheeling them into the air in a scurrying rush. Ben leaned heavily against her leg, using her body as support while he kicked out sideways, in the middle of some private martial-arts game. Isabel felt surrounded by the vast New York hum of activity, the cars rising irrepressibly and endlessly up over the horizon, the cold invigorating air moving past, her own son raggedly kicking his leg toward some unseen foe—she had the sense of life churning all around.

Watching the oncoming traffic, Isabel wondered, as she did every morning, if they'd missed the bus. She wondered this no matter what time they arrived, but particularly on mornings like today when they were almost late, when getting Ben up had been particularly hard. These winter mornings were still dark when she had to wake him. Poor Ben was groggy, heavy with sleep, a deadweight against his pillows. It was painful to drag him unwillingly up from those depths into the cold morning world.

Why did young children have to be at school so early? Fretful and tired—what was the point? Why didn't their schools start at ten, when they'd be rested, brushed, happy? It was something to do with the harvest, she'd read, the agricultural American past. Or no, that was summer vacation, when everyone went home to bring in the crops. It seemed unfair to the children, the early start to the day.

Though maybe, like everything else, the problem was the parents. Maybe if these tired children had responsible parents who maintained sensible rules and put their children to bed properly by seven-thirty, they'd be rested and bouncy at eight the next morning. But if you worked and saw your child only after you came home at night, that was not possible. Isabel never got Ben to bed before nine no matter how she tried, and often not before nine-thirty or ten. He furiously resisted the call to bedtime, turning sullen or suddenly charming, wheedling, large-eyed, winning, asking the last-minute interesting question, knowing that his parents' hearts weren't in it, that they secretly wanted him to stay up, too. But it was Ben who paid the price, tired-eyed and listless the next morning.

A yellow silhouette rose up over the crest of West End. Isabel hoped it was the bus until it descended, revealing itself as a taxi.

"When will we take a cab, Mommy?" Ben asked, watching the same shape.

"Ten more minutes," Isabel said.

Eight-thirty was the cutoff, when they would assume they'd missed the bus. Isabel took his hand, looking down at him. Sensing her anxiety, Ben sighed dolefully, theatrically hanging on her, leaning against her leg like a refugee.

She looked up the avenue again, watching the shifting rows of cars and trucks appearing in the distance. She could take a cab right then and not keep tired Ben standing in the cold for another ten minutes. But the cab would be expensive, and wasn't there also some sort of principle involved? Shouldn't she wait for the bus, follow the plan? Each time they took a cab, she not only spent money on the ride but wasted the money they'd paid for the bus. But was money the real issue? If it was a question of Ben's well-being, how could she even hesitate? On the other hand, she didn't know if it really was a question of Ben's well-being. Was it harmful for him to stand, warmly dressed, in the morning air for ten minutes each day? Might it not be actually healthy for him?

Isabel could not decide. Like so many decisions about children, the problem seemed to resist analysis, clarity, logic. And it would end up being made by chance, or inadvertently, because of something unrelated. Then there would be unintended consequences. You would never know afterward how to assess it, whether it had been the right choice. What about the tube the doctor had inserted in Ben's ear when he was three because of all those infections? The doctor had said the tube was the only way to deal with them, that it was wholly safe. Now there were reports that those tubes damaged the inner ear and compromised the immune system. Or something like that: anyway, now you wouldn't dream of putting one in. It was impossible to keep track of all the crucial and bewildering information aimed at you. It ended up swirling around in your head like bright confetti in the gutter.

Isabel shifted her feet, stamping to warm herself. The wind swelled coldly against her thighs.

These minor, immediate worries ran through her mind: that they had missed the bus; that it was hard on Ben to wait in the cold; that Ben did not get enough sleep; that he was not doing well in math; that she herself was cold. Beneath these concerns were deeper, more troubling ones that were always present: about Michael and about herself.

Isabel was thirty-five, and they had been trying for eight years to have a second child. The first time had happened so easily; pregnancy had slipped into their lives so quickly; her body had been so confident and assured, and everything had worked so flawlessly that she was still incredulous that she could not repeat this. Each month when she learned again that she was not pregnant, felt the relentless seepage between her legs, saw the hateful blood again, she felt stunned. Each month it was a new blow.

Isabel was now on her fourth doctor. David Samuels was a famous fertility specialist who charged astronomically high fees and had an office on Park Avenue. He was small and plump, with honey-colored skin and dark liquid eyes. His fine black hair was dense and short, like felt. He wore crisp white lab coats, and he listened attentively. Before he spoke, he set his elbows on his desk and laced his fingers together in a way Isabel found reassuring.

Isabel found everything about Dr. Samuels reassuring: what she felt for him was reverence. She believed in him. She believed he would cure her, that through his arts he would magically release her from barrenness. Underneath this belief, this fanatical streak, was another, equally primitive fear that he would fail, that she would never be permitted to have what she yearned for.

That morning when she woke up, Isabel had stretched her hand to the nightstand without sitting up. You were supposed to take your temperature before doing anything to make your heart speed up or your temperature rise, anything at all, even sitting up in bed. Isabel took out the thermometer and flicked it, liking the hard, decisive snap of her wrist. She read the silver stripe against the toothed row of calibrations: below ninety. Isabel slipped the cool rod under her tongue and lay still, waiting for the liquid metal to expand. On the day of ovulation, the temperature dropped two degrees, declaring the body prepared. It happened without fail, and Isabel looked forward to it each month. It was a moment of hope, possibility.

Each day carried risk. Each time Isabel saw a pregnant woman on the street, or passed a woman with a baby carriage, was a blow. Each time she met the fact that she herself was still not pregnant and other women were, that other women were continually granted the gift of children, it was astonishing, unfathomable. Each time it happened, she felt dazed by it, stunned.

And Isabel could sense the second child somewhere present. The beloved daughter seemed already to exist somewhere in the ether. Isabel had already given her a name. She longed for this child. The daughter would complete the family, and, Isabel secretly believed, she would cure Michael. This baby's arrival would heal something in him, would complete something that was unfinished. The baby would be a balm to his heart.

Isabel knew her belief would not hold up to logic, but nothing about these matters was logical: not pregnancy, not emotions, not Michael's illness. It was a fact that Isabel needed this baby, and so did Michael. The yearning for a cure for their lives was always present. A strand of it was woven into her consciousness no matter what else she was thinking about, no matter what she was doing.

Frowning into the cold gritty wind, Isabel stamped her feet to warm them. Not too hard; she didn't want to dislodge anything. There was always the question of the mysterious interior, the possibility of something clinging inside, beginning to grow. It could happen at any time, any time. Isabel lived in hope.

That afternoon she had her third appointment with Dr. Samuels. This morning her temperature had dropped; it was the thirteenth day of her cycle. She would be examined to see if her body was doing what it should: turning rich and hospitable. Her secretions should be transparent and supple. She knew the mechanics, about sperm motility, egg viability. She knew how it worked, the majestic descent of the ovum, the frantic rise of the jittering sperm. The hormonal flows making this place smooth, that place furry. Isabel fervently wanted her body to perform.

The doctor's waiting room was beige, full of sleek furniture and glass-topped tables. On the tables were scrapbooks filled with handwritten letters of gratitude and photographs of tiny astonished infants held by radiant, exhausted mothers. When Isabel was alone there, she surreptitiously picked up a notebook and leafed through it. She pored over the pictures, the letters, the faces, examining everything. It was excruciating; it was also comforting. These were people who had reached the summit. Some sort of magic had worked for them; it could work for her. But Isabel kept this part of her life to herself. If she heard someone coming, she put down the scrapbook and picked up a dog-eared celebrity magazine. She would not be seen yearning.

She talked to no one but Michael about their struggles; it was too painful. When she cried in the night, she tried to make no sound, but Michael, feeling the tremor of the mattress, would awake, roll over and put his arms around her until she was quiet. When she cried in the daytime, it was in the ladies' room, or her own kitchen, or the back of a taxi, somewhere she could give way unseen, unexamined. She preferred to be alone. Michael, too, hoped for another child, and she was afraid to put too much of a burden on him with her sadness.

And all this, her own private ecological imbalance, the sense of something being wrong and damaged, added to Isabel's anxious sense of mission. It all seemed related to the environment being under siege, everything being haphazardly attacked by the frail plastic bags blowing aimlessly along the street, by the heavy diesel stench behind a truck, by the piles of radioactive tailings by nuclear power plants, sifting into the ground, the water. At home she read about pollution, about polymers and reproductive toxins: there were connections, apparently, or infertility wouldn't be such a growing problem. Why was the human sperm count declining all over the world? What was changing for everyone besides the environment, the way we treated our captive bodies, exposing them to toxic chemicals, electromagnetic waves, the lethal and miasmic cloud of pollution?

Now, over the crest of the hill, the yellow school bus appeared in the midst of a pack of cars and trucks, and thoughts of the taxi, Ben's chill, the fear of lateness all fell away. Ben, who loved the bus, cheered up at once. He dropped Isabel's hand and slid his parkaed forearm across his runny nose.

Isabel stooped down to kiss him quickly, before the bus arrived, so as not to embarrass him. Down at his level, face-to-face, she was reminded again that he was here, her actual flesh-and-blood child, beloved, vital, his head full of thoughts and emotions, his pink cheek smeared thinly with mucus. And just as Isabel saw him, Ben stopped seeing her, shuffling with impatience for the bus's arrival. Isabel hugged him hard, kissing his unsmeared cheek. His skin was cold, smooth, elastic, bright with life, and for a moment she pressed her nose into his cheek, her eyes closed, drinking in his small vivid presence. He leaned excitedly away from her: the bus had arrived. It stopped and the door slid open. Isabel smiled at the driver, a huge black woman who nodded impassively back. Ben climbed the steep steps, looking for his friends. The driver slid the lever, the door closed and Isabel set off toward the rest of her day.

When she reached her office, she hung up her coat and went down the hall for coffee. The office kitchenette was always slightly squalid; the counters lightly stained with coffee, scattered with sugar, littered with scraps of paper.

Netta stood by the coffeemaker, settling a filter into the pot. "Hi," she said. "We're two cups too late."

"I'll come back for both of us, then," said Isabel.

"Thanks," said Netta, "but I'll come back myself. I'm going to be in with Wallace."

At her desk Isabel started reading a report about pesticides. She was meeting later with a lawyer, and she turned the pages, highlighting passages. Three years ago, EPR had sued to stop the government from meeting secretly with the pesticide industry to set regulations. They had won, a triumph, but no matter how many pesticides were outlawed, chemical companies produced new ones. And now genetic manipulation was entering the world of agribusiness, another source of lethal chaos.

Isabel highlighted a paragraph and put two stars in the margin. Beside them she wrote, "Dioxin?"

When the coffee was ready, she brought back her cup. She looked at her watch: an hour before the lawyer, Lew Winston, arrived. After the meeting she'd order a sandwich then go uptown. She thought of Dr. Samuels and felt a tiny private flare of excitement.

Netta came in, her arms full of files.

"How was your meeting?" Isabel asked.

"Good," Netta said. "We're planning a symposium on ocean pollutants."

"When?" Isabel asked.

"Next fall," said Netta. She sat down, opened a file and began writing. The two women were alone, the office was quiet. Isabel sipped her coffee and wrote comments in the margins. Intermittently she thought of Ben, in his classroom or playing outside at recess. Reading about the Rockies, she thought about going out to Yellowstone next summer. Would Michael like that? They'd never been camping together. Would it be fun? She thought of scraping grease from a frying pan with a handful of leaves. How did you do dishes on a camping trip? In the margin she wrote, "Cellular damage." She looked at her watch. Ten more minutes.

Netta closed the last file, stood all of them upright on her desk and jostled them into a neat pack. Then she set them down and pressed her hands into the small of her back.

"I'm getting stiff," she said. "Why, do you think?"

"Yoga," Isabel said, not looking up. "The answer to everything."

"I'm stiff because of yoga?" Netta said. She tilted her head back, looking up at the ceiling and stretching her neck.

"You're stiff because of not yoga," Isabel said. "Or so I'm told. I have a friend who does yoga all the time, and it's amazing how limber and self-righteous it makes her."

"Mmm," Netta said. She closed her eyes and slowly rotated her head. "I need some of that."

"Hey there." It was Lew Winston. He was stocky and friendly, with reddish-brown hair, a long face and deep dimples. "I'm early, is that okay?"

Isabel began clearing a space on her desk. "Pull up a chair," she said.

Netta stopped rotating her head and looked at him, keeping her fists at the base of her spine. "This feels so good, I think I'm just going to stay like this," she announced to the room. "I can dictate, right? Who needs hands?"

"How much time do you have?" Lew asked Isabel. "When are you going to lunch?"

Isabel looked at her watch. "I have to leave at two for an appointment, but until then I'm yours." Saying the words "an appointment" was like speaking the name of a secret lover. Dr. Samuels: the dark felt helmet, the steady gaze. She felt the wash of yearning, greed, excitement. The assignation. At two-thirty she would be in his gaze, and he would save her. She smiled at Lew.

"Let's get going, then," Lew said, and he pulled a chair over. Isabel flipped the pages on her yellow pad back to the beginning.

"Are you all busy?" Another voice from the door, this one shy, female, pleased. Isabel looked up.

It was Ann Johnson, an intern who had worked at EPR the previous summer and fall. She was in her late twenties and married; almost as soon as she'd arrived, she became pregnant. Isabel had had to watch her shape swelling day by day. She'd seen Ann's face growing round and beatific, she'd seen the belly becoming large and hard. Each time Isabel saw Ann in a hallway, in someone's office, she wanted to turn around and walk away. It was chemical. Her face turned stiff and rigid; she wanted to say unkind things. She would make herself smile and speak pleasantly, but she could not bear to look at Ann, to listen to Ann's plans for the birth, the baby's room.

In her seventh month Ann told Netta, "I'm painting the walls blue. Even though I'm sure she's a girl. I know she's a girl." Ann patted the big curve of her belly, looking confident and possessive.

The words were like poison: *I'm sure she's a girl.*

A girl, too? Not only was she having the baby that Isabel wanted, but it was a girl. Everything Ann said echoed horribly inside Isabel's head.

Ann had looked over at Isabel. "Did you know, when you had Ben, that he was a boy? Some people say they just know."

It had taken Isabel a moment to answer. How dare Ann speak to her? How dare she discuss her burgeoning pregnancy? How dare she flaunt her wealth like this?

"No," Isabel had said, shaking her head, and looked down at her desk. "No." It was not so much an answer as a dismissal.

Ann's baby had been due around the New Year, and Ann left just before Christmas. Isabel signed the card that circulated through the office, a picture of a stork with a worldly, benevolent smile carrying a naked baby. Isabel wrote a banal message—"Best wishes from Isabel"—gave someone ten dollars toward the changing table and hoped never to see Ann again.

But now, horribly, Ann was standing in the doorway of Isabel's office. In her arms was a pink bundle, held with tender possessiveness.

"Ann!" Netta said, standing up, arms still behind her back but smiling, welcoming. "You've brought it in!"

Ann advanced shyly, beaming. "She's a girl," she corrected Netta.

"Oh, how wonderful! Let me see her!" Netta said, coming from behind her desk, her arms now outstretched. Ann met her and held out her own arms. Gently, Netta received the bundle, cradling it carefully against her breast.

"Oh," Netta said, admiring, cherishing, "look at her! She's beautiful." Her voice was softened.

The two women stood together, gazing down at something Isabel could not bear to see. Ann leaned toward Netta, her face eager, close. Netta bent her head. She swayed slightly from side to side.

"Are you beautiful," Netta whispered, her voice full of love. "Aren't you a beautiful girl?" Ann reached out to the bundle, touching something. Isabel still had not moved.

Without raising her head, Netta said, "Isabel, come and look at this ravishing child. She is simply—" She broke off. "Look at you! Is that a yawn? Are you yawning at me?" As she spoke, she smiled down and nodded.

Ann hovered. "Don't yawn in Netta's face, Cecily," she said proudly, "that's not polite."

Cecily! thought Isabel. The room was ringing with shock. Ann had named her. A girl, and she had given her a name. All of this was unbearable. The air before her shimmered with poison.

"Come over here," Netta said to Isabel. "Don't you want to hold her?"

Ann turned to look at Isabel, her round face beaming. Her long blond hair was tousled around her shoulders, tossed there casually like a wrap. She had a wide mouth, a broad face and long green eyes.

"Want to hold her?" Ann asked Isabel. "I brought her in so everyone could see her."

Lew Winston shook his head affably. "Go ahead," he said to Isabel. "I'm in no hurry."

Everyone looked at Isabel. They were waiting for Isabel to join in, to walk across the room and hold out her arms. The room seemed to glitter dangerously, as though every surface were cut glass.

"Here," Netta said, offering what she held.

There was no escape. Isabel stood and walked over. Ann smiled at her shyly. Netta held out the bundle. Isabel put her arms out, her heart pounding in her chest. The small creature was set into her arms: it was astonishingly, heartbreakingly light. It weighed hardly anything at all.

Isabel barely looked down, not bending her neck, not wanting to see. There she was, so tiny, the round smooth head, the patch of light downy fur. The smooth curved cheeks, the skin fresh, as though still damp and crumpled from the interior sleep. The eyebrows, faint but there forever, the lines of expression marked for life. The eyes, milky blue and liquid, were fixed steadily on Isabel. Above them was the smooth perfect arc of the eyelids, the tender fold of skin, the froth of pale reddish eyelashes.

It was the baby's gaze that was unbearable, calm, unblinking, wholly trusting. It was the feel of the baby in her arms that was unbearable, the nearly weightless burden, the tiny perfect quickened body, unthinkably someone else's, not hers, while everything in her longed for this. It was the life in her arms that was unbearable, this child with a whole life ahead of her, this whole person who was not hers, who had been denied her again. Isabel could not lift her head, could not look into Ann's eyes, Netta's, Lew's, all waiting joyfully and expectantly for her to smile, to speak. She could not say a word.

Chapter 18

Ordinarily the manager of a foreign bureau was chosen from among the leg men at *Bulletin*. The head of the Paris office would be someone whose territory had for years been France, someone who had gone there often to cover stories, who had worked with the bureau and its staff and was a logical choice to run it.

It was rare for a word man to be sent abroad; editors ordinarily stayed in the imperial city. But if an editor wanted to run a foreign office, he could make this quietly known. If he was successful and well regarded, popular with management, he might receive the post. A foreign office was a reward, a mark of esteem.

When Michael first arrived at *Bulletin,* he was assigned to topics from all over the world. During those heady years everything had seemed available to him; it had seemed that the globe was slowly spinning before his fascinated gaze, revealing itself for his delectation. Each new subject he examined, everywhere—Johannesburg, Los Angeles, Kuwait—revealed something marvelously unexpected, some revelation about the way politics worked or did not.

Michael became increasingly interested in Western Europe and England. He was fascinated by their relationships, by the way old alliances and antagonisms kept reappearing within new contexts, by the way a ghostly historical imperative hovered over contemporary exchanges. He focused particularly on England—its struggle between extroversion and introversion, its complicated relationships with Europe and the United States. He read voraciously about Britain's history and culture, its politics. He subscribed to dozens of English publications, from *The Times Literary Supplement* to *Modern Ploughing*. He liked the Brits themselves: he visited the London office every year, and he and Isabel took vacations in England, driving through the brilliant green countryside, walking the safe brisk streets of London.

Michael wrote about the U.K. with confidence and authority, and he began to be considered an expert at *Bulletin*. (He called himself a Limologist.) It was he who covered London's "Big Bang," the financial explosion of the mid-1980s that catapulted England out of its postwar genteel shabbiness and made it rich again.

"When it's six o'clock in New York, what time is it in London?" his article began. "The answer to that used to be, hilariously, 'Nineteen thirty-eight.' But things have changed in London Town, and today the answer might be 'Five or ten past the hour,' since the Brits appear now to be running just slightly ahead of everyone else."

Michael had risen to the position of senior editor and was popular with management. When he let it be known that he was interested in a foreign bureau, he knew he was a good candidate. He also knew that his medical history might stand in his way.

Twice, Michael had taken medical absences from work. The first time, only two weeks long, had been diplomatically described by his doctor as a "stress-related condition." That time he had stayed at home under supervision and on medication. But the second leave had been nine weeks long and had to be called what it was: clinical depression.

The day it started, Isabel had left for work before Michael got up. He usually rose first and went running before work, but that day it was raining heavily. Ben was dopey and sluggish, lying in bed without moving, his face in his pillow, his limbs boneless and heavy. He was resistant even to begin moving, and Isabel, exasperated, snapped at him. They left late and in a hurry, calling out good-bye to Michael from the hall as they went out the front door.

At work that day Isabel had been busy. She called Michael's office once and left a message. He didn't return it, but she'd thought he was in meetings or in a hurry, under deadline. She wasn't worried. Though apprehension was always present in her mind, she was always tamping it down, teaching herself not to listen.

It was not until the end of the day, on the subway going home, that worry crowded upon her. Sitting crammed among the heavy coats, she began to remember the silences of the night before, the sense of gathering darkness. Michael had been quiet for the last few days, and last night he had talked very little. During dinner Isabel and Ben had argued over video games and Michael had said nothing. After dinner he had gone alone into the living room, put on earphones, and stretched out on the sofa. Facing the night view of the river, he lay listening to jazz for hours. Isabel was asleep when he came finally to bed.

Now, she remembered the look on his face at dinner, how slowly he had moved and spoken, and alarm streaked lightly through her consciousness. When she had asked him for some water, he moved with ponderous precision, lifting the heavy china pitcher as though he had to focus on each muscle, each nerve. He watched the pitcher as he held it. Now Isabel could feel her heart beating, and she looked around the subway car, her chest tightening. Across from her was a tiny Asian woman, feet barely grazing the subway floor. Isabel stared at her, focusing on breathing. She felt her breath rising in her chest. She tried to calm herself, breathing slowly. The subway air was dense and fumy. The Asian woman across the aisle leaned forward, staring at the door. Her face was fierce, and her tight, closed mouth formed a contemptuous inverted "U."

It could be just a bad mood, Isabel told herself, watching the woman, *just a bad mood.* She tried to remember if Michael had spoken to her that morning. She'd been in that tearing hurry, afraid of missing Ben's bus. Had she said something, anything? Had he replied? Had he spoken at all? Speech, connection, was crucial when Michael was down. *He could be fine,* she told herself, addressing her panicky heart. Struggling up out of her seat, squeezing past a fat man in a raincoat, pushing toward the door as the subway slowed, she told herself she could be wrong. Michael could be fine.

As soon as she opened the front door, she knew. She could feel the black mood contaminating the air, his silence from the front hall.

"Michael?" she called. He didn't answer, but he couldn't hear her from the bedroom. If he was there. He was probably still at the office. She had really only spoken out of fear. If he was there, dreadfully, still in the bedroom, then even if he had heard her he wouldn't answer, she knew that. She walked down the hall, her footsteps loud.

The bedroom was dark. It was close inside; the air had been used up. The bed was unmade, rumpled, full of folds and creases. Under the covers was a body, hardly decipherable in the dimness, under the ridges and folds of bedclothes.

"Michael," Isabel said, standing in the doorway. She said his name differently now, her voice hushed.

She had learned what to do when she found him like this. First sit down with him, gently and slowly, to see what he could tolerate, if he could talk, could stand to be touched. If she was allowed to turn on the light or if this was too much, too transformative, too challenging. If he could not speak at all, if he lay frozen and mute. That was the worst. Carefully she eased herself down on the mattress beside him. He did not move.

That time Michael was sent to a private hospital in Westchester, a complex of low white brick buildings. These were linked by asphalt paths that wound across the meager lawns.

During the stay, Isabel drove up to visit him every afternoon. Usually she found him in his room, which had a bed, a bureau and a metal chair with round metal rods in the back of it, like bars. Michael sat heavily in the chair, leaning back and setting his own arms on the chair arms as though obeying orders. There was nowhere for Isabel to sit except on the bed, and this was so high that she had to make a little backward jump to get up on it. Michael watched without speaking. It made her feel awkward, as though she were performing for him in some way.

At other times she found Michael in the solarium. This had been built during the 1930s, when the sun was still curative and kind. Three of the walls were taken up with small-paned windows, and plants with dark arrow-shaped leaves sent snaky creepers up the frames. A row of stiff upholstered chairs faced the windows. Michael sat in the exact middle of the row. There were no other chairs in the room, so Isabel sat beside him as though they were on a bus. She turned toward him, but he looked straight ahead. He wore gray T-shirts, sweatpants and sneakers with Velcro-covered straps.

Michael's eyelids were heavy, as if he weren't quite interested enough in the world to allow it fully into his sight. He spoke slowly, as though near sleep. He seemed stunned. He turned his head carefully. He looked at Isabel, but it was not always clear that he saw her. Once, in his room, she thought he was looking straight at her, interested by what she was saying, and she had a moment of happiness. Then she realized that his focus had shifted. He was looking just past Isabel's shoulder, at the Monet poster on the wall—the blurred deep blue image of the pond at Giverny, lapped by lily pads.

"Michael?" Isabel said. He did not answer.

It seemed then that he was gone, that there was nothing left of him, and Isabel had no way of knowing he would return. She never took Ben to visit, not wanting him to see his father's stunned eyes, his underwater movements. When Ben asked when his father was coming home, Isabel told him she didn't know. She said he was definititely coming back, though. At the time she didn't know this was true. She didn't know if Michael was ever coming back.

"But where is he?" Ben asked sadly.

"In Westchester," Isabel told him, and put her arms around her son. She could not bear to look in his eyes. She tried to act cheerful in front of Ben, to protect him from the sight of her own fear and grief, to keep him from feeling fear and grief. Maybe that was not the right thing to do, but she didn't know what the right thing was to do. Should she tell Ben everything? Nothing? Michael's solemn doctors gave her no advice for dealing with her ten-year-old son, and she did not dare ask Theresa.

Michael was in the hospital during the late winter, when the ground was dead and colorless. The lawns were brown, the shrubs along the asphalt paths pinched and barren. Driving home on the darkening highway, Isabel wept, wiping at her eyes with one hand and keeping the other on the steering wheel. At the south end of the Sawmill River Parkway was a small gas station, and she pulled in there and parked off to one side. The light was gone by then, and no one could see her. She leaned against the steering wheel and put her hands over her face.

During these times, when Michael was ill, Isabel felt as though the whole planet were darkening. It seemed as though she could feel the earth moving out of the path of sunlight into the shadow of a final, deadly eclipse. She could feel around her the dying off of the endangered species; the poisoning of the sweet groundwater; the browning of the great evergreen forests, the taiga, along the northern rim of Russia; the dimming and dying of the coral reefs; it felt as if all these losses were spreading across the planet like darkness and sorrow, and the thought was too heavy for her to hold, too terrifying to confront.

But Michael recovered. When he was taken off the heavy drugs, his spirit returned. His eyes cleared and brightened, he went back to work. He was given different medications. The pharmaceutical industry kept on producing, and there was always the possibility that a new drug would be the solution. He saw different doctors: clinical psychologists, psychotherapists, more psychiatrists and psychopharmacologists. Isabel became expert at watching for early warnings and at taking steps to intervene, to stop a sudden plunge into despair.

And when Michael was back, he was back. He was funny, alive, quick, loving. It was as though these episodes had never happened, as though someone else had sat heavy-eyed in the metal chair, staring at the pond at Giverny. This alive Michael belonged to Isabel and Ben.

He sat with them at the kitchen table one Saturday morning, reading the newspaper out loud.

"How about this, Benny?" he asked. " 'Mysterious goat found on Upper East Side.' "

Ben looked up from his toast. "Goat? Did you say 'goat' or 'boat'?"

"Goat. Listen to this: 'Early morning birdwatchers in Central Park, their binoculars trained on the red-tailed hawks' nest, were surprised to see an unfamiliar silhouette against the urban dawn skyline. They watched with increasing excitement as a mountain goat, followed by a small herd of others, made its way unconcernedly from the stepped roof of one luxury building to the next, making small neat jumps from ledge to ledge along the row of Fifth Avenue residences.' "

"Mountain goats?" Ben asked, smiling, frowning, understanding that he was being teased, tugged along in the wake of his father's exuberance.

Isabel looked at Michael, who looked at the paper. "The animals were identified as a rare Asian silky-feathered angora—"

"Feathered!" Ben exclaimed, seizing on an error. Now triumphantly suspicious, he shook his head.

But Michael refused to be caught. He looked at Ben and shrugged. "That's how they're described, apparently. 'Feathered.' That's what it says here. I think they look like birds. I think they may be descended *from* birds, actually."

Michael went on pretending to read, spinning out the tale, and Isabel and Ben listened, admiring, delighted, beloved. This was Michael.

When Michael put himself forward for London, he had not had a serious episode in four years, or at least none the office knew about. Most of the time he functioned very well, and all of the time he functioned at work.

In the early nineties, after over a decade at *Bulletin,* Michael was asked to run the London bureau. It was a demonstration of company confidence, and he was elated. Isabel shared his excitement: England would be an adventure. She would find something to do, and EPR promised to keep her job for when she returned.

The bad part about London was the problem of Ben: that year he was to start boarding school outside Boston. Should they instead bring him to England and plunge him into an alien culture during this fragile adolescent passage? Or should they leave him in America at the school he'd chosen, three thousand miles away?

Michael thought Ben should come with them. "We're doing it, he should do it. Why wouldn't we bring him? Of course he should come. That will be home, that will be where we all live." He and Isabel were in the bedroom. Michael lay in bed reading a magazine, while Isabel walked about in her nightgown, tidying up, distracted.

"I know, but we're not going to live there forever," Isabel said. She spread a sweater flat on the bed to fold it. "All his friends will be in America."

"Except for his friends in England, whom he'll meet."

"But he's in a really good school here, Michael." Isabel flipped down the sweater's arms and tucked in the sides. "We won't be able to get him into a really good school in England, starting so late. A, he's American, and B, all these kids are put down for schools at birth. We're fourteen years late in applying."

"What is it you want?" Michael asked. He looked over at her. "Don't you want him to come with us?"

"Oh, I do, of course I want him with us." Isabel put the sweater into her bureau and shut the drawer. She turned to Michael. "I don't know what the right thing is to do."

"Why not ask him, my love?" Michael said. "He'll have a point of view. And it is arguably his life."

Ben, it turned out, was adamant.

"I'm staying," he told his parents. "I don't want to go over there and meet a bunch of people I'll never see again and lose all my friends here."

"But these are people you'll see again," Isabel said, now taking the other side. "If they're friends, you'll have them forever."

"No," Ben said, resolute, his head down. He was leaning in the doorway to their room, his hands in the pockets of his pants. "No way. I'm not going."

"Ben, it will be fun being in London," Michael said, nettled. "There are people who actually like going to live in exciting places. You act as though this is some terrible sentence."

Ben merely shook his head again. "I'll come over and visit you. But I'm staying here."

"But you'll be so far away, Benbo," Isabel said at last, admitting to the heart of the matter. "We'll miss you so much. We won't ever see you."

Ben grinned. "Well, isn't that sort of the point? Of boarding school?"

"It's not meant to be three thousand miles away," Isabel said.

"I'll come over for Thanksgiving and Christmas," Ben said. "And spring vacation. You can come see me in between. How often do you want?" He smiled at her. "Ma."

Ben was getting big, his shoulders widening, his frame shooting up, starting on its awkward shifts toward manhood. Isabel found his new size oddly impressive. She found herself deferring to him simply because he was tall and looked more powerful, more grown-up. Now the strange clothes he wore, the too big, baggy, tattered pants, the hulking running shoes covered with arcane insignia, the layers of floppy T-shirts and sweatshirts, all seemed outside her domain. They were things she could no longer challenge, though she'd have forbidden them at once when he was a foot shorter than she. Now they identified him as part of another tribe. Actually, it was mostly wonderful to watch. She was proud of his transformation, delighted that he had such a rich internal source of strength, independent of his parents. He was magically becoming his own person.

She smiled back at him.

Ben raised his eyebrows at her. "Ma," he said again.

In the end, since Ben was determined and they were not, they let him decide. They would go and he would stay, though Isabel dreaded the separation. What if they had a child in London? Shouldn't Ben be there for the birth of his sister? But that was an argument she did not make out loud.

Chapter 19

In London Isabel found a furnished flat on a quiet square in South Kensington. It was owned by a young couple called the Menzies, who were being sent to Tokyo.

Andrew Menzies, in his late thirties and said to be a financial wizard in the City, was tall and very thin, with stovepipe arms and legs. He wore impeccable dark suits and striped shirts with crisp white collars. He frowned reprovingly when he spoke, and shot his cuffs with an opulent glitter of links. His wife, Diana, was cool and blond. Walking Isabel through the flat, she wore an ice-blue sheath and low pale sling-back heels with black shiny tips. Her hair was short, modishly cropped to the nape of her neck. She walked ahead and talked over her shoulder, telling Isabel what they would leave behind.

Isabel wished the Menzies would take everything with them. The flat itself was light and pleasant, but the furniture was formal and the atmosphere glacial. The sitting room, as Diana called it, was pale and lifeless, with cream-colored carpeting and heavy brocade curtains, belted with thick knotted cords.

"These will stay," Diana announced. She waved at the floor-length curtains, fringed with gilt.

"Lovely," Isabel murmured, dismayed. She was not grand enough for these.

"And that," Diana said, pointing to a rigid upright sofa, stiff, narrow, in pale-blue-and-white-striped satin.

"Oh good," Isabel said. Worse: the surface would show every touch, though the sofa was so unwelcoming that no one would sit on it. Diana moved rapidly ahead, making announcements.

"What sort of a place have you found in Tokyo?" Isabel asked conversationally.

"It's rather nice, actually," Diana said, her voice brightening. "Some Americans had it. They're going back to New York."

"Musical chairs," Isabel said idly. "Too bad you're not going to New York."

Diana turned around fully for the first time and stared curiously at Isabel, her hand on her sheathed hip. " 'Musical chairs'?" she repeated. "It's too bad we're not going to New York?"

"I mean, you could have had our apartment. We could have traded places," Isabel explained, suddenly fixed in Diana's cold blue stare.

Diana raised her eyebrows and turned away. "Oh, yes," she said dismissively, "I see what you mean." She went on toward the kitchen.

Isabel followed, wondering if Diana was as rude as she seemed. Weren't the English famous for perfect manners? She, Isabel, must be reading the signals wrong; there must be some cultural gap she didn't understand.

"We're taking that," Diana said, waving at a small, pretty mahogany bookcase, one of the few things Isabel liked.

I should make a list, Isabel thought. She would have to learn how to weave their life into this new world. Perhaps she should put the striped sofa into storage, or ask Diana to. Would that be expensive? Offensive? She didn't want Diana to swing around on her again, hand on her hip. Perhaps Isabel could disguise the sofa, disarm it. Fat pillows in the corners, a shawl thrown over the back. Would that be charming? Or absurd? It would look odd and temporary, hybrid and awkward, but wasn't that how their life here would be?

"You should make a list of what I'm leaving," Diana informed her, not looking around.

They moved in October.

Their part of the city was quiet, full of handsome brick houses with white trim, shady garden squares fenced with black wrought iron. Everything was clean and well maintained. Isabel loved the somber elegance of the neighborhood, and of the city itself. She loved the red double-decker buses, ponderous and top-heavy, groaning along Piccadilly in clouds of sweet, lethal exhaust. She loved the buses' gallant color, the same red that was on the flag, the neat telephone kiosks, the guards at Buckingham Palace—a brilliant scarlet, brave and alive against the endless gray of the weather.

Isabel also loved the charming details of London—who would not? The tiny cobblestone mews, the freshly painted front doors, the window boxes of gay blooms. The glass milk bottles set trustingly in metal boxes on clean front steps, beneath the gleam of brass doorknobs. She liked the innocent assumption that these tidy domestic arrangements would be unchallenged.

The people made an entirely different statement. If the symmetrical architecture, the bright flower boxes and milk bottles, suggested stability and order, the faces on the street declared flux. It seemed that half of them were from the Indian subcontinent, people with liquid brown eyes, long, glossy black hair, heavy swinging braids. The women's heads were wrapped in shawls, and they wore short wool coats over rustling silk saris. Gleaming gold studs nestled by dark nostrils; exotic moons were set on dark foreheads.

The man at the corner newsstand had a dense glistening pompadour and large, restless, gleaming black eyes. He took Isabel's money with impossibly beautiful hands: narrow and graceful, with slender, coffee-colored fingers.

Isabel, standing in the crowded shop waiting for her change, briefly met his liquid gaze. He was young, maybe thirty. She wondered how long he had been in this cold, sprawling northern city, and if he felt at home yet. Was he settled in with cousins and parents and children, did he have his own safe neighborhoods, friends, restaurants, or did he still feel, as she did, alien and *dépaysé*?

For it was strange, how strange she felt there. England was America's cousin: didn't they share genes, culture, political institutions, language? But knowing the language only revealed how complete your foreignness was, how much you had to learn before you understood the English. Isabel felt rebuffed by the cool oblique responses, mystified by the arcane exclusionary codes that were somehow embedded in her own language.

But Michael felt no such sense of exclusion. He was a part of the international community, on the inside of everything. *Bulletin* had its elegant office in a modern high-rise near Pall Mall. There were three other writers there: two Americans and a friendly, laconic Brit. The secretary was a pleasant middle-aged Englishwoman.

Michael was elated to be in London and in charge. He was full of ideas: he wanted to invigorate his staff, infuse them with enthusiasm. He wanted to reveal and explain the soul of England to the world. He came home at night humming with energy. Daily he delivered new opinions.

"I'll tell you what's interesting," he told Isabel one evening. They were in the tiny kitchen, and Isabel was slicing beets. Michael walked back and forth on the tiled floor, holding a glass of water. "The way geography influences character."

"How do you mean?" Isabel asked. She was wearing a long wool skirt with a long sweater over it: in England women did not wear pants. Here they wore droopy ankle-length skirts or short tight skirts, but not trousers. Isabel had chosen the droopy look, with thick tights underneath. At home she wore a heavy sweater: London was cold. The whole city seemed permeated by a creeping damp that lay in the bones of the buildings. It was untouched by the inadequate heating systems— the ornate, ancient lukewarm radiators, the thin glowing coral lines in the electric heaters, the strangely tepid gas fires. Most of the time Isabel was chilled, hunching her shoulders and nursing her elbows.

Michael took a gulp of water. "The English are an island people. They're literally insular, detached. It has a profound effect on their foreign policy."

"How, for example?" Isabel asked.

"For example. They're deeply suspicious of the rest of Europe," Michael said.

"But so is Europe tremendously suspicious of the rest of Europe," Isabel said. She swept the bits of carrot together and carried them to the bin. "Isn't it? Aren't they all like that? Look at France and Germany."

Michael shook his head. "Not the same way," he said. "The rest of Europe shares frontiers and enemies, climate, landscapes, lots of things. And they've always had to get along with each other, they've had to work out differences over boundaries and trade. But England is separate. They share nothing with people on the Continent."

Michael drank lengthily from his glass, then went on, "Look at language, for example. Europeans grow up learning each other's languages. They're used to different prononciations, different rhythms, different syntax. They know all of it's real, their neighbors speak it. Europeans are famously good linguists; lots of them speak three or four languages. The Brits are famously bad linguists; it's rare for them to speak even a second language with any fluency. Even when they do, they're bad at accents and pronunciation. It's as though there's only one way to form words—the English way. It's a kind of linguistic colonialism. It's so interesting!"

Michael was full of ideas. He had theories about democracy, about racism, about agriculture and the British sensibility. He had notions about the Labour party and the Tories, about the constitutional monarchy. He was in his element.

Running a bureau was new to him, of course—supervising, preparing budgets and reports, holding meetings. Administration. Watching Michael navigate all this made Isabel apprehensive—change was risky for him—but this change seemed only to invigorate him. It was all part of the challenge.

Isabel herself was unable to get working papers. (Michael saw this as another example of British insularism. "It's like the canine quarantine laws," he said. "It's island policy. They want to keep foreigners out.") She found an environmental agency, however, that permitted a foreigner to volunteer three days a week.

The Landscape Trust had its offices in three large rooms on the ground floor of a shabby eighteenth-century house near Kentish Town. The furniture was battered, and the plaster walls were covered with fine cracks. The marble fireplaces had not held a flame in decades. A luxurious layer of dust blanketed the elegant moldings and cornices, and the marble-tiled floors were scuffed and dull. Still, the high ceilings and lofty proportions gave the place dignity, a sense of historical grandeur.

The head of Landscape Trust was an elderly Englishman named Trevor Moot. He had small blue eyes and bottle-thick glasses. He had a bulbous nose and pouched pink cheeks. Wild white tufts blossomed from his ears like wisps of down escaping from a pillow. Arriving in the mornings, he would unwrap a long red woolen scarf from his neck, bowing ceremoniously, as though greeting a monarch. The top of his head was quite bare and shiny from the cold air.

He was kindly and absentminded. "Oh, good *morning,*" he would say to Isabel, smiling and nodding. Sometimes after a moment he would add triumphantly, "Isabel."

There were two others in the office: an idle, fair-haired young man, Hugh Connor, who spent most of the day in his tiny dusty office with the door shut, making lengthy telephone calls to people Isabel suspected were his friends; and a middle-aged woman, Edwina Collinsworth, very brisk, with short tight blond curls and an air of cold and terrifying politeness. Isabel's friendly overtures toward Edwina met with limited success.

"We went down to see Petworth last weekend," Isabel told her soon after starting at Landscape Trust. "We just loved it. It's so beautiful, all that Grinling Gibbons carving, and then that whole roomful of Turners."

"Mm, you liked it, did you." Edwina gave her a tight, pursed smile. "Mm, yes," she said judiciously, "Petworth is rather good." She looked back down at her desk.

Isabel, who had meant simply to demonstrate goodwill, felt she was being chided for not having known that Petworth was rather good and, worse, for showing enthusiasm. Enthusiasm, apparently, was to be kept to oneself. As for knowing about things: it seemed that everyone in England had prior knowledge about everything.

The trust sent out newsletters describing environmental problems and soliciting funds. Little money actually came in, and it was unclear to Isabel what would have happened if it had: the trust didn't seem to lobby any more than it litigated. Its mission appeared to be educating the public in a mildly unfocused manner. But education was a good thing, and the office was a pleasant place to work.

In the morning, after Trevor hung his scarf on the coat stand and had or had not remembered Isabel's name, he would smile energetically at the room, rub his dry old hands together and stride into his grand but shabby office as though about to vanquish pollution that minute.

Isabel smiled back at him. She sat at her desk reading about hedgerows and listening to Hugh's drawling voice from behind his closed door as he made his complicated plans: "Is anyone else going to be there, do you know?"

Isabel did like learning the English perspective on the environment; she liked the affable Trevor and the indolent Hugh; she even liked tight-mouthed and diligent Edwina.

Life in London began to feel settled. Ben came for Thanksgiving vacation, and the fact of his presence in the apartment—"the flat"—changed the place; it became more familiar, familial. Isabel and Michael took Ben to their favorite places, surprised to realize they had them. They were making a life. They made friends, among them the laconic Brit from Michael's office, James Sutherland. They met American expats, and Isabel met some Englishwomen, friends of friends: Eva, a cultural historian, dauntingly brilliant and exceedingly kind, who took Isabel to museums. James's girlfriend, Cynthia, a young single mother, blond and outgoing, full of hilarious stories. There were others as well. London began to feel like a community, and Isabel like a member of it.

Coming in to work one morning, she told Edwina, "We saw the best movie last night. You must see it: *The Piano.*"

Edwina lifted her eyebrows. "*The Piano.* How interesting," she said, her voice bright. "I must make a note of that."

Isabel smiled. "Yes, you must," she said, "you'd love it." She no longer worried about seeming gauche and enthusiastic: she was American, she *was* gauche and enthusiastic. And who knew? Edwina might love the movie. Maybe a tempestuous feminist story of obsessive passion was what Edwina secretly longed for.

Isabel had her own secret longing, of course. She was hoping her body would quietly unlock, now that she was in a new part of the globe, tilted at a different angle from the sun. It might easily happen. People were always telling her to relax and stop thinking about getting pregnant, and then it would happen. Relaxing and not thinking about it was impossible, but she thought that here, in a strange land, anything might happen. Their life in England was an adventure.

One afternoon at work Edwina came past Isabel's desk carrying a cup of tea. She was slightly pigeon-toed, and her high heavy heels made a clumping noise with each step. She stopped, and Isabel looked up.

"Oh, Isabel," Edwina said, "I went to see that film you recommended, *The Piano.*" She pronounced it "piahno."

"Oh, you did?" Isabel asked, surprised. Now she felt faintly guilty: recommending the movie to Edwina, with her prissy curls and clumpy shoes, had been almost a joke. "Did you like it?"

"Very much," Edwina said in her clipped metallic voice. "Very, very much. It was really brilliant. Thank you so much for telling me about it."

Isabel stared at her. "I'm so glad," she said. Had Edwina seen the right movie? "I'm glad you liked it."

"I did," Edwina said calmly. "Very much. Thank you." She clumped off to her desk, her pleated skirt swaying modestly.

That night in bed Isabel told Michael about the exchange, mimicking Edwina's polished upper-class delivery. " 'Veddy veddy much. Thenk you,' " said Isabel. "It's a complete mystery. Either she never saw the movie at all, and she just saw me and thought it was something to say, or else Edwina has a much richer interior life than I thought she did."

"Of course she does. Englishwomen are hot as snakes, didn't you know that?" Michael said. "All that decorousness is just a ruse."

Isabel laughed. "Edwina, hot as a snake, is a wonderful idea. I'm going to start looking at everyone here in a new way."

"Hot as a snake," Michael repeated, musing. "Which reminds me." He slid his hand under her bare back.

When Isabel looked back at that time in London, it was impossible to remember when things began to change, but it seemed that, as she began to feel more free and comfortable, Michael began to feel less so. His excitement began slowly turning to tension.

She remembered hearing the first complaint about the American in Michael's office, Harold Benton. It was after dinner; Michael and Isabel were in their bedroom. Isabel was under the covers. Michael was still dressed, lying restlessly on top of the bedspread, his stocking feet crossed. He was watching television, changing channels with the remote control, and Isabel was trying to read. On the screen three frowning men in suits sat at a long desk.

"The situation is, quite frankly, alarming," said the man on the right. He spoke with great conviction, folding his arms. "It must not be permitted to continue unchecked. I call on the international community to take action."

Isabel looked down at her book.

"Here's what Benton did today," Michael said, his eyes on the screen.

"I actually must say I do not agree with my learned colleague," drawled the man on the left. "This is a matter that should be dealt with very carefully. The international community must not be drawn into it."

"Harold Benton?" asked Isabel.

Michael nodded. "I was in my office on the phone, having a conversation that was actually rather delicate. Benton walked in without asking and sat down. I looked at him and sort of waved at him to go away, to let him know I'd be awhile, and he nodded and crossed his legs. He just sat there during my whole conversation." Michael shook his head irritably. "Finally I hung up and asked him what he wanted, and he announced that he thought we should have an office meeting once a week."

"There are different methods of dealing with this sort of internal dispute," said the man in the middle.

"An office meeting?" Isabel asked. This didn't sound terrible, but she knew from Michael's voice that it was. She watched the three men intently.

"Every week," Michael said. "For one thing, I'm trying to make this place less bureaucratic, not *more*. For another, I'm running the office, not Harold Benton." He pointed the control and clicked, and the three men were replaced by a dark figure struggling along the rocky side of a mountain. ". . . high above the busy streets of Boulder, Colorado," an announcer said in a low, confidential voice, "there is another sort of lifestyle that Americans, particularly Coloradans, embrace." The camera pulled back to a long shot of the mountaineer, now tiny, flattened against a sheer red cliff.

"What did you say to him?" Isabel asked, looking now at the mountain climber. The tiny figure moved sideways, one limb at a time, finding a precarious hold on the rock, shifting its weight slowly.

Michael clicked, and the three men reappeared briefly, then disappeared. "I said, basically, no. I told him I want the writers to be independent," he said. "I want them to have time for their own projects, not to get bogged down in bureaucracy. And that I'd call the fucking meetings when we need them."

He clicked. On the screen was a farmer in a wide field, surrounded by a herd of unsettled sheep. The sheep made steady bleating sounds.

"Not anymore," the farmer said into the microphone held out to him. Isabel, who was trying to learn the regional accents, wondered if his was West Country or Welsh.

"He's so fucking arrogant," Michael said. "Who does he think he is?"

"Michael, if you want to talk, could you please switch off the TV?" Isabel asked. "I can't concentrate with it on."

Michael kept his eyes on the screen, but he clicked again and the sound stopped. The farmer's mouth kept on moving, and the sheep, too, kept lifting their heads and milling around, moving their mouths and crying soundlessly. Watching them, Isabel imagined the sound of their voices; she imagined them just below the level of her hearing. She imagined she could hear them intermittently. She wondered who the farmer was, and what the problem was.

"Who is Benton, anyway?" she asked Michael. "It sounds as though you already don't like him."

Michael shrugged, watching the screen. "Right. I don't. He's a protégé of Jeff Goodnoe, in New York, and he thinks he's God's gift. What I'm trying to do is give the writers a chance to expand their views. That's sort of the point of being here, expanding your view. But Benton is a superbureaucrat. He's always saying things like 'I think we should adopt a policy on this' or 'I'd be more comfortable if the office had a clear position here.' "

Michael clicked and the glottal stutter of the sheep filled the room, mindless, distraught. Were they merely thirsty, Isabel wondered, was the farmer's well dry—the result of global warming, horrible but known—or was there some new, more horrible sheep threat? Before she could hear the answer, Michael clicked. The mountain climber reappeared, inching his way up a giant overhang. It made Isabel sick to watch him. "He's going to fall," she said, "switch it off."

"He won't fall," Michael said. "They're never live, these things."

"How do you know?" Isabel asked. "TV loves grisly stuff. They're always announcing some horrible accident live from somewhere, or else they simulate it."

"This is a successful climber," Michael said, watching. The tiny black figure was on his back, hanging from his feet and hands, barely moving, inching along under the hideous jut of the overhang. "The guy's fine. He made it."

"You don't know," Isabel said, "you don't know."

The announcer said nothing, and in silence they watched the climber. The silence, the vast swing of air beneath him, the terrible slowness of the movements made it unbearable.

"Please, Michael," Isabel said, "please turn it off."

But Michael stared without answering, and Isabel looked down at her book, trying to block from her mind whatever was going to happen.

Benton's name became a code word between them, and whenever Michael said it, his voice turned insulting. Everything about the man was offensive to Michael.

"Have you ever *tried* having office meetings?" Isabel asked him once.

Michael turned on her. "Thank you for your thoughts on management," he said coldly. "I wasn't aware I'd asked for your opinion."

Isabel subsided, and after that, when Michael brought up Benton's name, Isabel was only sympathetic.

Twice a year the *Bulletin* foreign-bureau chiefs met in New York. Isabel went with Michael on these trips and watched as Michael's tension rose. The demands on him had changed. As a New York editor, he had never had to produce an annual budget or defend a management policy. Isabel hoped the magazine understood that administration wasn't Michael's forte; that it wasn't meant to be. He was a brilliant journalist, and the magazine was lucky to have him, in London or anywhere else. Didn't they know that?

On the flight back to London after the third meeting, Michael put a black sleep mask over his eyes, though it was daytime. He sat beside Isabel for hours, blinded and silent, though she could see from his hands that he was not asleep.

It seemed as though Benton's discontent began to contaminate the atmosphere in New York: the tension over the meetings grew worse. And in the second year Isabel noticed that Michael talked about his superiors in a new tone. In the past he had always talked like a favorite son about his father. Even when he was irritated or angry, he was certain of his position. "*Now* what do they want?" he would say good-naturedly, shaking his head. "Do they know? Not a clue." He was talking about men he respected, trusted, liked. But these days his voice was challenging and wary: "New York'll have something to say about this, I'm sure." He sounded hostile, embattled.

It was during the second year that Michael stopped coming home at night full of observations about the English. Now he came home silent.

Isabel had no one like Netta in London, no one to whom she could risk confiding her anxieties. As Michael's mood turned darker, Isabel turned inward. At home she was quiet and watchful. She missed Ben.

It was strange and disorienting, living without her son, like losing a limb: it was useless to remind herself that he would have been gone even if they had stayed. Isabel felt unbearably far away, and the time difference made telephone calls difficult. She could feel Ben's presence— vivid, warm, bright—but so removed, so unreachable, like a distant star. She savored his few brief letters, reading them over and over, learning the few mysterious bits of information he let drop about his new world. She loved the idea of Ben's progress, the way he was moving into his own life, but she missed him. She thought even more of a second child. Every time Michael complained about work, Isabel's mind went automatically to another child. All these tensions would be resolved by the arrival of a second child. The thought was like a talisman.

In the third year Isabel went to see a British doctor. He was a genius, a miracle worker. Everyone he treated became pregnant. Someone's cousin had gone to him after decades of infertility and had three children in four years. Well: someone in a foreign land might easily be more artful, his magic stronger.

Dr. Wickershaw was thin and gray, with a long, judicious face and lined cheeks. He listened to Isabel's history and then asked if she had considered in vitro fertilization.

Isabel had, of course. It made her skin crawl. The process was chilling: clinical removal of eggs and sperm from their hosts' bodies, then their public seclusion in vitro, urged chemically to mate, the resulting embryo replaced inside the womb. The whole thing seemed odious, monstrous: everything so unnatural, so radical. Isabel would never do it.

"You might consider it," the doctor said.

Isabel looked at him across the big mahogany desk. He waited for her response, and as he waited, she understood from his silence that this was all there was left. She had tried everything else during fourteen years. This was her last chance. He had no magic.

That evening she told Michael. They were in their bedroom. The Menzies had covered the walls in silver-leaf paper that shone with a dull luster, like the background of an Italian altarpiece. Isabel stood with her back to Michael, straightening the things on her bureau. She moved her hairbrush to the center of the linen runner. "I want to do it," she said. She could see Michael's face reflected in the hanging mirror. She kept her eyes down.

"In vitro," Michael said. "God."

"I really want to do it," Isabel said. Her voice was on the edge of trembling. She set the matching comb beside the brush. "I really want to do it." She did not dare turn around.

"Isabel," he said, "when are you going to stop? What's the end of this?"

"Don't ask me that," Isabel said, furious. "I want to do it."

"In vitro is so—extreme," Michael said, distaste in his voice.

"This is extreme," Isabel said. She started to cry. "Where we are is extreme. We have no choice, Michael." She had never felt so powerless, so abject.

"If you want to do it, we will," Michael said finally, but she could hear in his voice that this was the limit, this was as far as he would go.

When Michael came home from his first appointment, he told Isabel about the cramped bathroom in the doctor's suite, the nurse handing him a small glass jar.

" 'This is for your sample,' she said, and then she leaned down and opened the cupboard door under the sink. 'And here are these if you need them.' There was a stack of old porn magazines." Michael grimaced. "Then she shut the door, leaving me with the little jar and those magazines. The room was so small I could hardly sit down. It was revolting. Christ. I felt like a cow."

"I'm sorry," Isabel said.

"It's not your fault," Michael told her, but they both knew it was.

Isabel gave herself the hormone shots, sitting on the bathtub. Syringe in one hand, she twisted around struggling to grab her own buttock with the other. Her flesh shrank from the cold metal stab, but this was worth it. Anything was worth it.

During these months, Michael was working on a long article about the emerging European community and the English response. He came home quiet and preoccupied. Isabel, hugging to herself the notion of pregnancy, was preoccupied as well. The baby filled her mind.

"How's the piece coming?" she asked.

"Fine," Michael said brusquely; he seemed annoyed.

A certain tension began to emerge around discussion of the piece, and the next time Isabel asked about it, Michael said it had been shelved.

"What does that mean, 'shelved'?" Isabel asked.

"It means shelved," Michael told her. "It means I'm not working on it now."

Isabel wondered whose decision it had been to shelve it, but it was a question she was not ready to ask. She could not risk any discord during this precarious journey toward pregnancy. What if they had a fight at the last minute and Michael refused to participate? Isabel asked no risky questions. She made soothing comments and hugged her secret knowledge to herself. Now, when she passed a mother on the street pushing a baby carriage, she felt a secret affiliation, exultation. *Just a few more months,* she thought, glancing down into the carriage at the wrapped bundle, the alert pink face.

When the time came, Isabel, under anesthesia and in a hospital bed, was harvested of seven healthy eggs. Michael, under sordid conditions of sexual manipulation, harvested himself of a sticky plume of invisible sperm. Separate from both parents, behind the closed doors of a laboratory, among strangers, the mating process began.

Isabel lay in her hospital bed, weepy and tremulous with anesthetic but buoyant with certainty: *Seven eggs.* Michael came and sat beside her. He held her hand, his face somber. In the evening Isabel was sent home; that night she slept wrapped around Michael. During the night she dreamed of clambering along a rocky beach, searching for something, over and over. She woke each time to find Michael beside her. She was elated, hallucinatory: she was pregnant.

In the morning he left for the office. "I'll come home as soon as you hear," he told Isabel. "Call me right away."

Isabel nodded. She did not need to speak. She moved in a bright cloud. In the kitchen, in her bathrobe and slippers, she sat and read the paper. She had all morning; they'd said they'd call by noon. Isabel read an interview with the head of Covent Garden. She sipped her cold tea. She considered heating the kettle but felt a superstitious reluctance to move. She did not want to alter the balance of the universe with even an insignificant gesture. Everything was significant. For everything was aligned: she could feel the celestial spheres set perfectly in their courses. She could feel the perfect logic that connected everything, from this small painted kitchen in South Kensington to the radiant orbs spinning gorgeously in space. She could feel the perfection of the universe, could hear its inaudible humming. She was pregnant. She looked at the clock. She waited for the sound of the telephone.

The kitchen was silent. She looked again at the clock, leafed on through the paper.

When the telephone rang, Isabel did not move. Suddenly the sound was terrifying. Logic fell away, and she was no longer certain of anything. The phone hung on the wall by the window; Isabel sat still. It rang again and she stood. After the fourth ring, Isabel picked it up, closing her eyes.

"Hello?"

"Mrs. Green?"

Isabel knew at once from the nurse's voice—cautious, slightly monitory—what she had to say. Listening, Isabel stood at the window.

The sky was cloudy but bright. Down below, the owner's back garden was green and luxurious, the foliage glowing in the soft London light. In one corner, against the brick wall, was a big rosebush, apricot blossoms against glossy leaves. Isabel could not take her eyes from the roses.

"Yes, I see," Isabel answered. "It didn't. No, I see." She kept her voice perfectly controlled, as though this was the crucial thing. All her concentration went to keeping her voice pleasant. "I see," she said again. "Yes." At the end she said politely, "Thank you for calling."

When she hung up, she stood still.

The rosebush was massed against the dry porous brick. The plant seemed peculiarly vivid, radiating a sinister potency. And it was covered in those pale blooms; they were crowding one another horridly amid the foliage.

So lush, Isabel thought, *for a city garden.* How did they manage to grow here? The blooms, that strange pinkish yellow. Isabel leaned closer to the window, pressing her forehead against the cool glass. Then she put her hands over her eyes.

The four years in London were like the arc of the sun, and there was a point that Isabel missed as you might miss noon. Until then she still looked forward with anticipation, still felt that things were yet to come, looking forward to the rest of their stay in London. She looked forward to knowing the city better, learning more of its streets and neighborhoods. She looked forward to the next time they would meet with friends—to dinner at the Brasserie Saint Quentin with James and Cynthia, a new exhibition at the V&A with Eva. She planned to get the leak fixed under the kitchen sink, to introduce Ben on his next vacation to the son of new friends, to visit the Scottish Borders and the Welsh Marches.

That moment was like the point in a solar arc when the light imperceptibly changes from easterly, rising, to westerly, waning. Isabel's face turned to America, and what she began to feel toward England was a sense of dogged endurance, not what she had felt earlier—delighted anticipation. Without realizing it, Isabel had turned against London, the cold buildings, the dreary skies, the chilly faces. Partly she missed Ben and longed to live near him again. Partly London was the scene of her own failure. It was, worst of all—and this was the thing that held her heart in its grip—the fact of Michael's growing gloom. There were times when she understood that it was overtaking them.

Chapter 20

They moved back to New York in early spring. By then living greens had begun to emerge, miraculously, against the grays of winter. Even in the city's concrete landscape, the air softened, the trees turned fresh. Leaves began to open, pale yellow-green envelopes unfolding further each day, heralding lusher, more voluminous developments.

The furniture arrived, from London and from storage, in one long day of sweaty men in T-shirts trudging silently back and forth, wheeling trolleys through disordered hallways. Tables and chairs were carried upside down, legs and undersides bared. Hidden grime was exposed, puffs of dust eddied weightlessly in corners.

Everything was set in its old places. Boxes were unpacked, books put on their shelves, the apartment cleaned. Isabel and Michael were back in their lives, and she waited to feel comforted, reconnected.

But now New York seemed odd. The city seemed so big and impersonal, and the cars were on the wrong side of the road. The people were so loud and rude, so sloppy. The streets were so dirty and the traffic homicidal. Isabel couldn't be missing London—could she?

She'd once seen a list of stressful events in which moving was surpassed only by divorce and death of a loved one. But she was moving back home, not away, and forewarned was forearmed, wasn't it? Then why was she so nervy? Why did everything seem so risky, so uncertain?

Early one morning Isabel stood in her nightgown at the bedroom window, looking out. The buildings beyond, washed in deep blue shadow, blocked most of the sky. Between them an angular pathway framed a small restive triangle of the distant river. The combination—the somber vista through the darkened buildings, the remote scintillation of the water—struck at Isabel like fear. Where was the relief at being home? Where were their real lives?

It seemed that home had changed. The apartment had become strange in their absence. Everything seemed slightly altered. The dimensions of the rooms, the angles of the corners, the length of the hallways all seemed to have shifted. Lingering in the rooms was evidence of the tenants: a greasy mark on the living room wall, a deep scrape on the hall floor. The door on a kitchen cupboard now merely bumped against the frame before drifting to settle, slightly open, in midair.

The tenants had been perfectly pleasant, an academic couple in their sixties, with private means. The husband, a visiting professor said to be brilliant on European history, medieval to modern, was silent, tall and cadaverous. His wife was small, effusive and thick-waisted, with a piled mass of weightless, dyed black hair. They'd left behind no real damage, only intangible spoor: the invasive sense of them, their intimate strangeness seeping into every space. The woman had stood at Isabel's bathroom sink, her reflection in Isabel's mirror; had called to her husband, who lay on Michael's side of the bed. Their bodies had sighed, sweated, given off odors and sounds.

Isabel, waking in the middle of one night, was uncertain where she was, if the bed was against the right wall, if Michael was where he ought to be, beside her. And she still missed Ben. When they'd left America, he had been only fourteen, nearly a child: he was now eighteen, a senior at school, nearly a man. He was caught up in the swirl of adolescence: sports, strange scratchy music, weird baggy clothes, street slang, odd haircuts, an incomprehensible life. Drugs, presumably.

All the authorities urged you to talk to your child, but by the time he reached adolescence, the word itself—"drugs"—had acquired a peculiar and risky charge that made the subject strangely difficult. What was it you were meant to say? The fact that drugs were illegal complicated everything. How could you discuss them openly? If you asked your son what was going on and he said "We smoke dope every night," how did you respond? If you didn't try to stop it, you were tacitly condoning it, and if you did try to stop it, you were betraying a confidence. And if he said "I've never taken drugs," did you believe it? Or did you feel you'd made him lie?

Isabel had thought they'd reconnect easily with Ben—they'd visit him at school, he'd come home on weekends. He'd call often. She assumed that their closeness, interrupted temporarily by distance, would naturally be knit back together. But it was becoming apparent to her that this would not happen, that the interruption would continue and was due to something besides geography.

It was like moving: Isabel knew that teenagers separated from their parents, had thought she was prepared for it. *It's awkwardness,* she told herself; *he's trying to make up his own life.* But it was disappointing that his new life seemed hardly to include theirs. That he felt the need for them so rarely, that he called so seldom.

When he did call, Isabel was transformed, like an adolescent herself, by emotion. At the sound of his voice, the syllable "Mom?," Isabel stopped reading a report, folding laundry, balancing her checkbook. She set everything down and leaned back as though stretching out before a benevolent sun. She closed her eyes and listened with her whole self.

He called seldom. The pattern of calls and visits had been established while they were in London, and it seemed too late to alter them. Ben's old life seemed no longer to exist. When he came home for the weekend, he stayed in his room most of the day, asleep or on the phone or listening to pounding music or taking lengthy showers. When he finally emerged in the early afternoon, his hair slick, his face moist, he set off at once, pounding purposefully down the front hall. If Isabel heard him in time, she called out—"Benno? You're up?"—and he turned, momentarily caught.

"Hi Mom." He smiled, nodding, raffish in army pants, a shabby sweater, gigantic sneakers.

"Where are you going?" asked Isabel. An idiot's question.

"Just going to meet some guys. I'll be back later," Ben promised, and smiled again. As he spoke, his tall lanky body was in motion, walking backward toward the door; his shining face sweet, apologetic, gone.

"But they're like that, Bel," Michael said. "That's what kids are like."

Isabel wondered whether they'd done something to deserve this exclusion. She had worried about leaving Ben when they went to England, sending him into the care of strangers so far away when he'd been tender, still searching for form. He'd had to learn alone who he was, and now it was done, and maybe this separation would be there forever.

Maybe Michael was right, but what if it wasn't normal, this painful distance? And in any case, it was only Americans who thought it *was* normal that children should routinely turn hostile and antagonistic toward their parents. The French, for example, thought boarding school was inhumane and kept their children at home through college. And they didn't tolerate teenage insolence; French parents still had authority. Family life took precedence: the French had family dinners every Sunday, grandparents at the head and foot, aunts and uncles along the sides, family quarrels and conversations flowing up and down the table and through the years, connecting every member.

So why was this American way of adolescence accepted? Why should it become the model for the rest of the world? If all this was so normal—a child's withdrawal, his silence and distance, the sense of something unspoken and adversarial in the air—why was it so painful to her? And if it wasn't normal, what was the reason for it? What she didn't want it to be, what she pushed from her mind as a possibility, was Michael's moods.

The year they moved back to New York, Isabel was forty-three, and they had been been trying for sixteen years to have a second child. She still felt the longing tug toward motherhood, but hope ebbed with each month. It began to seem that something inside her had altered irretrievably. She felt lessened by this, shamed by the disastrous failure in London. She could not talk about it. She felt punished in some large and unnameable way.

Her life at work offered consolation. EPR had given her back her job, and she shared an office again with Netta. It was a relief to be in a place where projects were defined and goals specific. It was a relief to be working with Netta. Netta's compassion, her pragmatism, her ease in the world offered a kind of refuge.

Several months after Isabel's return, she and Netta went to a nearby sushi restaurant for lunch. As they left the office, they found themselves in a heavy autumn rain. They had coats but no umbrellas, so they ran along the sidewalks, splashing through the deep streams at the curbs.

Inside the restaurant they stood still for a moment, damp and breathless. Their shoes were sodden, their legs wet. They hung their streaming coats by the door. The room was small and crowded, the windows misted. Isabel and Netta were given a tiny table: their knees touched, then slid politely sideways.

"God, my hair's soaked." Netta raked it with her fingers.

"We should have those little pleated plastic rain hats," Isabel said. "Remember those?"

"There's a place in Vermont that still has them," Netta said. "A catalog. It's a voice from the past: open it up and you're in nineteen fifty-nine. They have manual typewriters, and rain booties, and little stick-on patches you wear at night to keep from getting wrinkles."

"I know that one," Isabel said, "I love it. It's one of the catalogs I keep."

"My mail is mostly catalogs," said Netta. "There are days I throw out every single thing that came."

The waiter came, a small Asian man in shirtsleeves and a crew cut. He poured them mineral water and took their orders.

"When I was at boarding school," Isabel said, "the mail was put out by class. My first year our mail was set out in alphabetical rows on the grand piano in the common room. I remember coming in after lunch that first day and being amazed that every letter was handwritten. They were like rows of precious stones. It made you homesick just to see them."

Netta shook her head. "I never see a handwritten letter. Who writes me?" she asked rhetorically. "Bills and catalogs, that's all I get." She drank from her mineral water. "Actually, I love the linens catalogs. I'm a complete sucker for them. I keep a pile of them by my bed and look through them at night. It's like eating chocolates. An addiction."

"The linens," Isabel agreed. "What is it about them? Those immaculate rooms, the sheets turned back, the pillows plumped. The folded quilt, the flowers on the bedside table. It's so unbelievably comforting."

"Mitch says it's like men looking at lingerie catalogs."

"It is," Isabel said. "Domestic porn. Fantasy. I only like the white sheets. Pure white, not the white-on-white patterns. And I don't like that slippery sateen finish. I like the other kind—what's it called?"

"Percale?" Netta said. "The kind we grew up with. The sheets that feel rough when they come out of the dryer."

The sushi arrived on neat laquer trays.

"Or off the clothesline," Isabel said, and had a sudden flash of memory: her mother in the backyard in Bedford Hills, taking in the sheets. Isabel must have been small: her mother's head and shoulders were silhouetted against the sky. Her mother's skirt belled and emptied in the wind. The clothesline made shallow loops between the warped wooden poles leaning up to meet it. On the grass was a wicker basket half full of folded sheets.

Her mother's legs were spread for balance, her arms lifted. The cloth flapped against her grasp, the sheets bucked and rippled in the wind. Her mother unclipped each one, folding and doubling until the boisterous, snapping flag became a neat white packet, quiet but still somehow buoyant, full of sun and air.

For no reason, Isabel—at the memory of her mother's figure rising against the sky, of the soft swelling and emptying of her skirt, of the wild geometry of the swooping line, the rough sunny feel of the sheets—felt her eyes fill.

Netta watched her kindly. "I'm sorry," she said after a moment. "What is it?"

Isabel shook her head, pulling hard against the current of tears. "It's the sheets," she said finally, "drying on the clothesline."

This was ridiculous, and she began to laugh, still crying, and choked on the combination of breath and sobs.

It could not be the sheets. But why was this sea of emotion so near, so troubling? For the tears, once started, would not stop.

"It's moving back here, I guess," Isabel said. She shook her head, trying to clear it, then she crumpled completely and laid the chopsticks down beside her tray. She put her elbows on the table and set her face in her hands. "It's Michael," she said.

"I'm sorry," Netta said again.

Netta knew about Michael. Her husband, Mitch, had given referrals, had advised on treatment and therapies, had approved the place in Westchester. Netta waited while Isabel wept.

When she could talk, Isabel drew a long breath. "Things are really bad," she said. It was a relief to speak the words. "At home it's awful. And something's gone wrong for Michael at work."

"How can you tell?" Netta asked.

"For one thing, they've given him a smaller office."

Netta tilted her head, considering. "That might not mean anything."

"At *Bulletin*?" Isabel said. "It means everything. Everything. The offices are calibrated exactly to people's standing. When he left, Michael had a big office with two windows. Now he has a small one with only one. It sounds small-minded, but it's an emblem. And there are other things like that, but Michael won't talk about them. Or he tells me things but I'm not allowed to answer. He gets furious if I say anything."

"Like what?" Netta asked.

"Oh, you know. There are meetings he isn't invited to. People have lunch together and they don't ask him."

"How does he know this happens?" Netta asked.

"He sees them going off together. He watches—" Isabel paused, her breath catching. "He watches people in the halls. I have this feeling that he looks out and watches the other offices, other people's doorways, to see who comes out and who's been talking to whom."

"It sounds really hard."

"It sounds like a crazy person," Isabel said miserably. "What if he's hiding behind his door looking out through the crack? Or something worse? I don't know what he's doing." She stabbed her straw into the glass of mineral water, releasing a silvery spume of bubbles.

"How does he seem at home?"

"Awful. He doesn't talk," said Isabel. "It's like living with a zombie. He's angry all the time. He eats dinner without looking at me, and if I try to talk to him, it makes him angry. If I don't talk, he's angry anyway. Everything makes him angry. After dinner he puts on earphones and lies down and listens to jazz. Which he's always done, but now it's as if he isn't there. Or as if I'm not." She set the heels of her hands into the corners of her eyes.

Netta put her elbows on the table. "Is he seeing a doctor?" she asked. "Has he seen anyone since you got back?"

"He won't tell me," Isabel said. "He gets furious if I bring it up. I don't dare ask him. I don't know who he's seeing or what he's taking. And the new doctor won't talk to me because that's his rule. Michael's old doctor retired while we were in London, and I called this new one who took over the practice, Dr. Stark, and left a message asking him to call me back. And then he left a message on my machine in this horrible disapproving voice, as though he were the principal and I'd been bad. He said he would have to ask me not to call him again unless Michael gave him permission. He said Michael was his patient, not me, and I would be interfering with the treatment if I tried to talk to him.

But I can't ask Michael, because he'll get furious. So I don't know what's going on. I have this feeling that there's something I should be doing, but what is it? I feel as though I'm inching my way along a cliff in the dark."

She looked down at the table, at the pale wooden chopsticks. She aligned them side by side, matching the smooth tips. She spoke without looking up. "I'm so frightened."

In the steamy restaurant, with the midday clatter of dishes and talk all around them, the small table cramping their legs, Isabel's fear was like a sickening cloud. As she spoke the words, as she named it—fear— it swelled around her, enveloping, suffocating.

———

Usually Michael arrived home by six-thirty, except on Fridays. On other nights, when he stayed late, he let Isabel know beforehand.

The night he came home so late was a Tuesday. Isabel arrived just after six o'clock. She'd stopped at the supermarket on Broadway and walked home afterward. It was dark by then, mid-January, and the streetlamps were on. The air was chilly and damp, but not bitter. The sidewalks shone moistly, and the streetlamps had shimmering haloes. The groceries were heavier than she'd thought, and she set them down once or twice on the way, then again outside the apartment as she looked for her key. She opened the door and stepped into the hall, calling out, "Michael?"

She stood listening, but there was no answer, and she closed the door behind her.

In the kitchen she unpacked the bags, setting the things for dinner on the counter. She went into the bedroom and listened to the messages on the machine: the repairman needed a part before he could fix the washing machine; two hang-ups; a prerecorded promotion of a Catskills resort; the real estate broker from Bridgehampton. Isabel wrote down the broker's number, erased everything and went back into the kitchen. It was nearly seven. Michael would be home any minute, and she started making dinner.

At seven-thirty, wondering if there was something she had forgotten, she called Michael's office. Was he on deadline? Had he told her he was working late? She was put through to his voice mail, which said, "Hello, you've reached Michael Green at *Bulletin*."

The voice was wonderfully familiar. It was a shock to hear it like this, so direct and intimate, the words spoken so deeply into her ear but not meant for her; this message was meant for a stranger. Isabel closed her eyes, listening, struck by the difference between this steady, confident Michael and the one she had become so used to.

"Please leave a message," Michael told her pleasantly, "and I'll call you back."

There was a purposeful beep and an electronically attentive silence. Isabel said nothing, held by his voice, suspended in the listening space. She wanted to leave no message, no trace of her presence—it would annoy him—but still she waited, the phone against her ear. She was reluctant to break the connection to that other Michael.

She considered hanging up and calling again just to hear his voice, to pretend he was talking to her. It felt illicit, though; there was something covert and greedy about it. It was a kind of theft. She would be taking for herself the warmth and courtesy that Michael had intended for strangers.

But she longed to hear that voice. Still listening to the silence, her head bowed, she leaned in to the phone. She might call once more.

"What are you doing?"

It was Michael, using the other voice, the one she heard most often.

Isabel turned. Michael stood behind her in the kitchen doorway, his overcoat open, his collar rumpled.

"I was just calling your office," Isabel said, embarrassed.

"Why?" Michael asked.

"I wondered why you were so late," she said.

"Late?" Michael asked challengingly. He looked at the clock. Seeing him stare like this, accusingly, at her, Isabel felt the black weight of his rage and knew what was coming. There was nothing she could say that would not draw this rage upon her.

"I'm hardly late," Michael said, and left the room.

Isabel looked at the food laid out on the counter: the glutinous slab of swordfish lying on the waxy paper; the plastic bag of spinach; the clutch of new potatoes. They seemed strange, set against the white Formica, and she was caught in a rising tide of panic. Everything seemed unknown. She thought wildly, *How can I do this?*

When dinner was ready, she called Michael. He sat down without looking at her. He began to eat slowly, gazing at his plate. Isabel, studying her own, heard him chewing: a slow interior grinding, not quite even. When he took another bite, there was a pause; then it began again. She heard him stop and wondered what had happened. He wasn't taking another bite, he hadn't swallowed, but he wasn't chewing. What was he thinking? She didn't dare glance at him. It seemed like eavesdropping to listen to his chewing.

Listening to the irregular surfaces of his teeth bearing down on his food became intolerable. She moved in her chair to make noise. Now she could hear herself chewing, the sound of her own swallowing, the uvular gulp. Inside was her throat, larynx, stomach, then the slimy crumpled length of the intestine. Beyond that, worse. She set down her fork and leaned back. Michael was chewing again. He reached for his glass; she heard the wine go down his throat, an enclosed rush.

"Want some more swordfish?" Isabel asked finally.

Michael shook his head. "No thanks," he said. He did not look at her. He wiped his mouth and set down his napkin. He took hold of the table edge in both hands, gripping it as though about to stand. His gaze was fixed on something in the middle of the table. He did not rise; after a moment he took his hands away. His eyes were still focused on the table.

Isabel, to gloss over this, obscure it from them both, set his plate on top of hers and carried them to the sink. That gesture—his seizing of the table to rise and then not rising—was alarming. It seemed as though they were moving toward some sort of precipice.

She wanted to steer them away from it to safer ground. She found it easier to talk with her back to him. Standing at the sink, she began rinsing the dishes, raising her voice above the sound of the water. "The agent from Bridgehampton called about that place. We have to decide about next summer."

Michael said, "Next summer?" There was something odd in his voice, something unmoored.

Isabel went on. "I was thinking we should make some plans."

After a moment Michael said, "Right."

She had not expected him to agree and turned to look at him. He was still staring at the table, but when she turned, he raised his eyes to hers and nodded.

"Right," he repeated. But his answer seemed disconnected from what she had said, as though he were existing somewhere else, involved in some monstrous mental calculation that absorbed all his attention. Whatever he said to her was ancillary, irrelevant.

"The rental starts the first of July," Isabel said. She turned off the water. In the sudden silence Michael's wordless concentration expanded, filling the room. She could feel him being elsewhere. He said nothing.

"Michael?" she said. "Are you paying attention?"

"Of course I am," he said, but he was not. He was listening to something interior. "The rental starts on the first of July. We'll go out then."

Isabel stared at him, trying to make sense of him, trying to make him take hold of something. His absence ballooned like darkness, filling everything. He was gone.

"Michael, what is it?" she asked. "Are you taking something?" Her breath was tight in her chest.

His face did not change.

She walked back to the table, stood facing him and put her hand on the back of her chair. She felt as though she were walking into a heavy wind and the elements were massing against her. "Michael, you're frightening me," she said. "If you won't talk to me, I'm going to call Dr. Stark."

The last resort. She was holding up Dr. Stark like a flame against this darkness. She was bluffing, of course, she could not call Dr. Stark; but hearing Michael repeat her words in this way, making them absurd, made her feel weightless, as though she were cast loose into churning waters.

"Dr. Stark?" Michael repeated. He raised his eyebrows and his face was iridescent with contempt.

Isabel stood motionless at the table. It was not enough to have him turn so strange and irrational: he had to turn against his wife as he did so. He had become cold toward her, he had become her enemy. He was weakening her with his hatred. At the moments when she needed to be strongest, he derided her, denying her position, her worth.

She stood silent, facing her cruel-eyed husband. She thought there was something crazed and pathetic about herself. She was like a dog who did a trick over and over for a master who used to praise him for it but now beat him for it; a dog who continued to perform the trick, hoping that the master would return to his earlier behavior, longing dumbly for the return to the other, happier, life, doing it over and over and being beaten each time, not learning. She couldn't help herself; she couldn't stop believing that if she kept on being herself that Michael would one day return to being himself.

"Michael, I can't go on like this," Isabel heard herself say. Now the silence was broken, but Michael said nothing. She heard herself go on. "I'm going to leave you if you don't stop."

There was a silence. Isabel's heart grew larger in her chest. She waited for Michael to speak.

He stared at her as though she had just appeared.

"You are," he said. "You're going to leave me." It was impossible to tell if he was asking a question or reiterating.

"Yes," Isabel said, drawing breath.

"I see," he said. He was at least looking at her, connecting his gaze with hers.

Isabel stood watching, waiting for something more. The kitchen itself seemed to become attendant, the hanging lamp, the table and the wooden chairs, the dull gleam of the white-tiled walls. The porcelain sink under the window, the nighttime lights outside. Everything was gathered there for a purpose, bearing witness to this moment.

"You have to do something," Isabel said. "You have to change."

"I'm seeing Stark tomorrow," Michael said.

"You are?" Isabel asked.

He nodded.

She stared back. It was too good to be true. But it might be true.

"When did you make the appointment?" she asked.

"Three days ago," Michael said, and stood up. "I'm seeing him at ten-thirty tomorrow morning." The small muscle in the corner of his jaw was clenching and clenching, but he looked straight at her. Even if it wasn't true, she could hold him to account for it. She could call Dr. Stark in the morning and verify it. It would be a start. They could go on from there.

"All right," she said. "Good."

Michael left for the living room. Isabel stood over the sink and turned the water on hard. They would get through tonight, they could do that. In the morning she would call Mitch and Dr. Stark. She would declare herself, she would insist. She was still washed in fear, but she was taking steps.

When the dishes were done, she went down the hall to the living room. From the doorway she could see Michael's crossed stockinged feet on the end of the sofa. He was listening to jazz. He was gone for the evening.

Isabel went back to the bedroom. She lay on the bed and tried to read reports. She had difficulty concentrating. She stared at the same lines over and over, she underlined headings, she went back to the beginning and started again.

At eleven Isabel brushed her teeth and put on her nightgown. She went into the living room. Michael was still stretched out on the sofa, hands folded on his chest, feet crossed. His gaze was absorbed and dreamy. Isabel, standing unseen at the head of the sofa, was touched by his expression. He looked happy. Maybe he was happy. She stood in her nightgown, reluctant to disturb him. It was dark except for the one bright lamp by his head. Across the room stood the big windows full of the dark sky. In the distance were the lights across the river.

Isabel put her hand on his shoulder, and Michael looked at her upside down, the narrow black cord trailing loosely from his ear. It seemed as though he was smiling at her, and she smiled back.

"Are you coming to bed?" she asked, though he could not hear her. She folded her hands next to her cheek and closed her eyes, miming sleep.

Michael smiled at her again, she thought, and nodded.

Isabel stepped back and Michael sank again into the music. She could hear its jingling hiss. She stood watching him. He was looking again into the distance. She thought of how she knew his body, every part of it. She had touched him everywhere, his shoulders, ribs, the smooth rise of anklebone, the mounds of his buttocks, the hard slant of his jaw, the musky hollows of his armpits. The dull red birthmark on his hip. She had seen him naked thousands of times. It seemed astonishing to have such an intimate knowledge of someone else. What was it for, this knowledge? Over such a long time, nearly twenty years, she had seen his skin change, his silhouette alter; he had been hers to watch. She owned him, as he owned her.

She left him listening. Back in bed, Isabel read for a while, waiting, but sleep swept over her and she put her book down beside her face on the pillow.

When she woke, the light was still on, the other side of the bed still empty. She got up and went down the hall to the living room.

He was not on the sofa. The light had been turned off, and it took her a moment to see him. He was standing in front of the windows, looking out across the Hudson to the grids of New Jersey high-rises. When she saw him, she understood at once.

"What are you doing?" she asked. She couldn't keep fear from her voice.

Michael turned to her. "Nothing," he said, his voice distant. "As you can see."

But she felt his urge streaking through her like a siren.

They stared at each other. She did not know what to do. She could feel her heart now, her breaths starting to deepen. She felt bone-fear: this was real. Walking across the room, taking his arm, touching him at all felt dangerous. It was too late to take his arm. She could not allow herself even to think of his intention, the words were too threatening to allow into her mind. She thought if she said nothing, if she did not move, it would not be true. There was a chance it would not be true. Below them, out in the darkness, was the chill black sweep of the Hudson. On its surface were oily swirls moving fast; she could picture them in the dark.

"Will you come to bed?" she asked.

She could feel him escaping.

"In a while," he said, and turned back to the view. His body blotted out the lights on the opposite shore, declaring itself only by the absence of illumination. Isabel waited. She did not know what to do.

"I'm not going to leave you, Michael," she said. "I'm not. You know that." It seemed late to say this, the words felt inconsequential. Her earlier words had been absorbed, and her voice had no presence. It was as though he were still wearing the headphones.

She could feel him across the room in the grip of something. He was consumed by it; he couldn't spare her a look, a turn, a word. A current had swept him up, taken him. She was onshore waving, calling out from the distance. She was too far away to reach him. She walked across the room to him and took his arm.

"Michael," she said steadily, "I'm not going to leave you. Come to bed."

He stood still. She felt him weighing her presence, her insistence, against something else.

"Come to bed," she said again, and he turned docilely.

In bed she pressed against him, and he let her. He let her breathe in the smell of his shoulder, press her face against his neck. He was still. She kept her arms tightly around him; he permitted this, but it felt as though a ballast had shifted within him, an interior weight. Some kind of equilibrium had been lost and she could not right it. She kept herself curled tightly around him. She did not sleep. She saw the clock at 1:35, at 2:08, at 3:20. Outside it was very still. What she had to reach was 10:30, she thought, she had only to get through to 10:30.

When she woke, Michael was gone. She felt the draft and knew before she moved what had happened, though it was not something she could believe. She stayed still, listening for him in the bathroom, for the rushing sound of plumbing. She waited for him to come back from the kitchen, the living room. She could not bear to get up. Around her was silence. As long as she did not get up, nothing had happened. She did not want to speak out loud in the darkened apartment, did not want to use her voice. She felt the air around her, pressing against her, holding her still. She did not dare swallow.

She got out of bed. She slid open the closet door; it rumbled on its tracks. She took her bathrobe from the hook and tied the cord around her waist. She moved slowly. She could feel the draft from an open window. The bedroom window was always open at night, but this was a cross draft. It was moving through the apartment, there was something open elsewhere. She felt her heart again, rising up in her chest, pounding. She walked into the hall. She was barefoot, and the floor was cold and gritty against her feet. She could not bear to call out. She did not want to hear no answer, no other voice. She walked down the hall to the living room.

The big window was wide open. The empty space where the glass had been was rich and velvety. She could see the lights on the far side of the river. She could feel the wind. She stood still in the doorway. She did not want to walk over to the window. It seemed as though all the air in the world had come, chill and turbulent, into the room.

Part 5

As the fire burns . . . it releases the energy that the plant has gathered from the sun and stored up as plant tissue. The tissue decomposes as it is heated by the fire . . . releasing combustible gases that burn as a free flame. This in turn heats the remaining solid matter to drive off more combustible gas. . . . Much of the heat is carried away as hot gas, up into the smoky buoyant plume above the fire. But much, too, escapes as radiant energy from the bright flame, returning to the form in which it was released from the sun and captured by the living plant. In the form of radiation, the energy flees with the speed of light and travels in straight rays until absorbed by matter. When it is absorbed, this energy raises the temperature of the matter which has captured it. . . . So the fire spreads.

—Dr. Frank Albini, physicist,
U.S. Forest Service, Missoula, Montana

Chapter 21

On Thursday morning Isabel was awakened by the light, though it was not bright. It seemed to come from the canopy of the sky instead of the sun. This light filtered wanly through the trees and pressed against the cabin. The woods outside were still.

Isabel was alone in Whit's room. She listened: there were no sounds in the cabin, nothing from Paul. She wondered if he had gotten up, gone to the lodge without her, declaring by that separatist act their separation.

She looked at her watch, squinting in the gloom: quarter of seven. She lay still under the covers, dreading the day. She wished she could leap past it, move at once into her future. If the car were hers, she could leave now.

She thought of Whit. She was in his room, in his bed. She wondered if, up at the lodge, he was lying awake and thinking of her.

But she put away the thought of Whit and resolutely rolled over. Paul was right. They had betrayed him. And it was she who had started it. She could not defend herself. Was this the kind of person she was, wholly unreliable, disloyal? Driven by emotional impulse, hormonal whim? (Though a part of her was secretly proud to discover this underground current, to learn she was still running at full spate when she'd thought that river had gone dry.) But how could she have failed so profoundly to be honorable? She would put him from her mind now.

She could hear the slow beginnings of the day outside, the soft rustle of leaves in upper branches, the coarse alarm call of a jay. It was oddly quiet: there were no other birdcalls. The air was motionless.

She dressed quietly. In the kitchen she drew an almost soundless stream of water, eased the kettle onto the stove. When she had her steaming mug, she slipped out the front door, avoiding the walk down the hall past Paul's room. She made her way around the side of the cabin to the porch. The air was heavy and dry, with an acrid tang. Isabel settled herself in the chair. The cold body of the mist lay in drifting swathes along the surface of the lake. The sky was pale, with a high filmy ceiling. There was the jay again, raucous, now down by the shore.

She heard sounds from inside the cabin. When Paul opened the door, she turned her head to him, waiting.

Paul slowly sat down beside her. He looked horribly tired. He hadn't yet shaved, and his cheeks were grayed with stubble. His eyebrows were heavy, low over his eyes, and his eyes seemed set deeper into his skull.

"Good morning," he said formally.

"Good morning," Isabel said.

The distance between them now was vast. He was someone she never known. It was unimaginable, the notion of pressing against his skin.

"I've been thinking about all this," Paul said. He spoke with deliberation. "I'm going to ask you to reconsider."

Isabel's heart sank.

"I think you're acting hastily." His stranger's profile was set toward the lake. "I think you've become caught up in something by chance, by a sort of accident. I don't want our marriage to end because of something—" he paused "—because of something that went out of control. I want to ask you to try again."

He leaned back in his chair without looking at her.

"Paul," Isabel said, "it's my fault, what's happened. But it's over. This won't work."

There was a silence.

"How do you know?" His voice was now faintly belligerent, as though he might be able to bully her into knowing something different.

"I'm the wrong person," Isabel told him.

"The wrong person to get married? Or the wrong person to marry me?"

"Probably both," Isabel said. She turned to look at him. He had laid his head back against the chair and closed his eyes. His collar was open, and his throat, with its strange awkward lump, was bared to the air. Seeing him like that, still and sightless, his throat exposed, frightened her.

"Paul," she said, and he opened his eyes.

"What," he said. He still did not look at her.

"Don't blame yourself," she said.

"I don't want this," Paul said. *"I don't want this."*

On the lake the mist was thinning and rising. The jay cried and was answered in the distance.

"What is it?" Paul asked. "What happened?" His voice was tight; he held something inside his chest. He stood up and came over to her. He leaned over Isabel and tried to gather her up to him. "How can you do this? Please," he said, and his voice dropped. "Please."

His knees pressed against hers. Isabel's legs were beneath her, and she could not stand or move. As he leaned, the rocking chair tipped backward and Isabel put her hand on his shoulder, holding him off.

"Paul," she said, "I'm so sorry."

"What can I do?" His voice was unsteady.

Isabel shook her head.

Paul pushed himself away from her and, without speaking, went down the porch steps. He took the path to the lake. When he was out of sight, Isabel could hear the swishing of the branches as he passed them, his footsteps on the soft dry earth.

Isabel sat without moving. The day was just beginning.

The lake began to shimmer as the sun moved higher. The scents of pine and bracken drifted in the still air. Now even the jays were silent in the cool darkness of the trees. In the lake, the ghostly fish—stipple-backed, white-bellied—descended soundlessly, dropping into the quieter, dimmer regions, farther from the glare of noon. The animals in the woods—raccoons, muskrats, foxes, deer, mountain lions, if they were there—were making their way to earth, to burrows, to cool dark groves of trees, to rocky caves, to their shaded, secret sanctuaries, as the day rose up into the world.

When Paul came back, Isabel was inside their bedroom, kneeling in front of her open suitcase. Paul stood in the doorway.

"Don't pack," he said, his voice determined.

She was setting in a pile of T-shirts. She looked up. "Why not?"

"I don't want you to leave yet."

"What do you mean?"

"Stay until Saturday. Then we'll both leave together, a day early. There's no way for you to leave alone now anyway, there's only one car."

"It's a bad idea," Isabel said at once.

It was a terrible idea, the two of them staying on in the cabin together, estranged and hostile.

"I want to make this as easy as I can for you," Isabel said. "I want to do whatever is most—"

"Humane," Paul said. "But you're still killing me."

Isabel sat back on her heels and folded her hands in her lap. "I thought you wanted me to leave."

"What I don't want is for my whole family to be an audience to this sordid and humiliating mess. I don't want to tell them now. You can spare me that."

"But you don't want me here," Isabel pointed out. "Last night you wanted me to leave right then." She wanted to go. She could not bear his presence.

"Don't you think you're doing enough damage?" Paul asked. His voice rose. "Aren't you doing enough by walking out on me?"

Isabel said nothing for a moment, then, "All right. All right. What I'm doing is terrible. But don't make me—"

"*Don't try to bargain!*" Paul's voice was angry. "What you're doing is terrible, right, yes! Don't try to get past that! Let's stop right there: *what you're doing is terrible!*"

Isabel folded her arms. "I'll stay until Saturday."

"Thank you," Paul said, furious.

Isabel leaned over and lifted out the pile of T-shirts. *Two more days,* she thought.

They gathered later in the morning for a picnic hike up a mountain; everyone went except Charlotte. Outside the lodge Isabel nodded communally to Douglas and Whit, her glance not lingering. On the trail Isabel was last, behind Paul. She walked with her eyes down. *A day and a half,* she told herself. She watched the soft dark earth of the trail, the heels of Paul's gray leather hiking boots walking away from her.

By lunchtime they had reached the bare crest of the mountain.

They spread out along the rock; Isabel kept Paul between herself and the others. The view stretched around them, the wooded hills lapped into the distance. To the north the sky was smudged, an airy darkness lying lightly above the distant slopes.

"That's where those fires are." Douglas squinted toward them, hands on his hips. "You can smell them." The others turned, scanning the distance.

"It doesn't look bad from here," Paul said.

"Question of wind," Whit said. "They might burn out on their own if there's no wind. If it comes up, that's trouble."

They stood silent, watching. There was no wind now. The air was completely still. Nothing stirred in the woods below.

"It feels so dry," Douglas said.

Whit turned away from the view, moving back. "It is," he said. He took out his water bottle and tilted it against his mouth, closing his eyes. Isabel found herself watching him: the lifted chin, the closed eyes, the water trickling around his mouth. The lips pressed together, as for a kiss. Of the two, the wife's betrayal was the worse. It was the wife who had made a vow of fidelity. The brother had been born into it. He'd promised nothing.

Isabel turned away from Whit. Listening to the others talk, she felt invisible. No longer a member of this clan, she was hardly here. Standing on the rocky uneven slope between Paul and his father, she set her hands on her hips and closed her eyes. The sun was warm on her face, her soft cotton shirt comfortably damp with sweat. Above her was the sky; she felt a liberating rush. She was done with all this. She was done with willing herself to feel something she could not. She was done with this failure. For a moment she felt giddy. *A day and a half,* she thought, *and now less.*

Later, in the cabin, she and Paul barely spoke. They walked up to the lodge for dinner in silence.

Conversation that night was muted. Even Charlotte seemed subdued. Isabel held to her resolution: she hardly looked at Whit, and met his eyes not at all. He was quiet.

Afterward, back at the cabin, Isabel and Paul faced each other awkwardly in the hall.

"Well, good night," Isabel said.

"Good night," Paul said.

Isabel hesitated, then said, "I wish you well."

Paul looked at her, his eyes narrowed. He shook his head and turned away. From her room she could hear him moving angrily about. She undressed quickly and pulled her cotton nightgown over her head. Sliding between the cold sheets, she shivered, wishing she'd brought a warmer nightgown. She hadn't thought she'd be sleeping alone.

She dreaded telling her father; she dreaded the furrow of disapproval between his brows. She dreaded telling Ben.

—

After Michael's death, Isabel had not called Ben at once. There had been times, that awful night, when she could have. After the departure of the silent ambulance, its red light circling slowly in the darkness. After the departure of the two somber-faced policemen, who had crossed the living room with heavy footsteps to examine the window frame. *The window frame.* She had watched them squatting to dust it for fingerprints, nausea stirring inside her at the thought of Michael's fingers. She could have called Ben before the trip to the hospital, when she'd walked through the dead fluorescent glare of the hallways to sit in small offices, empty in the middle of the night, where she'd filled out forms, then waited before being sent on again. Again and again she'd wanted Ben, his voice. There had been times when she could have called, but she had waited until it was light. She hadn't wanted Ben to hear in the dark.

She called very early in the morning, barely daylight. She was back in the apartment. In the morning there would be more official business. She couldn't leave to go and get Ben, though she would have liked to: driving through the dark, the car eating up the distance between herself and her son. But she could not leave the city. In the early morning she came back alone to the apartment and opened the front door onto its silence. She was afraid of the window—had anyone closed it? She went past the living room door without looking in.

In the bedroom she sat on the bed and called Ben's school. The phone rang, then a recording came on. Isabel scribbled the number to call in the margin of a magazine. She dialed again.

"Security," a man said after clearing his throat.

She asked for Ben. "I must speak to him. It's his mother," she said. "It's an emergency." As she spoke, she wondered if she had said it right.

The emergency was not his mother but his father. She should have said, "I'm his mother, there's an emergency." She was holding on to the telephone with both hands. Light was beginning to edge along the silhouettes of the buildings.

The guard put her through to the housemaster, Bill Wainwright.

"I'm sorry to call so early," Isabel said. "I have to speak to Ben. It's an emergency. There's been an accident."

"I'm sorry," Wainwright said, and then, unforgivably, instead of going right to get Ben, he asked, "Can I ask you what's happened?"

"There's been an accident," Isabel repeated, suddenly furious. It was her business. And what should she say? She couldn't use the actual word. "There's been an accident," she repeated. "His father is hurt." It was as far as she would go.

"I'll get Ben," Wainwright said, and put down the phone. It took a long time. There was no sound, and Isabel sat on the bed imagining Bill Wainwright at his closet, pulling on his bathrobe, tying the sash, trying unsuccessfully to find slippers, striding off barefoot down the corridor. Up the steps to the next long corridor with its dark wainscoting, past the closed doors all the way to the end. Standing outside Ben's door, knocking quietly at first, trying not to rouse the others. But quiet knocking would not rouse Ben. Opening the door to Ben's room. Isabel knew how Ben looked asleep, his mouth slightly open, his body twisted like a contortionist's among ropes of knotted bedding, asleep in that druggedlike, unconscious adolescent way.

Isabel sat on her bed waiting, now patient. Outside, the early yellow light rose against the shadowy buildings, spreading cool dawn across them. She imagined Ben coming out, sleepy, dazed, already frightened, following Bill Wainwright with his trailing bathrobe tie and his bare feet, the two of them walking past the closed doors to Bill Wainwright's room, where the phone lay on the table.

Ben's voice came on without warning. "Mom?" he said.

Isabel, who had thought she was prepared, now could not answer. Ben waited.

"What's happened to Dad?" he asked.

"You have to come home right away," she said. "The school will help you get here."

"What happened?"

"Your father fell," she said, and stopped. She willed him not to ask the next question, she wanted not to say it, not to make it real in daylight. "You have to come home. Bring your books and things. It may be awhile."

There was a pause. She wondered if Bill Wainwright was standing beside Ben. She imagined Ben's wild hair, the innocent sleep-filled face now grave. She ducked her head, cradling the phone in the hollow of her neck.

"Mom?" Ben's voice had deepened.

He was not a child, she could not treat him as a child. It was for herself that she was holding back the words, not for him. She couldn't ask him to make the trip not knowing, sitting on the train, staring out the window, not knowing.

"What?" she said.

"Is he alive?"

She still could not say it. She listened hard into the phone as though waiting for Ben to speak. She could not say the words. Her fingers were clamped tightly around the phone. She could not speak at all, it seemed. She could hardly believe she was sitting alone on the rumpled sheets of the unmade bed. She looked with disbelief at the sun coming up in that unholy dawn. She was alone and speechless, in the middle of her life. She listened to Ben; he waited to hear the words.

"Mom?" he said, his voice strange.

Isabel had waited to answer, because this was the last moment that his father would be alive for Ben, and she was filled with love and sorrow for her son.

"He fell," Isabel said again, and hearing herself speak the words, they were real, and she saw the loved body dropping swiftly through the dark air, and she understood then that it had happened. "No."

Now, lying in the cabin bunk, tucking her legs beneath her nightgown to warm her cold feet, Isabel thought of telling Ben about the end of her marriage to Paul. It would be bad. She would be ashamed to tell him she'd made such a mistake, but it would not be as terrible as that phone call. Nothing would be as bad as that.

She and Ben were closer now. Michael's death had brought them together. And something had shifted: Ben had become kind to her. The adolescent sullenness had gone. Isabel had wondered about this change, why it had happened. She wondered now if part of Ben's resentment had been at Michael's moods. They had terrorized the family, held all of them hostage. The moods had been so terrible that they had silenced Isabel, and she could never bring herself to talk to Ben about them. Or maybe the reason was much simpler: maybe now Ben felt sorry for his mother. Isabel didn't want his pity, but she wanted her son back; was grateful for his return.

That morning, seeing Ben's face had been like coming into sight of land. And Isabel remembered, later, that awful day—when had it been? There were people still in the living room, there'd been people in and out all day—the lawyers, the police again, a social worker. She and Ben were alone in the bedroom, and something—what was it?—had started them laughing. She remembered looking over Ben's shoulder as they laughed, at a watercolor on the wall. It was crooked, and she thought that in a moment she would straighten it, and she felt such relief that there was something she could fix so easily, but just then they were both laughing, helpless. What was it? They were screaming, weak, tears streaming down their faces, bending at the waist. Something about lunch, something about the cold cuts.

Afterward Ben sat down on the bed. There had been that tipped picture waiting for her to straighten it, and the feeling of safety, the two of them.

Since then she'd told Ben everything: Michael's ominous, darkening mood, his promise to see the doctor. She'd told him everything except what she'd said to Michael, her threat. She could not tell him that. How could he forgive her for that? She could not forgive herself.

———

On Friday afternoon, everyone went out on the water. Isabel still did not meet Whit's eyes and barely spoke to him.

Sitting in the bow of the canoe, facing away from Paul and separated from everyone else, only the empty lake beyond her, Isabel hardly had to speak at all. She looked out in the distance to the green water, the wooded shores, the treetops moving slowly in the wind. The wind had begun to rise and ruffle the surface of the water. The sky was pallid and opaque, veiled with haze. She heard the voices of the others behind her, talking about the fires still burning to the north. The voices echoed across the water. Isabel slid along ahead, separate from them. She heard Douglas say something, then Charlotte's laugh ringing out across the water. Tomorrow she would be gone from here, in a new life.

That evening Isabel dressed for dinner in a bright sweater and earrings to mark the occasion: their last night. Outside in the darkness the trees murmured, the low restless sound of branches moving against one another.

Paul and Isabel again walked up to the lodge without speaking. Around them the black woods stirred and shifted, the tops of the trees swayed slowly. When they reached the front door of the lodge, Paul stopped abruptly on the steps. He turned to Isabel, and she thought he might say something kind.

"Don't ever think," he said, "that I will forgive you." He went up the steps and held the door for her to pass through.

The others were in the living room by the fireplace. The fire lit up the room, the dusky brocade of the sofas, the dull gilt of the picture frames. The big lamps glowed through their pagoda-shaped shades. Overhead, the swan's breast had a glossy sheen.

"Here they are," Charlotte said when Paul and Isabel came in. "We're inside," she announced unnecessarily. "Too cold tonight to be out. Feels like fall. Doesn't it? The evenings have turned cool." She wore, festively, turquoise cashmere, a strand of pearls. She and Douglas were on a sofa beside the fire. "Come sit," she said, and waved Paul and Isabel toward the facing sofa.

"It's only about one degree colder than when I arrived," Whit observed mildly. He sat in a big chair beside his parents, his legs crossed casually.

"But we've been here longer than you have. It's much cooler now than when we first came," Charlotte insisted. "It's different now. Chilly. You can feel it."

"Your mother likes to feel the seasons changing," Douglas said to Whit.

"Of course I do," Charlotte said. "Don't make me sound like someone from a lunatic asylum. Everyone likes to feel the seasons changing. What's the matter with that?" She rattled the ice in her glass mutinously.

Charlotte was right, Isabel thought, everyone did like to feel the seasons change. And it was true that everyone treated Charlotte like a lunatic, no matter what she said or how sensible it was. Isabel felt a surge of affection for the older woman, her energy, her enthusiasms. She would miss her.

Looking at Charlotte, Isabel could see Whit to one side. He was holding his glass on the broad arm of the chair. His hair was wet, just combed and glossy. He looked clean and glowing. He glanced at her, then away.

"What about the fires?" Paul asked. "What does Eddie say?"

Douglas shook his head. "It's not good. They're still out of control. I listened to the news and talked to the police. They're on alert. If those fires get up over that long ridge, they'll barrel straight down this valley and everything will go. It's because of the wind, it's so high."

There was a silence. They felt the presence of the fires, voracious, blazing against the night.

Charlotte shook her head. "They'll get them stopped," she said knowledgeably. "They always do. Firefighters up here are *crack*." She clicked smartly with the side of her mouth.

"We hope so," Douglas said. He looked at Isabel, changing the subject. "We're so sorry you're leaving early."

"Yes," Isabel said, "it's a pity." She felt Whit's eyes on her again; she looked steadily at Douglas.

"A real pity," Paul said, unsmiling. There was a pause, and he added, "Isabel has some things she wants to do before Monday." Isabel understood that she was being blamed for their defection. She wondered what Whit thought.

"Well," Charlotte said briskly. "Since it's your last night, I've asked Miriam for something special."

Paul said nothing, so Isabel answered. "How nice of you. Is it a surprise?"

"Venison," Charlotte said with satisfaction. "Frozen, of course. Eddie does a lot of hunting during the season, and we buy from him. Always have some in the freezer. I thought tonight was cold enough. And it'll make you feel a part of all this up here." Charlotte lifted her drink in an encompassing gesture and smiled at Isabel. "So you'll come back."

"How nice of you," Isabel repeated, feeling fraudulent. "Thank you." Paul frowned studiously at the darkened windows. Whit looked at him, then away.

When they went into the dining room, Miriam came in with a big platter.

"Miriam," Douglas said, "what's Eddie finding out?"

"He's still calling around," Miriam said. "He'll come in when he's done." She offered Charlotte the platter.

"Thank you, Miriam," Charlotte said. "Here we are. This is from the place." She laughed and said to Isabel, "Family joke. There was someone we knew years ago, Hasty Jackson. Lived in Far Hills, and he used to say that about everything at the table, even things that weren't possibly his. 'This is from the place,' he'd say, even though everyone knew he didn't have any peach trees. Or peonies, or whatever it was. Finally someone called him on it. Said, 'Hasty, these can't be from your place. Tomatoes aren't ready up here.' And Hasty said, without even blinking"— Charlotte blinked her short pale lashes several times—" 'I never said *what* place.' So now we always say everything's from the place."

Isabel smiled: family lore. The stories, the way the world was seen from here. She would become a part of it, and she would come off badly. She would be the wife who'd run off so outrageously. Her name would be mentioned at this table in the future. She realized with a beat of gratitude that Charlotte had said nothing unkind about Louisa.

Miriam stood beside Isabel as she ladled the dark steamy chunks onto her plate.

"It's good, this stuff," Douglas said. "You can't beat wild venison."

"Is there any other kind besides wild?" Paul asked.

"Must be," Douglas said. "Don't you think? Someone must be raising deer for meat. Some Texan on a ranch. Whit? You know about this sort of thing."

Whit shook his head. "I know there are some game operations, but I don't know much about them."

What does he know, Isabel thought. She felt the wish to learn Whit, to know what he knew. Probably she never would. She might never see him again after tomorrow. This thought gave her a swift moment of pain.

"Oh, come on," Paul said. "You *do* know about this sort of thing." His tone was unfriendly, and Whit did not answer.

"Hope you don't mind eating venison," Charlotte said bossily to Isabel. "Some people don't like it. They think deer are too beautiful. Think of Bambi."

"Isabel doesn't mind," Paul said before she could answer. "She'll eat anything."

"That's very bold of you," Whit said to her.

"Isabel is very bold," Paul said bluntly. "Isabel is stupefyingly bold. Nothing stops her."

Isabel could feel his ire rising. She looked down at her plate.

Charlotte nodded. "Isabel probably wouldn't have run from that bear," she said, "unlike what's-her-name. What?"

"Marilyn Hornby," Paul said.

"Actually," Whit spoke up, "Marilyn Hornby was not the coward she's made out to be."

"Didn't she run from that bear?" Charlotte asked.

"The revisionist," Paul said sardonically.

"She did run from the bear," Whit said. "We all did. We ran for our lives. There's nothing cowardly about that." Whit looked at his mother, then Paul. Not at Isabel, who was, since he was talking, watching him. "But otherwise Marilyn was actually quite fearless. She conducted a solitary nocturnal expedition, for example, into my room, uninvited."

There was a silence. Paul watched Whit.

"Where she was completely unwelcome," Whit went on. "I tried to make her leave, but she refused. We ended up having a serious struggle: she was determined to stay."

The candle in front of Isabel guttered suddenly. A drop of wax ran down the white column to the rim of the brass candlestick.

"Marilyn went into *your* room that night?" Paul repeated.

Whit nodded, looking steadily at his brother. "She did. It was an amazingly low thing to do. Vile, actually."

"That's not the way we saw it," Charlotte said.

"No," Whit said. "I know that."

"I don't believe it," Paul said.

"No," Whit said. "I know you don't. But that's what happened. I had to wrestle her out into the hall. I was trying to get her out before anyone heard us."

Charlotte shook her head, remembering. "God, it was awful."

"You went into her room, you bastard," Paul said.

"Actually," Whit said, "I did not. I never would have done that. I had nothing to do with her."

Paul stared at his brother. Afraid of what he would say next, Isabel spoke.

"Paul, stop it," she said. "It's over."

There was silence.

"Isabel's right," Paul said, calm, furious. "It's over. She's leaving me. We're going to get divorced."

Douglas and Charlotte stared at Isabel.

"I'm sorry," Isabel said.

"Don't be ridiculous," Charlotte said crossly. "You don't know what you're talking about." She drained her glass and set it down; the ice cubes slid and shifted.

"I'm sorry," Isabel repeated. She put her hands in her lap, like a bad child.

Douglas frowned deeply.

"It's not Paul's fault," Isabel said. "It's mine. I shouldn't have agreed to get married. It was a mistake. I was trying to get over—what had happened. I thought this was the way for me to get back into life. It wasn't. It was the wrong reason to get married."

Charlotte and Douglas looked at her with profound disapproval.

"How could you be so stupid?" Charlotte asked finally.

"I don't know," Isabel said. "I'm sorry." She looked anywhere but at Whit, who now was watching her.

The door opened from the kitchen. Miriam put her head through.

"Mr. Simmons," she said, "Eddie would like to talk to you."

Chapter 22

Douglas looked up. "Right now?"

Miriam nodded.

"Of course." Douglas stood up. "Does he want to come in?"

Miriam came farther in, and Eddie appeared in the doorway behind her. Eddie was barely taller than his wife, broad and solid, with heavy jowls and deep-set blue eyes. He wore an old red plaid shirt and dark green pants. He moved quietly.

"Good evening, Eddie," Douglas said.

Eddie nodded around the table. "Evening, Mr. Simmons. Mrs. Simmons," he said, then pressed his lips neatly together, as though sealing off the words.

"Tell us the news."

"The fires," he said. "They're heading this way."

"Ah," Douglas said, serious. "Reason for alarm. Who have you talked to?"

"Troopers and the parks people," Eddie said. "Just now I was on the phone with Charlie Alcorn. He's a trooper. They're starting to talk about evacuating this area."

"We're not leaving," Charlotte said absolutely. She shook her head. "Alarmist."

Without expression Eddie looked at her, then back at Douglas.

"Where are the fires right now?" Douglas asked. "Where are they sending people?"

"There's one been burning for three days about fifty miles northeast of us. Just above Bendleigh. Seems it's going to miss Bendleigh itself; it's going straight south. If it keeps on in this direction, it'll come right through this valley. They've been trying to contain it, and they thought they'd got it out yesterday, but they didn't. It came back again, farther down and bigger, and now it's spreading. This whole county is bone-dry, and the woods are going up like kindling. The fire is still a ways off, but if the wind comes up and it starts moving, none of these roads will be safe. They all of them go through the woods. The troopers want everyone who can to get out of this area as soon as possible."

There was a silence.

Charlotte looked down and began cutting vigorously at her venison. "I've been coming here for seventy-four years," she said. "I'm not going to be chased out of my house by a lot of policemen."

"Eddie," Douglas said, "what would you and Miriam like to do?"

"I want to get that hose out and spray the roof down," Eddie said. "Give it a good damping. That'll protect it from flying sparks. Then I'd like to take Miriam and get back to Casco. That's where we're supposed to go. They had that little rain, and it's closer to the highways. That's where they'll start any kind of evacuation. My advice, you all should leave." Eddie pressed his lips together again.

There was another silence. Everyone was watching Eddie. He looked steadily at Douglas.

This is really happening, Isabel thought.

The fire lay somewhere to the north, bright against the forest darkness, its orange brilliance lighting up the black skeletons of trees.

"Let me talk to the trooper," Douglas said. He followed Eddie back into the kitchen. The others waited. They could hear his voice coming from the kitchen. When he came back, his face was sober.

"Let's get started on that roof," he said.

Isabel went outside with the men. She stood shivering and holding two flashlights, aiming the beams in front of the others as they worked. The men moved slowly in the dark, uncoiling hoses, dragging them across the ground.

"Where's the ladder?" Paul asked.

"In the boathouse," Eddie said from the shadows.

"Give me one of those," Paul said to Isabel. He took a flashlight and set off. Douglas vanished along the side of the house to turn on the faucets. Eddie and Whit stood apart, away from the wall, aiming the empty nozzles into the darkness. Waiting, silent, they looked expectantly up: there was an urgent rising gurgle. The water spat, hissed, then rose toward the roof. The spattering on the shingles sounded like rain.

Douglas reappeared, picking his way. He stood between the others and looked up.

"Cedar shakes," he said ruefully. "We could've used asphalt shingles for that roof. A lot cheaper, and now it would be a lot safer." The spray turned to mist as it fell.

"It's a wooden house," Whit said, "in the woods. That's the risk, not what the shingles are made of."

"They should have put the fire out up at Bendleigh," Douglas said sternly, "that's what they should have done. Letting these fires burn like that is criminal. This environmentalist stuff is irresponsible."

No one answered. Eddie and Whit moved the nozzles back and forth, sending languid arcs up into the air. Isabel could just make out Whit's shape.

The night sky spread royally overhead. Isabel, her eyes adjusting to the darkness, looked up. It was perfectly clear, and in the black felt of the sky, the stars were thick. The falling spray misted her face. Below the house was the lake, shining in the moonlight. The wind was rising. The trees were beginning to shift, creaking faintly. The high branches were moving, lifting and falling with an airy hushing.

It took over an hour to wet down the roof. They took turns spraying, and Eddie held the flashlight for Isabel while she went inside for a coat. There were only two small-gauge garden hoses, and for each section of roof, the hoses were dragged along the wall to a different outside faucet, then reconnected. Paul brought the ladder from the boathouse and leaned it against the roof. He climbed slowly up into the darkness, holding the heavy snake of hose in one hand. Isabel could not shine the beams high enough to help him.

The wind continued to rise, the tossing upper branches heaving and pitching against the sky. The sound of the wind in the trees grew louder, rising over the soft patter of water on the shingles.

When they had reached the northern end of the house, closest to the cabins, Miriam appeared from the darkness.

"The troopers just called," she said, her voice raised.

"What'd they say?" Douglas asked.

"They want everyone this side of the lake out," Miriam said. "The wind is up and the fires are spreading. They're moving this way. It's the wind. It's getting higher: like a thunderstorm, only no rain."

"All right," Douglas said. "Where's Mrs. Simmons?"

"I think she's gone to bed," Miriam said.

Douglas shook his head. "All right," he repeated. "Eddie, it's time for you and Miriam to go on home. No reason for you to stay until we're done. We can finish up, we're close anyway. You and Miriam go."

Eddie said nothing. His hose trained steadily up, his head was tilted back; he was watching the spray.

Whit came over and put his hand on the hose. "Eddie, give that to me," he said. "You go. Go on. You have your own house to look after. Leave us. We only have two hoses, anyway, and there are three of us here. You're not doing anything we can't do."

Eddie did not move.

"Eddie," Douglas said, "go. Really. This'll take us fifteen more minutes and then we'll go. You and Miriam go now, please. I appreciate you wanting to stay, but it's unnecessary. I'm going in to get my wife, and by the time she's down, Paul and Whitney will have the roof finished. There's no reason for you to stay. And it's dangerous." His voice was tense.

Eddie took a step back and lowered his hose. Whit took it from him.

"Go," Whit said, "go."

Eddie looked troubled. "I've worked here all my life. My father worked here all his."

"Please, Eddie," Douglas said, distracted. "I know. We appreciate what you're saying, but we don't want you to stay here just for us."

Whit put his hand on Eddie's shoulder. "Please go," he said. "We'll be done in a few minutes, and there's nothing more you can do. Think of Miriam. Get her out of here."

There was a pause, then Whit spoke again, more gently. "Fire's the one thing," he said. "We can't beat it. Go."

Eddie frowned, then stepped back, yielding the hose to Whit. He put his hands awkwardly in his pockets. "You all have enough gas?" he asked.

"We filled up the truck on the way home," Whit said.

"My car has lots of gas," Douglas said. He was at the side door, opening it. "I'm going to get my wife. Go on, Eddie, go. Please."

Eddie took another step back, looked up into the dark sky and frowned again in the dim glow of the flashlight. "I don't like leaving while you're here," he said.

"But you should," Whit told him. "Please get Miriam and go, Eddie. We'll see you in Casco. Just go. Tell them we're coming right along."

Eddie turned reluctantly. "All right," he said, "you finish this and get out of here."

"That's the plan," Whit said.

Paul, invisible on top of the ladder, came down slowly backward, the light revealing him feet first. On the ground he slid the ladder sideways and settled it against the roof.

"Paul," Isabel said, "we're supposed to leave. Eddie's just left, and your father's gone to get your mother."

"What happened?" Paul asked. His face was lit from below by Isabel's flashlight, which cast wild shadows up onto his cheekbones, his chin.

"The state troopers just called. They want everyone out," Isabel said. She was beginning to breathe fast. "Eddie wanted to stay, but your father told him to go. He says to finish the roof and then to go. I'm going to get our stuff. Is there anything you want? What shall I get?" Her chest was rising and falling as though she'd been running.

Paul looked around: only Whit was left, making steady arcs into the air with the hose. "No, nothing," he said. "Bring the car." He climbed back up the ladder.

Whit moved farther away into the darkness, spraying.

Isabel took a step toward him. "Is it crazy to stay on and finish here? Should we all just leave right now?"

Whit shook his head. "It's only a few more minutes. We're almost done, and this could save the house."

From inside they heard raised voices, shouts.

"Go on, get your stuff," Whit said, his voice urgent, and Isabel turned and fled into the black woods.

She hurried down the path, the flashlight bobbing and weaving, its beam glaring suddenly close against a roughened trunk, then glancing away into the dimness. Overhead the treetops were tossing loosely, swiping widely against the sky. The dryness of the wind was frightening: these wild surges were like a gale, but where was the rain? The arid wind felt deadly.

In the cabin Isabel shone the flashlight wildly around the kitchen before she remembered the light switch. The cabin, lit up, seemed oddly disordered. It seemed impossible that when she was last here—three hours ago?—she had felt sluggish and trapped. Now she felt electrified. She changed into jeans and sneakers and a sweater. She grabbed a duffel bag, wondering what to take. Nothing was important, or everything was. Wallets, glasses, keys. Socks. Underwear. She yanked open drawers, searching for anything that anyone might need, sweeping things into the open bag. An extra sweater, pants. She felt as though fear were closing off her vision, as though she could see only directly in front of her. She thought she heard footsteps and stopped to listen, but it was the wind. Now the bigger limbs were beginning to move, swinging hard against one another.

Oh please, she thought, *please.* She found Paul's running shoes. At this moment she was his wife. She thought of his face, lit by the flashlight, shadowed against the sky.

"I've got everything," she said out loud. She zipped the duffel shut. Was every second important? How did you know? Either the fire was coming or it was not. She thought of being inside the pickup, driving through those woods, the branches scraping hard on both sides of the windows. She thought of the fire, incandescent, furious.

In the car she turned the ignition key too hard, and the engine whined crazily. She started over. She turned on the headlights. Everything seemed alarming; the sudden flood of whiteness was like an explosion.

She parked outside the lodge. Their car was not full of gas; there was just over a quarter of a tank. Was that enough? How would they know how far they'd need to drive? She heard voices from inside the house and went in. It was Charlotte and Douglas.

"I will not!" Charlotte's voice was loud and adamant.

"I don't care what you want to do," Douglas said firmly. "We're leaving here now."

They were in the living room. Charlotte was in a white high-necked nightgown, long and flowing. She was barefoot. Douglas was gripping her forearm, pulling at her. Charlotte slapped angrily at his hand. "Take your hand off me," she said to Douglas imperiously.

Douglas said to Isabel, "Go and call the boys, would you. We're getting out of here." He had a canvas bag in one hand, and with the other he held tightly to Charlotte's arm.

"Douglas, take your hand off me!" Charlotte said, her voice rising again. She spoke with breathtaking contempt. "You complete ass."

Douglas pushed at her steadily. "I may be anything you say, but you're coming with me," he said, propelling her toward the door. "We're leaving."

Paul came in from outside, his face smeared. "What's up?"

"Paul, tell your father to take his hands off me," Charlotte said. She twisted suddenly away from Douglas. He grabbed for her but missed, and Charlotte bolted, running from the room to the staircase beyond. Douglas was behind her, but he'd been unprepared and she was surprisingly fast.

"Charlotte!" he shouted after her. "Damn you!"

"Go help him," Isabel told Paul. "Quickly, help him!" Paul went out after them. The seconds were ticking by, the trees outside weaving, the high branches swaying heavily.

Whit came in from the porch. "Let's go," he said. His face, too, was smeared, his hands covered in pitch and dirt. "What are we waiting for?"

"Your mother doesn't want to leave," Isabel said. "She ran back upstairs. Your father and Paul have gone after her."

"Is she drunk?"

Isabel nodded.

From upstairs there was more noise: a banging door, running footsteps.

"I'm not, I'm not," Charlotte shouted.

"You are, too," Douglas answered.

A tremendous crash and a cry.

"Don't do that," Charlotte screamed. Her voice rose to a shrill keening sound. There were footsteps on the stairs.

"We're all ready," Isabel told Whit. "Our car is in front. Do you want to come with us?"

Whit shook his head. "I'll go with them," he said. "They may need help."

Isabel nodded again. It was like war, everything was being stripped away.

Charlotte appeared in the doorway like an aged Ophelia. Her head was high, and she swayed slightly. Her arms were held by Douglas and Paul. The three faces were intent and furious.

"Damn both your eyes," Charlotte announced. Her steps were reluctant. She was being forcibly walked ahead. "Damn everyone's eyes."

"Get the car," Douglas said to Whit.

By the time the trio made its difficult way out onto the front step, Whit had driven the Volvo station wagon up from the garage. He pulled in behind Paul's little red sedan and got out.

"We don't have enough gas in the Volvo," he said, coming around to the others. "We filled up the pickup, but we can't all fit in that. We'd better all go in Paul's car."

"I'm not going anywhere," Charlotte said loudly. She swung her head back and forth. "You can't make me leave my house, Douglas. This is my house, it's my family house!"

"Get in," Douglas said. He and Paul flanked Charlotte, moving her toward the red car. Barefoot, she winced at the gravel. Paul held his mother's arm with one hand and opened the door with the other. Charlotte, just as she was being drawn into the car, kicked out at her husband. The nightgown moved gracefully with the action, like a dancer's dress.

Douglas ignored this. "Get in."

Charlotte, her head high, turned. "Damn you, Douglas, for doing this to me," she said. "This is the place that I love. That I *love.*"

Douglas, his hands on her forearm, leaned close to her. "For doing *what* to you?" His voice was fierce. "Do you think I like being your keeper, Charlotte? You think I want to be the only sane one in the family? The only grown-up?" He shook her arm in his two hands. "I'm trying to save *your life.* Now *get in.* Get in the car."

"Douglas," Charlotte said; her voice broke and then, horrifyingly, turned to sobs.

For a moment no one moved, and then Douglas said, "Charlotte." He put his arm around her and said, "Come on. Get in."

Now she allowed herself to be handed into the backseat. Paul and Douglas, their faces somber, climbed in on either side.

Whit got into the driver's seat, Isabel beside him. No one spoke as they drove off. On either side of the driveway, the trees tossed against the night sky. The only sound inside the car was that of Charlotte, sobbing.

Chapter 23

As they drove off, Whit reached for the radio, releasing a sudden blare of sound: rock music from the local station, sixty miles away. Whit lowered it at once to a muted, rattling whine.

"If you hear talking, turn it up," he told Isabel.

Everyone was looking straight ahead, watching the dirt road reveal itself in the darkness, as though each of them was driving, responsible for deciphering what came next.

Around them the forest had gone wild. Along the verge of the road, shrubs and grasses waved and swayed. The ghostly undersides of leaves shone in sudden rippling shudders. Leaves and twigs were hurled against the windshield.

Rounding a corner, the headlights lit up a doe, with brown velvet body and narrow elegant legs, walking steadily across the road. A spotted fawn hurried at her heels, his nose stretched forward, his ears laid flat. The doe turned and looked at them, her diagonal ears pricked, her eyes phosphorescent in the headlights. She turned again and walked on, hurried, stepping toward the dark woods and invisibility. The fawn, on long fragile legs, bounded behind her, white tail whisking.

Around them the wind rushed through the woods. Isabel wondered how they would know what was happening: if the fire was approaching, which way it would be safe to go. She thought of the lake, its expanse dark and cool behind them, more distant with each moment.

The jittery sounds of music gave way to talk, and Isabel turned it up.

". . . high winds driving them on, in spite of attempts to control them. Manateck, Acatawah and Hamilton counties have sent in firefighting teams to assist the state. Anyone in the region southeast of Bendleigh is urged to contact their local police for instructions. Communities are now being evacuated. For more information, please call one of the following numbers."

"Does anyone have a cell phone?" Whit asked.

"I do," said Isabel, and pulled it from her bag.

She dialed. The screen displayed the numbers, then turned blank and gray. She dialed again. The screen flashed monotonously: WAIT FOR SERVICE. She waited; the screen went blank. She tried a third time.

"Nothing," she said. "I can't get through."

"That's the trouble with emergency phone numbers," Paul said. "In an emergency you can't get through. No one can."

Isabel turned off her phone and slid it back in her purse. Cell phones: the notion that you could speak to someone who was safe made you think somehow that you yourself were. She thought of that poor man freezing to death in the Himalayas, talking to his wife, halfway around the world.

Isabel wondered how long it would take them to reach Casco. Watching the dim roadscape so intently, muscles tensed at every turn, it now seemed hours—days—since they had left the lodge. Whit turned on the windshield wipers to clear a scrabble of leaves and the tail end of a branch. Were there more of these now, these bits of torn-off trees, or was she imagining it? She looked, straining, into the darkness. The dimness seemed thicker now, too, more intense, didn't it? Or was she imagining that?

"Is it getting darker?" Charlotte asked suddenly. She had stopped sobbing.

"Smoke," Whit answered.

They were hurtling along on the loose gritty surface. The air was thickening, and the smoke was entering the car. They could smell it now. Isabel tried to breathe shallowly.

"If it gets worse, how will we decide to keep going or to turn back?" she asked.

"Turn back?" Paul repeated.

"To the lake," Isabel said, and again felt its presence behind them.

"If we can get through to Casco, we should," Whit said.

"They'll have helicopters there," Douglas said. "That's what the trooper said. Casco will be an evacuation center. He said to get to Casco."

"But we might be cut off from behind," Isabel said. "If we turned back now, we could go out on the lake."

Afterward, when you heard about them, it was easy to see which decisions had been poor ones: you could tell by who survived. But at the time all those judgments must have seemed sensible, considered, well planned: Napoleon choosing the wrong hill to march up on the way to Moscow; Lee exposing his flank or whatever he'd done at Gettysburg. Hiding in a closet instead of bolting out the back door. At the time these had been rational decisions.

No one answered Isabel, and Whit did not slacken his speed. There were more slaps against the windshield; Whit flipped the wipers on and off. The air was growing dense and abrasive, filling up Isabel's throat. She swallowed against it.

"We should have brought something to breathe through," Isabel said. "I should have thought of it." Rooting through the cabin, her mind had been blank. Why hadn't she thought of towels, scarves? She had brought only shoes and sweaters, underwear. Nothing related to fires. She should have brought bottles of water, thermoses, anything wet. Too late. Her mind had been flailing: she'd had no idea how to focus it.

Isabel had heard once about a woman who was obsessed by fire. She planned carefully what she'd do in one, making lists of what to save: photographs, jewelry, favorite objects. When one night her house finally did catch fire, the woman sprang up and stripped the blanket from the bed. In it she set the two big telephone books, the White and Yellow Pages, and folded the blanket carefully around them. Carrying the heavy bundle, she fled through the smoke-filled rooms. It was all she saved.

When Isabel had first heard the story, it seemed hilarious and absurd. Laughing at stories like this was one of the ways in which you separated yourself—sane and sensible—from the ineffective and ludicrous. But now, in this landscape, the story was plausible. Fear did strip your mind of reason.

She thought of the deer and her fawn, moving through the darkness and the wind, away from the smell of smoke.

The air thickened, steadily darkening. Paul coughed suddenly. Isabel breathed slowly, flattening her nostrils against the smoke.

The road seemed never to change. They were always driving through the same long tunnel of tree trunks, lit by the glare of the headlights. Always the twin shallow troughs of the tire tracks on either side of the gravel ridge. Always the scene was dim grays and blacks, all color drained away. Always above was the high tossing blackness of the trees.

Douglas coughed, a helpless bark.

Whit looked steadily ahead, pressing on.

The road curved to the left, and as they followed the turn, the road went on, then on and on, turning and still turning, the curve sharper and sharper. The car was straining to keep contact with the surface, straining against the wide centrifugal drift. They could feel the car readying itself to slide sideways, to lift into the air. Isabel saw the tree trunks approach, closer and closer, as the car turned and turned. They could feel the wheels on the dry gravel, on the edge of skid. *We'll skid off or we won't,* Isabel thought, *it's a law, it's physics.* She felt oddly removed, at once fatalistic and terrified.

For long moments everything was slow. There was time for thought and reflection. Suddenly everything sped up to a hectic jumble, and then everything was over in seconds: Whit putting on the brake, locking the car into deceleration, trying to break its headlong hurtle without losing traction.

It was at the end of the curve, when they could see the road going finally straight again. As they came around the final segment of the curve, the rear tires lost traction, lifting smoothly and neatly into the air. The car slid into the shallow ditch alongside the road, and then up again and over its far side, like a boat over a wave, coming to a stop a hand's breadth from the line of tree trunks.

When the car stopped moving, there was silence. Their headlights, now skewed by the ditch, lit up not the road ahead but the rows of darkened columns along the edge of the woods. The depths beyond were impenetrable. As they watched, into the open channel of the roadway bloomed a billow of smoke.

"Oh, God," Charlotte said. She began to cough.

"Turn up the radio," Paul said.

Isabel turned the knob to hear the man's sober voice. ". . . increasingly high winds. The National Parks Service is bringing in firefighters from other parts of the Northeast. Evacuation of the following areas is being called for: Bendleigh, Willow Run, Ordway, Casco Corners,

Hillbrook, Medway and Grant Springs. In order to make sure that these areas . . ."

"What do we do now?" Charlotte asked. "If Casco Corners is being evacuated, should we still try to get there?"

"Of course we should," Douglas said, his voice sharp. "That's the whole point. We'll be evacuated with everyone else."

"What if we get there too late?" Charlotte asked. "What if we get there and they've all gone? In helicopters and things? What if everything's on fire there?"

Whit put the car in reverse and turned to look at the road behind. He accelerated gently. The noise of the engine rose; the wheels spun. He shifted to forward; the wheels spun again. He opened the door.

"Isabel, take the wheel," he said. "Paul, let's go."

Isabel slid over, and the men got out and set themselves against the rear of the car. She put it in gear, and as they began to lean, she pressed slowly on the gas pedal. She could feel them push against the dead mineral weight of the car. The engine noise rose; Whit and Paul pushed. Nothing. Isabel cautiously stepped harder on the gas. The wheels caught, spun, caught again. She could feel them strain. Slowly the car's chassis slid up out of the ditch.

"God," said Charlotte. "This is terrible."

Douglas said nothing. Isabel stopped the car and slid back across the seat, and Paul and Whit climbed inside. The air was denser now.

"This is terrible," Charlotte said again.

No one answered. Whit drove slowly ahead. The smoke was thicker; they could see less and less of the road in front of them.

"Douglas," Charlotte said, "I want you to answer me. I think we should turn back."

"Well, I don't think we should," Douglas said forcefully.

"But we're going right into the thick of it," Charlotte said. "We're heading straight for the fire. We're going to find at some point that we can't go on, and then it may be too late to go back. I think we should turn back now."

"And do what?" Douglas asked. "What do you have in mind?"

"Get into the canoes and go out on the lake."

"And then what?" Douglas said. "Sit in canoes waiting for hours, days, while the whole Adirondacks go up in smoke around us? We won't know what's going on. We've been told to evacuate."

A heavy branch hit the windshield, the leaves flattening against the glass. Whit turned on the wipers and they thrashed rhythmically, hitting the branch. Still it did not move, fixed in front of them, cutting off the nightscape beyond. After a moment Whit stopped the car, skidding slightly on the loose surface. He opened the door and pulled off the branch, hurling it sideways into the darkness.

When he started again, Charlotte spoke again. "Whit, I want you to stop. It's getting worse ahead."

Whit slowed, then stopped, the car. He turned around in his seat. "Okay," he said, "we need a group decision. Let's look at the situation. If we go on, we're depending on the firefighters and the police, the experts. If we go back, we're on our own.

"The lodge is down in a hollow by the shore. Fire burns more slowly downhill than up, so it should be relatively safe, unless the wind drives the fire on and the whole valley goes up, in which case the lodge will, too.

"Driving on to Casco means going up over the ridge and down into the next valley. The fire's being driven by the wind, which is mostly from the northeast, though it's also gusting in swirls. If we get to the ridge above Casco and find it's worse down below the ridge than it is here, then I agree we should turn back. But if the fire is still above the town, burning slowly down toward it, or skirting it and staying up along the ridgetops, then we'll get there safely and we'll be evacuated with everyone else, maybe by helicopter. They probably will have dug firebreaks around the town by now, and they'll have trucks with hoses. They have pretty sophisticated ways of saving people nowadays."

There was silence.

"If we keep going now," Isabel said, "we may not have enough gas to go back later, if it turns out we need to."

Whit looked at the gas gauge: the needle was slanted, on its way toward the red. He nodded. "That's a point."

Douglas said firmly, "I think we should rely on the information we've been given. We've been told to get to Casco."

Ahead of them the headlights seemed suddenly to brighten, reflecting off a muscled cloud of smoke that drifted straight into the car. The light shone back into their eyes.

"We can't see," Charlotte pointed out.

"How would they get us out of Casco?" Isabel asked. "If it's really bad, they wouldn't be able to land helicopters. Especially at night, with all the smoke. I mean, what is it that we think they're going to do for us?"

After a moment Paul said, "Try calling the number again."

Uncertainty had entered the car.

Isabel dialed the number. The screen flashed WAIT FOR SERVICE, then went blank. She tried a second time, then turned it off.

"We know we'd be safe if we go back," Isabel said. "We don't know we will be if we go on." She spoke diffidently: she was an outsider. "Those deer were heading back toward the lake."

No one answered.

She was beginning to feel claustrophobic. Fear was rising into her throat. The smoke roiled before them in steady billows, changing shape, bullying its way across the open roadway. Overhead the trees tossed. The wind was incessant.

"We don't know that we could get back now if we tried," Whit said, but in his voice was the possibility of change. "We may have already been cut off. It depends on the shape of the fire. If it's already crossed this ridge farther up, then it may have come down into our valley, and it may already have crossed the road behind us."

Behind them was the lake. Isabel thought of it with longing.

"We should go back," declared Charlotte. "We'll be safe there, even if the house goes. This way it's getting worse every minute."

It was true. The air in the car was thick and choking, the smoke seeping in through the air-conditioning, settling in their throats. Douglas coughed.

"Maybe we should go back," he said reluctantly.

Whit looked in the rearview mirror. "You want to turn back?" he asked.

"No," Paul said loudly. "We should not go back. We've been told to evacuate. These troopers know what they're talking about. They know we're on the lake. They'd have told us to get out on the lake and stay there if that was the safest thing. They knew where the fire was, they knew where it was going."

"Things change," Douglas said doubtfully. "That was two hours ago. Everything may be different now."

"With this wind," Whit said.

"We should go on," Paul said strenuously. "This is how people die.

Why do you think you know better than the police and the firefighters?"

No one answered him.

Charlotte gave a dry cough. "Paul, please," she said. "Don't make
this worse than it is."

"Me! You're drunk and crazy," Paul said angrily. "You have no right
to tell anyone not to make things worse than they are. You're all crazy.
Look, we're nearly there. We've been driving for nearly an hour, we're
nearly at Casco. We've practically made it. Going back along this road
is madness. This wind is from the northeast. The fire may have crossed
the ridge behind us already and may be driving right down that valley
between us and the lodge. We'll have to go right into the middle of it,
and then we'll be completely fucked."

"But we're *not* nearly in Casco," Whit said. "We've been going much
more slowly than you think, because the visibility is so bad. We're not
even halfway there." He paused. "I'm beginning to change my mind."
He looked again at the gas gauge.

"Well, I haven't," Paul said. "And I don't want to die because all of
you can't make up your minds. We've already made our decision, and
if we unmake it, we'll be trapped. Maybe we should have stayed at the
lodge in the first place, but we didn't, and now we have to get to Casco.
We're committed. Now it's our only chance."

"But what will happen there?" asked Isabel. She imagined the scene:
boiling flames, clouds of smoke, chaos, burning buildings, the town
empty, everyone gone. Or worse, sirens screaming, red lights circling,
police cars parked uselessly at angles as the fire surged around them:
everyone trapped. Which was worse? The lake lay behind them.

"We don't know what will happen there," Paul said. "But we know
what'll happen behind us. The troopers told us to get out. We know that
our valley is exactly where the fire was headed. It's insane to go back
into it now."

There was a long silence.

"We have to decide," Charlotte said.

They all knew it. With each second the fire was surging forward
somewhere, its red maw illuminating the landscape, devouring it.

Chapter 24

Isabel's body was filling up with fear. It seemed to have entered below her waist and moved upward, invading and constricting, through her stomach, her chest and her throat. Her body was turning fixed and rigid with it. She could barely breathe, barely swallow. Each movement seemed risky.

"Can we even turn the car around here?" Charlotte said. The road was narrow, set between unbroken lines of trees.

"If we decide to, we can," Whit said.

"Let's do it, let's go back," Charlotte said. "The worst that can happen is we'll catch cold sitting out in the canoes all night long."

"The worst that can happen is that we drive straight into the fire and we die," Paul said.

There was a silence: The Fire.

They had not seen it. Their knowledge of it was still only intimation, through the high tossing of the branches, the ferocity of the wind driving toward them, the heavy drifting clouds. But the fire had become a presence in their minds. They were frighteningly aware of it, of its lethal incandescence, its dreadful speed, its monstrous, unthinkable size.

"I think we should go back," Whit said suddenly.

"Christ," Paul said, leaning forward, furious. "You're crazy, Whitney. You're going to kill us all. And it's not just us. They may be waiting for us in Casco, did you think of that? They may be holding up the evacuation. There may be people staying, waiting for us."

There was a silence.

"Eddie's gotten there by now," Paul went on. "He's told the troopers we're coming. They all know we're here. We may be putting other people in danger if we turn back. If we don't show up, they may send someone out to find us."

"But we don't know that," Charlotte answered. "We have to save ourselves. It doesn't make sense for us to die trying to get there just because someone else might think we're coming. We have to save ourselves."

After a moment Douglas said, "I think I agree."

At once Whit turned the wheel hard, as far as it would go, starting the cumbersome turn.

"Goddamn it!" Paul said, shifting angrily in his seat. "You're all crazy. You're going to kill us! We're not going to make it back! Can't you see that?"

"Paul, we have no reason to think we can make it going on," Douglas said.

"You think that just because Whitney lives in Wyoming, you have to listen to whatever he says about this! The Mountain Man!" Paul was shouting now. "But Whitney's wrong! This is a matter of common sense, this isn't some arcane wilderness lore!"

"Paul, no, you're wrong," Charlotte said, upset. "That's not what—"

"You think whatever I say is wrong and whatever Whitney says is right," Paul said furiously. "You think he's God. But you're all going to die because of it. And he's not going to save you!"

Charlotte and Douglas both spoke Paul's name at once, placatory and urgent. Instead of answering, Paul opened the door and stepped out into the roaring darkness, slamming the door hard. He moved quickly in front of the car, his shape bright in the headlights. He held a flashlight in his hand and he was walking fast, heading toward Casco.

"Get him," Charlotte said urgently. "Whit, go after him."

Whit swore and wrenched the door open. He threw himself out of the car, running into the headlights after Paul. He reached his brother and grabbed his shoulders. Paul turned. His face, in the glare, was contorted. He shouted something at Whit.

The two men were facing each other, and Whit grabbed Paul's

shoulders again. In the car they could not hear what was being said, but everyone could see the two angry faces. They saw them shouting at each other, they saw Paul's arm rise and his fist strike out at Whit's face. They saw Whit's head twist, his chin lifting into the air at the blow, his body stalled.

Whit staggered backward, then recovered and started off again after Paul, who was striding off. The smoke swirled and billowed, muffling their forms. Whit flung himself again on his brother's shoulders, but Paul was ready this time and twisted—in the car they thought this was what he did—away from Whit, but the two were now farther away, and the smoke kept drifting and eddying. The smoke cleared for a moment and they could see Whit, running away from them along the road, but they could no longer see Paul, and then the smoke closed in again and they could see neither, and then not even the trees along the road, and then they could hardly see the front of the hood. They waited in silence, seeing nothing for what seemed like a long time.

"Paul's gone crazy," Charlotte said, her voice tight. "We have to get him back."

"Drive after them," Douglas said to Isabel. "Move over, Isabel, quickly, drive after them."

Isabel slid over and drove slowly forward again. They could see no one ahead, nothing. The forest spread out into the night, vast, and black, black. Isabel's breaths were short, and she could feel them in her throat.

"Be careful," Charlotte said. "Don't hit them."

Isabel could not speak. She could do nothing but strain her eyes ahead, into the smoke and darkness, inching the car into the glare of its own lights. They could see nothing.

"Goddamn it," Douglas said forcefully. "Damn them."

"How can they be doing this?" Charlotte said.

Isabel drove carefully, staring ahead. There was nothing, no movement, no figures, only the tree trunks along the road. Isabel had no idea where they were now. It seemed they had been driving forever, since birth.

She stopped finally. "How far should I go?" she asked. "What if I've passed them?"

"You're right. Stop," Douglas said. "Stop. They're goddamned fools." He sounded distraught.

Charlotte began to cry again. "Where are they?" she asked, her voice cracking. "Douglas, what are they doing? We have to find them."

Isabel opened her door and got out. At once the air was unbearable, scouring her lungs, and she shut the door behind her. She cupped her hands at her mouth and shouted, "Paul! Whitney!" Her voice was nothing. She could hardly hear it herself. "Paul!" she screamed. "Paul! Paul! Come back!" She tried again, then stopped to listen. Above, the trees thrashed. She could hear nothing but wind. Ahead, in the headlights, the smoke pulsed and billowed. She got back into the car, slamming the door.

"You can't hear anything," she said. "I couldn't hear my own voice."

"Use the horn," Douglas said.

Isabel set her hand hard on the horn. Blaring it, she looked from side to side, back and forth, into the woods. She stared ahead. The drifting smoke was disorienting. The ground ahead was obscured sometimes, and without the trees, without anything at all to moor it, it felt as though the car itself were tilting, as though the landscape plane were shifting. The trees appeared, ghostly and transient, then vanished. The upper shaft of a tree appeared, sailing into sight like a ship; it turned visible, showing its lower branches, its trunk nearly to the ground, then suddenly a new gust obscured everything, roiling across the windshield and covering it in opaque gray. Isabel kept pressure on the horn. When her hand cramped, she changed hands.

Charlotte wept angrily. "They're crazy," she said. "Douglas," she added accusingly.

Douglas said nothing.

When they felt the impact on the car, they all jumped, though it was slight. When the dark figure appeared at the window, they were startled, and in fact the face leaning into the window was terrifying, covered in black and glistening. The figure opened the front door: it was Whit. Isabel slid over and he climbed in.

"I've lost him," he said. "He's gone."

"You haven't lost him," Charlotte told Whit. "He's here somewhere. Get him."

"I know he's here somewhere," Whit said. "But I can't find him. I shouted and shouted. He ran into the woods after he hit me. That punch threw me off balance, and he got just enough of a head start so I couldn't reach him before he went into the trees. After that I couldn't see him. I couldn't hear him, the wind is too loud. Finally I stopped and shouted. But he's gone. He won't come with us even if we find him. He's in a rage."

"What did he say to you?" Charlotte asked. "Before."

Whit paused. "He said he'd rather die without us than live with us."

Douglas drew in his breath. "What's the matter with him?"

After a moment Whit said, "The horn was a good idea. You were way ahead of me, and I didn't see the headlights. I couldn't have found you if it hadn't been for the horn."

"It was your father's idea," Isabel said.

Whit's breathing filled the small space.

Charlotte leaned forward. "We have to find him," she said.

"Yes," Whit said. "How?"

"Let's go back," she said. "You said you were behind us. Turn around."

"I was," Whit said. "But I don't know which way he went, or where he is by now."

Isabel thought of Paul moving through the smoky woods. Even with a flashlight, it would be easy to walk into a low branch, to slice open a cheek, to stab an eye. The footing, off the path, was treacherous. You jarred your teeth, you bit your tongue: every step was higher or lower than you'd expected. You had to make your way as though blind. There was no path. Paul would be finding his way through deep woods.

The smoke would close around him. Paul was deliberately putting them behind him, heading deeper into the blackness. Isabel felt her throat fill: these were tears. She coughed to cover them.

"Hit the horn again, Whit," Douglas said.

"Isabel, you lean on the horn while I turn the car around," Whit said. "He's somewhere behind us. He'll have to change his mind sometime."

Isabel held the horn down while Whit spun the wheel. He turned the car slowly around in the narrow road, inching back, stopping, twisting the wheel, inching forward. This time, if they were stuck, it would be Whit and Douglas trying to push them out. Their power had been diminished.

Isabel looked at Whit's face. "You're bloody," she said.

"Just my nose," Whit answered. "I'm all right." He swiveled the wheel. "Stay on the horn. I want him to know where we are."

When they had reversed, Whit drove slowly along the road, stopping every few feet. Isabel held the horn. Even inside the car, the blare was faint against the roar of the wind.

"Can he hear that?" Charlotte demanded.

"It's all we have," Whit said.

"This is terrible," Charlotte said. "We have to find him."

They drove along slowly, stopping, starting. Isabel shifted her hands on the horn.

"Get out and shout," Charlotte said. Whit turned off the engine and got out. He stood beside the car, cupping his hands at his mouth. They could hear him faintly, calling his brother's name into the storm. He called it over and over.

It was Douglas who said it finally. "We have to go." His voice was low and somber.

"We can't leave Paul," Charlotte said.

"He doesn't want to come with us," Douglas said. "He'd come out if he did. He's left us on purpose."

"But we can't leave him," Charlotte repeated, louder. She was no longer drunk; fear and adrenalin had consumed the alcohol. "Douglas, we can't leave Paul here in the woods."

The door opened and Whit climbed in again. "What do you want to do?" he asked, shutting the door.

"We can't leave your brother here," Charlotte said.

"We can't stay much longer," Douglas said.

"He'll die if he stays," Charlotte pointed out.

"We'll die if we don't leave," Douglas said.

There was a silence.

"It's your fault," Charlotte announced. Her voice was calm and bitter, and it was not clear whom she was speaking to. "If you hadn't left him, he wouldn't have done this."

"Charlotte," Douglas said warningly.

"It's true," Charlotte told him. "You know it. He's gone crazy. He's furious because this woman has left him. It never would have happened if she hadn't done this."

Isabel looked straight ahead.

Charlotte leaned forward and spoke nearly into Isabel's ear. "What did you think you were doing?" she asked. "How could you have been so cruel?"

"Charlotte—" Isabel began.

"And don't call me Charlotte," Charlotte told her. "You have no right."

Without turning, Isabel asked, "What shall I do? What would you like me to do now?"

"There's nothing you can do now," Charlotte told her. "Nothing you can do."

"Charlotte," Douglas said again, "stop it. Isabel didn't want this to happen. She doesn't want anything to happen to Paul. None of us do."

Charlotte gave a short derisive bark.

Even if Paul had changed his mind and decided to come back to the car, Isabel thought, *he might not know which direction to take.* You lose direction in the dark, in the woods. Even if he found his way out, found himself on the road with the fragile beam of light illuminating the gravel path, feeling the welcome flatness underfoot, he still wouldn't know which way the car would be on the road. He wouldn't know which way to turn.

You are making my life a misery.

He was now picking his way among tree trunks, coughing in the clouds of thickening smoke. He would be moving slowly, holding his head down to keep his nose and mouth clear of smoke, squinting and blinking. He would be unable to see, deep in the woods, with a forest fire approaching.

But it's possible for him to survive, Isabel told herself. Weren't they near enough to Casco for him to reach it, going straight on? Or if the fire went the other way, if it blew west over the ridge and headed down toward the lake and the lodge, wasn't it possible that Paul would be all right? That he might blunder through the woods all night and, in the morning, be nothing worse than cold and filthy, damp and hungry?

What Isabel didn't want to imagine was the fire coming through here, the fire roaring through these woods. It now seemed everywhere, a great dominant presence, like the sky. It didn't have a particular site; it seemed about to descend on them from everywhere, impossible to avoid, like a solar shadow moving over the landscape. They were small and lost in the blackness. It would descend where it would. There was no recourse for them, no escape. But where was it? It was all around them, in the roaring wind and the billowing smoke. It would come when it did. It was biblical in its scope, its incomprehensible size, its lethal potency.

Whit turned up the radio: static.

"What do you want to do?" he asked his parents.

Isabel opened her door and got out, closing the door behind her. She stood in the road and put her hands to her mouth. "Paul!" she screamed into the roar of the wind. She screamed his name over and over. "Come back!" She turned in one direction, then the other. Her voice became quickly hoarse. Smoke was drawn down into her lungs, drying out the shaft of her throat. She stopped finally to listen. Whit was giving intermittent blasts of the horn, long and short, long and short. In between the blasts Isabel strained her ears, hoping for something.

She could hear nothing but the wind. She took a step into the smoke, straining into it. She couldn't tell what she was seeing: a dark shape. Was it a figure? She took another step. Certainly something. She stepped again. The smoke swirled around her. She shouted his name over and over. She paused, listening. She could hear nothing but the wind, the heaving trees.

She could feel Paul's presence nearby. He was there, somewhere just beyond her vision, behind that row of tree trunks, inside the scrim of trees, on the far side of the road. She walked forward, groping with her feet, lifting her voice. She saw something through the shifting clouds and began to run.

"Paul!" she shouted. *"Paul!"* She ran slowly and clumsily, stumbling as she crossed the unseen ridge between the two dirt tracks. "Paul!" She was surrounded by smoke, and she paused, disoriented. The grayness had covered the world, the horizon was gone and now, oddly, her balance. She staggered and stepped sideways to catch up with herself, falling. She felt herself going over, and the air in front of her was opaque, there was nothing to hold on to; she staggered farther, lurching toward the fall. *"Paul!"* she screamed. *"Paul!"* As she fell, she flung out her arms and twisted, trying to save herself, turning in the air to catch hold of something. As she turned, looking back, she saw that the car was gone. She was separated from everything, cut off for good. She screamed his name. He was out there in the dark, his head down, trying to breathe. Her throat—raw and scraped—filled with fear and smoke.

She had sprawled sideways when she fell. She struggled to pull herself upright. She knelt, swaying, trying to sit up. Something hit her shoulder gently. Someone leaned over her, and hands groped carefully along her body.

"Paul!" she shouted, turning toward him.

An arm went around her shoulders. She was being pulled up.

"It's me," Whit said, holding her steady. "Paul's gone." He began to walk her back to the car. Isabel shook her head, wild.

"No," she said, and then shouted Paul's name again. She screamed it over and over, but Whit kept her going toward the car. He opened the door for her, handing her inside.

Back in the car, Isabel leaned her head against the door frame. Tears rose in her throat, and she heard herself sob suddenly out loud.

"Oh, cry," Charlotte told her. "You're why he's done this."

"Stop it, Charlotte," Douglas said. His voice was low. "We have to go now. We have to leave."

This time no one answered, and Whit started the engine. The car started to head slowly back toward the lake. Everyone leaned forward again, staring into the billowing clouds, watching this time not only for a horrid orange glow but for a figure.

It was possible. Paul could have gotten turned around. He could have been heading back unintentionally through the woods. He might step into the headlights, unhurt, ready to rejoin them, at any moment. That was what they were looking for.

Chapter 25

They crept back along the road through the dark woods. The smoke drifted at them amid the trees; the headlights shone harsh against the dense tumbling clouds.

Staring straight ahead, Isabel thought it was possible to believe that Paul was still in the backseat. Without turning around, she could believe it.

The car went carefully around a long curve.

"We're leaving our son to die," Charlotte said.

"Stop it, Charlotte," Douglas told her.

"He'll die in the woods," Charlotte said, and sobbed.

"*Stop it,*" Douglas said, more violently.

"Oh, God," Charlotte said, her voice wild. "Why are we doing this?"

No one spoke. Ahead lay the interminable road.

"It's you," Charlotte said to Isabel. "It's your fault."

"Charlotte, that's enough," Douglas said angrily. "Leave Isabel alone. None of us could stop Paul. He was determined to go on. That's what he wanted to do."

"He wanted to stop living," Charlotte said. "That's what he wanted, because of her. His beaming bride."

"He's doing what he wanted," Douglas said. "Whit tried to stop him."

"He's committing suicide," Charlotte said. "She made him."

"Stop." Isabel closed her eyes.

"Don't say that, Mother." Whit looked at Charlotte in the rearview mirror.

"No one commits suicide by walking into a forest fire," Douglas said vehemently. "Don't make this into something it isn't."

"Douglas, we're killing him," Charlotte said, giving another sob. "We're killing Paul, we're leaving him to die."

"Charlotte," Douglas said, warning.

She ignored him and leaned toward the back of Whit's head. "It's your fault, too, Whit," she told him. "You've always taken his women."

"I have *not* always taken Paul's women," Whit said, his voice rising. "I have *never* taken Paul's women. I've been accused of it for thirty years because of something that didn't happen. I had nothing to do with that girl, *nothing*. I never looked at her. When she came into my room that night, I told her to leave, and when she wouldn't, I pulled her out into the hall. That's all I did! Christ."

"He's never forgiven you," Charlotte said accusingly, as though Whit had not spoken.

"I know that. *I know that*," Whit answered. "Why do you think I live out west? You think it's a pleasure for me to come back here? This family offers nothing but blame. Paul has never forgiven me for something I didn't do, he resents everything I *do* do, and you two are still waiting for me to start my career. I'm forty-five years old! I'm in the *middle* of my career, for Christ's sake. I have tenure! I have a distinguished chair! This *is* my career!"

"Now, take it easy, Whitney," Douglas said, his tone forbidding.

"I do take it easy," Whit said, lowering his voice. "I take it easy by practically never coming back east. What is there to bring me here?"

"Oh, blame us for everything," Charlotte said.

"I don't blame you for everything," Whit said forcefully. "There's a lot I don't blame you for."

"Like what," Charlotte said, challenging.

"Okay. I've never married: not your fault."

"Well?" Charlotte said. "Whose fault is it?"

"It's no one's fault, Ma, there are things that are no one's fault," Whit said, shaking his head. "I fell in love with a married woman. She was very unhappily married, but she wouldn't leave her husband. She had leukemia, and she didn't want to get divorced. She grew sicker and sicker and then she died. I had to watch it happen and I couldn't help. It took six years. She died in the hospital, and her husband was with her. No one told me. I heard about it the next day from my department secretary. She thought I already knew." Whit stopped for a moment. "So that was the worst thing that's ever happened to me," he went on, "and it was not your fault. There's a great deal I don't blame you for."

"What are you saying, then?" Charlotte asked.

"What I'm saying is that you two make it hard for us to be around you. Me and Paul," Whit said. "You deny everything that doesn't fit into your world. And you have no idea what my world is like, or Paul's, either, and you have no interest in learning."

Behind her Isabel could feel Douglas and Charlotte, mute and furious, punishing their son with iron silence. Beside her she felt Whit's anger, but she could not attend to this, to any of it, she could only half hear what they were saying. How could they be saying these things now, hurtling through the woods, through the thick clouds of smoke? It hardly mattered what was being said inside the car. Nothing inside was more important than what was happening outside; nothing could be this large, this significant, this frightening.

A big branch fell heavily onto the road just in front of the car.

"Is that a spark?" Isabel asked, fear hitting her chest. "Is that branch smoldering?" She could not say the word "fire."

They all were silent, straining their eyes. It was impossible to see clearly through the clouds. They could not see a spark, but the branch itself seemed to be smoking. If the fire was moving through the tops of the trees, if it had begun leaping like this through the woods, it was bad.

Whit drove over the branch, which thudded and cracked heavily beneath the wheels. He stepped cautiously on the accelerator. The smoke was so thick they could see only a few feet ahead of the car.

"Be careful," Douglas said.

"I'm *being* careful," Whit answered.

"Of course he's being careful," Charlotte told Douglas.

"I know he is," Douglas said. "I know you are, Whit." His voice was distracted.

We're all distracted, we're wild, Isabel thought.

It was impossible to be calm, to concentrate on anything because of the fear splintering their minds, because of this large real terror: death. It was coming toward them from all sides. Death was quite near; it was very real.

Charlotte gave an odd choking laugh, or a cough. It hardly mattered, now that they were all so intent on the road, on the wild furious landscape, the tossing grasses and shrubs, the drifting, sinister masses of smoke. Staring so hard was hypnotic: they could not shift their unblinking gazes or spare any attention from this, the nearing sense of death.

You are making my life a misery.

He was somewhere in the black woods, far behind them. They had chosen different paths, but still it was possible that he would be all right. Everything depended on the course of the fire and the wind. He had a flashlight; he could find the road. Maybe he would live and they would not. Isabel did not dare approach the word, not even to think it, of what might happen to him, to them. Saying the word, even thinking it, was too unsafe: it might attract the thing itself. *He might be all right,* she told herself, *he might be fine.*

They felt the road begin to rise.

"Thank God," Charlotte said. "We're nearly there."

Isabel turned to her. "Do you have any clothes?" she asked. "Did you bring a bag?"

Charlotte stared at her coldly.

"We may have left it behind," Douglas said finally. "I don't remember having it after she ran back upstairs."

"I brought some things," said Isabel. "They're in the trunk."

"I don't want anything from you," Charlotte told her.

"Charlotte, for God's sake," Douglas said angrily. "You're in your nightgown."

"Here's the driveway," Whit said. "We're here." As he turned the car off the road, a small branch landed on the windshield. It was fuming with thick white smoke, and as it hit the glass, it burst into flame.

Whit turned on the windshield wipers, swishing the branch quickly onto the road. He stepped again on the gas. They were heading up the long curve toward the lodge. The smoke had closed in, dense and choking. There were no longer any spaces of clear air; it was continually dense.

The house came into view, looming like an ocean liner. The windows glowed a pale orange. For a moment this looked eerily like fire, as though the invader had already arrived and was leering at them from the windows of their own house. But the light was steady; it was not fire, it was only the lamps in the empty rooms.

"I can't breathe," Charlotte said.

They inched along the driveway, too slowly, past the lodge, heading down toward the boathouse. Behind them was something unknown. No one looked out the rear window for fear of what they might see: an inferno. As long as they looked straight ahead, they were still alive. Behind them they could feel the forest's lethal radiance, the heat. The world behind them was shimmering with terrifying heat. Destruction was near, they could feel it. They did not turn; looking would make it real.

At the boathouse path Whit stopped and they got out. Once out of the car, the smoke was upon them. They choked, their throats rasped, they groped through it.

"Hold hands," Whit ordered, "we're going to walk together. We can't lose anyone."

He took one of Charlotte's hands, Douglas the other, but Isabel dodged back to the trunk. Her eyes stung. She lifted the lid, scrabbling for the duffel. She could hardly see her hands; the air in her chest was solid. She slung the bag over her shoulder and turned. The others were gone.

"Where are you?" she called.

Douglas answered, "Here. Come on."

Isabel groped toward his voice, shuffling across the gravel. She saw his figure faintly through the smoke, his hand outstretched. She seized it, and they moved down the path in a line.

"My feet hurt. I can't walk on this gravel," Charlotte announced.

"You have to," Douglas told her grimly.

"I brought clothes," Isabel said. "Sneakers and jeans."

"You can't buy me," Charlotte answered.

They groped their way along the path toward the boathouse. Behind them the roaring seemed to be growing louder: was it louder? Or was it that they were so exposed, listening so hard?

Somewhere in the woods, Paul moved among the trees, smoke in his lungs.

"Don't look back," Whit called out. "We're almost there."

They could feel the lake ahead, its cool dim presence. Clouds of smoke might muffle its surface, but the deep green lake was there.

In the boathouse they stumbled clumsily until Whit found the light switch. The sudden glare was a surprise: the world had been dark until now. They could see that the air was solid with smoke. As the men tugged the canoes from the racks, Isabel unzipped the duffel bag, taking out jeans and a sweater, sneakers. "Here."

"I want nothing from you," Charlotte told her, and folded her arms over her nightgown.

"These are Paul's," Isabel said.

"Charlotte," Douglas said, taking his wife by the elbow. "Get in the canoe." The boats were now in the water; the roaring behind them was rising.

"*Get in,*" Whit said urgently, "*get in the canoe.*"

The two men took hold of Charlotte.

"Don't shove me," she said.

Douglas climbed down into the rocking boat. Whit handed Charlotte down to him. Isabel stood on the dock; Whit climbed into the *Weetie.*

"Here," Isabel said again, but Charlotte stared up at her without speaking and the *Elsinore* began moving away. Isabel leaned out over the water and threw the bundle past Charlotte, into the bottom of the boat. "*Take it,*" she said.

"Get in! Get in!" Whit shouted at Isabel. "Get in the canoe! Now!"

The roar was growing, the sound was flooding around them. Noise was taking over the whole world, a wall of it rising and blotting out everything else, a sweeping wave. It took over everything, Isabel's understanding of the world and the way to see it and even the way to stand up in it; she staggered, nearly falling from its impact, and Whit reached up and grabbed her arm.

The roaring was everything. The whole world was turning into sound, there was only that great solid wall, and heat was a part of it. The heat and smoke and roaring were connected, and the smoke was boiling around them now, thick and white and furious, full of tiny unfurling rumples, like the smoke on the branch before it burst into flame. She could hardly see anything. She had lost sight of Charlotte and Douglas; they had vanished into the thick whiteness.

Whit was shouting. His mouth was open and his eyes were full of urgency. At his pull she jumped, too fast, falling dangerously into the canoe. It rocked violently, and then Whit moved behind her. He was pushing off, and the canoe gained stability through its own forward movement, the seesaw lessening as they slid quickly along the dark water.

She heard Whit faintly. "Paddle!" he yelled at her. "Paddle!"

She set her blade into the water and they pushed together through the smoke, stroking hard and fast, blind. They could see nothing ahead. *Setting out upon the face of the waters,* she thought.

"Hurry," Whit called out from behind her. "Don't look back." His voice sounded strange, and Isabel wondered if he was about to cry. Was he thinking of Paul, was this grief? Or was it urgency and fear? She had never heard Whit cry, did not know how that voice would sound. She thought of the woman he had loved. Had he been able to visit her in the hospital? She knew nothing of all this, his past, his whole complicated life, full of vigor and incident, pain. Learning it lay ahead.

It was hard to hear anything against the terrible high roaring. This louder noise was more than the wind. *It must at last be the fire,* she thought, which had found them, sought them out, discovered and pursued them out here on the surface of the lake.

The air they were breathing was lethal. Isabel would not let herself think of Paul again. She felt the strain in her upper arm and changed sides. She had never paddled so hard.

Somewhere near them, Charlotte wept without restraint. "Oh, God," she cried into the night air, *"oh, God."* Douglas did not respond. No one did.

The two canoes moved steadily away from the shore. They had lost sight of each other at once, and as they paddled through the darkness, Whit and Douglas called out, staying close.

"Hall-oo," Whit called out, two notes, rising.

His father answered him through the smoke, like an echo: "Hall-oo." They could not see where they were going, but once on the lake, this hardly mattered; only that they stayed together.

As they moved farther out, they began to see through the smoke. Isabel could see the water ahead of her, faintly shimmering. The air was clearer now; Isabel's breathing started to slow and ease. Her arms ached, but each stroke took them farther from the roiling chaos, that terrible roar.

They still looked only ahead, not back toward the great clouds of smoke. They headed into the wind, and the air was cleaner. There was a faint glow from the sky, and the surface of the lake held a dim nocturnal shimmer. The water was calm.

They kept on. Looking into the gloom, Isabel thought she saw something off to one side, moving on the water.

She squinted at it in the dark. It was elusive, whatever it was, flitting in and out of her vision. Was it real? Maybe it was only the fluttering of a strained optic nerve. It was like a faint star: she could not fix on it. She lost it, found it again, lost it, kept it. It was coming nearer, drawing itself into a dark animate point, tugging behind it a liquid "V" of ripples. Heading for the far shore, it would cross directly in front of their canoe.

"Look," she said, her voice quiet, and Whit stopped paddling.

In the faint glow they could see the pallid gleam of its eyes, just above the water, pale green and phosphorescent. As the creature drew closer, they could make out its smooth round face, the straight blunt nose, the flattened ears.

The lion was breathing out loud, a faint steady rasp. His mouth was open, as though snarling, and the two curved canines glimmered white. His eyes were wide. On either side of the mouth was a waterfall of whiskers, air and bubbles trapped among them.

The lion moved steadily past the canoe. His chin was just above the water, his white goatee dripping. He looked straight ahead, giving them not a glance. His shoulders surged against the water. He was intent on saving his own wild heroic life. *Go on,* Isabel thought, urging him on, willing him to safety. *Go.*

She pictured him as he reached the other shore, his feet at last touching muddy bottom. She pictured him walking up through the shallows, rising from the lake, his long rangy body dripping, his pelt sleek and dark, heavy with water. His thick tail carried low, uncurled. She pictured him on the shore, gathering himself, then shaking, up and down the length of his body. Drops of lake water flying into the darkness, spattering against the dry leaves like a shower of rain. Lighter now, his damp coat patchy and scuffed, the lion stepping into the new landscape.

Go, Isabel thought again, urging him on. *Flourish, succeed. I'm with you.* She pictured him moving into the waves of wooded hills that lay beyond, rippling on toward the west.

She was with the lion, she was with the whole elegant imperiled earth as it moved, spinning, through the bright blackness, sounding its harmonies out into the reaches of space. *I'm on your side,* she thought.

She felt privileged to be witness to the mysterious workings of the planet. Even with destruction bearing down on them, there was a terrible magnificence in the earth's workings. These were the secret harmonies. *What were they?* she thought. *How could we possibly know?*

The lion was moving past them, and the back of his head was nearly invisible against the dark water. The "V" of ripples followed, widening across the surface.

Saving yourself, that was the thing. The obligation was to survive. *Michael was ill,* Isabel thought suddenly. *I couldn't save him.* Then: *It's over.* The thought was a revelation. Something stopped ticking in her brain.

There were things that were no one's fault: Whit's words fell on her like balm. Michael had been driven by pain and had made his choice. His body was now earth, and nothing she did could alter that. *You do what you can,* her father had said, *you don't blame yourself.* These words clicked into some secret interior place like deciphered runes. Isabel felt the unloosing of weights, a physical lightening.

As the lion disappeared into the gloom, Isabel raised the curved blade of her paddle and held it high in salute. Lake water slid off the blade, shining in the moonlight.

"There he goes," Whit said, pleasure in his voice. Isabel turned to look at him through the dimness; she thought she could see him smile. They could not move. They could not touch or even stretch toward each other without destroying the fragile equilibrium of the vessel as it sat lightly on the water. They sat still, looking at each other, smiling invisibly.

"Hall-oo." Douglas's call was long and drawn out. The second note rose and fell mournfully, like a loon's.

Whit answered. "Hall-oo. We're here, we've stopped."

"Hall-oo." Douglas was coming closer.

Whit answered, and in a moment they saw the *Elsinore* gliding toward them.

"I think we're safe here," Whit said.

They were now far out on the lake, and it was quiet again. Small intimate sounds were now audible—blades dipping and withdrawing, drops falling back on the water's surface, wooden creaks from the thwarts.

Watching Charlotte and Douglas approach, slowly dipping their paddles, Isabel thought of Paul. *Let him be safe,* she thought. *Let him find the road and follow it out. Let the wind shift, the fire pass him by.* She pictured the fire roaring up over the ridge and going straight down the other side, leaving the road and woods to the east untouched. She pictured Paul walking along the road, the low beam of the flashlight weaving back and forth. Once on the road, he could walk on to Casco. If he kept his head down, if the wind kept the smoke away, he would be safe. He might even be picked up by troopers before he reached town. He might right now be in the backseat of a cruiser, taking long drafts of oxygen from a metal canister. Isabel could feel the breath in her own chest, sweet and restorative. She willed him safe. *Go,* she thought, *go on. Save yourself. Survive.*

The *Elsinore* slid toward them. Charlotte and Douglas appeared, silent. Their faces glowed a flickering red against the deep shadows of the night, and Isabel and Whit saw these crimson reflections like a bright warning before they turned and looked behind them. They turned back toward the shore, toward the low hillside and the lodge stretching before them, incandescent. It was safe at last to look, but the world they knew was gone.

Chapter 26

The landscape was transformed.

Bleached and blackened, without color or movement, it was alien, unearthly. It was entirely silent. Even the wind made no noise, sweeping across the bare hillsides.

The contours of the earth were revealed: the abrupt folds of gullies and ravines, the smooth steep rise of the hillsides, the empty line of the summits. The undulating waves still swept toward the horizon, but without the vivifying layer of forest.

There was not a single surviving tree, though stands of blackened ones stood bare and bristling, rigid, thickets of skeletons. Fallen trees lay in thunderous disorder. Standing trunks and fallen logs were silvery black, charred and alligatored. The burned wood had lost its density. It was without substance, rigid and inert, lightweight.

The surface of the ground was thick and gray with sifting, suffocating ash. Any impact, any movement—the soft thudding to the ground of a timber shaft, a swirl of strong wind—produced a dry explosion, a cloud of gritty mist. The ash muffled the earth in a dense and airless layer. There was no color, there were only the shades between the radiant pallor of mineral dust and the dense deadly luster of charcoal.

There was nothing in the landscape that was alive, there were no cells that held moisture. There was nothing flexible, nothing supple or yielding. There was nothing that was both solid and soft, nothing that offered solace or shelter or nourishment. The landscape was wholly arid: there was nothing that breathed.

—

The property, all eight hundred acres, was sold by the family trust to the state of New York. Because the property was entirely within the boundaries of the Adirondack State Park, this meant that by law the land would revert to wilderness. Sweetwater Lodge could never be rebuilt.

No one in the Simmons family had considered rebuilding, though everyone had wondered if Charlotte would.

She did not.

"Move on," she said, and she and Douglas bought a condominium in Martha's Vineyard. Her brothers and their children were no longer interested in the place, nor were Paul or Whit. The sale of the property was performed through lawyers. No one wanted to see it.

Wholly burned forestlands take decades to recover. At first activity is nearly invisible. Narrow shoots of grass strike up thinly through the soft covering of ash. These come from seeds blown in by the wind, or seeds that were buried deep enough to survive the conflagration and have been struck for the first time by direct sunlight. As these tentative green shoots become established, they form root masses, gradually extending outward to create a meadow. Fireweed, as its name suggests, is one of the earliest plants to arrive, with its tall magenta spires and its bushy, leafy habit. After the establishment of grasslands, woody plants appear, shrubby saplings, their miniature leaves unfolding in the spring, the narrow trunks expanding with each year. Wild shrubs continue the task of making shade, extending the green protection of their leaves over their own small plots of earth. Earthworms rise near the surface of the ground, starting their slow sightless work, making castings, aerating and enriching the soil. Birds arrive on burned land before animals do, dropping down onto a berrying shrub. After grass starts growing, deer come through to browse, and field mice burrow among the roots. Once green hosts are present, insects appear. The smaller animals, opossums, raccoons, squirrels and foxes, construct dens. Their populations have been decimated by the fire, however, so reestablishment on the land will be slow. Recovery takes decades—it takes five hundred years to produce a climax forest—but it begins at once.

No one in the Simmons family saw this.

Paul never returned to the region, and for the rest of his life the word "Adirondacks" caused him a brief flare of pain. In the summers he began to travel. He went on hiking trips with his son or small adventurous groups in rugged landscapes. These groups climbed mountains all over the world—New Zealand, Bhutan, Peru.

Whit received a national award for his study of large western carnivores and was elected head of a distinguished scholarly consortium. He came east increasingly rarely.

Whit and Paul did not see each other for many years. When they finally did, it was by chance, in an airport, late at night. They sat across from each other at a distance, in a half-full departure lounge, before a delayed flight from San Francisco to Tucson. A voice on the loudspeaker gave out flight numbers and gate changes, asked standbys to come forward. Teenagers curled awkwardly on the seats and slept, bare feet tucked under blue-jeaned legs. The waiting passengers leaned back in their seats, tired, resigned, and looked through magazines. They flipped pages, glanced up, glanced down.

More than an hour into the wait, Whit raised his eyes from his book to find someone's gaze on him from across the room. It took him a moment to recognize Paul: his brother's hair had become gray, there were folds beneath his chin, and over his face there seemed to be a strange mask of lines. Whit felt a tiny sense of shock and aggrievement, pain that his brother should be so changed, so assaulted. The two looked at each other across the rows of seats, but neither moved nor spoke. After a time Whit looked down again at his book. The woman next to him—his wife—was asleep, her head against his shoulder, her throat trustingly exposed.

When their flight was announced, Whit turned and quietly spoke her name.

"Isabel," he said; she awoke.

They gathered themselves for departure. Whit closed his briefcase, pulled on his coat. Isabel searched for her book, wrapped her scarf around her neck. When they were ready to leave, Whit looked across the room again.

Paul sat motionless, watching them without expression, and after a moment Whit turned away to follow his wife. Isabel, unaware, was already moving toward the boarding gate. Paul waited until they had gone through before he stood. At the other end of the flight, he stayed in his seat until the plane was empty. When he made his way off at last, Whit and Isabel had vanished into the seething airport crowds.

During the winter following the fire, Isabel had given up her job at EPR and left New York for good. She had received a grant to study riparian-edge ecosystems in the watersheds of the Medicine Bow Mountains, in eastern Wyoming, with a particular focus on drought conditions, which continued.

ABOUT THE AUTHOR

ROXANA ROBINSON is the author of two previous novels, *Summer Light* and *This Is My Daughter;* a biography of Georgia O'Keeffe; and two short-story collections, *A Glimpse of Scarlet* and *Asking for Love*. She has received fellowships from the National Endowment for the Arts, the MacDowell Colony and the John Simon Guggenheim Memorial Foundation. Her fiction has appeared in *The Best American Short Stories, The Atlantic, Harper's, The New Yorker* and *Vogue*. She lives in Westchester County and New York City.

ABOUT THE TYPE

This book was set in Bembo, a typeface based on an old-style Roman face that was used for Cardinal Bembo's tract *De Aetna* in 1495. Bembo was cut by Francisco Griffo in the early sixteenth century. The Lanston Monotype Company of Philadelphia brought the well-proportioned letterforms of Bembo to the United States in the 1930s.